I0762118

Other books by

Paul W. Feenstra

Published by Mellester Press

Boundary

The Breath of God (Book 1 in Moana Rangitira series)

For Want of a Shilling (Book 2 in Moana Rangitira series)

Gunpowder Green

Into the Shade

Falls Ende short story eBooks

1. The Oath
2. Courser
3. The King

Falls Ende full-length novels.

1. Falls Ende – Primus (eBooks 1,2 & 3)
2. Falls Ende – Secundus
3. Falls Ende – Tertium
4. Falls Ende – Quartus
5. Falls Ende – Quintus
6. Falls Ende – Sextus

Leonard Hardy Series

A Sinister Consequence

A Questionable Virtue

A Gentleman at Heart

Falls Ende - Sextus
First published in 2025 by Mellester Press

Falls Ende – Sextus ISBN 978-1-067010-14-0 Softcover
Falls Ende – Sextus ISBN 978-1-067010-15-7 Hardcover
Falls Ende – Sextus ISBN 978-1-067010-17-1 Epub
Falls Ende – Sextus ISBN 978-1-067010-16-4 Kindle
Falls Ende – Sextus ISBN 978-1-067010-18-8 Apple Books

Published in New Zealand
A catalogue record of this book is available from the National Library of New Zealand.
Kei te pātengi raraunga o Te Puna Mātauranga o Aotearoa te whakarārangi o tēnei pukapuka

With heartfelt thanks.

Cover Design by Mea

Published by
Mellester Press

FALLS ENDE
SEXTUS

by

PAUL W. FEENSTRA

PROLOGUE

Chreig Charrach, Ireland. 1143.

A wall of impenetrable fog rolled in from the northern Sea of Atlas[1], masking the stealthy approach of six heavily laden *curach*[2]. Budoc Ó hAllmhuráin[3], the war band's leader, or *Ceann Fine*, needed to blindly navigate his craft across the bay and find a suitable place where his small flotilla could safely put ashore. Aboard each craft, armed warriors, all Irish clansmen, had serious misgivings about their landing. Not because they feared the perilous rocks that surrounded the peninsula where they headed but for the devilish and unthinkable fate that awaited them on arrival.

A fisherman with expert local knowledge was unwillingly conscripted and, under his surly guidance, successfully navigated Budoc and his armed troop over the calm, flat waters of the bay and through the thick, low fog to arrive without incident.

Like ghostly spectres, the six *curach* materialised from the greyness, silently manoeuvred around jagged rocks and cautiously approached a small gravelly beach. Inside the craft, wide-eyed, nervous clansmen tightly gripped their oars and squinted towards the shore, hoping they wouldn't confront the unimaginable.

Once ashore, Budoc's clansmen were ordered to slaughter any villagers they encountered. At the same time, those who fled would be herded towards another handful of Budoc's

1 *Sea of Atlas – Atlantic Ocean*

2 *Curach – a wooden framed boat over which animal hides are stretched.*

3 *Ó hAllmhuráin – Pronounced O'Halloran.*

men who'd set out overland during the night. They now lay in ambush, waiting to prevent anyone from escaping by blocking the only safe route from the sparsely wooded outcrop. As intended and decreed by a parish priest, no one must survive.

Budoc wasn't particularly thrilled about acquiescing to his priest's holy demands to complete this perilous mission. The parish priest had repeatedly insisted that he take a group of heroic men and, without mercy, slay the pagans who possessed otherworldly powers and dwelled without God on the rocky outcrop of land known as Chreig Charrach, or *rugged rock*, as it was aptly named.

"They practice sorcery, worship demons, and perform other forms of hideous and devilish rituals," advised the all-knowing priest. "Undoubtedly, ye will encounter fiendish monsters, vile and evil serpents, and even lurid spells will be cast over ye," he warned before embarking on a vigorous sacrament of extended prayers and devotional proclamations.

Immediately before their departure, Budoc and his men were liberally doused in blessed water, but according to the Irish chief, the priest's exhortations weren't enough, and copious amounts of mead were consumed to further fortify themselves against the horrors they would surely encounter. By the time Budoc's jittery men departed, most were inebriate.

Chreig Charrach was a rocky wind-swept peninsula, three miles from Galway, about two miles in length, and only a quarter of a mile wide. Low-growing vegetation grew in abundance around the peninsula's coastal perimeter, while inland, a few hardy trees provided some shelter from dampness and wind. It was an unforgiving finger of land and uninhabitable for most, but not all.

The early morning stillness of the peninsula was pierced by Crundmáel's frenzied cry. "Macha, run! They come!" he yelled as he bolted protectively towards her in fear for both their lives.

At the warning, Macha stood upright. She'd been harvesting lichen and mosses that grew plentiful within the woods and frantically sought to identify from where the attackers came. Around her, other villagers began to flee in abject fear as panic set in. Abandoning her basket, she bent low and ran to a fallen tree as Crundmáel caught up.

"Is Budoc and his men," Crundmáel gasped. He looked around for a safe place to hide or run, but Budoc's clansmen had already formed an impenetrable line near them. "We must get to the *curach*," he whispered. His voice quaked in fear.

The serpents and demons that they were assured of encountering never materialised. No one cast a spell over them or vanished into a puff of smoke, and so emboldened and somewhat relieved, Budoc's warriors gained confidence and took the opportunity presented to them.

Sanctioned by their priest on their holy cause and without moral demand for conscience or thoughts of remorse, the clansmen began their brutal and methodical slaughter. It didn't take long; the village numbered no more than seventeen. Only the women were temporarily spared; they'd first serve another, more carnal purpose. While hysterical appeals for mercy were ignored, peaceful unarmed men, the young and even the elderly were quickly executed.

Around Crundmáel and Macha, pitiful screams pierced the air, only to be drowned out by laughter and nervous bravado until they, too, ceased. Crundmáel protectively held Macha's hand as they fled the carnage, but they'd not managed more than a few paces before a hatchet slammed into his back. With a loud and painful grunt, he pitched forward. Unable to free herself from Crundmáel's grasp, Macha fell awkwardly as she tried to protect her stomach and unborn child. Before she could wriggle free, Budoc's heavy foot pressed hard onto her chest. She was caught, and Budoc bared his teeth in a vulgar smile.

Macha wasn't a comely young woman; her nose may have been too long for some and her ears a little too wide, but she had something about her that gave others pause. If her complexion wasn't as smooth as some young women, then it was her grey eyes that distinctly marked her as unique. They concealed little and spoke of inner strength, courage, and determination. Her man, Crundmáel, whose last vestige of life seeped out beneath him, had genuinely been in love with her. He couldn't articulate it well but had previously told others how she had wit, quickness of mind and an understanding of life that others could only dream of.

It was those eyes that Budoc looked away from. For the briefest moment, and before his thoughts were dominated by pure lust, he briefly experienced doubt.

Budoc laughed away his misgivings, bent down and ripped away the small utility knife attached to the belt at her waist. He wasn't foolish; Budoc was an influential clansman leader who achieved greatness through cunning, strength and intimidation. He led and protected his people; in turn, they dutifully respected and feared him. They listened when he spoke because he was a chief, a *Ceann Fine,* and it would take a clever and strong man to overcome him. He shook his head and threw the knife away. It was small and insignificant, however, it could still have caused him harm, but now she was defenceless. He untied his breeches and lowered himself to his knees before her.

Macha was frightened beyond belief but did not resist or fight Budoc. She had one thought only, and that was to protect the life of her unborn baby. When Budoc pushed up her skirts, Macha innocently raised her hands to protect her head from the blows she knew would come.

He had no thoughts of what the woman's hands were doing; his attention was focused on other matters. Clansmen ran past, offering lewd encouragements, and within moments, Budoc and Macha were alone.

When Macha heard the rumours that Irish clansmen would come for them, she tied a lethal dagger in a sheath and hung it behind her neck, which lay partly hidden beneath her hair and tunic. And Budoc and his men did come, and with them, they brought death. She knew they would violate women even if they were with child - it was the way of these violent men and others like them. Their arrival this grey morn caught the villagers unaware, but Macha had prepared and was ready for them – she couldn't succumb, she wouldn't.

Feigning despair, with her hands at her neck, Macha moved her head from side to side as she desperately sought purchase on the bone-handled blade beneath her hair. Eventually, she found the hilt, and as Budoc continued to look down and fumble beneath her skirts, she saw her chance.

It went against every fibre of her body; killing was contrary to her beliefs, and she'd devoted her entire life to healing the ailing and injured. And now, she confronted a most challenging predicament: the survival of her baby was paramount.

With the narrow-blade dagger firmly in her grasp, her hand shot out with lightning speed and stabbed at his exposed neck, then brutally wrenched to the side as she pulled it free. The chief recoiled in horror as dark, red blood spurted. Instinctively, he swung out an arm in defence. It was a futile attempt. Macha avoided his powerful swinging limb by rolling to the side and, with all her strength, stabbed again, hard between his ribs. Such was his surprise that he never yelled in alarm as he slumped over the still form of Crundmáel.

Macha rolled to her knees and gently stroked the face of her beloved husband. Crundmáel was dead. She whispered a few silent words before carefully standing and replacing the dagger into its sheath at her neck. Driven by pure fear of the clansmen, she bent low, clutching her extended belly and ran away from them, towards the ocean and beyond. Grieving would come later.

With absolute certainty, Macha knew when the body of Budoc was discovered, the clan would come for her and leave no stone unturned in their search. They would avenge the death of a *Ceann Fine*, and she knew from experience the Irish had long memories. With nothing but the clothes she wore, she ran as fast as she dared.

Hidden between large rocks in a gravelly depression at the beach lay a *curach*, a smaller version of the boats that Budoc and his men used. Macha and Crundmáel intended to escape on their tiny craft when the clan came for them. They'd selected the location carefully, hiding it from view and knowing the gravel beach wouldn't damage the animal skins covering the boat when launched.

The *curach* was light, and Macha dragged it over the small, rounded stones towards the water. Behind, she heard cries of alarm, and she looked over her shoulder to see clansmen angrily brandishing swords sprinting towards her. They'd already discovered the body of Budoc, and she didn't have a moment to lose.

She gave the boat a firm and final push and nimbly climbed aboard. Within moments, the tiny boat was headed into the fog. She wasn't in danger of being followed as the clansmen's boats were beached on the other side of the peninsula. Macha shivered as she heard the vile, obscene, shouted threats. She believed them; these men were truly evil and would do to her what they promised. Sixteen men, women and children had perished under the sword of their false Christian precepts.

Her oars dipped in the water, and the small, flimsy craft bobbed away.

Once safely enveloped by the fog, she paused and held her stomach to feel her baby's reassuring movement. She knew it was a boy, and she and Crundmáel had previously decided to name him Cathal.

With an aching heart, Macha quietly resumed paddling through the fog towards the unknown.

CHAPTER ONE

Five years later,

Beneath the forest canopy and from suitable vantage points along the edges of the well-frequented road, highwaymen lurked in the shadowed leafy perimeter to prey on unwary travellers. Less than a half day's walk from where the outlaws waited lay the bustling town of Brycgstow[4], and Melcher Turner, the leader of the ragtag band of highwaymen, believed that merchants and other well-heeled travellers would soon pass by. If they didn't have coin, they'd have other valuable items his highwaymen could liberate, food being high on the list of priorities.

Of annoying interest were a solitary woman and boy who dawdled along the short stretch of road where his band of robbers waited. The boy pointed to various plants and impressively named them, as his mother responded with encouragement. It was apparent they weren't in haste, and occasionally, the boy would stop to investigate a leaf or bush that held his interest and question his mother about them. Melcher wanted the couple to move on, but they weren't in any hurry. He knew the woman probably had nothing of value, but her presence could prove problematic if any wealthy merchants happened by. He silently wished they would hurry along – They didn't.

Melcher had little patience. Five days earlier, an impulsive

4 *Brycgstow – Place by the bridge, or more commonly known as Bristol.*

merchant defending his hoard slashed his arm with a knife, and the nasty gash continued to cause him increasing discomfort and growing worry. The wound was now corrupted and beginning to fester.

"Eric, I think it best if we snatch her, take her off the road before she is seen," said Melcher through gritted teeth as he suffered another painful spasm up his arm.

His second-in-command nodded, "Aye, I shall see to it." He spared his leader a sympathetic look before he slid backwards and out of sight into the forest.

Macha knew that men loitered beneath the leafy branches. She also knew there was little she could do; they couldn't run because they'd catch her and Cathal easily. She whispered to her son, who walked a step in front and warned him to keep pace beside her where she could hold his hand and keep him close. The best they could do was appear unthreatening, continue as if nothing concerned them, and hopefully, be left alone. It wasn't to be.

Suddenly, two filthy armed men appeared, and although they did not brandish swords, they were still intimidating. Without a word, they roughly grabbed her and Cathal and quickly thrust them into the forest, away from prying eyes. Neither she nor Cathal cried out or protested and allowed her captors to lead them away. Macha knew events were out of her control and was acutely aware of the risks of travelling alone, and she accepted them. The men led them deeper into the forest to a campsite where horses were tied.

One of the men grabbed some rope, his intentions all too obvious.

"Must ye bind us? We give ye our word not to run," Macha implored.

Her captors remained silent.

She was tied to a tree, and Cathal was bound by a rope looped around his waist. Even hardened outlaws found it challenging to be cruel to a young lad and spared the boy any undue distress. The last thing anyone wanted was for him to begin wailing, and they knew he wouldn't run far from his mother.

Later, as the shadows lengthened and the sun began to dip beneath distant hills, the highwaymen returned to their makeshift camp. Spirits were high, and the mood was jolly as a man cradling an injured arm stepped up close to her. She didn't look away and, instead, assessed him. She took in his skin pallor and the colour of his eyes and saw his face looked flushed.

"Why is it a peasant woman travels alone with a boy along a dangerous road?" he asked.

She inclined her head. "Why not, good sir? I must be somewhere, isn't here better than there? And here is where ye found me."

Despite the pain from his arm, the man grinned at the enigmatic reply. Macha didn't return the smile.

"Ye have family?" he asked.

Macha shook her head.

"My name is Melcher, and I lead these brave, good fellows." He waved his good arm toward his men, preparing food and building a fire. "We've been most fortunate this day, and we have food to fill empty bellies."

Macha didn't react and remained expressionless.

"Do you judge us? Is this why you cannot answer?" he accused.

Macha held the outlaw's eyes. "I do not judge, fer that serves no purpose, and I care not to explain myself, fer ye have better things to do like take care of yer arm before it takes ye."

Melcher's eyebrows furrowed together. "Ye know about

potions?" he asked.

"Some," she nodded in affirmation, "but I can do little with my arms bound and tied to a tree."

Cathal watched and listened but said nothing

"What are ye called?"

"I am Macha, and this is Cathal," she finally said after a lengthy pause.

Melcher nodded thoughtfully. "Untie her."

Immediately, an outlaw ran over and began to undo the bindings.

He watched as she was untied and felt a compulsion to explain their situation to her. "We are not bad men, Macha. We take from the rich to feed ourselves and others like us who have nothing. We take their bulging purses and purchase food. Most of us have families and children who cry from hunger."

Macha believed Melcher. She'd seen the look of desperate men like this before. They had wives, children, and farms that either produced no food or what food was grown were taken by greedy lords or knights. These weren't bad men; they were desperate men. Free of her bonds, she slowly stood and stretched her cramped muscles. "There is enough light for me to gather what I need fer yer arm." She made no assurances that she'd return to the camp, as the thought of running away hadn't even occurred.

Melcher grimaced. "There will be food fer ye and yer boy when ye return." He turned away and slowly walked to the fire.

"Why did ye let her go? That will be the last we see of her," Eric questioned.

Melcher sighed loudly and eased himself onto a log. "I think not." He looked at his friend. "We are blessed to have her here. Ask me not why, fer I have no answer. I cannot explain. But return, she will, and she will do right by us."

Macha and Cathal remained with the highwaymen for two months. Together, mother and son treated the unfortunate who needed care and visited nearby villages to help the poor. Macha refused payment and asked for nothing in return for her ministrations. Cathal grew quickly, and she willingly accepted offers of clothes for him but not for herself.

Melcher and his men treated her well, protected Cathal, and yet weren't overly familiar and kept their distance. Melcher's arm fully healed, and then the whispers began. Furtive intimations that grew into bold speculation. At first, outlaws spoke quietly amongst themselves and then later, with newfound courage, boldly concluded Macha was a witch.

One morning, Macha approached Melcher, who was readying to ride out. "Cathal and I will take our leave," she simply said.

Melcher was surprised and caught off guard. "Er, I, I..."

"It is time. We must be on our way, and ye have no need of us. Yer men grow weary of me."

Melcher had heard the rumblings and nodded. He understood her reasoning. "Very well, I thank ye, Macha, fer all ye have done."

Macha didn't acknowledge the compliment and turned. With Cathal close at her side, she began to walk away when she paused and looked back at Melcher. "It would behove ye to leave the forest too. Ye and yer men aren't safe here."

"Methinks there's more to be had, Macha," Melcher replied. "We will stay only a week or two longer."

With Cathal at her side, she smiled and walked from the forest onto the road to Brycgstow.

The sun hadn't reached its zenith before a large group of armed knights thundered past. She pitied Melcher and his loyal followers; she knew the knights came for them.

Brycgstow was a thriving port town serviced by the Avon River and reliant on trade from Scotland, Wales, Ireland, and the New World. Macha's clothes were threadbare, no longer repairable, and urgently needed replacing. She hoped to find paying work so she could purchase what she needed.

The town was more extensive than she believed possible. People were everywhere, and the narrow streets were busy. Even as a five-year-old, Cathal was curious and gawked in wide-eyed fascination at what he saw. She clutched him tighter and ensured he was secure at her side, especially when people approached.

Hawkers were trying to sell overpriced trinkets, or shifty-eyed pickpockets looked for easy victims. Cathal was particularly intrigued by a young bard with a melodic and tuneful voice who sang for coin. She pulled him away, not wanting to loiter and become an easy target. Macha felt hemmed in, almost trapped, and she longed for the open countryside and a return to nature, but first, she needed to find work. Cathal began humming the tune he'd heard from the bard.

Ahead, she saw a merchant-tailor selling the clothes she sought. She wandered over to learn the cost and saw the merchant was a dark-skinned man with a thick, full beard and long black hair neatly tied back. Most unusually, he wore colourful clothes not typically worn by merchants or peasants. They were distinctive. She paused as a customer approached the merchant, and they began haggling over the cost of breeches. The merchant was resolute and would not drop his price below the already discounted amount, while the customer was becoming more agitated and frustrated.

As the customer's anger increased, so did the volume of his yelling, and soon, a crowd gathered and, hoping for some excitement, watched the heated exchange. Interestingly, the merchant remained respectful and polite and did not indicate annoyance or anger.

Macha was impressed; the merchant had control of his emotions without showing weakness, and when provoked, he held his tongue and did not offer insult. Although she observed him warily inching back into the protection of his shoppe. The Customer wasn't having any of it and followed the merchant, shouting a barrage of unkind insults and slurs. The merchant had help; another man, also dark-skinned with long hair, who observed closely but did not interfere. Fearing violence, Macha tried to walk away, but the throng of bloodthirsty spectators intent on some afternoon entertainment made it difficult as they pressed inwards.

In frustration, Macha turned around to face the merchant and pulled Cathal in front. Behind, spectators jostled for a better position. She'd had enough. "Halt!" she yelled. "Stop this foolery!"

The unexpected command from a stranger drew all attention to her, and even the merchant and angry customer paused, turning to her in puzzlement.

She nudged Cathal forward and took a step closer. "Why do ye bicker? Ye wish to sell yer breeches," she raised an arm and pointed at the merchant, "and ye want to buy them." She moved her arm and indicated to the customer. "But why quarrel?"

"This merchant demands more coin than I have, and his wares are good but not worth what he asks. He is dishonest!" exclaimed the customer with renewed enmity.

Some sympathisers in the crowd jeered in support of the customer.

“Does he speak the truth?” Macha asked the merchant.

The merchant shook his head vigorously from side to side. “My cloth is the finest in the land; it is strong and will last. I reduce price fer him, and he still complain. I want happy customer, not angry man yelling, so I ask him to go.” He said with a strong, unfamiliar accent.

Behind Macha, the crowd had largely lost interest and was already dispersing. She gave Cathal another gentle push forward, and she followed. “Kindness will help ye. When ye insult a man, he takes offence.”

The merchant looked unsure. “Offence? I make no offence. I not want unhappy customer.”

Macha turned to the disgruntled customer. “Can ye buy breeches like this in other places?”

The man shook his head and hawked at the ground before turning away to leave.

“Then the price of breeches is fair, is it not?” she asked.

The man was trying to save face. “Aye.” He stopped. “I suppose, but I don’t like to be told to go. It isn’t kindly fer a merchant.”

Macha looked at the dark-skinned merchant and raised an eyebrow.

He bowed at the waist. “I am sorry, good sir, I mean ye no ill will.”

The customer looked unhappy and made to be on his way.

“Then sell him yer breeches and be done with this foolishness,” Macha demanded. She was tired and wanted to leave.

The merchant nodded again and held out the breeches the customer sought.

The customer reluctantly paid the merchant, took the breeches and hurried away. Macha grabbed Cathal’s hand and was about to leave.

“If ye work fer me, then I pay ye.”

Macha stopped and slowly turned back to face the grinning merchant. "I only have need fer a tunic, fer my clothes are beyond repair. Nothing more or less."

"Then ye should choose a fine garment now, fer I need ye to look fair."

"What say ye, Cathal?" she asked.

Before replying, the boy turned to the merchant and then nodded.

Macha learned that Darshan Baghmar and his brother Suvrat had voyaged by ocean from a faraway place called India. They brought an assortment of cloth and clothes made from silk and wool. They traded silk for quality wool in various ports along the way and learned how to blend the two vastly different materials to produce a durable cloth that was both strong and finely woven. While Darshan assumed the role of peddling their wares, Suvrat was the master behind blending, weaving and design.

Macha found the two men deeply religious, disciplined and surprisingly gentlefolk. They allowed her and Cathal to sleep in a room where they stored their fabrics and offered to share food. When time permitted, she peppered them with questions and discovered they didn't eat meat, were non-violent and abhorred killing any creature, whether an insect, animal or human. They laughed heartily when she told them she respected and admired their devotion. However, Darshan told her they were not devout at all, and their religion of *Jainism* required a level of commitment they could not adhere to, which was part of why they left their birthplace of Pataliputra in India.

Macha helped Darshan to sell his fine clothes, while Suvrat, along with some local women they'd hired, created garments more suited to the tastes and pockets of local clientele. Cathal spent time helping Suvrat, who took delight in the inquisitive nature of the young boy and, as he worked, began teaching him about the world.

In the beginning, Macha had only intended to work for as long as it took to pay for the new clothes she needed, but privately, she relished the conversations she had with the brothers. Their beliefs, founded in Jainism, struck a chord with her, and during the evenings, she and Cathal listened intently as the brothers told her of life in a faraway place she could only imagine. The days turned into weeks, and Macha understood if she didn't leave soon, the Irish clan would eventually find her. It was time to think about moving on.

CHAPTER TWO

Macha was afforded a half-day off work a week. During that time, she would pack food, and she and Cathal would head for the forest to harvest various plants she used for potions or as dietary supplements. During this time, Cathal was schooled, and like a sponge, he absorbed and retained everything. His perspective and awareness of life had recently begun to change, and she believed it was the positive influence of the Baghmar brothers. Privately, she was thrilled. Cathal started to conceive that life and all its living forms were treasures to be respected and cherished. He was still far from his sixth birthday, yet his mind comprehended much more than boys twice his age and even many adults. She knew he was unique and intelligent, and like her, his sense of logic was uncommon; even the simplest of challenges were now met and overcome with omniscience, without emotion.

During their walk from the forest and back to the clothing shoppe, Macha began to feel uneasy. The impression descended over her like a black shroud and made her shiver. She protectively pulled Cathal closer, and as the sun's lingering rays dipped below green wooded hills, they cautiously approached Baghmar's shoppe. Smoke from cooking fires and food odours wafted down narrow streets, but her thoughts focused only on what lay ahead. Outside the shoppe, a small crowd had begun to gather, and with craning necks, townsfolk inquisitively gawked at the shoppe entrance. With trepidation,

Macha cautiously edged a little closer to see better and then saw men inside, and they didn't need clothes.

Suddenly, a morbid scream pierced the early evening stillness and was quickly cut off. Moments later, two burly men stepped from the entrance and, like discarding garbage, tossed a body onto the street. In the diminishing light, she recognised his clothes and saw enough of his face. It was Darshan. Blood slowly oozed from his neck to pool beneath his unmoving body, and she felt the sorrowful burden of responsibility. This wasn't a simple robbery; it was the Irish, and they came for her.

She turned from the vileness, pulled Cathal away, and within moments, they disappeared into the growing darkness and the labyrinth of narrow streets.

"We must leave here, Cathal," Macha told him.

Unlike boys of a similar age, who'd ask why? Cathal just nodded and accepted his mother's decision.

"We will travel by ship to Frankia..."

"Will they not find us there?" Cathal asked.

She looked down at her son and his discerning look as he stared innocently back at her. Her love was overwhelming, and she pulled him close. "They will not find us if we keep moving, fer yer destiny is assured, and I will keep ye safe. We cannot return to Brycgstow, so we shall make our way to South Hamtun; there, we will find passage."

When Macha and Cathal left Baghmar's shoppe to forage in the forest five days ago, she wore her new tunic, a cape, and carried what few possessions she owned in an oversized hold-all bag she slung over her shoulder. She even had more than enough coin to pay for passage to Frankia. The Baghmar brothers were hospitable and generous; Cathal's clothes were new and would keep him warm and dry, at least until he outgrew them.

Mother and son successfully avoided all villages and any contact with people as they headed east towards South Hamtun. The favourable weather made travelling and sleeping outdoors easier, but Macha was ever vigilant.

She avoided the obvious places to spend the night and instead chose locations that were somewhat exposed but well away from paths, streams and shelter that travellers commonly sought.

One late afternoon, shortly after they cleaned themselves in a stream, and were heading away when they heard horses and the clink of metal - the unmistakable sound of a group of armed men.

With Cathal's hand firmly in her grasp, they ran towards some exposed boulders a short distance ahead. Horses couldn't climb rocks, and men were inherently lazy, and Macha determined it would be most unlikely that they'd dismount to search amongst the boulders if they had no reason.

They reached the rock formation and squeezed into a narrow crevice when the riders appeared. Three of them rode past the boulders where they hid and headed towards the stream where they'd been only moments before. She heard their Irish brogue.

She understood that someone must have seen her and Cathal and informed the three clansmen. The riders paused at the stream and allowed their horses to dip their heads and drink.

When the three Irishmen dismounted and began to set up camp, Macha was devastated. It would be a long and uncomfortable night. *Why are the Ó hAllmhuráin clan so determined to see my death*? She wondered.

Over five years had passed since that fateful day in Chreig Charrach when she protected herself and killed Budoc Ó hAllmhuráin. A *Ceann Fine* was an important person, but to bear a grudge for so long was astounding. Macha didn't understand, and with the complexities swirling around in her head, she eased herself into another more comfortable position between damp boulders and settled down to wait until the Irish warriors departed.

Eamon Ó hAllmhuráin[5] threaded his way around large stones placed by a long-forgotten civilisation around a section of cliff tops known as Cliffs of Aran on the island of Inishmore. He'd travelled by boat, under sail, to reach Inishmore, one of the Aran Islands that guarded Galway Bay in Ireland. Behind and some distance away, half a dozen of his men waited, under strict orders not to follow.

Below, from where he stood, powerful greenish-blue waves, borne on the Sea of Atlas, relentlessly pummelled the cliffs with the endless patience of timeless persistence. In desperation, the spray reached upwards like ravenous tendrils, trying, again and again, to reach him. Eamon took an involuntary step away from the cliff top just as a voice spoke.

"Ye could leap."

Eamon almost jumped in fright. He never heard the druid approach, "I prefer to live, Felix," Eamon replied. The druid frightened him, and he hoped he adequately masked his fear.

Felix was a druid; some said he was a sorcerer who could cast spells or perform magic healing. Other brave souls whispered that Felix was a wizard who could turn people into stones or even animals. However, the Church said it was pure nonsense, and such men with supernatural powers didn't exist – it wasn't Christian. Priest Flann said druids were scoundrels who preyed on the gullible and weak with trickery and

5 *Ó hAllmhuráin* - O'Halloran

sleight of hand. But then, priest Flann had never met Felix; if he had, he would think differently. Eamon knew a Welshman who claimed he'd witnessed Felix turn a beggar into a rock. Eamon didn't know how much was true, but he expected his life to end every time he met Felix.

Felix didn't immediately reply. Instead, he allowed the forces of nature to unsettle the clansman. During the pause, the incessant wind tugged at his robes and pulled the coarse cloth tightly around his thin frame and bony legs. Felix wasn't an old man; he was quite young, but his hair had turned prematurely grey, propagating the look of being patriarchal and wise. He waited until just the right moment when he gauged Eamon Ó hAllmhuráin would speak next and turned his head to face him. "Why does he still live?"

Eamon closed his mouth and swallowed. He could taste the saltiness of the ocean, and then he felt a weakness in his knees, and his legs almost buckled. The ocean's spray reached for him, and it felt like he was being poisoned. He gagged, took an unsteady step backwards and wiped his mouth with the back of his hand before replying. "They, er, were seen east of Brycgstow, but my men lost her."

The druid sighed and turned away to stare at the expanse of ocean. Felix knew he was on precarious ground and must tread carefully with the clansman. The only reason Eamon Ó hAllmhuráin continued to acquiesce to the druid's demands was that he was being blackmailed and didn't have the fortitude to be courageous and disobey.

Felix showed Eamon a bag of coin and instructed him to return to Galway and immediately call on Priest Flann. With a little incentive from the bulging purse, and in the name of the Church, the priest could influence the powerful Ó hAllmhuráin clan to continue to pursue Macha and her son and see their death. Felix didn't care if Macha lived or died; it was the boy's life he sought. The priest had the authority under the guise of his holy prattle and could easily demand the clan continue to seek retribution for Budoc Ó hAllmhuráin's death all those years ago. Eamon reached out to take the purse.

"T'is getting difficult to talk to Priest Flann," shrugged Eamon, "he grows weary of this vendetta. Why is the boy's death so important to ye? Why not just let it be?"

"Difficult, ye say?" the druid asked as he stared vacantly out to sea. "Let it be?" He jostled the purse as he considered his options, delaying handing it over.

"Aye, five years is a long time to seek vengeance." Eamon declared, feeling a little better and more confident now he'd seen the purse.

Felix came to a decision and nodded, but not in agreement. He shuffled a half step closer to the cliff top. "Ye need to see this."

Eamon's eyebrows furrowed together, and he curiously moved closer to the edge to peek at what drew Felix's interest.

Felix was lean and tall. His limbs were long and sinewy, and despite his gaunt, unhealthy façade, he had surprising strength. As Eamon stepped forward, Felix placed a hand on his back and pushed.

Eamon's terror-stricken shriek was carried away by the wind, and his life suddenly and painfully ended on the rocks far below. A powerful wave surge dislodged the body, and within moments, the savage seas consumed him; all traces of the Irishmen vanished.

Unmoved, Felix turned and, still jostling the purse, began walking away. He had another, better way to access the priest.

Macha felt she was constantly looking over her shoulder,

fearing that the Ó hAllmhuráin clan would come for her and Cathal. She wanted to have Ireland safely at her back and England between them. She felt some relief when they finally set foot on Frankia, but not enough to sleep soundlessly; she was worried.

Macha was focused, and she knew the more distance she put between Ireland, the safer she'd feel. An inner voice told her to head to Clugny, just north of Lugdunum[6] , but that same voice gave her no answers or explanations.

She didn't know why they needed to go to Clugny; perhaps she'd overheard someone talk about the town. It mattered not; they had to go somewhere, and Clugny became their destination. With haste, she and Cathal began their long trek inland.

Macha quickly discovered that communicating with the locals was a problem, and she and Cathal did their utmost to learn and speak the language of the Franks. It wasn't easy for her, but Cathal picked it up quickly, and by the time they reached Clugny, he spoke like a true Frankish boy.

Macha and Cathal tended to the sick and injured along their inland route. It wasn't because she felt an obligation to aid people in need, but more about a sense of duty. She had the knowledge and the expertise. Why *should I not help people when I can*? She thought.

Clugny wasn't a large town, but it was dominated by one important feature, a sprawling abbey appropriately called *Abbaye de Clugny.* Cathal stood at her side near the gated entrance. The imposing metal gates were closed during darkness and opened at sunrise. People came and went throughout the day, and men and women were freely permitted to enter. A stranger informed her the abbey was a place where educated monks could tend to the sick. Compelled to discover more,

6 *Lugdunum – Modern day Lyon, Frankia.*

Macha decided to enter.

A visitor pointed out that the sickly were treated inside a building called *Maison Dieu*, conveniently situated not far from the entrance and easily accessible to those who sought care.

When Macha pushed open the door, she was met with a vile medley of obnoxious odours. Sufferers moaned in cots arranged around the perimeter of the gloomy room and were attended to by overbearing monks. She stood near the doorway, taking in the sights before a monk approached.

"*Mademoiselle*, how can I assist?" asked the pasty-skinned monk.

"I wish to offer good cheer to the inflicted and do what we can to ease their pain and suffering," Macha respectfully replied.

The monk's expression changed to one of suspicion. "They have no coin, and we offer a service, a charity to the poor; such is the will of God. No coin changes hands," he affirmed. He gave Cathal a long, hard look, believing mother and son were robbers.

"We seek no coin or favour, only that we may ease the burden of discomfort fer these wretched souls," she added.

The monk thought long and hard. "What are ye called?"

"This is my son Cathal, and I am Macha."

"Irish?" he asked.

Macha nodded.

"Ye may enter, but be quick and don't interfere with the poorly or our ministrations."

Macha bowed her head in thanks, adjusted her head covering and, with Cathal in tow, walked to the first patient.

As requested, they didn't stay long. But on their departure, Macha asked the monk if they could return the next day. He seemed happier with her intentions and agreed.

Once outside in the fresh air, she turned to Cathal. "Foulness thrives in stagnant air, and they need to open the shutters and clean the floors."

Macha and Cathal returned each day, and with them, they brought fruit, which they handed to each bedridden patient. It wasn't much, but the gift and meaning were well taken, and soon, the monks ignored her and her son. On her visits, she came to learn more about the monks and those they cared for, and while she felt the holy men meant well, their belief that spiritual activities would heal was laughable. Macha believed that foulness and corruption eventually killed, and to avert death, the monks needed to prevent defilement from happening. Instead, the cultured monks offered Christian prayer and some elementary medicinal nostrums. Once or twice, she made a subtle suggestion to aid a stricken patient, and the attending monk took her advice, but she would be banished if she openly meddled in the affairs of the monks and patients. She knew not why, but it was essential for her and Cathal to be able to continue to come to the abbey and offer solace and comfort.

CHAPTER THREE

A lone Knight Templar and his sergeant entered Clugny and immediately began shouting for townsfolk to make way. Not far behind them, a contingent of Templar Knights approached shepherding a wagon. They were in a hurry, rode quickly and wouldn't slow down. In fear of being trampled, people scattered, and the narrow thoroughfares emptied as the Templars charged through.

The Templars were filthy, travel-weary, and had no patience for anyone too slow to move out of their way. With urgency, they thundered through the streets, and the wagon carrying an injured knight followed; there could only be one destination - *Abbaye de Clugny.*

Cathal held his hands to his ears as the mighty destriers passed them by; the stark white mantles bearing the red cross the knights wore were soiled and some tattered, evidence of recent battles. It was a sight to behold because these men were fighting monks and perhaps the most fearsome warriors in the known world.

Long after they passed, Macha stared after them, her mind in a clutter. She shook her head to clear the fog and to bring order to her thinking; it did little good. She'd never met a Templar before, although she'd heard of them, and as most folks did, Macha knew a little about their vows, but for some inexplicable reason, she was drawn to them and the abbey. The mystery lay within the abbey's walls, and she determined the answer lay with these fighting monks.

As they had on previous days, they entered the abbey grounds. However, today, Cathal was unusually distracted and lagged a step or two behind, staring at things that fascinated a curious young mind. She paused, waited for him to catch up, and gently pushed him forward. She was tense and anxious and did not understand why she felt as she did.

When they entered the hall, she felt a change. She looked around the room and immediately saw the monks fussing over a new patient. *The knight in the wagon?* She wondered. The hall was dark, and the stench was potent. She leaned down to her son, "They should open the shutters and replace the straw," she tut-tutted again.

Cathal felt the oppressiveness and reached for her hand as he stared at the cot where the newcomer lay.

As always, she made her way around the room and spoke briefly, providing a smile and kind words to the men under care. To those who could eat, she gave them an apple, a simple gift that she thought would help. Again, her mind was distracted as she felt the need to aid the stricken knight. He was in some distress and threshed incoherently, the agony of his wound almost too much for him to bear.

Eventually, she made her way to the newcomer, who was bathed in sweat. He was a young man with a severe leg wound that festered. The attending monks had just walked away, briefly leaving them alone. With a practised eye, Macha assessed his skin colour and felt the heat from his body without even touching him. The injury was grave, but if she could help the knight, she'd need to inspect the wound. Macha noticed his clothes, which confirmed he was a Templar. But this only added to the complications because she knew he couldn't communicate directly with her. His religious order didn't permit him to talk directly with women.

Macha quickly looked around the room to see if anyone was paying her attention. They weren't, and she eased herself onto her knees beside the cot. With care, she removed the soiled cloth wrapped around his thigh. Macha spoke softly and calmly, hoping the man wouldn't fight or resist. The wound was ghastly. It festered in corruption and mattering, and his entire leg was swollen and seeped foulness from the horrific gash.

She pointed out various details to Cathal, who watched with fascination.

Satisfied no one was paying her attention, she bent forward to sniff the wound. She was so engrossed that she never heard the footsteps of approaching men and jumped when one of them spoke.

"What is it ye are doing? This isn't permitted," the monk said quietly. He never spoke loudly in the hall, but his disquiet was evident from the tone of his voice.

With her hand, Macha moved aside a strand of hair that fell over her eyes and looked up at the monk intently. "This wound is devilish; it must be–"

"We will attend to the leg and remove it forthwith," interrupted the monk.

The surgeon, the other man with the monk, stepped closer and looked at the exposed wound. He didn't react to the ghastly inflamed slash that festered.

Cathal looked over at the Templar and saw him open red-rimmed eyes.

The woman took a breath, "I can save his leg. I have not much time, but save it, I can," she offered with unwavering conviction.

Both the monk and the surgeon shook their heads simultaneously. "Nay, it is too far gone; he will die if it is not removed," the monk responded.

"He may not survive the amputation," she replied.

Neither man couldn't disagree with her assertion.

The knight groaned; the involuntary sound escaped his lips, and all heads turned to him. "Cut it off, please. The pain…" he croaked.

"It is not too late, I can save it," Macha pleaded. "Allow me two days. In two days, ye will see an improvement. If I fail, do as he wishes, but two days is not much to ask."

"Not if ye are him," the surgeon moved his heavy bag of surgical tools to his other hand and pointed to the knight. "Fer two days in agony is a lifetime, is it not?"

Cathal had been watching the knight intently and spoke to him for the first time. "She can, she can heal ye, kind sir," he appealed and then vigorously nodded in naïve childish support of his claim.

Macha reached over and pulled her son closer. "Sir, with the Lord's guidance, I *can* heal him." She turned from the monk and looked down at the young man. "I know ye are miserable with torment, but grant me this, let me heal ye?"

The knight wouldn't break his vows and speak to the woman. He shifted his gaze to look at the boy, who stared innocently back at him with wide, open eyes. He held the boy's gaze for a moment or two. Slowly, he exhaled. "Grant… grant her two… two days."

She rose from the cot. "I will return soonest." Without waiting for the monk to challenge her or the patient's decision, Macha grabbed Cathal's hand and strode quickly from the hall.

"Can ye heal him, Mama?" Cathal asked. He had to run to keep up with her.

"Aye, we must," she responded.

Cathal was quiet a moment, "Must we?"

She slowed down, crouched before him and grasped his shoulders. "Aye, we must." She took a deep breath. " I don't know why, Cathal, but you and I will make him better."

Cathal scrunched his eyebrows together as he tried to understand what she said.

"I cannot explain it. But that man," she pointed back to the abbey, "must live, and it is within us both to ensure he does."

"How do ye know?"

Macha exhaled, and her shoulders slumped as she shook her head. "I know not, but it is a feeling, nothing more, nothing less."

Cathal scratched at something behind his ear. "Then we must hurry, mama."

Felix made his home in ancient Roman ruins on the island of Inishmore. It was most convenient, and the stone structures, or what remained of them, offered suitable shelter from the harsh weather that pummelled the wind-swept isle and provided him with the privacy he sought.

People came to him for various reasons, and nearly always in secret. If the Church knew that a parishioner had sought the help of a druid, a sorcerer, punishment would be severe. Mostly, his visitors needed healing, and he was more or less successful in providing healing potions and remedies. Less frequently, he'd be asked to cast a spell or two. Of course, this highly specialised task required a much greater endowment, and as a result, the druid had no shortage of coin.

Payment came in many forms. Sometimes food, coin, clothes or even favours. While favours couldn't feed or keep him warm, they were a suitable form of recompense, especially if the indebted had position, power or knowledge, as was the case of the man and woman who sat apprehensively near the fire before him.

Felix had a seaworthy craft propelled by wind and a loyal servant who ferried people, or himself, backwards and forwards to Galway when needed. The servant had just arrived, delivering two people he was most anxious to see.

After endless prayers and numerous consultations with their parish priest, Conall and Aine Ó Flaithbheartaigh[7] failed in their dreams to be blessed with the birth of a healthy son, although they now had four fine daughters. In desperation and without the knowledge of the Church, the couple had previously arranged to see Felix and sought a magical potion to ensure Aine would finally have a boy. Felix made good with his concoction, and much to their delight, Aine and Connal now had a male heir. However, Felix had not received payment because it had been deferred. As told to the couple, he would call on them when it was time to collect, and it was now that time.

"Aine Ó Flaithbheartaigh, I have need of ye," Felix stated as he chewed on the leg of a well-cooked rabbit.

Aine shared a concerned look with her husband, Conall, before answering. "Aye, how can I help, ye?"

Felix threw the bone away and wiped his hands on his robe. "It is a simple task and requires a journey to Frankia."

"Frankia?" Conall repeated. "It is dangerous to travel alone…"

Aine looked shocked. "I have children and a husband and–"

"Connal will take care of yer children while ye are gone," Felix interrupted. "But ye will travel with one other." He looked over his shoulder. "Mánús!"

"Aye, Master!" came a distant response, and from behind a wall, a figure emerged. He walked up and stood patiently beside the fire.

Aided by the fire, Conall and Aine saw that the man looked

7 *Ó Flaithbheartaigh - O›Flaherty*

peculiar … something about his face. One eye was noticeably lower than the other.

"Mánús will travel with ye," Felix informed.

"Fer what reason does Aine need go to Frankia?" Connal asked with the sound of desperation creeping into his voice. He lowered his head in despair.

"Ye and Mánús will travel to Frankia and find Macha Ó Brollacháin–"

"Macha is dead!" cried Aine.

Felix laughed. "Nay, she is indeed alive and in Frankia with her son. Ye were close friends, and she will allow ye to find her."

Connal raised his head. "Nay, this is unfair. What ye ask is beyond the cost of the potion ye gave us." He stood as his anger erupted. "We will not do yer bidding!" And he thrust out a hand and pointed at the druid. "Find another, we have five children who need their mother–"

Mánús tensed and, in defence of his master, prepared to lunge at the man.

"Sit," instructed Felix with authority. "Ye will do as I bid or forfeit the life of yer son!"

It was Aine's turn to cover her face with her hands. "Nay, ye cannot do this, ye cannot. T'is cruel and unjust," she pleaded and began to weep.

Perplexed by where Macha and her son were going, Felix had turned to his craft. Aided by powdered seeds from the plant commonly called the African Dream Herb, he'd filled the bowl of his clay pipe and smoked before he slept. This induced vivid dreams that the druid would later interpret and seek answers to where Macha and the boy hid.

Whilst dreaming, he'd fly and soar over wooded hills, river valleys, and vast expanses of oceans. What he discovered was disappointing – he learned where Macha wasn't. She wasn't in Ireland, England or anywhere near him. After a few nights of dreams and almost exhausting his valuable supply of seeds, he deduced Macha was in Frankia, not near the coast, but safely inland; she couldn't be anywhere else.

"Frankia is a large place, the search could last years," appealed Connal in a more subdued tone.

"Ye, will leave on the morrow," stated Felix, rising from his seat. "And ye may not return to yer home until ye find Macha and her son," the druid warned before walking back inside the ruins.

"Nay, ye cannot do this," Connal appealed as Mánús led Aine away.

Macha and Cathal returned to the abbey soon after their departure, armed with herbs, leaves and various other unidentifiable substances to help their patient. Without seeking permission, she again carefully removed the Templar's soiled bandages and gently cleaned the exposed gash as best she could. Someone had roughly sewn the wound closed with plant fibres, but the fine strands had separated in a few places, and the injury had reopened. Once she'd cleaned the corruption and the surrounding area with clean water, she placed leaches along the length of the gash and lightly wrapped the leg with a clean cloth. Cathal watched the process closely.

Occasionally, the knight opened his eyes but was delirious and seemed unaware of Macha's administrations. When she was finished, she sought the monk and explained that in two days, she would return. "Until then," she resolutely stated, "do not remove the cloth or touch the wound." While she spoke softly and respectfully, the tone of her voice was firm and left no room for misinterpretation.

The monk saw no reason to argue with her. In his opinion, the knight would most likely die either way. He nodded his head in agreement. "It will be as ye ask."

Macha turned to leave and then paused and again faced the monk. "What is he called, his name?"

"Odo, Sir Odo Brus," he replied.

"Odo Brus." Macha slowly repeated.

She left the hall with Cathal lagging and the name Odo Brus swirling around her head.

Macha and Cathal had passed a soothsayer in Clugny who sat beneath an awning and purported to tell the future. She had not given the hawker a second thought; however, her desire to seek answers overcame scepticism, and after leaving the hall, she decided to visit him.

The soothsayer was an older man of unknown age, with slick prattle and quick eyes, who sat cross-legged on an old threadbare rug. When she approached, the man's expression and demeanour subtly changed, and he waved an arm and invited them to sit before him.

Macha opened her mouth to speak, but the soothsayer spoke first.

"I knew ye would come," he simply said, foregoing his usual slippery jargon. He gave Cathal a long look. "And ye have a curiosity and learning that is most uncommon." He smiled, "Watch and listen carefully, and I will explain to ye."

Cathal nodded.

The soothsayer turned his attention onto Macha. "Fear not, fer I do not create the future, I do not change time or affect life, I watch only. I see things as if I'm looking through an open shutter, and I tell ye only what my eyes see. Do ye apprehend?"

"I, I think so," Macha replied.

The soothsayer seemed to relax, "Then tell me, child, what is it ye wish to know?"

Macha wasn't sure about the man, but then, what did she have to lose but a coin for some brief entertainment. "What can you tell me about Sir Odo Brus?"

"Odo Brus, Odo Brus…" the soothsayer repeated. He closed his eyes, continuing to speak the injured Templar's name. When he stopped, he pulled a small bag with a drawstring, much like a purse but bigger, from a larger bag at his side. He shook the bag vigorously, undid the drawstring and upended the bag. A handful of old bones fell upon the rug.

"Hmmm." The soothsayer said and leaned down to see more clearly.

Macha and Cathal watched intently as the man silently stared at the bones. Without a word, he picked them all up, placed them back in his bag and shook it again. As before, the soothsayer tipped the bones out and bent low to inspect how they fell and were arranged. After a long pause, he scooped up the bones, returned them to the bag, and tied the drawstring.

"I, I, er, I apologise. I saw nothing. I, er, I must go."

"Wait," Macha cried, "What did ye see? Ye must have seen something? Tell me, please."

The soothsayer shook his head, picked up his bags, and stood. "I must go. Er, my rug."

Macha and Cathal stood and stepped aside, and the soothsayer bent down, grabbed his rug, and quickly walked away. He uttered not another word.

CHAPTER FOUR

On the afternoon of the second day, Macha and Cathal returned to the abbey and, as she usually did, began making her rounds and visiting the patients in the hall. She gave fruit to those who could eat, offered words of encouragement with a smile, and moved on to the next. Eventually, she arrived at the litter of the injured Templar.

She looked closely at his face and wondered who he was and why he was so important to her. The soothsayer hadn't been helpful and, luckily, never asked for coin. Her visit with him had been a complete waste of time.

The knight groaned, and she again focused on him. While his eyes were closed, Macha could see the young man was still afflicted and deeply troubled. She leaned forward, gently touched his brow, and felt his skin was hot. Frowning, she focused on his leg and carefully removed the bandages.

Her expression never changed when the wound was revealed. It was no surprise to see the change; she expected as much. Carefully, the leeches were removed, and she leaned forward and examined the gash. As she was apt to do, she spoke to Cathal, pointed to various places of the injury, and explained what she observed. She was succinct and, with patience, carefully instructed him. Although still young, the boy was learning and would acquire all the knowledge and skills she imparted to him over time.

Much of the redness and swelling had decreased, and while still inflamed, the leeches had done their task and eaten the dead skin and toxins; the miracle of their unusual gift never failed to amaze her. "Man kills, nature heals," she simply told Cathal. "Never forget."

She reached into the bag she always carried and removed a small parcel wrapped in cloth she'd prepared earlier. She unfolded the package and carefully placed it on the bed, removed various items, and meticulously arranged them over the exposed wound. Captivated by her ministrations, Cathal watched closely.

Earlier, she'd pounded roots into a pulp, and with the utmost care, she placed the mash directly over the gash and sutures. Then, over that, she positioned moss, lichen, and an assortment of crushed leaves of various sizes and descriptions. Finally, she rebandaged the leg, and her patient hadn't stirred.

Once Cathal helped clean up her mess, they walked to the door to leave when the monk approached. "How fares our sufferer?"

Macha averted her eyes as she knew her presence made the monk uncomfortable. "There is improvement, but he still ails. I have replaced the dressing, and I implore ye, please, do not remove it fer another two days. He is recovering."

The monk looked thoughtful. "Let me see." He walked towards the Templar knight to have a closer look. It was plainly evident the knight rested and appeared less troubled. Indeed, there had been some improvement, as she claimed, and notwithstanding his prediction, the wounded knight's condition had not deteriorated. He nodded. "Very well."

She respectfully dipped her head and hurriedly left the hall, clutching Cathal's hand. "He fares well and will improve a little each day, Cathal. But we must continue to keep the wound free of filth."

Cathal didn't reply; he was staring towards the open gate of the abbey at the soothsayer who stood waiting for them.

No doubt come for his coin, she thought. She went to walk past the man when he stepped out in front of her.

"May we speak?" he asked pleasantly.

"Two days past, ye rushed away and said nothing of what ye saw without explanation," she stated.

"Aye, that I did, but this is why I wish to speak with ye now."

"Then ye have something to say?"

He nodded. "I do."

There was a large tree a short distance away, and Macha pointed to it. "We can talk there."

When they arrived, Macha remained silent, folded her arms, and waited for the soothsayer to explain himself.

"Your request wasn't easy, and I needed time to think and put into words what I saw," he began. "Divination isn't simple or always straightforward, and it requires time to say the right words."

Macha wasn't impressed with his waffling, and her expression must have revealed her less-than-kind thoughts.

"Er, let me explain. If I ask ye to describe the colour red to me, how will ye do this?"

Macha shrugged, "I don't know."

"Ah, then ye see, I am faced with finding a way to interpret to ye what I see so that what I say is exactly what I saw."

Macha exhaled loudly.

"Odo Brus is exceptional. He is destined to be hated by some, feared by many, and er, will leave a lasting legacy of righteousness," the soothsayer explained.

"Then he is a bad man, a villain?" she asked.

"Nay, or rather to some people, he may be bad, but to most, he is a man of virtue. Where I struggled is because it isn't so much about Odo Brus. It's about his legacy, what happens long after he dies."

"Then Odo must die?" Macha clarified.

"Nay, nay, he must be allowed to fulfil his fate."

Macha paced backwards and forwards as she tried to make sense of the soothsayer's visions. "Then Odo Brus is a good man?"

"Aye, I believe so."

"What if he dies before he has fulfilled his destiny or fate?" she asked.

The soothsayer shrugged. "I know not. But I guess evil will thrive. With the absence of good, then what remains?"

It was a question that didn't need to be answered.

"Why is Odo Brus linked to me? Why do I feel this way about him?" Macha asked.

"Oh, but my child, he isn't linked to you."

Macha looked surprised and stopped her pacing to glare at the soothsayer.

"Odo Brus is linked to him," he pointed to Cathal. "His fate is shared with Odo Brus." The soothsayer stepped to the tree and leaned against the trunk.

Macha's mouth opened. "And this is their destiny … together?" she asked with a slight shake of her head.

"Nay, when people think that God has planned their future, and therefore we cannot change that future, then that is fate. Destiny encourages people to act, move forward, and determine their individual future, so we have a hand in creating our future."

This man was confusing.

"Then this Templar knight and Cathal are linked together through fate?"

He smiled. "Exactly."

She had more questions, a lot more. "Is there anything more ye can tell me about Odo Brus and the destiny, er fate of my son?"

The soothsayer shook his head. "Nay, that is all I saw, and ye know everything. Time will aid ye, fer then ye can look again into the future."

"Aye, only if ye are with us."

"Nay, if I so choose, my destiny could be elsewhere," he laughed, "but my fate is with ye and yer boy," the soothsayer grinned. He rubbed his chin and pondered the matter. "I can teach the boy and show him how to see. I know this because he has the ability, fer yer son is special."

Macha was aware Cathal was different. Did she trust the soothsayer, or did he have other less-than-wholesome desires? "Where will ye teach him?"

"It matters not to me where it suits ye," he replied, moving his head to look down at Cathal. "And what say ye, boy?"

Macha looked down at her son and gave him a nod.

"If it is well with ye, Mama, then I would like to see better," Cathal responded.

It was agreed Soothsayer Lohier Blanc would instruct Cathal in practising *cleromancy* in the small room Macha rented on the outskirts of Clugny.

When Macha and Cathal returned to the abbey, she saw the knight was awake and attentive. She was still reeling over the soothsayer's claim about this man's fate and desperately wanted to talk to him. However, that was forbidden. Observant of Templar protocols, she did not speak to the knight and dipped her head to avoid eye contact as she lowered herself onto the filthy straw-covered earth. She began to hum a melody as she focused on his leg.

As carefully as she could, she slowly unwound the bandage, peeled the remains of the moss, leaves, and pulp from the gash and studied it.

Ever curious, the monk wandered over, stood behind her

and looked over her shoulder at the trauma. He crossed himself and muttered a few words of prayer. "T'is but a miracle," he said, shaking his head in disbelief.

"What? What has happened?" the knight asked the monk.

From the folds of his robe, the monk produced a cross and clutched it tightly to his chest. "God has seen fit to spare yer leg and life, Milord. I believe it not, but my eyes do not deceive." With the realization of a new thought, his eyebrows furrowed together. "Did ye cast a spell, use sorcery?" He stepped backwards and raised the cross protectively to ward off evil spirits.

Macha had heard the accusations more often than she cared to remember. She shifted position slightly to see the monk better. "Did ye see what I removed from the wound? They were from plants and roots, and ye did not hear incantations fer I uttered none. This man is healing because of nostrums from the earth." She ignored the ridiculous allegations and turned back to the knight's leg.

The monk gave her reply some consideration. He had not heard her cast a spell... If she had, then indeed, someone would have heard and told him. He relaxed and exhaled, swallowing away his fear and turned to the knight who looked at him inquisitively. "Yer wound is healing, Milord. I believe it not, but this woman has given ye back yer leg and life."

"Then I offer my gratitude and thanks to her and God," the knight stated.

Cathal watched and listened to the exchange with curiosity, then turned his attention to his mother, who began repacking the wound with her unique combination of root pulp and leaves. The monk continued to observe as the Macha finished her task and rewrapped the leg with a clean, unsoiled cloth. When completed, she eased herself upright, back to her feet, reached inside her bag, and handed Cathal an apple.

Self-consciously, Cathal turned to the knight. "Milord?"

In response, the Templar blinked open his eyes.

"Mama says I should give ye this." he handed the apple to the knight and took a step back closer to his mother.

The knight didn't immediately respond but held Cathal's gaze for a few heartbeats. "Tell yer *maman* I am very grateful fer all she has done to help me. God has blessed her with this gift of healing, and I am forever in her debt." He looked at the apple. "Thank ye fer yer help too."

Cathal's cheeks reddened.

"My name is Odo Brus; what is yer name?" suddenly asked the knight.

Cathal turned his head, squared his shoulders, and stood straighter. "Milord, my name is Cathal," he said proudly.

Odo was exhausted and wanted to sleep. "I hope to see ye again, Cathal."

The knight never heard Cathal mouth the words, "We will."

Macha reached down, grabbed Cathal by the hand, turned and began to walk from the hall. The monk watched a moment, then called after her. "Wait!"

She stopped, and the monk approached.

"Why is it ye do this and come to these men and help?" he asked.

"Because I can," was her simple reply.

The monk laughed, "So can I, but that is not the answer I seek."

She sighed softly. "If ye saw a man, a woman, or a child fall to the ground before ye, would ye stop to help?"

The monk looked puzzled, "If they weren't heathens or unclean… then, er, of course."

"Then how is it ye know if they are heathens or unclean?" she asked.

The monk thought of a suitable response.

Undeterred, she continued. "Ye pass judgement on them, I

do not judge, fer all are worthy of help, and because I can help them, then I do."

The monk scratched at something on his neck and found himself staring at her back as she and the boy departed the hall.

Cathal, a step behind his mother, turned to look over his shoulder at the knight named Odo Brus. He smiled at him and then followed his mother from the hall. They needed to hurry because he was beginning lessons that afternoon.

Again, Macha's plans didn't go as hoped. Initially, she didn't want to linger in Clugny longer than necessary. However, she was treating locals in need of care regularly, and now with Cathal taking lessons from Soothsayer Lohier Blanc, she decided it would be best to stay in Clugny a while longer.

Every day, Lohier visited them and spent either the morning or afternoon with Cathal, patiently guiding and advising him on the complex art of *cleromancy.* Cathal absorbed everything he was taught, and when the lesson was over, Lohier questioned him about what he'd learned, and he'd answer with confidence and accuracy.

CHAPTER FIVE

Aine resisted, protested and fought Mánús at every opportunity as they departed Ireland. She was a strong-minded woman, and she wouldn't easily succumb to the will of Felix and his peculiar roughneck manservant or whatever he was. She had a family: four daughters, a son, and a husband who would have to provide and care for them all in her absence. It wasn't just; she felt she'd been betrayed and tricked by Felix.

The only reason she eventually allowed Mánús to lead her away was when he had unkindly reminded her that her son would die if she did not do as asked. The potions that the druid Felix gave her were potent and enabled her to give birth to a healthy boy. At his will and leisure, Mánús claimed, the druid had the right to take her son's life as she had never repaid her debt to him. It broke her heart but not her spirit.

"The sooner we do as Felix asks of us, then you can quickly return to yer family, and the lad will be unharmed," Mánús told her.

Felix had provided Mánús with ample coin, and the two of them had spent weeks travelling across Frankia, visiting one town after another and enquiring after an Irish woman and her five-year-old son. They'd had some reported sightings, which turned out to be nothing, and a few positive responses eventually led them to Clugny.

Aine had begun to give up. Part of her still believed Macha had been slaughtered on *Chreig Charrach* by Budoc all those years ago and felt this ridiculous search was a waste of time. She wanted nothing more than to go home to her family and husband, whom she missed so much. Aine was weary, homesick and tired of the escapade forced upon her, so she was momentarily stunned when she first glimpsed Macha from a distance. She truly believed her dead.

They'd begun to wander the streets and markets in Clugny, asking after Macha and the boy. Mánús believed she was close and became more watchful. Aine had a basic knowledge of the Frankish language, while Mánús didn't and, no matter how hard he tried, couldn't make any headway in learning Frankish. In addition, people were suspicious and reluctant to talk to him because of his facial deformity. Talking to locals was generally left to her.

Just as they were about to leave the market, she saw Macha. She froze, and then Mánús gave her an unkindly shove from behind.

"What is it?" he asked.

She thought quickly. "Tis this day a year past that my son was born." She watched as Macha disappeared into the crowd.

Mánús grunted and pushed her again to keep her moving.

She thought about telling Mánús what she saw, then decided against it. Macha was here in Clugny and had no idea that she and Mánús were in search of her. Somehow, she must find a way to speak to Macha without Mánús knowing.

Felix had sent them to Frankia to find Macha and the boy and trusted that Aine would identify Macha, as Mánús did not know what she looked like. The threat of losing her son if she disobeyed Felix was reason enough. However, there had to be a way to warn Macha without having either of their sons killed. Aine hoped Macha would return to the market around the same time the next day.

"Ye are in danger," informed Lohier when Macha returned from the market with food. She'd begun going to the market alone when Cathal was with the soothsayer, and she placed her trust in him and knew he posed no risk to her or Cathal. He was a good man, sincere, and gifted. He also became a friend, and they spent hours talking and learning from each other.

Macha looked fearful. "Then we must take our leave. Cathal, it is time," she said.

Lohier shook his head. "It will not serve ye well. Ye will be in as much danger if you leave or stay. Makes no difference."

Macha rushed up to him. "How do ye know? What have ye seen?" she pleaded.

Lohier placed a hand gently on her shoulder. "My child, two people come fer ye and Cathal; if ye run, they will know where." He shook his head, trying to make sense of it all. "It's like… It's as if they know what ye will do next and where ye will go. I believe they've been guided."

Macha turned away and walked to Cathal, who sat on the rushes on the floor studying bones. "Then what can I do to protect myself and Cathal against two Irish clansmen, Lohier?"

"Two Irish clansmen? *Non, non*, Macha. It is a man and a woman who seek ye."

Macha looked incredulous and turned to sit on the edge of her cot. She needed to think.

As usual, Macha visited the market around the same time as Lohier instructed Cathal. She kept an eye open for anyone who showed more than a casual interest in her but saw nothing to cause concern. When she had everything she needed and was about to return to her room, a woman casually stepped up beside her.

"Macha, it is I, Aine," she said, barely above a whisper. "Don't look or acknowledge me. A man, a tall man standing near us, has been sent here, and he will kill ye and yer boy."

Macha froze. She recognized her old friend's voice and, to hide her fear and trembling hands, picked up some onions to inspect them; her mind raced as she thought of options.

"Macha, I will try to return here alone tonight to this place when it is dark. If I cannot come, I will try the next evening or the next and explain to ye." Aine casually walked away, and after a moment or two, Macha risked looking up and saw the man Aine described. He was tall, and his face looked deformed as one eye was lower than the other. She tried to steady her nerves as she slowly ambled back to her room.

Lohier compulsively rubbed his hands together, something he did when upset. After a short while, he looked up at Macha. "And ye trust this woman?"

"Aye, she is a dear friend. If she wanted to cause me harm, then she would have let the man know who travelled with her that I was there, and she didn't." Macha met Lohier's probing gaze. "I will meet her, fer I need to know why the clan is so determined to see my death after so many years."

Lohier grimaced and took a deep breath. "Macha, my dear child, it is not the clan who seeks yer death. I have seen, and what I saw does not bode well. The man and woman who come here fer ye were sent by a sorcerer." He raised his hand to ward off the question he knew she would ask. "Nay, I know not who this sorcerer is, but let me tell ye, he seeks…" He turned his head to look at Cathal.

Macha's hand flew to her mouth, and she swallowed away the fear. She took a moment to think. "Then it is settled. Can ye look after Cathal when I return to the market square?"

Lohier nodded. "Of course."

The market was a daily occurrence, and the vendors typically occupied the same spaces and stalls. To make it easier, they left their awnings in place overnight, and Macha stood patiently beneath a canopy where the light of the moon wouldn't expose her while she waited for Aine to appear. She didn't.

Macha returned the next evening and again on the third evening before she finally saw movement and a woman's silhouette walking towards her; it could only be Aine. Macha waited for her to approach, then firmly held her by the elbow and led her down a nearby alley away from prying eyes.

"I thought ye and Crundmáel dead, killed by that gobdaw, Budoc," began Anne after a quick hug.

"Aye, I almost was. But I managed to escape and have my baby. Crundmáel was killed by Budoc. But Aine, why are ye here looking fer me? What does this all mean?"

Aine looked around to ensure no one had entered either end of the alley. "My son will die if I don't find ye," Aine began with a flood of tears. "He will kill my wee boy.

Macha grabbed Aine's shoulders and leaned forward. "Who, Aine? Tell me, who sent ye, who is behind this?"

"The druid, Felix. He sent me and his servant Mánús, and he is here to kill ye."

Macha shook her head. "Felix, the sorcerer?" She knew of the man, as most everyone had, but nothing more. "Nay Aine, Felix seeks not my death. He wants to see the death of my son Cathal," she removed her hands and let them hang at her sides. "But I don't know the reason."

Aine shrugged. "And I don't know, Macha, what can we do?"

"Ask the servant why; he may tell ye."

“I have, and he says nothing. Aine looked anxious. “I must return Macha, or Mánús will ask questions. Can we meet here in two days, at the same time?

“Aye, ask him again and with luck, ye may have word fer me,” Macha replied as they walked from the alley and almost collided into Mánús. He recovered quickly, reached out, grabbed Macha, and pulled her into his body. Aine screamed and then shouted at him to let Macha go.

Mánús sneered, “Where is yer boy? Where-is-he?” he grunted and violently shook Macha, believing that a good shake would loosen her tongue.

Eventually, he stopped shaking her, and with one arm firmly around her neck, he extracted a knife with a very long blade.

“No,” Aine shouted and leapt for him.

Even with one arm wrapped around Macha, he was quick. He pivoted, and his arm shot out and slashed cruelly across Aine’s stomach and up her chest. It was an unnecessary, vicious strike delivered with the single purpose of killing. She collapsed onto the ground as her lifeblood drained from her body.

Macha was trying to fight Mánús and had her hands up around his arm that encircled her neck. She wanted an opening so she could reach her knife that still hung down her back.

Before Mánús could reposition himself, he was attacked by another. This person was stronger than the woman, and Mánús eased his hold on Macha so he could focus and defend himself from the new threat.

Macha slipped free and onto her knees as Mánús fought like a man possessed. He spun wildly and tried to stab the new assailant. After a moment, he stepped quickly to the side, and Macha saw it was Lohier.

“Nay, stop!” she cried as she pulled her knife from its sheath around her neck.

Lohier was no match for the much younger and stronger manservant and never stood a chance, but he created a distraction, and for Macha, it was enough, but too late. Lohier failed to step away from the scything blade, and Mánús saw the opportunity and lunged. The long blade slipped between the ribs of her dear friend Lohier, the soothsayer.

Macha wasn't finished. With strength and wild determination, she leapt onto the back of Mánús as he pulled his knife free from Lohier. But the Irish woman was a step ahead. She reached around her assailant's exposed neck and, with her knife honed to a razor sharpness, easily sliced through Mánús's throat, and he, too, collapsed to the ground. In futility, he tried to stem the blood flow with his hand, but he could do little.

On hearing the commotion, someone yelled, and Macha heard questioning voices approach. She ran. Just like when Budoc attacked and killed the villagers on Chreig Charrach almost six years ago. She ran for her son.

She found Cathal alone in her room and, without explanation, grabbed their meagre belongings and his hand and disappeared into the night, heading towards the forest where she knew they'd be safe. She didn't have to explain much; somehow, Cathal knew what had happened. Not because he'd mastered interpreting the bones but because Lohier had told him what could happen when he left Macha's room each time she went out to meet her friend from Ireland. Cathal had been forewarned. But being forewarned didn't help his grief at losing Lohier.

Macha abhorred violence; she hated killing any living creature, even for food, and she had imparted her beliefs to her son from an early age. However, killing an evil man and fleeing into the safety of the woods did not provide solace. She was deeply afflicted and tried to reconcile the death and violence that followed her.

As usual, they avoided towns and villages and kept their distance from others, preferring to live from the land in solitude. Macha believed the druid Felix wouldn't rest until Cathal died, and befriending people only put them at risk.

Late one evening, she pulled Cathal close. "Ye will have to learn to protect yerself. Men seek yer death, Cathal. Fer, I know not why, and one day ye may come to understand the reasons. But to do nothing and allow these men to harm ye is wrong. Violence is the way of man, and ye must learn to defend yerself from a simple bully, a quarrelsome knight, or a druid, intent on seeing yer death. Do ye understand?"

Cathal didn't move as he thought about what his mother had advised. He didn't comprehend and couldn't understand; he was too young. He shook his head.

"One day ye will, and when ye do, then learn to protect yerself."

CHAPTER SIX

They ventured north into the forests of Bohemia and south to the warmer climates of Iberia, avoiding unnecessary contact with people when convenient. It wasn't the life Macha wanted for her son or herself, and years passed without incident. It would be reasonable to expect that Felix had given up hope after all this time, and it was Cathal who changed her perspective.

After the death of Lohier, Cathal continued to learn and practice with the bones. He was never without them, and after a while, Macha even forgot to question what he had discovered from them.

It came as a surprise when Cathal turned to her one evening. "We must return to Ireland, *Maman*, only then will we find peace."

Macha looked at her son in surprise.

"Felix waits fer us, and we must confront the man. Only then will we know what ails him." He reached out for her hand. "*Maman*, if we do not return, we will forever live in fear."

She knew he spoke the truth and had deftly avoided making the unpleasant decision earlier, but she was frightened. Facing Felix was the most horrifying thing she'd ever had to do. The thought of returning to Ireland was daunting and made her feel ill.

"The bones?" she simply asked.

Cathal nodded. "West is where our fate takes us."

The following day, they walked through the forest towards the coast.

Two months later, Cathal and Macha stepped foot in England, and without delay and urged by Cathal, they began their journey across England and towards Ireland.

Cathal was becoming more assertive and firmly insisted on leading the way. It was like he followed a marked path - as if he knew exactly where he needed to be. Macha didn't question or resist and followed a step behind.

One week after arriving in England, they were walking along a well-used path when Cathal stopped unexpectedly. Macha walked up beside him. "Cathal?"

"Do ye hear it, *Maman*?"

Macha inclined her head and listened. There was nothing to hear but the breeze in the trees and birds chattering. "Nay, what do I listen fer?"

"Someone ails, fer I hear moaning," he stated with ever-growing confidence.

Again, Macha strained to listen and shook her head.

Cathal cautiously edged towards the side of the trail and began walking around low-growing bushes towards a stand of trees near a stream. Macha followed curiously. He paused and pointed. She quickly caught up and saw where he indicated. It was a man who was severely injured and tormented in disordered incoherence. He was in danger of hurting himself as he writhed and wildly flailed his arms.

"Come," Macha said and, without hesitation, went to the man's assistance.

"Odo!" cried the man over and over again.

Macha recognised his face immediately; it was him, the same man, only older. She grabbed Cathal's arm and turned to face him. "Is this why we are here?"

Cathal nodded.

"Do ye remember him? He is the man we helped in the abbey, the Templar Knight all those years ago?" she asked.

"He is no longer a knight; he, er, he looks…"

"Aye, he has seen bad times," Macha said as she dropped to her knees beside the injured man."

She was in danger of being seriously hurt as the man thrashed about. Without being asked, Cathal lay across his legs, and Macha pinned his arms. After a few heartbeats, the thrashing eased, and the man tried to rise.

"Odo," he cried, "Save me!" It sounded like a croak. His eyelids flickered open, and he tried to sit up and struggled. "Where is my sword and bow? The blackness slowly dissolved into familiar shapes, and he saw and recognised her immediately. It was the woman from the abbey in Frankia, and she held his arms and spoke his name.

"Odo, all is well," she said calmly. The sound of her words … reassuring and soothing.

His chest rose and fell in desperation, and his heart raced.

"Odo, we are here to help ye," she said.

He saw her smile and then felt a weight on his good leg. He looked down and saw it was the boy; her son lay over him.

He stopped struggling. "I, I…" was all he could manage.

He felt the lightness as the boy moved from his legs, and the woman released his arms. Slowly, his breathing settled, and he swallowed thickly, his throat parched.

She held a clay bottle to his lips, and he drank greedily. The cool water helped, and slowly, his mind returned to lucidity, and he could focus on the present. "My leg, I suffer greatly," he managed to croak.

"We will help ye and are not here to cause ye harm," she

comforted. “Yer mind has taken ye to dark places, but everything is as it should be; fear not.”

Odo looked at the boy, who innocently stared back. Suddenly, his face creased into a friendly, boyish smile, and he immediately relaxed and felt the tension ease. But the pain in his leg didn’t. “My leg,” he cried.

Macha removed the soiled cloth from around his leg, cleaned the wound and then gave instructions to Cathal, who ran off. Within a short time, he’d returned with an armload of greenery.

Odo felt ill and shivered uncontrollably.

Macha was pleased with what Cathal brought her, and she took time to instruct him and point out various essential details. As he always did, Cathal listened with interest and occasionally nodded as she sorted the items he brought. Eventually, she reached into a leather bag, extracting a mortar and pestle, and began rhythmically crushing the plants and roots into a paste.

She hummed as she ground and fused the substances together. The melody and sound of her voice was uplifting and put Odo at ease as the torment of his nightmare was still raw and unsettling.

When the wound had been treated and a clean cloth strip wrapped around his leg, Macha sat back against the tree and closed her eyes.

“How is it ye come to be here?” Odo asked.

“We head fer Ireland, …to home,” she simply stated.

“But I last saw ye in Frankia, at the abbey that was, uh, years ago.” Odo turned to look at the boy. He’d grown since he saw him last.

“Aye, we go where needed and do what we can to help.”

She paused a moment, then opened her eyes and studied him closely. "When we saw ye in the abbey, ye wouldn't speak to me."

"Aye, a lifetime ago." His leg throbbed, and his teeth chattered.

"And ye still live."

"Aye, thanks to ye and Cot... Cet..."

"Cathal," he replied.

"Aye, Cathal. I owe ye my gratitude, and ye too. What are ye called?"

"I am Macha," she dipped her head. "And now ye are a priest."

"I am, but ye know me as Odo, and I am known here as Oswald. Please, I ask ye–"

"We will call ye Oswald, as ye ask," she suddenly said as if anticipating his request.

Odo was exhausted, his leg was painful, and he shivered. He closed his eyes. This woman and boy were confounding.

Cathal built a fire and set traps for food. There were instances where the fire wasn't enough to keep him warm, and at other times, Macha observed that Oswald was hot and broke into sweat. She and Cathal remained at his side and tended to him as best they could. She used the stream to wash the robe he'd soiled and cleaned the dirty bandages while Cathal hunted for food and wild vegetables. Oswald lay beneath a blanket that kept him warm, and he felt immense gratitude that Macha and Cathal had come to his aid – again.

As their patient slept, Macha and Cathal spoke quietly. "Ye saw this?" she waved her arm towards Oswald. "Through the bones?"

Cathal nodded. "I feel it now and know this man and I are

somehow, er, connected. But I have no notion as to why. Do ye know, *Maman*?"

"I wish I did, Cathal."

"When will we learn? Will the sorcerer tell us?"

Macha felt a chill and wrapped her cape tightly around her shoulders. "I know not."

That night, Macha was plagued by vivid dreams. Unknown voices told her things that made no sense, and she saw things that meant nothing to her. Bothered by the unusual experience, she told Cathal in the morning as Oswald slept. But typically, of a boy, he had no insights. The bones provided no clues to the outcome of their encounter with the druid.

After two days of torrid nightmares and discomfort, Macha noticed Oswald's condition improving. After the second night, Oswald finally slept soundly and woke feeling refreshed and stronger, informing her that the wound's throbbing had eased considerably.

"The poison has mostly gone," Macha told Oswald. "But ye need to eat and regain yer strength. If ye must, then tomorrow ye can be on yer journey if ye travel slowly."

Oswald nodded reflectively. "Aye, I will heed yer advice and wisdom." He scrutinised Macha carefully. "How was it that ye found me here, fer the road is some distance away?"

The images and voices she'd dreamed of two days earlier flooded back into her consciousness.

She held his gaze a moment and glanced at Cathal. "Methinks, Oswald, that ye found us. We were travelling, and yer cries and torment alerted us to yer need."

"Is this what ye do, help the sick and ailing?" Odo asked.

Cathal sat back against a tree, cleaning a rabbit's skin. He looked towards his mother and listened to her response.

"Is it not our duty to help those in need? We could have

passed ye by when we heard ye cry out," she shrugged. "But methinks ye are a good man and would do the same fer anyone – fer a peasant or noble." Her head turned and followed the flight of a murder of crows as they flew past. "We do what is right, not because we must."

"Then ye follow yer faith?" Oswald asked.

"Of course, but not as ye do. Men decide yer faith; my faith is determined by the world around me and the laws of nature." She saw the look of puzzlement on his face. "Who created this?" She spread her arms wide. "Our God did. Not mortal men with their judgements, prejudices and greed."

Oswald reflected on her words.

"Use the world around ye, Oswald," she added. "Did ye see the crows that flew past here moments ago?"

He did see them and thought nothing of it, they were birds, just birds flying away to feed. "Aye, I saw them."

"They flew from south to north silently. That means all is well, and they were not alarmed or frightened. Does that mean I am a witch?"

Oswald was shocked. No one openly spoke of witches. His mouth opened, and he stared at her.

She smiled at his reaction. "I am not a witch, but I use what God created – the birds, plants, trees and animals to help me, and then I help others."

Oswald relaxed as he understood her point. "Ye had me fearful."

She laughed, and then her expression turned serious. "Why is it ye have become a priest?"

Cathal paused from his task with the skin and turned to him with curiosity.

He thought carefully. "Because, Macha, I have dedicated my life to protecting someone." He saw the corners of her mouth twitch.

"I see ye have suffered greatly. Yer eyes tell a story of pain and suffering, not through a wound from a sword or lance. The hate within ye festers like the poison in yer leg, allow it to pass. If ye don't, it will destroy ye," she advised.

"That pain and my memories keep me alive and remind me why I do what I must." Oswald turned away and couldn't look at her.

"Acting on emotion may see yer death," she simply said.

Oswald looked alarmed, and his head spun. "What did ye say?"

Macha swallowed. She'd lived through this conversation in her dream and knew exactly what to say. It was like she was being guided. "Ye heard me, Oswald, and ye know what I mean. Protect yer son as best ye can. But do not do so at the risk of yer own life, fer ye have much to give him. If ye die, he has nothing."

Oswald's eyebrows knitted together as he pondered what she told him. He exhaled slowly. "I try hard not to make decisions based on my past and anger," he said. "But it is not always easy."

Slowly, she raised a hand and pointed a finger at him. "Be warned, yer greatest enemy is the bishop. He will seek yer death and that of yer son. It matters not where ye go or travel to; his shadow is long, and the darkness will follow. He will not rest."

Odo felt his heart begin to race.

"In the morn, we will leave," she suddenly said. "We will not see ye again, but God will be at yer side. With yer help, yer son will survive and leave his mark on the world, fer he is special."

"What do ye speak of?" Odo shook his head.

"I tell ye these things because the knowledge is plain fer all to see. But ye cannot see the stories nature has to tell." She spread her arms wide to encompass the area around them.

"Cathal, do ye see what yer ma sees?" Odo asked.

He nodded emphatically. "*Maman* teaches me."

"Then my son will live, and I have no reason to fear?" Odo asked Macha.

She shook her head and laughed. "Nay, Oswald, I do not predict the future. I said, if ye help yer son, then he will survive."

"But you predicted ye would never see me again. Ye can't possibly know that."

"Aye, except, we journey to Ireland, and ye will remain near yer son. It isn't likely I will see ye again, she laughed.

This conversation was too much for Odo, and he wanted to rest and think. This woman was an enigma, a contradiction...

The next morning, Macha and Cathal inspected the wound, repacked it with a fresh layer of herbs and small crushed leaves, and then rewrapped Oswald's leg. He didn't know what herbs and plants she placed over the gash in his leg; however, whatever they were, they had helped. When finished, Macha told him he could safely continue his journey if he didn't overdo it, rested frequently and tended to his leg.

"Only clean cloth; do not use soiled rags," Macha insisted. "Wash the wound with fresh water twice daily, just as we have done. Ye will heal quickly now."

"Many thanks to ye, Macha. Last time we met, ye saved my leg, this time, ye saved my life. I am truly in yer debt."

Macha smiled and turned to follow Cathal, who led the way.

"Why is this man, Odo or Oswald, so important to us?"

Macha walked a few steps more before answering. "Methinks Felix will know."

"The sorcerer? The man who wishes me dead?"

"Aye, that is why we return to Ireland," she replied.

CHAPTER SEVEN

Felix stared blankly into the fire that burned in a large pit within the ancient ruins on the island of Inishmore. He sat quietly, transfixed by leaping tendrils of ever-changing rhythms and colour, while a manservant occasionally stoked the fire with peat and driftwood. Large moss and lichen-covered boulders sheltered him from the wind and rain that lashed the exposed isle, but he had no thought about the weather or the damp chill that found its way through his clothing and into his bones.

After the fire was again fuelled, the manservant didn't move away, and he shuffled closer to his teacher and paused with his head respectfully dipped. "They come, *Sacart* [8]."

Felix reluctantly tore his gaze from the fire, made brief eye contact with the servant, and then turned his attention back to the dancing flames with a sigh. He loathed the Norsemen with a passion, and while hesitant to admit it, he was even frightened of them. Their Gods were powerful, unforgiving, and cruel. Although he didn't shy away from cruelness, the *Ostmen*[9] were savage and unpredictable, and he lamented the day he became beholden to them. They arrived this evening to seek progress on a simple task he'd promised to deliver. Sadly, he'd failed, but not for want of trying.

Borne on the wind, he heard their voices long before he saw them. Loud and disrespectful, the Norse valued nothing except bravery, violence and their Gods – life meant nothing.

8 *Sacart – Irish for priest.*

9 *Ostmen – Is what the Vikings called themselves*

It wasn't to be respected or honoured, it was a temporary existence between *Valhalla* and *Hel*, or as they called it, *Midgardr*, the abode of mankind. Slowly, Felix eased to his feet, clasped his hands together, ensured his expression did not convey his feelings and stared blankly at where he knew they would appear.

They were seldom without weapons, and true to form, twelve heavily armed warriors from the north rounded a large boulder and clumped towards where he waited.

The Norsemen's leader, a brute of a man called Nels One-Ear, stepped up to Felix, clapped him hard on the shoulder, and laughed. "Ahh, Druid, is good to lay my eyes upon ye."

Felix recovered from the blow. "Aye, is good ye have come," he croaked.

"Is it?" Nels One Ear's expression hardened, and his eyes narrowed. "This rock ye live on isn't fit for whores or dogs," he growled. Behind him, his men settled on rocks and logs surrounding the fire for warmth and to dry out.

"It isn't safe fer me to live anywhere else, the Church would welcome my death," Felix offered in reply.

The Norseman's look softened, "Then we share something, eh? Fer the Church would joyfully see us all killed," he laughed.

The druid grimaced. He knew the Norsemen weren't welcome in Ireland, and since their defeat at the battle of Clontarf many years before, the invaders sought to regain a footing on Irish land and make it their own. If Ireland's rulers knew of this meeting, he'd be executed as a traitor without delay. Before him, Nels One-Ear stood arrogantly, with his hair shaved close to his scalp at the sides to brazenly show off his battle-earned deformity of having only one ear.

Nels returned his look. "We've travelled far and have thirst. Bring mead, wine or that cat's piss *metheglin* ye Irish love to drink." Behind Nels, his men murmured in support.

Felix knew the *Ostmen* would remain on the isle until they were sober enough to launch their longboat and be on their way. As planned, he had his servant hide all the wine, metheglin, and food. If Nels and his men had no food or drink, they would leave sooner – or so he hoped.

Nels looked around and saw Felix's manservant. "We have a thirst and empty bellies, bring food and wine!" he commanded.

Ever polite, the manservant lowered his head. "Milord, we are poor and have nothing to offer ye."

Nels turned to Felix in question.

"It is as he says, we have little food and nothing to offer ye. Please, sit. Warm yerself fer the night is not hospitable." He indicated a place near the fire.

Nels settled onto a smooth rock warmed by the fire. Once seated, he looked at one of his men and subtly motioned his head. The warrior nodded, poked another in the ribs, and indicated that he would follow. The two Norsemen wandered away to search for food and drink as Nels turned back to Felix, his expression serious. "I believe ye have news fer me?"

Felix stroked his beard as he considered his response.

"The boy?" reminded Nels.

"Aye, the boy," Felix turned to the reassuring warmth and security of the fire. "He still lives, Milord."

Nels One-Ear didn't immediately react, but then he slowly leaned forward with elbows on his knees and turned his head to stare at the druid. All other conversations stopped; the Norsemen remained silent as they watched their leader.

Felix continued. "I have been thwarted, there are other powerful forces at work, and the boy and his mother remain unseen. It is..."

"Ye told me this was easy fer ye." Nels One-Ear's voice

took on a hard edge as he interrupted the druid. "What of yer spells and incantations? Are they worthless or just the trickery of a market hawker?"

Felix looked indignant as Nels' men laughed. "Nay, the boy's mother is careful and she..."

Nels One-Ear raised an eyebrow while waiting for Felix to finish his tepid excuse.

Felix believed a few exaggerations to embellish the truth wouldn't hurt. "She has protection; the powerful forces of unknown Gods watch over her and the boy."

The Norseman leader feigned a sympathetic look. "Which Gods do ye speak of? Nigh on two years past when we last came here, ye said the boy was as good as dead. Ye said it would be a week or two or even days. Tell me why, Druid, why should I believe ye will honour our bargain?"

Behind them, the voice of his servant could be heard squealing. Felix swallowed. "I know not which Gods she calls on, but they must be displeased with me, Milord."

Nels One-Ear laughed, and his men joined. "I doubt it."

"When I told ye I could find him... I spoke truthfully. I did locate him as the vision was clear." He shook his head in mock despair. "And I nearly had him." Felix looked into the eyes of the Norseman with desperation. "And then, like a blindness, he disappeared from my sight."

Nels One-Ear turned away and looked into the fire as he considered killing the druid. He thought, *something suitably horrific, like slow roasting him over the fire.* But he needed Felix. The druid had proven himself in the past; if he were dead, all would be lost. Nels One-Ear stood. "I will return, and next time I come here, make sure ye have proof – the boy must die." *And then I will kill ye.* Nels smiled at the thought. He was thirsty, hungry and couldn't wait to leave Inishmore. He stood. "Finish this, Druid."

The twelve Norsemen stomped into the rain and darkness, and with their departure, Felix felt relief. The manservant staggered from behind an old column, clutching the side of his head as blood mixed with rain streamed through his fingers. Nels One-Ear's men had cut off one of the servant's ears.

Felix ignored the servant's wound and thought about the Norseman leader. If he could inform the right people where Nels One-Ear made his camp, then that would eliminate a significant problem. Legions of Irish warriors would descend on Nels and his people and slay them without mercy. If he were dead, his problems would be over.

"Bring my pipe and some African herb!" shouted Felix as he strode towards the circular, thatched roof house he slept in.

Felix placed the empty pipe on the ground, lay on a bed of animal fur, and was asleep in moments. As expected, he soon began to experience lucid and vivid dreams, but this time, he could not see where the Norsemen made camp and couldn't send word to local lords and have his problem dealt with. Instead, the druid clearly saw the woman and the boy. He hadn't been able to see them in his dreams for some time, and he'd been honest when he told Nels One-Ear of his dilemma. The sight of the boy gave him no satisfaction; however, what he witnessed gave him pause, and quickly, his explicit dream turned into horror, and he woke with a start. Bathed in sweat, Felix threw water over his face and stumbled from his small house. It was still dark, but already a greyness seeped from the east. The rain had stopped, and the fire was out other than a few glowing embers. He threw some dry wood onto the ashes and sat down with his head bowed, resting against his hands.

His dream had been explicit, and typically, his dreams

weren't open to complex interpretation. He'd seen what was happening, and it gave him a chill. The woman and the boy had appeared to him when before they'd been hidden and cloaked in darkness, but tonight, he'd seen them clearly and observed where they were headed. It was here, to Inishmore they came. They wanted a reckoning, and he, the mighty druid Felix, would suffer if they were given that opportunity.

If the woman and boy were coming here, how would they know where to come? They must have sight, he reasoned, and that gave him pause. He couldn't reconcile why he feared the woman and the boy. When Nels One-Ear demanded the death of the boy and his mother, he'd made some discreet enquiries and learned that Macha was a devoted healer and had learned from respected masters, druids like him. Whereas she did not cast spells or practice sacred rituals. She wasn't a *Cailleach*[10], but others didn't know that, and it gave him an idea. *Felix* stood and wrapped his cape tightly around his lean body and walked towards the cliffs. The freshness of the air and the early light of dawn would give him clarity of thought.

Nels One-Ear's men had found Felix hiding some years earlier when the Norsemen had a powerful presence in Ireland and were going to slay him. He had no defence against the Norsemen, and his magic and wizardry left no impression on them. He'd pleaded, begged and grovelled for them to spare his life. With some reluctance, they'd taken him to Nels One-Ear, a clever and astute warrior and leader who'd immediately seen the benefit and agreed to spare his life on one condition: that he, the druid Felix, would see the death of the healer Macha.

Felix readily agreed and understood if he failed, then Nels One-Ear would kill him. With the help of clansmen, he bribed

10 *Cailleach - Irish for witch.*

priests to wage war against the unchristian healers who lived amongst them. A small community of healers lived on the rugged peninsula of land called Chreig Charrach. They were harmless, did no wrong and healed people who required care. It was easy to manipulate Christian priests to believe those people were heathens, evil sorcerers and witches who killed good Christians in satanic and barbaric rituals.

His plan had worked, and aided by the clan, Chreig Charrach was attacked, but Macha escaped and disappeared. The clan were furious because she'd killed Budoc, a noted and respected leader, and it had been easy to encourage the clan to pursue and kill her. But time heals all wounds, and the clan eventually lost interest. It was a visit by Nels One-Ear, who provided the bad news. Macha still lived and had a son. Nels insisted Macha must still die, but of more importance, it was her son who must also be killed.

Felix had repeatedly questioned Nel One-ear why the death of the woman and boy was so important.

Aided by the dream herb, Felix had again seen the woman and boy, and the fact they were coming to him gave him every reason to be concerned. He couldn't fully decipher his feelings but held her in high regard. Not because she was familiar to him, no. As far as he was aware, he'd never met her before. She was a survivor and overcame so much. She had strength and wisdom that he couldn't challenge. Perhaps he'd been mistaken, and she was a *Cailleach,* a witch, and if she was, then she was powerful and could easily influence his death. He'd seen it in the eyes of Nels One-Ear; if he were victorious and saw the death of her and the boy as agreed, then Felix also knew that Nels would kill him. Keeping her alive kept him alive.

The cold wind whipped his robes against his legs, tugged at his hair and made his eyes water. Despite the discomfort,

Felix remained standing at the cliff face. Huge rollers smashed against the rocks far below, sending spray upwards, reaching for him in a confusion of endless futility before falling away to dissolve into the cauldron of the ocean below.

CHAPTER EIGHT

Macha and Cathal made their way to Pul[11] on England's north-western coast. They were used to travelling alone and wisely avoided villages and towns when possible. In addition to Druid Felix, she still feared retaliation from Budoc's clan all these years later, and if recognised, interaction with locals could prove unwise. She explained to Cathal they would detour away from any settlements she'd previously visited to minimise contact. As usual, Cathal accepted his mother's decisions without question or complaint. He was curious to learn more about the druid and to meet the man he'd heard so much about.

Passage was secured on a small trader that took them across the Irish Sea to the town of Duiblinn[12]. After all this time, Macha again stood on Irish soil and felt nothing; her anger had simmered away years ago, and now her concerns and fears lay solely for the wellbeing and future of her son.

Without dawdling, she kept her head covered and made their way through the settlement and past the many Norsemen who, alongside the Irish, now peacefully inhabited the coastal port town. They headed towards Galway, one hundred and thirty miles away, where she knew Druid Felix could be found or, as Cathal enigmatically suggested, where Felix would be waiting.

"Waiting?" Macha asked, "Waiting for us?"

Cathal nodded, "Aye, he knows we travel to Galway to find

11 Pul - Blackpool

12 Duiblinn - Dublin

him."

"And ye know this, how? The bones?"

"Aye."

Macha repositioned the large bag she carried to the other shoulder and continued walking, lost in thought. Cathal never ceased to amaze her, and now she doubted her decision to come here and seek out the druid. She looked over her shoulder and watched Cathal walking a few steps behind, typically, he appeared unperturbed.

"Do ye fear Felix?" she asked.

He looked up at her and shook his head. "Nay, should I?"

Her look softened at his response. "Nay, fer he is just a man."

As strangers, mother and son received a few curious looks but nothing hostile or alarming, and they were ignored except by the hawkers peddling wares who eagerly sought customers with loose purses and coin.

The days merged, and after two weeks, they finally approached the outskirts of Galway. "We will sleep here the night, and in the morn, we will enter the town," she stated with some apprehension.

As usual, Cathal wandered off to set traps for rabbits and collect wild onions and other essentials for their evening meal while Macha began to lay leafy branches on the ground where they would sleep when she heard a noise and turned, expecting to see her son. It wasn't.

Two armed men stepped from behind a tree with swords raised, and Macha froze. What do ye seek?" she asked, masking her fear.

The men didn't answer. Instead, they looked beyond her towards a third man who appeared from behind. He was tall, lean, and his eyes were bright and intense. He wore a simple, filthy robe similar to what a Christian priest would wear, but without the holy adornments, and with increasing dread, Macha knew he was the druid, Felix.

The druid took a few steps closer to Macha and silently appraised her as his men approached. She couldn't run; she was trapped. Cathal had yet to return, and she hoped he'd see the men at their camp and keep away.

"Ye have saved me the trouble of finding ye," she spoke with confidence she didn't feel. "Fer I am here in Galway to seek ye out."

The druid cupped an elbow with a hand and stroked his beard. "Then it seems this meeting benefits us both; is this not so?" He didn't smile, nor was there warmth or friendliness conveyed by his demeanour.

Macha was thinking furiously of a way to protect herself. The two men with swords were close but not close enough that she could attack them with her knife. Annoyingly, the druid was also out of reach.

"Why is it ye seek me?" Felix eventually asked.

Macha laughed. "Because ye sent my friend, Aine, to kill me. Why? Fer what reason?"

The druid ignored her question. "Where is the boy?" he asked.

"He is long gone, and ye will never find him." She bravely held his intense glare and didn't back down. "But why, tell me, Felix, grant me this simple request, fer I cannot see a reason that ye would see his or my death? I have caused ye no harm. Can we not discuss this?"

Cathal had seen the three men approach the campsite but couldn't warn his mother of the approaching danger. Instead, he hid, and then once they passed, he ventured out and crept silently closer so he could overhear the conversation and hopefully offer some assistance.

Felix conceded the woman had a point and felt telling her wouldn't change anything, and he hoped the boy would soon return. *He must be close,* he thought. He signalled to his men, and they stepped up to Macha, forced her to her knees, and stood threateningly behind her.

"Search for the boy," Felix instructed, and one of the armed men quickly walked off to disappear into the trees.

Macha just felt the odds improve slightly.

"It isn't ye. I seek, it is yer son–"

"What has a boy done to deserve the attention of a druid?" Macha shook her head and, at the same time, felt the reassuring weight of the knife that hung from her neck.

Cathal was as close as he dared without fear of discovery and could easily overhear the druid—the armed man who left the camp headed in the opposite direction. For now, he was safe.

"Ah, well, ye see now, it isn't me. I'm beholden to others and bound to do their bidding," Felix replied.

"Budoc's clan?" Macha asked.

The druid shook his head and laughed. "Nay, I encouraged Budoc's clan to seek revenge against ye, but my bond is with another. It is the Norsemen who seek the death of yer boy."

Cathal's eyebrows furrowed. *Norsemen? Ostmen*?

Macha laughed. "Ye jest, Felix. I have never encountered or had dealings with men from the north. Why do ye lie to me?"

Felix looked around the campsite. Already, the sky had begun to darken as evening approached. "Where is the boy?"

Macha shrugged, "Tell me, druid, who is this Norseman that seeks my son's death?"

Felix stared at the woman for a dozen heartbeats before deciding whether to answer. "Nels One-Ear."

Macha was perplexed. "I do not know this man."

Silently, Cathal mouthed the Norseman's name. *Nels – One – ear.*

"Yer son. Where is he?" Felix demanded again. She knew where her son was. He nodded to the remaining guard, who reached down and slapped Macha hard on the side of the head.

In reaction, Macha cried out in pain, and naturally, she raised her hands to her head and fumbled beneath her hair for the knife.

The druid had lost all patience and stepped closer to Macha and leaned forward. "Where is he?"

This was what she wanted. Macha was quick but not fast enough, and she never knew the guard behind her had the tip of his blade held mere inches from her neck. As she pulled the knife free, she simultaneously lunged at Felix, but the guard was ready and thrust his sword deep into her back as Felix frantically backpedalled.

Macha collapsed to the ground with her knife spilling from her grasp. She cried out a single word, "Run!" before her heart stopped beating.

Cathal stared in total disbelief at his mother. In the diminishing light, he saw a black stain generously spread across her back. She hadn't stirred, and he doubted she would move ever again as he knew the sword thrust was fatal. He fought the temptation to rush to her and offer comfort and aid. He bit his into his cheek and resisted the impulse to cry out. Tears streamed down his cheeks as he stared at her inert form. But as much as he wanted, he couldn't help her; it was too late. He was frightened and his mind in turmoil. His mother's last word was a signal they'd often spoken of. It meant he had to run, not to the nearest town or settlement for help, but far, far away. As she instructed, he had to run to distant, unknown lands where he couldn't be found - ever.

"Find him!" Felix screamed.

The other guard ran from the camp as Cathal slid further into the lengthening shadows beneath a leafy bush.

The moon was high in the night sky when he finally rose from his hiding place. The druid and his men had departed some time ago, but fearful of deception, Cathal waited in case they returned. They didn't, and deeming it safe, he slowly stood, half expecting to hear yelling and see armed men charge him.

Cathal tied the sheath around his neck, just as his mother had, and slid the knife securely into it. Her bag had been upended, and possessions scattered. He quickly retrieved as much as possible before burying her in a shallow depression and covering her body with rocks. He wept for his loss; he cried for the love he felt. Macha O'Brollacháin, his mother, teacher and protector, was dead, slain by the will of the druid, Felix. He felt empty, and the loss was painfully unbearable. Cathal sat beneath a rocky overhang, some distance from their campsite, until the greyness of dawn. When he rose and, with his vision blurred by tears, ran as fast as he dared.

Felix didn't want *Ostman* Nels One-Ear and his men returning to Inishmore to create more havoc, so he prudently thought it best to report the partial completion and success of his obligation directly to him. The woman's death didn't sit well, and something about her unsettled him, but he could not reason why. The boy wouldn't go far. He was now alone, frightened, and would naturally gravitate towards settlements and people. He'd offered a healthy reward to anyone who could provide information about his whereabouts, capture, or better yet, show proof of his death. Buoyed by confidence, Felix sent word from Galway that he wanted to meet the Viking warrior and, rather than return to his haven on Inishmore, waited near

Galway for a reply. It took five days before Felix received word Nels One-Ear would meet with him at Scath Na Mara, a small coastal fishing village outside Galway, in three days.

Felix hoped someone would see the boy by then and report to him. His attempts at using the dream herb to locate him proved futile, and with every passing day, his confidence waned, and he began to doubt he ever would find him.

Inclement weather delayed the arrival of Nels One-Ear, and on the morning of the fifth day, a Viking longboat appeared from the haze and ground upon the rocky shore with a clatter as oars were stowed. With the long boat secured, Nels One-Ear and a score of men leapt ashore and strode arrogantly towards the waiting druid. The Norseman, Nels One-Ear, known to the Irish as a schemer and troublemaker, was not welcome in this part of Ireland. To ensure their safety, Nels ensured vigilant guards were posted.

It was cold, and Felix wrapped his cape tightly around his lean body as Nels clomped towards him. The sight of the brutish Viking warrior only added to the druid's anguish.

"I hope ye have news fer me, Druid, fer I travelled far to be here?" exclaimed Nels as his men surrounded Felix.

Felix took a deep, cleansing breath and then slowly exhaled. "Aye, and ye will be pleased to know that the woman is dead–"

"–and the boy still lives," interrupted Nels and cocked his head to the side.

If Felix was expecting gratitude or appreciation from Nels for slaying the woman, he was disappointed, as the Viking did not acknowledge the partial completion of his task. "Aye, fer now, if the weather, outlaws or starvation doesn't kill him, then I will, fer I have placed a bounty on him."

"A bounty?" questioned Nels, and he raised a single patronising eyebrow. After a lengthy pause, he straightened and rubbed his chin. Metal adornments in his beard rattled.

He believed his window of opportunity to kill the boy had closed. Felix had failed, and this posed a problem. Nels was acting on instructions; he'd been given simple instructions. Find the woman called Macha O'Brollacháin and ensure she doesn't give birth to any children. Purely by chance, he'd happened on the druid some years earlier when other Norsemen claimed the isle of Inishmore and found the druid and a large group of followers living there. Nels ordered Felix to be spared on one condition: that he use his skills and resources to find and kill the woman. The whimpering druid readily agreed, and to motivate him, Nels had everyone else slaughtered.

A low whistle by a guard alerted him that people were coming. He couldn't risk remaining at the beach and needed to set off.

Nels One-Ear knew the druid had made an honest attempt to kill the woman and cleverly used the Church and had clansmen do his bidding – that was then. But now... He sighed and glanced around. Aware they needed to depart quickly, he looked at the druid. "Ye come with us," he simply ordered.

His men closed on Felix, and with squeals of protest, the druid was dragged aboard the long boat, and they set off with haste.

With its single sail hoisted, the longboat made its way past Inishmore, met the deepening swell and entered the Sea of Atlas [13] in a cloud of spray. Shortly after clearing western Ireland and turning northward, Nels became weary of Felix's snivelling. With a prearranged signal of a simple nod, Druid Felix lost his head, and his body was tossed overboard; his head followed soon after.

With the warm sun at his back, Nels One-Ear tried to think

13 Sea of Atlas – North Atlantic Ocean

how to find the boy. He had an obligation and needed to provide results. It was time to report back to Scotland and visit with *Mormaer*[14] Harald Maddadsson, the Viking ruler of *Orkneyjar*[15].

14 *Mormaer – Leader of any seven provinces of Celtic Scotland divided.*

15 *Orkneyjar – Norse for Orkney, the Orkney Islands, Scotland..*

CHAPTER NINE

Cathal knew to stay away from people; his mother had drummed it into him, and he was adept at avoiding contact. He could even creep undetected through a forest and even surprise animals if he was downwind where they couldn't detect his scent.

He lay upon a flat rock deep in a forest that provided a perfect view over a house built entirely of logs. He didn't know exactly where he was, but it was in a remote, sparsely populated hilly region somewhere in southern Yorkshire near the Sheaf River. He'd been watching the house all morning and had seen no activity. He believed it safe to climb down from the rock and make his way past the dwelling. If he wanted to continue farther and deeper into the isolated hills, he had no choice but to pass directly in front of the house.

He was filthy, his clothes were torn and barely covered his body, and as usual, he felt the familiar pangs of hunger wrench at his insides. Accustomed to the feeling, he ignored them and slid backwards out of sight from the house.

Since the death of his mother, he'd been devastated and consumed by grief. The despair had blinded him to common sense and logic, and he'd done everything his mother had requested of him – except take care of himself.

After her death, he spent the entire first-night catatonic. Completely unresponsive and unaware – he was numb. Cathal's sense of loss was encompassing, and while Macha had lovingly spoken and prepared him for this moment, for a nine-year-old, her passing represented a free fall into a dark, forbidding abyss. From that moment when he witnessed her death, everything about his life changed – it had to change, but the depth of his fall gave him no opportunity to grasp the reality of his position. Emotionally, Cathal was hopelessly lost.

Eventually, a speck of light offered a tenuous handhold, and he unconsciously grasped it – survival and instinct began to dominate his actions. He whispered sorrowful goodbyes and reluctantly crept away from his mother's grave to return to the comfort of the forest depths to start his long trek back towards Duiblinn. He ate sparingly, and then only when his strength faded. His need to survive superseded anything else.

He found a coastal trader, similar to what he and his mother had taken to Ireland from England, and during darkness, he crept aboard and hid beneath a pile of rope in a forward storage locker at the bow. Physically exhausted and emotionally spent, Cathal slept for most of the voyage and patiently waited for nightfall before sneaking ashore once they'd arrived.

He headed in an easterly direction and then south into the hilly region that dominated this part of southern Yorkshire, where he hoped to find somewhere remote enough to hide. Beyond that, he'd not thought about any plans or his future.

When he'd slid back along the rock far enough and was out of sight from the house, he turned and froze. Before him stood a man, silent and questioning. The man carried only a long wooden staff; otherwise, he was unarmed. They stared at each other—the boy, almost naked and filthy, and the stranger, impassive and curious.

Cathal was trapped. The rock he lay upon sat at the top of a small cliff, and his only escape route was where the man stood beside his mother's bag. Neither spoke, and for Cathal, time stood still as his mind considered his options, and there weren't any.

"Ye look like ye could do with a good meal," the man eventually said. "I have food and won't harm ye." he turned away and began walking down a narrow path towards his home built from logs.

Cathal's stomach spasmed at the mention of food, and he also knew that he should grab his bag and flee to safety. But he was weak and exhausted, and the tempting offer of food overrode caution. Common sense told him he should run away from the stranger. He stared at the back of the man as he walked down the path.

The house had been built carefully. It was sturdy, had a high thatched roof, and was considerably larger than the ordinary cruck homes in which peasants lived. More importantly, it looked inviting. The man had disappeared inside, and Cathal could hear him whistling as he pottered around. He stood outside until the smell of cooking food was almost unbearable. He took another tentative step closer, hoping to see what horrors awaited him. After another step, he stood by the door and craned his neck to peer inside. The man was alone and stood by a table. A simmering pot hung over the hearth.

"I am called Gryffen. Were ye blessed to have been given a name?" the man suddenly said.

Cathal reluctantly tore his gaze from the pot on the hearth to the man and back to the pot. He swallowed away saliva and turned back to the man called Gryffen. He hadn't appeared hostile in any way and carried no weapons that he could see. The staff he carried earlier leaned against the wall outside the house. "My–" Cathal coughed. He hadn't spoken a word in weeks, and his voice sounded hoarse. "My name is Cathal," he finally managed to croak.

Gryffen moved to the hearth and ladled food into a bowl

with a large wooden spoon before placing it on the table. "It is a pleasure to meet ye, Cathal, but I dare say if ye don't sit yerself down… er, its best eaten hot."

Cathal was still uncertain. He saw the steaming bowl, and again, his stomach protested.

Gryffen filled another bowl from the pot and sat down at the table. "I'm used to eating alone, and it matters not to me if I eat by myself. But when there are two bowls on the table, well then, it is churlish not to join me. Would ye not agree, Cathal?"

Cathal had chosen not to set traps to hunt and cook rabbits as he usually did when his mother was alive. Lighting a fire would only draw unwanted attention, so he opted to nibble at this or that when he had the opportunity and told himself he'd eat a good hearty meal when it was safe. But he'd never felt secure in the weeks since her death, and now he was undernourished and starving. Try as he might, there wasn't a reason not to eat the offered meal that smelled so good. He stepped inside the house.

"Ye might want to eat slowly and take yer time, or ye'll be poorly," cautioned Gryffen with a smile as he took a mouthful.

Cathal sat as close to the door as he could.

Gryffen slid the bowl over. He didn't probe or ask questions and allowed the boy to eat. When the bowl was empty, Cathal looked at his host, his unspoken words an appeal for more.

Gryffen shook his head. "Ye may want to wait a while; yer stomach will thank ye," he laughed. "There's a brook out back, ye may want to clean yerself. I have some clothes if ye want, but they might be a little big. Best if ye cover-up, as the nights are cool up here."

With a nod, Cathal grabbed his mother's bag, held it protectively to his chest and went outside. He had no intention of staying. However, Gryffen was correct, and he did need to clean himself. Macha had always believed filth led to illness, and Cathal had numerous minor cuts and abrasions all over his body, and some had reddened. If not taken care of, they could begin to fester.

The meal had provided him with energy and improved clarity of thought. As he scraped and washed away the weeks of grime and filth from his body, Cathal decided to leave as soon as he was finished.

Gryffen suddenly appeared at the stream carrying a small bundle of clothes, giving him a start. He almost leapt away.

"They'll be a bit big, but if ye can wait til morn, then I reckon I can tailor them to fit ye better." He placed them on a nearby rock and returned inside.

It was decided he would stay here for only one night, then in the morning, after the clothes were tailored a little, he would continue onwards.

As it turned out, Gryffen was an adept tailor and made suitable adjustments to the breeches he gave Cathal, and much to his relief, they no longer required to be held up when he walked. His plan to leave was delayed when Gryffen reheated the leftovers from the previous evening's meal. Cathal was still ravenous; his stomach had not protested during the night, and the smell of simmering food again consumed him. After he ate, he'd say farewell.

"You need to eat, Cathal. Look at ye, all skin n' bones. Gotta eat, lad."

They hardly spoke, and Gryffen was content to give Cathal space. He sensed the boy had undergone a recent tragedy and was emotionally fragile. And if he admitted to himself, it was pleasant to have company, even if the boy wasn't a talker. As Gryffen had used the last of his meat to cook the previous evening's dinner, he needed to obtain more and asked Cathal if he wanted to come.

Cathal looked unsure.

"Be a big help if ye can help carry it out fer me and cut it up. What say ye?"

Cathal wanted to depart, but... He nodded. "Aye, I can help."

Gryffen produced a bow and a quiver full of arrows, and the two of them wandered out and headed further up the valley to an area where Gryffen knew deer loved to come and feed in open areas of wild grasses. Of surprise to Gryffen was Cathal's stealthiness.

It didn't take long when Cathal tugged at the back of Gryffen's capuchin and pointed. Gryffen hadn't heard a thing, but closer scrutiny showed a deer grazing in the murky shadows directly ahead, unaware it was being stalked. It was a long shot, somewhere around one hundred yards, and Cathal was perplexed when Gryffen silently knelt, pulled an arrow from his quiver, licked his fingers, and carefully stroked the fletching before notching the arrow. The distance was too great, surely, he'd miss.

Gryffen rose from concealment, exhaled slowly and let the arrow loose.

The deer never moved, and the arrow flew true, piercing its heart, and the deer fell where it stood. It was a masterful shot. Cathal had never seen such accuracy and guessed that Gryffen was once an archer. He looked at Gryffen with a newfound respect.

Without delay, they carried the carcass back to the log house, where it was skinned and butchered into portions. Some meat was prepared for drying, but it was still too much for Gryffen to store as it would turn rancid long before it could be eaten, and together, Gryffen and Cathal divided the meat into parcels that Gryffen would trade or sell. They spoke sparingly and only when needed. Gryffen observed Cathal was noticeably more relaxed and less guarded.

"If ye can help me more, I'd be grateful to ye. I need to carry this meat down where I can trade it," Gryffen began. "Yer help would be most welcome."

It made sense to Cathal. It was a large deer, and even after cutting it up, there was more meat than one person could easily carry. "Aye, we can do this together, but I do not want to enter the village and be seen, so I shall wait close by if that suits ye?"

It did, and the next day, without wasting time, Gryffen, carrying his staff and Cathal following, set out, each with a load of valuable meat on their backs, and trekked down from the hills. It took all day, and eventually, they arrived at a village. Cathal waited out of sight at the outskirts while Gryffen carried his load into the settlement. He returned soon after, picked up Cathal's smaller load, and disappeared again.

Cathal anxiously waited.

"We should leave now," Gryffen said quickly after returning.

Cathal looked at him and saw he was flustered; something bothered him.

Gathering the items he bought or traded for the venison, he stomped off.

Cathal followed. "Something ails ye? Is it me?"

Gryffen walked a few more steps in silence and stopped, then dropped to a knee to better face Cathal. "There are some people who torment others because they can. They do not look fer the good in folk. Instead, they search for the bad in them, and if they find none, they choose to believe anything – often the first thing that comes to mind, and then they spin a yarn. Nay, Cathal, it isn't ye." He smiled. "Come, fer we have flour and wheat and can make bread."

They spent the night in the forest, and Cathal opened up and spoke more and told him about plants and nature. He explained how man kills and nature heals. When Gryffen asked where he came by this vast knowledge, Cathal grew sullen and wouldn't elaborate.

In the morning, Gryffen noticed that the boy had overcome whatever had bothered him the night before, and they continued back to the valley that he called home. Gryffen knew that Cathal intended to leave. He'd told him so. However, with each passing day, he came to understand the enigmatic boy more and more. It was apparent Cathal was not like other boys of a similar age. He was reserved but not shy, and he had confidence but wasn't cocky. He was insightful and had an exceptionable understanding of people and life, and Gryffen believed that whoever had taught Cathal was the reason for the boy's deep-hearted sorrow.

They safely arrived at Gryffen's home without incident. There was work to do, and Cathal volunteered to help.

"I will depart on the morrow, Gryffen," Cathal told him that night after their evening meal.

Gryffen nodded. "If ye must, ye know yer own mind. I will be sorry to see ye go, lad."

And as usual, Cathal had another excuse and stayed another night and then another. He always had a valid reason to delay his impending departure.

CHAPTER TEN

Jarl Harald Maddadsson, the Viking ruler of Orkneyjar, was not in a good mood, but then he seldom was. The stubborn Scots wanted him gone and their lands back. His advisors groused about this or that and squabbled about petty things of no consequence that took time away from the things he enjoyed doing. To add to his disquiet, he'd been receiving more pressure to forsake his Norse Gods and adopt Christianity. From a practical perspective, dealing with one God would be easier than trying to placate dozens. However, Harald was circumspect and wouldn't speak of his thoughts to anyone. Even thinking about it made him uneasy.

Orkneyjar, where Harald ruled, was not his first choice as a place to govern, as it lay to Scotland's north, a long way from anywhere worthwhile. He wanted better lands farther south, as being annexed to the north only made him feel inferior to the other *Mormaer* who ruled the remaining six provinces. For many years, Harald sought ways to weaken southwestern Scotland in the Gall-Gaidel[16] region. If he could only obtain a foothold for his forces there, then launching attacks on Ireland and England's north would be straightforward. Unfortunately for Harald, he'd had no success, but it didn't stop him from trying.

All was not lost for Harald; as he usually did when facing a dilemma, he called upon his Nordic Gods for guidance. His

16 Gall-Gaidel - Modern day Galloway

Gods spoke through Ivar, a Gothi[17], a spiritual man deeply devoted to his beliefs. Some years ago, Ivar first came to him with the notion that he could strengthen his military presence further south. According to the mystic, a group of Gods called the *Vanir* had allowed him to glimpse the future. With this valuable gift, Ivar saw a mighty warrior emerge and seize power, eventually uniting Scotland to fight a common enemy. Harald scoffed at the notion, and Ivar clarified that Scotland would never be truly united, however, under the leadership of this man, there was no place for Vikings to rule. The Scots would eventually prevail, which displeased Harald.

Harald urged Ivar to ensure this mighty warrior never succeeded in uniting Scotland. Ivar diligently consulted with his Nordic Gods and was frustrated at the outcome, never learning the name of this mighty warrior. He persisted and eventually discovered that an Irish woman would give birth to a son who would save the life of the mysterious Scottish warrior. Ivar simply reasoned that if the woman died, then she would never give birth to the son. It was a practical solution that would appease Harald.

When Ivar returned to Harald and explained his elementary plan, Harald readily agreed but was not interested in the details. He instructed him to take care of it, waving Ivar away.

Emboldened with Harald's blessing, Ivar assigned a young Viking warrior called Nels One-Ear to ensure success. Ivar was fully aware that the mission that Nels embarked on would take time. The mystic was patient and had seen signs indicating Nels would succeed – the Irish woman would die.

After many years, Harald finally raised the subject of the Scottish warrior to Ivar and demanded detailed answers on

17 Gothi – Originally a term used for a Norseman responsible for religious elements of pagan ritual. A Priest..

progress. It had been some time since Ivar had heard from Nels One-Ear, and eventually, he managed to send him a message requesting him to report back.

Nels One-Ear arrived at Orkneyjar by longboat and immediately sought Ivar, the Gothi. After pleasantries, Nels quickly explained how he'd worked hard to identify the woman and learned her name from the cryptic clues he'd received. He was quite pleased with himself and proudly informed the priest of her death.

"Ye slew her?" asked Ivar as he turned his back to Nels and knelt before an enormous carved statue depicting one of their many Gods.

"Er, nay, not I, but a man called Felix. He slew her," stated Nels with confidence.

"Then ye have done good work," praised Ivor and began lowering and raising his head to honour the God the carved wooden statue represented. He never saw Nels grimace.

"Milord," Nels began, "While the woman is no longer alive, she, uh, she did bear a son, and he still lives."

Ivor paused at the shock revelation and turned his head to look at Nels. "She has a son, and yet he is still lives? How can this be?"

"I believe she had help."

"Help?" Ivar rose unsteadily and faced Nels. "Help from whom?"

Nels felt uncomfortable. "I was told she had, er, supernatural help."

Ivar's eyebrows furrowed, and he rubbed his chin beneath a scraggly beard as he digested this vital information. After all, he knew anyone who receives assistance from the supernatural shouldn't be taken lightly. "Who, who told ye this?"

"It came from the Druid Felix."

"Ye employed a druid?" Ivar asked.

"In a manner… he er, he was indebted to me."

Ivar began pacing as he continued to rub his chin. "Then surely, this druid can assist ye in finding her son."

"Aye, he tried but could not locate him."

"Then return and pressure him, insist!" shouted Ivar as he stepped before the larger man and paused, glaring up at him.

"That isn't possible fer the druid no longer lives," Nels replied in a voice barely above a whisper. He held his breath as he waited for a response.

Ivar's face creased in consternation. "What say ye?"

Nels noisily exhaled. "The druid is dead."

Ivar turned away, walked to the statue, and paused as he considered his options. After a dozen heartbeats, he spoke. "Then I shall ask the Gods, and when they tell me where this boy is, ye shall take as many men as necessary to find and kill him."

"And this is what *Jarl* Harold wishes?" asked Nels One-Ear with a respectful head dip.

Jarl Harald Maddadsson wasn't impressed when Ivar reported what he'd learned from Nels One ear. He was having another bad day and had little time or patience for the *gothi.* He sucked noisily on a gap where a tooth should be. "I do not want to wait another ten years, Ivar. If we wait longer, the boy will have grown into a man and have sired his own family. The Scots must not grow stronger!" he thumped his fist on the armrest of the throne he sat upon and momentarily glared at Ivar before dismissing him.

To expedite the matter of locating the Irish woman's son, Ivar, the *Gothi* decided to perform a ritual *blót*[18] sacrifice; this

18 Blót sacrifice – Is a sacrificial exchange where a sacrifice is made in order to receive something back.

would please the Gods *Odin* and, undoubtedly, the *Vanir*, who would respond in kind. Ivar decided a child, a boy, would be honoured, and as such ritual practice dictated, he would be hanged from a tree.

Harald was informed and was imminently pleased; not only could he see an end to the burden he felt over the Scottish warrior, but his people were always convinced they were better off after a sacrifice. It would become a festive event, reasoned Harald, and hopefully improve the surly disposition of his people.

If Ivar felt pressure to ensure he could interpret the *Vanir's* response to his plea and locate the Irish whelp, it didn't show. With vigour, he set about finding a suitable boy and preparations were made.

Almost anyone who had an opinion believed that *Odin* would be pleased with the sacrifice and pass on his appreciation to his subordinate, lesser Gods, the *Vanir*. This was what Ivar counted on because he fully expected to receive insights into the whereabouts of the Irish boy immediately after the ritual.

When the day arrived, the young boy was sacrificed in front of enthusiastic spectators who feasted and sang in drunken revelry after the formal ceremony. Harald was satisfied because he knew Odin was pleased and keenly waited for Ivar's news on the Irish lad.

Ivar wasn't having much luck. The Gods had forsaken him and wouldn't respond to his requests. There were no signs or cryptic messages, and nature didn't unfold and share its secrets with the priest about where the Irish boy hid.

For five straight days and nights, Ivar pleaded with the Gods to share their knowledge. When that failed, and his dignity in tatters, he resorted to begging. Exhausted and delirious, he finally launched into a hysterical tirade of abuse-laden profanities aimed directly at the Gods, where he accused them of being spurious and illusory. Around that time, the last vestiges of his sanity deserted him. Harald ordered warriors to take the disconsolate priest to his longhouse and surmised the Gods were displeased and, as punishment, had taken Ivor's mind.

Jarl Harald Maddadsson wasted no time and appointed an older, sombre man named Arne Thorvald as his new spiritual advisor. Arne was more aggressive and, by some, was considered extreme, and he wielded his spiritual knowledge and authority like a well-honed sword.

Of course, Arne claimed he knew better than his predecessor and set about placating the offended Gods and seeking favour. Goats, sheep and even pigs and cows were slaughtered in lengthy sacrificial rituals that lasted days. Harald kept a close eye on Arne, as the cost of killing valuable animals was not a trivial matter to be ignored. When Arne finally came to see him, Harald was more than a little anxious and eager for news.

"Ye bring good tidings, Arne?" asked Harald with a measure of hope. He leaned forward on his chair as his new high priest stood before him. Fresh blood stained Arne's priestly robes, and he looked fatigued. Harald wondered if the Gods were also going to take Arne's mind.

"Ye hound me and ask that I come see ye. As if I had better things to do. It would be better if ye spent more devotional time communicating with the Gods, then ye would understand," Arne began. "But ye will tell me the sacrifices cost too much coin and that ye have no time to learn from our Gods." He shook his head in disapproval.

"Have ye news? The Irish boy?" Harald reminded him, ignoring the taunts.

Arne paused a moment to collect himself. "Aye, some. He lives in a forest amongst the hills. But I know not where this forest or hills are."

Harald leaned back in his chair. "The hills ye speak of, are they near here or in far-off lands?"

Arne shook his head. "Wherever he is does not require a sea voyage."

"Ah, then he is close," Harald stated with a rare smile.

Arne didn't respond and stared blankly at the *Jarl.*

"What is this, have ye nothing more? I sacrificed a boy, costly goats, sheep and a cow, and that is all ye have to say?" Harald's good mood and smile were short-lived.

"Yer impatience displeases the Gods," admonished the priest.

"I want answers, and all ye tell me is to be patient?" Harald's composure with the *gothi* was deteriorating quickly.

"I speak fer the Gods, and the last time ye wanted answers, and as punishment fer yer rashness, a priest lost his mind. And now ye confront me? Perhaps ye should save yer complaining fer others – they may care to listen," Arne stated. He folded his arms and, in challenge, boldly held eye contact with the *Jarl.*

Harald stood. "Find the boy!" he yelled and angrily stomped off. *Perhaps the Christian God was more agreeable,* he thought.

In frustration, Harald sought counsel from Baldr, the wise. Baldr had been the one who initially encouraged him to pursue the Irish woman all those years ago. While old and decrepit, Baldr's mind was as sharp as a well-honed axe, and his perspective was always balanced.

When he arrived at Baldr's longhouse, his woman told him Baldr was ill and unable to speak. Harald asked to be informed of Baldr's condition and then walked away to the gravelly beach to contemplate and ponder. He was beginning to doubt the wisdom of continuing a search for an Irish boy who may or may not have a profound effect on the destiny of his people. With his hand resting on the head of his axe, tucked into his belt, Harald stared out to sea and wondered if it was all worth it.

CHAPTER ELEVEN

10 years later.

Voices, the sound of boisterous men drifted upwards to where Cathal was scraping lichen from rocks. The lichen, when dried, was used to make a powder that he used to treat minor wounds to prevent corruption. It was unusual for people to be in the hills this far from the nearest village. Sometimes, the odd solitary hunter would wander close, and as soon as they saw Gryffen's home, they would turn away, knowing the game they sought wouldn't be near a dwelling.

Because these men made no attempt at stealth, indicated they weren't hunting game. Cathal surmised they were up to no good. Of concern to him was that Gryffen had gone to the village and had been due back late the previous day, and he'd not yet returned. With the sound of approaching strangers and their unknown intentions, he was becoming anxious.

With care, he lowered himself to his belly and slid close to the precipice to peer down into the valley without being seen. Locating the three men didn't take long, as they made no real effort to be stealthy.

One was armed with a bow and carried a sheathed sword; another held a spear, while the third had a large club dangling from his belt. They were young, perhaps a year or two older than himself, and from their clothes, Cathal determined they were peasants, which offered some relief, as they were definitely not *Ostmen*.

Cathal crawled back out of sight and considered his best

options. If they continued on their current path, they would soon come across Gryffen's unprotected home. Most people would avoid the dwelling and not wish to upset the residents, however, the three young men heading up the valley didn't appear to be the type to observe those courtesies. With his mind made up, he grabbed his hemp bag and staff and ran towards home.

In the ten years, Cathal had been with Gryffen, a few people had stumbled onto the house, and there had never been any unpleasantness. Sometimes, they were hurt, having fallen and injured themselves or lost seeking directions, but none had ever been a threat. Fully aware that people could arrive at the house with hostile intentions, Gryffen had discussed with Cathal what to do when that moment finally came.

With that thought foremost on his mind, Cathal stood outside Gryffen's sturdy home, just beyond the door, resting easy with his staff when the three unruly young men approached from the forest.

They were surprised to see him and stopped their incessant chatter as they stared at the gangly young man silently appraising them.

"Who'd be ye?" asked the leader of the three as he lowered his hand to the hilt of his sword.

Cathal determined the man's question wasn't worthy of an answer. So, he simply didn't reply and continued his scrutiny.

They whispered to each other and then laughed loudly at something Cathal couldn't hear.

The young man with the club separated from his friends and boldly stepped closer to Cathal and squinted. "I ain't seen ye a'fore."

"Are ye lost?" Cathal asked. "Keep heading down the valley; it will take ye back to the village." He may have appeared outwardly relaxed, but inside, he was frightened. If these men were peasants, they'd have responsibilities and should be working and not be here, up in the hills. They were outlaws and clearly sought opportunity.

In reply, two men stepped towards him and separated slightly to simultaneously attack him from the sides and front. To Cathal, it was apparent they wanted to loot the house, and he was the only person who stood in their way.

In any other circumstances, he would have walked away and avoided a confrontation. But here, while Gryffen was absent, he was the only thing preventing these men from robbing and destroying the house. He felt obligated to Gryffen and had a sense of duty and loyalty to the man who'd become like a father.

"We ain't lost," snarled the leader as he unsheathed his old, rusted sword.

Cathal casually shifted his feet and weight in preparation for what would come next. These young men were hasty, impulsive and lacked common sense.

"Now!" shouted the leader as he rushed at Cathal, wildly waving his sword.

Cathal didn't immediately react and waited until the outlaw came closer and kept an eye on the other two, who were slower and lagged a step behind. Then, without offering a warning, he spun his staff until it was parallel to the ground, with one end tucked under his arm, then lunged forward and shoved it firmly into the chest of the on-rushing sword-wielding outlaw. The outlaw didn't expect the sudden move and couldn't prevent the oak staff from striking him hard on his sternum. The sword fell to the ground, and with both arms clutching his chest, dropped to his knees with a painful grunt. Cathal bent low, spun, and simultaneously pulled the staff, and it arced across the ground to strike the second outlaw across the back of his legs with a loud whack. With a yell, he crumpled to the ground.

The danger hadn't passed; there was still one more. Cathal nimbly side-stepped and straightened as he challenged the third outlaw who thrust a spear at him. Cathal swayed back, pushed aside the spear and skilfully rapped the outlaw firmly on the back of his hand with his staff. The spear clattered to the ground as the outlaw clutched his hand with an undignified yelp.

Before they could respond, Cathal picked up the sword and spear and threw them aside out of reach.

"If I told yer once, I told ye a hundred times, Cathal, ye held the *bō*[19] too low!" shouted Gryffen as he emerged from the forest gloom. He also wielded a staff and ignored the three outlaws on the ground as he approached Cathal, raised his oak staff into a horizontal position to the height of his elbows, and demonstrated what he described. "Here, at the elbows, that is the correct position," he instructed with a grin. Inwardly, he was proud. He'd seen how swiftly Cathal had handled the three outlaws and prevented the situation from escalating. He finally spared a look at the three pitiful men. "Why are they here?"

Cathal shrugged. "Not fer hunting," he replied with typical word economy.

Gryffen gave the outlaw leader an unkindly prompt with his foot, which saw him topple over. "If ye leave now, ye may make it out before dark. On yer way, lads, don't bother comin' back and don't forget yer weapons."

Cathal and Gryffen watched the three men scamper away. "I doubt we'll see them back again." He turned from the outlaws as they disappeared into the forest, facing Cathal, and placed a hand on his shoulder. "Ye did well."

Cathal didn't acknowledge the compliment. "I was expect-

19 Bō – is a hardwood staff weapon used in Asian martial arts.

ing ye back last evening…"

"Aye, before I left the village, I overheard a conversation and suspected these men would come." He sighed and spared a look along the forest perimeter. "I thought it best to wait and see if they were brave enough to come up this far. I followed a safe distance behind. All is well, eh, and they won't bother us anymore."

"Cathal turned to follow Gryffen's gaze. "I'm not so sure. Those larrikins are a problem, and you'll see this won't be the end of them."

Gryffen knew enough about Cathal's peculiar insights to take his warning seriously. He sighed. "Come, let's make sure those three leave, and ye can help me with the wheat and other things; they're hidden a little way back."

Gryffen sat on a chair and stared vacantly at the far wall. Cathal had retired some time ago and was soundly sleeping. Cathal's prediction about the outlaws being a problem was concerning. Over ten years ago, he'd encountered a lost little boy and taken him in his care. He'd fed, taught and instructed the boy. He'd provided him with a roof, warmth, and food, and in return, the boy had grown into a most unusual young man who became like a son.

But Cathal was wise beyond his years; he had a talent for helping those in need and had the skills to heal even the most complex injuries and sicknesses. Gryffen unconsciously rubbed his arm where it had broken a few years ago. It was a painful break when he slipped on wet moss and fell over a bank. He'd been alone and feared death, but Cathal instinctively knew something was wrong and found him. How, he didn't know, but the boy just knew.

Gryffen wasn't a hermit who preferred to live a solitary

life in the hills above Yorkshire - far from it. He'd once been an archer and pikeman and been rewarded lands for his heroic deeds. Admittedly, only a small estate in the Diocese of Lindisfarne[20], but nonetheless, the land had been his. The Right Reverend Chlodomer, by Divine Providence, Lord Bishop of Lindisfarne, claimed that Gryffen of Dearthington[21] obtained the lands illegally and, on behalf of the Church, took possession of his property along with the land of many others. Gryffen's protests fell on deaf ears, and he vehemently challenged the bishop's decision by confronting him in the church, a foolhardy decision he'd regretted ever since.

Humiliated, Bishop Chlodomer Dunhelm, a man of little patience and even less humour, wasted no time and excommunicated, *vitandus*[22], Gryffen for his indiscretion. Any attack on clergy was considered a serious offence, and excommunication was somewhat automatic. Gryffen's actions were interpreted as severe, and any verbal or physical attack, especially against a bishop, would be dealt with harshly. Consequently, Bishop Dunhelm proclaimed Gryffen of Dearthington's name to be struck from all records and any and all other wealth currently owned by him to be forever held by the Church.

Before the Church could seize anything, Gryffen took what he owned and vanished, fleeing north to the nearby Yorkshire uplands where he was unknown and eke out a solitary life. That is, until the day he happened upon the young boy known as Cathal, and his life forever changed. The boy had been remarkable, and since that day, they'd become close, like father and son.

On that day, when Gryffen fell and broke his arm, he knew enough about severe injuries to believe his life would be over.

20 *Lindisfarne – Modern day Durham.*

21 *Dearthington – Modern day Darlington*

22 *Vitandus – latin, to be avoided.*

He'd fought in battles on windswept moors and witnessed brave warriors, many good men who subsequently died from their injuries. Festering wounds that seeped foulness eventually took a man's spirit and invariably deprived him of the will to live. Laying in a hidden crevice with a broken arm for a night wasn't just a reminder of his mortality; it was a pain-filled nightmare, a requiem of lament where he celebrated and welcomed his death.

As he embraced the torturing darkness, Cathal found him. How? He didn't know because the young man didn't know where he'd gone, but find him he did. Cathal cared for him with a tenderness and empathy that heralded unselfish compassion. The injury left scars, not just on his leathered skin but inside his mind. Not only did Cathal mend his broken and shattered bones – it was like it never happened. He had a complete and total recovery.

At that time, he saw it as a sense of duty or perhaps loyalty, but now he came to see it for what it truly was – love. The paternal love a father has for his son and that silent declaration forever altered their relationship. Everything that Gryffen knew, everything he'd ever learned, would be passed on to Cathal; it became his responsibility and one he embraced with pure dedication and commitment. Since then, he'd often questioned whether he was educating the boy or Cathal was teaching him.

However, Cathal was vulnerable and needed to learn how to protect himself.

To aid with strength and flexibility, Gryffen suggested that they begin practising basic manoeuvres with a staff.

Years earlier, when Gryffen was considerably younger, a man from the east, from a warring nation of warriors called

Nihon[23], came to live in the tiny village where he grew up. The man, simply known as Rei, claimed to be a priest and chose to remain in England because his entire family and clan had been overcome and slaughtered by another, and he wasn't welcome to return to the land of his birth. Rei was non-violent, which seemed at odds with the culture of his birthplace.

However, Rei was masterful with a stave, and eager to learn from him, Gryffen convinced Rei to teach him the art. He'd been an enthusiastic and willing student. The unique skills and discipline required to master the simple wooden staff served Gryffen well and shaped his fighting ability with many other types of weapons, and it was this vast knowledge he'd taught and passed on to Cathal.

The boy had been a good student, and they practised tirelessly. Eventually, Gryffen began to teach Cathal the sword and like everything else he did, Cathal excelled. Cathal's reflexes were quick and his coordination astonishing. He was a natural. The lessons continued, and Gryffen passed on his fighting skills to the eager young man who wanted nothing more than to have the ability to defend himself. Today had been an example of that, and Cathal had wisely chosen not to inflict any injury on the three young men other than to wound their dignity.

He could have easily killed them; Cathal had the skill, but the young man had shown maturity and caution. He'd accounted for himself, and Gryffen glowed in pride.

Living a solitary life in the hills had mellowed Gryffen. Where once he'd been quick to respond to a threat with aggression, he was now more considered, valued life and had tried to impart that to the young boy. It wasn't that his teaching fell on deaf ears; far from it. Even as a boy, Cathal respected all living things and killing any creature was always a last and

23 *Nihon – Modern day Japan.*

reluctant resort.

Gryffen grew to understand the young boy who grew into manhood. Cathal had told him of his early life with his mother Macha and even about the *Ostmen* who sought his death, and Gryffen understood; he knew what it was like to be hunted. There wasn't a day when he didn't think about his past life and what could have been.

It wasn't always easy; Cathal was complex and was never one to engage in lengthy chatter. He was stubborn, enigmatic and a loner. All those years wandering through the forests of Ireland, England, and Frankia had left an impression. There wasn't a place Cathal would rather be than gathering mosses, roots, leaves, lichen and anything else that grew beneath the canopy of his beloved forest. To Cathal, the forest was more than a refuge, it was his home and where he felt safe.

They'd argued but never spoken an unkind word in anger. They'd laughed until tears rolled down their cheeks, and more importantly, they nurtured each other, offering support and love when needed. On dark, wet nights, when they remained cloistered inside their warm log home, they told fanciful, entertaining tales.

Gryffen rose from his chair, quietly opened the door and stepped outside. Sleep wouldn't come easily this night as his mind was on the three men he had sent hurriedly on their way earlier in the day.

CHAPTER TWELVE

Cathal upended his bag, and bones of varying sizes and shapes spilt onto the floor. He sat cross-legged and bent low to examine the position and relationship of the bones to each other after they settled. Gryffen stood behind him, his arms folded, cupping his chin, and watched anxiously.

He'd come to respect Cathal's mystical knowledge, and more frequently, the insights he provided after studying how the bones fell were, more often than not, accurate. At first, Gryffen had been sceptical, as he wasn't convinced by claims of foretelling the future by the ridiculous notion of studying bones. In the beginning, he'd laughed when Cathal first began the practice. After all, it wasn't Christian, and priests had vehemently rejected such pagan rituals as evil. However, the priests weren't here to witness the accuracy of Cathal's interpretations when they came true. Cathal wasn't evil, nor was he a druid. It was simply a skill he was taught, nothing more.

"Well, can ye see anything?" he asked.

Cathal straightened and looked up at his mentor. "Men come, many armed men, perhaps a score." He held Gryffen's questioning gaze. "They come fer ye because of yer past. We have time and can leave here long before they arrive."

Gryffen lowered his arms and turned away, stepping closer to the open door as Cathal scooped up the bones.

"And to where can I go? There is nowhere fer me to run, Cathal. They come fer me at the bidding of the Church. Most likely, I must face judgment for my rash sins, as there is little else they can do. The villagers will now know who I am and will not allow me to enter their hamlet, nor will they speak or trade with me. Excommunication means I am more than an outcast; I've been condemned to the devil and the eternal fires of hell. My life here in the hills is over."

Cathal stood and stepped up beside Gryffen." Will ye allow them to take ye? Will ye defend yerself?"

Gryffen turned and gripped Cathal's shoulders. "I fear no one, but many years past, I made an error and spoke with anger instead of with my head. I accept that, Cathal. It isn't yer burden; it is mine, and mine alone. Perhaps ye should take yer things and leave before they come – spare yerself from any unpleasantness. Ye are young with a full life ahead of ye, while I have lived already. I love ye like a son. Ye deserve better; ye have a duty to fulfil yer destiny, as I have fulfilled mine to help ye." He released Cathal from his grip and turned away with moist eyes. "I do not fear what the Church will do, fer I would give my life to see ye succeed."

Cathal's mouth was open, and he mutely stared at Gryffen. Finally, after an age, he shook his head in denial. "Nay, nay, we can leave here together and be miles away before they come. We can–"

"Nay, Cathal," Gryffen interrupted. "There is nowhere fer me to go, and the Church will find me. Ye have done no wrong, and is best if ye leave, and then ye cannot be drawn into or be tarnished because ye lived here and ignored the Church's edict of excommunication."

"But–"

"What happens if the Vikings hear word of ye? There will be talk, and they will listen…"

"It has been years, and I've not seen anything… Perhaps the Vikings have forgotten."

"Do ye think they have forgotten ye, Cathal? After all that has happened and the lengths they have gone to see yer death." Gryffen lowered his voice to just above a whisper. "What if these men making their way here to our home were Vikings? What would ye do?"

Cathal didn't reply.

"These men who come will not harm me here; they will take me to face further judgment. The Church will decide my fate, and if I repent and show them the error of my ways, they might reconsider, and all this worry is fer nought, eh." Gryffen placed his arm around Cathal's shoulder and smiled. "The priests always tell us how the Church is compassionate, and I will seek forgiveness, fer my actions were hasty and ill-considered. And ye, Cathal, will hide nearby, and when the men have taken me, ye can wait fer my return."

As predicted, they came. At first, a lone woodsman silently appeared from the forest. Close behind, a dozen armed villagers, many of whom Gryffen recognised, stepped nervously into the clearing—no doubt enlisted by the sheriff and all oath sworn to assist in his capture. It was a *posse comitatus*[24]. A few moments later, another man lumbered breathlessly into the clearing to stand in front of Gryffen's home. Dressed differently than the others, Gryffen believed he was the sheriff.

Gryffen was ready and had prepared. He grabbed a leather bag, slung it over his shoulder, reached for his staff, which rested against the wall, and opened the door. "Is a fine morn to be out in the woods," he said cheerfully. "You've come fer me, and ye'll not have me create a fuss; I'll go peacefully with ye, Sheriff." He glanced around and recognised one of the three young men who'd been up here causing mischief a few days ago.

24 Posse Comitatus – Old English practice consisting of a shire's able-bodied private citizens summoned to assist in maintaining public order.

"Aye, that's him, uncle," said the mischief-maker, pointing at Gryffen as he stepped outside. "But there is another, younger, his son."

"I'm not the sheriff," the red-faced man replied, still short of breath. "I am here at his behest." He nodded to the swordsmen, and six armed men immediately rushed him, tossed his bag and staff aside and tightly bound his hands. He turned to his nephew. "We came here only fer him."

Gryffen felt relief, Cathal was safe. "It will be less bothersome fer ye if ye untie my hands, allow me to find my way down. I'll slow ye down," he suggested.

"Milord," began the woodsman, "He speaks the truth. With tied hands, he has no balance and will slow us down, fer he cannot climb or walk over slippery rocks."

"That's enough! We'll rest here a moment, then continue back down. His hands will remain bound."

Now that Gryffen was tied up and posed no threat, the heavyset man determined it was safe to approach the prisoner and wandered over. "Er, have ye ale?"

"Ale? Up here? Nay, Milord," Gryffen replied.

One or two unknown men snickered at the absurdity of the request.

"What 'bout the others, Master Oakes?" a swordsman asked.

"Oh, aye, bring them all down," replied the overweight man, still miffed his prisoner had no suitable refreshments.

A swordsman signalled with a whistle, and within moments, another ten villagers who'd had the house surrounded appeared. Gryffen noticed a few carried bows and immediately felt concerned for Cathal's safety.

The group leader, Oakes, sat down in the shade, removed his rather ornate hat and wiped his brow as his men fidgeted, eagerly waiting for the order to depart so they could return to their homes.

"Very well, let's return, make haste, quickly now, he clapped his hands together to encourage his men to respond. "Burn it!"

"Pardon me, Milord?" questioned the nearest swordsman.

"Burn it, dam ye!" Oakes yelled.

"I don't think we should, Milord, not until the sheriff–"

"I care not what the sheriff says. Up here, I represent the law – see to it."

"Nay, ye can't'" appealed Gryffen. "T'is my home." He struggled against his bindings in protest before being struck on the head.

What began as a tiny flicker quickly became a roaring blaze as Gryffin's home was set alight. Cathal fought the impulse to cry out by biting the inside of his cheek. His house, the only home he'd ever really known, was being burned, and there wasn't anything he could do to prevent its destruction. From his vantage point across the valley, a thick column of smoke rose above the forest canopy and dissipated in a southerly direction. Why? For what purpose or reason is it justified to destroy a man's house? Cathal wiped his eyes to clear his blurred vision and slid back along the rock he lay upon. Everything he owned lay in the bag a few feet away. He swallowed away his emotions and reaffirmed his resolve. With his bag slung over his shoulder and a firm grip on his staff, he carefully descended from his hiding place and, from a safe distance, followed the sheriff's men down from the uplands.

Gryffen had been wrong; having his hands bound did not slow their progress as they made their way down from the Yorkshire Uplands. Master Oakes had been the cause of their ponderous descent. Frequent stops to rest and an unhurried pace meant Cathal could easily keep up, and the danger was in being discovered as he almost ran into Gryffen's guards.

It took forever, but finally, the posse entered the village to retrieve their horses and a wagon they left in the care of a hostler. Master Oakes had made it quite clear that he was not fond of sitting astride a horse. Seated upon a wagon was more dignified and added prestige to his countenance and the successful completion of the mission he'd been tasked with. Gryffen was chained to the wagon and knew there was little chance of escape.

It was almost nightfall when they rode into Dearthington, a market town governed by Lord Oliver Hansard. Gryffen was quickly locked in the bailiff's gaol, a small, squalid room used for a multitude of purposes, and one of them was holding prisoners. He'd been held in rooms like this before, many years ago, and they hadn't changed much, and unfortunately, this one was entirely secure.

When Cathal arrived in the village, the *posse comitatus* had already departed. He quickly learned they had ridden for Dearthington, a town about twenty miles northeast. To avoid being recognised by the three troublemakers he'd encountered a few days before, Gryffen had recommended that Cathal wear a hooded cape. It mattered not to Cathal what clothes he wore as long as they served their functional purpose. As suggested, he'd donned the cape over his clothes, covered his head and been able to interact with the villagers without being recognised. Although he suspected one or more of the young men were with the posse that came for Gryffen.

He spent a warm, comfortable night in the familiarity of the forest before departing for Dearthington early the following day.

It took Cathal three days to arrive in Dearthington. He'd stopped to aid a young girl with a stomach problem, and he quickly determined she'd eaten spoiled food. Her family was most grateful and offered him a meal, which he accepted, and a token payment, which he politely refused. After tending to her for half a day and offering assurances little Olive would again be well, he set out as quickly as he could for Dearthington. What awaited him, he didn't know, but he would do what he could for Gryffen.

Excommunication was a horrific punishment, and he'd been condemned by the bishop with bell, book, and candle and been deemed an outcast of the Church. More importantly, he knew that as a Christian, excommunication meant he had no hope of salvation. Despite the unkind and constant reminders of his situation, Gryffen worried more about Cathal than himself. What Master Oakes did by setting his house on fire was cruel and uncalled for. There was no need, but Master Oakes, a milliner[25], had exceeded his authority when he ordered the house burned, perhaps because one of the three young men was related to him. But how would Cathal cope with no place to call home? What would he do?

Gryffen decided that it would be best if he repented and offered a sincere apology to the bishop. Bishop Chlodomer Dunhelm would undoubtedly want to see him, knowing he appealed for compassion and mercy. But in all fairness, he had wronged and humiliated the bishop and failed to offer due respect afforded to an important man of God. When someone brought him food, he asked them to pass on his request to meet with the bishop, and Gryffen prepared to wait for the summons and hoped the unpleasantness would soon be over.

25 Milliner – A hat maker.

A house could be rebuilt, and his valuables were safely hidden and out of reach from anyone.

Bishop Dunhelm felt it best that his prisoner understood the error of his ways, and a day or two in confinement would serve him well. After two days, he sent for the man.

"Yer Excellency," stated a cleric, "The prisoner is in the vestibule."

Bishop Chlodomer Dunhelm drained his goblet of wine and dabbed at his mouth with a cloth. "Very well. Has the sheriff sent his man?"

"He has, Yer Grace, and he is in the vestibule guarding the prisoner, as ye asked."

"Have ye spoken to him? Does he know what must be done?"

"Aye, Yer Grace," replied the cleric bowing at the waist.

Bishop Dunhelm stood, steadied himself, and rearranged his robes and mozetta[26] before slowly leaving his private quarters inside the castle. The bishop temporarily lived as an honoured guest of Lord Oliver Hansard at Walworth Castle while Durham Cathedral underwent some repairs. The bishop, a cleric and two men-at-arms left the castle and slowly made their way to Saint Cuthbert Church, a short distance away.

They entered the church through the warming room, unhurriedly around the garden and into the nave. Earlier, the bishop ensured no one was inside the church, as he wanted privacy. The sound of four men walking through the church added a touch of drama and tension towards the unfortunate prisoner who waited on the other side of the doors just ahead.

An exile from the Church, or someone excommunicated, wasn't permitted to enter a Church; the only place they could be was in the vestibule, a room between the outer door of the

26 Mozetta – A hooded cape that bishops wore when not performing any ceremonies.

church and its interior. It suited the bishop that the prisoner could come close to entering the church – but not entirely.

Bishop Dunhelm nodded, and the two men-at-arms thrust open the doors. Ahead stood the prisoner he'd not seen in many years, guarded by a trusted man the sheriff provided. The humiliation he'd suffered at the hand of this despicable creature still left a sour taste in his mouth, and he'd never forgotten the disgraceful outburst and the torrent of unfounded accusations Gryffen of Dearthington had made inside this very church. People had laughed at him; some had even sided with the man, but one thing was clear: Gryffen of Dearthington would pay the price of his reprehensible act. Such was his anger that he felt his cheeks flush and his hands tremble.

He took half a step forward, separating himself from the cleric and men-at-arms, meeting the prisoner's inquisitive gaze. He looked older than when he saw him last, but his eyes, the insolence, were still there.

"Dearly beloved, avenge not yourselves, but rather give place unto wrath: for it is written, Vengeance is mine; I will repay, saith the Lord."

A chorus of amens from his men completed the scripture.

Not understanding what was happening, Gryffen looked at the bishop with hope.

CHAPTER THIRTEEN

Against his better judgement and own advice, Gryffen dropped to a knee and averted his eyes. "Yer Grace, if I may speak, fer I wish to offer regret and heartfelt sorrow fer my behaviour and words towards ye." He didn't wait for permission to speak and continued. "At that time, Yer Excellency, I spoke rashly with the undisciplined voice and naivety of youthful foolishness. I offended the Church, Yer Grace, and also ye. I wish to repent and serve penance for what I have done, fer Christ speaks to me."

Bishop Dunhelm raised an eyebrow. The man was genuinely unhinged. *Christ doesn't speak to excommunicated peasants.* This was turning out better than he'd hoped. He puffed out his chest. "I exiled ye from the Church to provide ye with the opportunity to reflect on what ye did and how ye offended God, and now ye seek penance all these years later and only when ye are caught? How convenient fer us both, eh." His voice rose in anger, and the cleric gave him a subtle touch on his arm, a gentle reminder to maintain decorum. "If ye felt pain and remorse, why did ye not come to see me earlier? Or better yet, fulfil yer obligation and hand yer wealth to the Church as required." Bishop Dunhelm did his best to look aggrieved and solemnly shook his head. "God is disappointed in ye, as am I, and ye have let us all down."

"Yer Grace, I have no wealth. Back then, I had only a horse

and left it behind in the village. My lands were taken from–"

"That isn't true," snapped the bishop. "Yer lands were forfeit to the Church for unpaid levies, and I'm told ye had hidden wealth, coin, treasures and jewels stolen from nobility in Frankia when ye fought there."

Gryffen knew the bishop lied and had listened to the flapping tongues of gossipmongers. Years ago, in a bold effort to obtain more land for the Church, the bishop had created an additional levy and intentionally not informed the landowners. When the amount was sufficiently high and landowners could not pay, he'd coldly confiscated their land.

His knee was beginning to ache from the cold, hard stone floor. "Yer Grace, if I had these riches ye speak of, then over the years, they would have surfaced. The village where I trade receives meat and hides from me as payment for tools and wheat. I am poor, without means except for hunting."

The bishop silently acceded that Gryffen had a point. No unexplained jewels or treasures had ever surfaced from the Yorkshire Uplands. It was logical to assume that if he had such wealth, he would not have need to trade meat and hides for wheat and tools; he would have purchased them. "I'll have someone search yer home, ye may still have them hidden."

Gryffen shook his head. "Yer Grace, Master Oakes saw fit to burn my home – it is gone, destroyed."

"What say ye? Does he speak the truth?" spluttered the bishop.

The cleric shrugged his shoulders. "I know nothing of this, Yer Excellency, but if it pleases ye, I will find out."

"Of course, it pleases me!" yelled the bishop. His face reddened with the exertion and not from the quantity of wine he consumed, as the cleric believed.

The bishop collected himself. "Then ye are still in debt to

the Church fer unpaid levies. Can ye pay?"

"I will pay, Yer Excellency. I have no coin to settle debt this day, but I will; ye have my oath, I swear to ye," Gryffen pleaded in desperation. "The Church is compassionate and can offer me grace – is this not so?"

"Only if they are members of the Church, and I recall, that ye, Gryffen of Dearthington, are excommunicated." Bishop Dunhelm looked at Gryffen in disgust and turned to walk away. "See to it." He spared the sheriff's man a subtle nod and re-entered the nave as the inner doors shut loudly behind him. Gryffen rose awkwardly and rubbed his knee as the guard shoved him towards the outside door.

Cathal arrived in Dearthington and, after a few subtle inquiries from a drunk, learned that a man, a stranger, had recently been locked up in the town gaol. Finding the gaol didn't take long, as most unruly drunks had spent a night or two locked inside and many, more than once.

He needed to speak to Gryffen and find out what was happening. Things had obviously changed; the destruction of their home had seen to that, and of pressing concern, was Gryffen in danger?

Cathal stood in the shadows of a nearby building and waited for the right time to enter. As the sun began its slow descent into the western sky, an armed man, with the assured swagger of confidence and self-importance, entered the building where the gaol was housed and exited a few moments later with Gryffen.

From where he stood, Cathal could see that Gryffen looked unharmed, but the sword-wielding man was none too gentle and pushed Gryffen hard, causing him to stumble a few times. He had no idea where Gryffen was being taken, and all he could do was follow.

Cathal assumed it was to meet the bishop when they entered the Church of Saint Andrew. This was good news and is what Gryffen had hoped would happen. Cathal remained out of sight and waited nearby with a measure of hope for a good outcome. He heard indistinct voices but couldn't tell what was happening. His patience was rewarded when the Church's main doors were thrust open a short time later, and Gryffen stumbled out after receiving another firm shove in his back by the same aggressive guard.

Most unexpectedly, they didn't follow the route back to the gaol and detoured away. It was almost entirely dark, and Cathal had no problems remaining undetected, but he was puzzled as to where the guard was taking Gryffen. If they followed in their current direction, it would lead to the town's outskirts, which didn't bode well.

Cathal closed the distance as much as he dared, and neither Gryffen nor the guard knew of his presence.

Ahead of them, the guard continued to push Gryffen, forcibly encouraging him to move faster, and he couldn't tell if they were speaking to each other. Suddenly, they veered left down a narrow but frequently used path. It was quiet, and no other people were around. Anyone they'd previously encountered kept their distance from the unfriendly guard as they passed him by, and now, in the stillness and blackness of the night, the hair on the back of Cathal's neck rose.

The stench was almost overpowering. The guard had taken Gryffen to where townsfolk discarded their rubbish, where raw sewerage accumulated, and where dead and decaying carcases and even people were left to rot in a trench of putrid filth.

Cathal now understood why Gryffen was led here. With a warning yell and his staff fully extended, he sprung from behind a bush and charged the guard, ten yards away, but it was too far; there was little he could do to save Gryffen – he was too late.

Even in the darkness and by the moon's dim light, he could see the guard's sword arcing down, towards Gryffen's unprotected neck. The sound of impact was sickening, and before he could prevent it, Cathal saw the guard raise his foot and push the headless corpse into the vile, effluent-filled trench.

Having completed his duty, the guard turned to face the onrushing threat. Cathal screamed in fury and, with the end of his staff, struck the guard's turned head beneath his chin with all the force he could manage. With a crack of splintering bones, the guard's head snapped sideways, and, with the force of the strike, he toppled to slide into the filth and settle in the thick sludge beside Gryffen's body.

Cathal sunk to his knees and buried his head in his hands. The unnecessary death of Gryffen was too much for the young man, and in total despair, he slowly stood, turned his back on Gryffen, and walked away.

Sometime later, distraught and overcome, Cathal wandered in a daze along a main thoroughfare from Dearthington in a north-westerly direction towards the Yorkshire Uplands. It wasn't his plan to return; it was the only place he had to go, and he didn't know what else to do. Unaware of his surroundings and his mind in turmoil, he almost stumbled into the path of a horse-drawn cart if not for the panicked warning of the peasant. He laboured onwards, unseeing and uncaring.

The sun was high in the sky when he stepped into a hole in the road and almost fell and lurched to the side to regain his balance. He hadn't heard the sound of approaching horses and was surprised when a large horse roughly shouldered him aside.

"A pox on ye, halfwit!"

Cathal stepped aside and, in confusion and surprise, turned to look. Six armed knights on coursers rode by.

"Have ye nothing to say?" questioned the rider whose horse struck him.

Cathal hadn't anything to say and walked on in silence.

"A muttonhead," yelled another knight, which solicited a laugh from the others.

The first rider reined in his horse and turned around to face Cathal. The others followed suit and blocked his path.

"Cat got yer tongue?" asked another.

Cathal paused and rested against his staff as he appraised the six knights. They carried no banners or anything which identified which lord they served. Typically, at the sight of knights, Cathal learned to hide, and he would have today had he been more attentive. Like most knights he encountered, these were spoiled young men of a similar age to him, full of cockiness and only too keen to show off.

"It pleases me to be on my way," Cathal eventually replied.

A few knights laughed. "It *pleases* ye?" repeated a knight with exaggeration.

Cathal shrugged. He didn't want to play games with these men, so he walked forward to pass between two of their horses when a sword was lowered and poked him in the chest. Not enough to draw blood, but enough to alert him of danger. A warning.

"Methinks ye should drop to yer knees and beg forgiveness. Ye were most ungracious, and ye almost fell in front of my horse… ye could have injured it, and these are costly animals. Are ye whiffled[27]?" the knight slung a leg over his saddle, slid to the ground and handed the reins to a friend.

Cathal took a step backwards to create some space. He

27 Whiffled – Medieval word for drunk.

knew the situation was deteriorating quickly. Other than the knights, they were alone. No one was near to offer assistance. "I offer ye my apology, and I meant no disrespect, Milords. I wish only to continue my journey and not cause any ill will." He subserviently lowered his head.

"Then ye are hard of hearing, fer ye were told to fall to yer knees," said the dismounted knight who swaggered towards Cathal with his unsheathed sword angled across his chest. He paused two steps away.

Cathal took another step backwards and stopped. "I have apologised and ask kindly if ye will allow me to be on my way?"

"Nay, fer ye have offended us." He turned to look back at his friends. "Isn't this so?"

There was a chorus of 'Ayes.'

"Then again, fergive me. I do not want to see ye aggrieved, Milords." Cathal again dipped his head in respect and hoped the gesture was enough.

"On yer knees!" shouted the knight.

Cathal saw the knight's grip tighten on his sword, and in response, he subtly changed his foot position while his staff remained upright and resting on the ground. He could hear Gryffen's voice in his ear. *Never lower yerself to yer knees in front of an armed adversary.* Cathal shook his head.

The mounted knights were all leaning forward on their saddles with a measure of excitement at the prospect of entertainment at the expense of a disrespectful peasant.

The knight with the sword swung it around to point it at Cathal's chest. "On yer knees!" he bellowed.

Cathal didn't move.

The knight was quick. Suddenly, the sword swept across to slap Cathal alongside his thigh. But the only thing it struck was his staff.

The unexpected move by Cathal caught the knight unprepared, and a quick look of puzzlement flashed across his face. In nervousness, he compulsively spun the sword so the hilt rotated in his hand.

Behind the knight, a couple of his friends whistled. "We have some sport this glorious day, after all," one yelled.

Cathal's stomach was tied in knots. He couldn't take on six knights and achieve a victory. Perhaps one or two, but six?

Again, the sword slashed outwards. This time, it wasn't intended to be a humiliating slap; he intended to inflict a deadly wound. As before, it failed to hit its target and swished harmlessly past where Cathal had stood only moments before.

"This is folly, Milord; let's continue with our day. I see no reason fer blood to be shed," Cathal implored.

The knight's face was a mask of concentration, and Cathal knew what to expect next. Gryffen had taught him about mastering a sword, and he knew the various strokes, slashes and thrusts used to kill or maim. He understood the techniques of a modern swordsman and, more importantly, learned how to defend against them. The knight's stance and grip gave away his next move, and Cathal anticipated when and how the knight would strike.

With both hands using an opposing grip, the sword came straight at him at about chest height. Depending on where Cathal moved, the knight could change the direction and push the blade one way or pull it back in another. The knight didn't expect Cathal to remain stationary and for the staff to briefly come alongside his sword, move underneath, and then back over the top, which twisted the blade from the knight's grip. The sword clattered to the ground, but Cathal wasn't finished. He spun entirely around and struck the knight, hard, along the back of his knees with his staff, and the knight crumpled to the ground. Cathal kicked the fallen sword away. The knight was left speechless and looked at Cathal in confusion.

"I ask that ye leave me in peace," Cathal raised his voice. "What ye do is folly; go about yer day."

In response, the remaining five knights dismounted and handed all their reins to the smallest of the six knights.

Cathal turned to walk back in the direction he originally came from. But the sound of running footsteps was the harbinger of doom. He could have picked up the fallen sword, but then he would be fighting four sword-wielding knights with the same weapon, giving them more of an advantage. With his staff, he could manoeuvre easier and faster and force them to keep their distance and hopefully not be injured in the process.

Cathal sidestepped and simultaneously discarded his bag, tossing it away. He straightened and faced four angry knights. He quickly glanced around and saw a structure he hadn't previously seen a short distance away. If he could make his way there, he could protect his back. This place looked familiar; it was the place he'd stopped to aid the stricken girl, Olive. It mattered not where he was, and the peasant farmer and his wife wouldn't be stupid enough to interfere with knights.

The four knights were soon joined by the fifth, who'd retrieved his sword and was entering the fray. The sixth knight who held the horses reins was yelling encouragement to his friends. The five knights fanned outwards, and Cathal struck first.

His plan was basic. Rather than fight all five knights at once, he intended to position himself to fight and incapacitate one knight at a time. He went for the knight on his extreme right side. He faked swiping the staff across the knight's mid-section, and when the knight took an evasive step, Cathal struck him hard across the side of the head. He fell. Then there were four.

Cathal kept moving to his right, keeping the knight who was originally on his left the farthest away. He used a similar tactic, and again, another knight collapsed. Then there were three. They taunted him, offering insults and slurs, as they wanted to make him angry so he'd forgo caution and fight with emotion. He didn't.

Gryffen had tirelessly warned him about that. *Never fight with emotion; ye will most likely los*e. Gryffen's words resonated in his head, but he was dead, murdered.

He sensed movement behind, but before he could turn, his world went black.

CHAPTER FOURTEEN

When Cathal blinked open his eyes, his first sensation was excruciating pain. It felt like he'd been stabbed repeatedly in the chest by a dozen red-hot pokers. When he tried to raise his head to see better, he couldn't. The pain was unbearable, and his heart was racing. His breathing was irregular, and his skin clammy… he knew something horrid had happened and tried to recall all the details … The knights and the fight… it must have been them. No plausible reason came to mind other than the brief fight. But he hadn't killed or even wounded anyone; the knights had their pride intact, other than a few would have some severe bruises. Again, he tried to raise his head and failed. He was losing strength. He tried to turn his head, but even that was becoming an effort. He felt weak and shut his eyes.

Someone was talking to him, and he opened his eyes and saw one of the knights sitting astride his courser, staring down at him. He tried to focus on what he said.

"… a pagan, nothing more than a heathen shaman," the knight said. "We have opened ye up, bared yer soul fer the world to see. Ye disgust me!" spat the knight. Behind him, other knights sat upon their jittery steeds and watched with baleful expressions. "Let this be a lesson to ye, fer a Christian would not practice sorcery or witchcraft, and fer yer crimes, we have decided to let ye live – fer now, but ye will take our message with ye fer the short time you have left. May God have mercy upon yer soul, fer we don't expect ye to live through the night."

Cathal closed his eyes…

Maman leaned over him and looked down at him with pity. "It is not yer time, Cathal," she said. Her loving voice… so soothing and comforting. "Ye have much to accomplish," she continued. "Now is not the time–"

She appeared the same as when he last saw her. "*Maman*?"

She placed a finger across his lips. "Hush, ye need yer strength, Cathal, and ye can overcome this." He tried to raise an arm to touch her, but the effort was too much. His chest felt like it was on fire.

"Save yer strength," she said.

Cathal forced his eyelids to open and saw a woman bending over him with a blood-soaked rag. It was a lot of blood, and nothing made sense… *Maman*… this woman… the pain. Sleep.

The water was an elixir, a tonic of life that had an immediate effect. He swallowed and opened his mouth for more, and it dribbled in, and again he swallowed, savouring the feeling. He willed his eyes open and saw the woman. She was not much older than he, and it was her, the mother of the girl he'd helped. Behind her stood her man with a thoughtful, serious expression.

Even breathing was agony, and the act of talking seemed impossible. She must have understood his questioning eyes and need.

"Cathal?"

He blinked in response.

"Ye must listen. Those bastards cut ye open like a side o' beef." She pointed to his upper chest. "From here, to here. To just below yer belly." Her finger moved down and back up again. "Then across." She moved her finger horizontally across his chest.

He could see she struggled. He blinked rapidly, encouraging her to continue because he knew there was more.

"They…" She took a deep breath and then exhaled slowly. "They pulled the skin back so yer insides are exposed." With the back of her hand, she wiped away the tears. "We, we don't know what to do. Her husband coughed and turned away.

He felt *Maman*'s presence, her words, what she said to him … then peace and he closed his eyes, willed away the pain and gave the matter thought. He licked his lips; the water had helped. With eyes tightly closed, he used his breath to speak, and it was nothing more than a whisper. "Am – I – cut – inside?"

He felt her move closer as she leaned down and placed an ear near his mouth.

He repeated. "Am – I – cut – inside?"

"Are ye cut? Inside, yer innards?" she confirmed.

He blinked rapidly.

Her husband stepped closer. "Nay, fer they knew what to do. I saw no damage. It looks t' me like the sods carved a cross onto yer skin, then they peeled ye open and left ye to die."

Cathal knew he would die when the wound festered and became corrupt. It was inevitable. The pain clouded his thinking, and it was difficult to focus. He forced himself to relax. "Water."

He needed water, which would give him strength, and when he felt it dribble into his mouth, he swallowed as much as he could. After a dozen heartbeats and some laboured breaths, he spoke again and gave them instructions.

While he waited for them to complete the tasks he'd asked them to do, he remembered all their names. Isolde was a beautiful name, and if he could have told her, he would have. Her husband's name was Piers Haynes, and their daughter, who had been ill, was Olive. The distraction helped. Thinking about his injuries caused him stress and his body to tighten up, and that caused him more misery.

The water helped, and he'd drunk as much as possible. After a while, he felt some strength returning and believed he'd lost a lot of blood, which Piers and Isolde confirmed. He still lay where the knights had left him to die. But soon, he hoped to be moved to Piers and Isolde's cruck house.

Through the pain, he'd asked to be taken to their home. They would slide a plank underneath and carry him back. Isolde was the wife of a freeman farmer and had more strength than some men he'd met, and he knew she could manage.

He also asked if they had found his bag. They nodded and added the contents had been emptied and lay scattered beside the road he'd travelled along. Of interest, they told him, was his small bag of bones. They'd been emptied onto a pile, and Piers said that judging by the smell, they had all pissed on them. It mattered not to Cathal; they were just some smallish bones, and he could easily find others. But it began to make some sense for him.

While waiting for Piers and Isolde to return, he thought about what had happened and why. The only conclusion that made sense was that during the fight, the knight holding the reins to the horses had crept up behind him and hit him with a rock or the hilt of his sword, which explained a rather tender, sore area on his head.

After that, they must have emptied his bag and discovered the small bag of bones, which offended their selective sense of Christian values. Because he also carried herbs and other plant-based remedies in his bag, they'd incorrectly assumed he was a druid, or shaman, a devil-worshipping heathen who cast otherworldly spells with evil potions. Pissing on the bones was nothing more than a statement of hate, and the cross they carved on his chest was an act of pure evil.

When Piers and Isolde returned with a sturdy plank, Cathal asked for more water. He drank his fill, and by the time they were ready to slide the plank beneath him, he felt he could manage what was to come next, but the pain hadn't lessened.

He couldn't remember being moved to the cruck house; the movement had caused so much agony his mind shut down. When he regained his senses, he lay in the byre on a bed of straw with his head propped up. From this position, he could see the extent of his injuries and was aware that his chances of recovery were slim unless he began treatment immediately. Unfortunately, this involved Isolde, and he needed her help. She had responsibilities to her husband, to the Lord of the Manor, and they needed to complete the work assigned to them. She and Piers had work to do, and pulling her away from those tasks could have repercussions that could affect whether they could provide food to eat and perhaps even receive a harsh word from the reeve. Life as a peasant wasn't easy; they worked from when the sun rose in the morning until it descended in the evening. Sunday was decreed a day of rest, but usually, other duties needed completing, and there was always work to do.

With Isolde's help, the contents of his bag were laid out around him and under his whispered direction, she wiped away blood and thoroughly cleaned his wounds. Olive watched with childish curiosity when Isolde began to sew him back together again. The pain was intolerable even after taking mandrake and poppy, and he fought the impulse to physically jerk each time Isolde poked the bone needle through his skin.

Isolde was masterful; her sewing skills and previous experiences attested to the neat stitching and efficient manner of her work. When finished, Cathal instructed her to spread a salve mixed with honey over the wound and stitches before applying clean cloth to dress his chest and abdomen.

Exhausted and still in enormous pain, Cathal slept.

During the following days, Olive learned to administer to their ailing guest, and Isolde instructed her to gently pour water into Cathal's mouth and spoon-feed broth. When lucid, he kept a close eye on the wounds in fear of corruption and foulness and ensured that fresh, honey-fused salve was reapplied with every daily change of dressings. The difference was noticeable; after a few days, his strength returned, and he could manage the discomfort more easily. When feeling brave, he could even move his arms a little, but the pain from severed muscles on his abdomen was excruciating.

He didn't move for fear of stressing the sutures and the healing wounds. When he soiled himself, Piers and Isolde didn't grizzle. They dragged him to the side, away from the mess, and wiped him clean before changing the filthy straw. They never complained, protested or said anything unkind to him, but Cathal knew his presence here would impact their productivity and potentially put them at risk if the knights returned.

After the fifth day, Piers sat beside him to talk, and Cathal broached the subject. "Will they return? And have ye seen them, the knights who did this to me?"

"If they come here to look, they'll find ye easy 'nough,

Cathal," Piers replied. "Buts if they come askin', they won't get nothin' but blank stares from us."

Cathal looked puzzled.

"O'er there, yonder," he raised an arm and pointed to another cruck house some distance away, "is my brother's home. Behind 'is house is me Da and Ma. O'er there," He pointed in another direction, "is Isolde's family. Everyone knows ye are here, Cathal, and they all knows what ye did t'help Olive. How do you think we find food to feed us all and keep ahead of our work?"

Cathal would have shaken his head if it didn't hurt. "How?"

"Cause they all be helpin' a bit. If them bastard knights come back, they ain't gettin' help from the likes of us. Nope, everyone will clam up." He pointed a grubby finger at Cathal. "But if they look fer ye, we can't hide ye, and find ye they will."

Cathal was silent as he digested what Piers told him. These poor people had already sacrificed so much, and if the knights returned, they had put themselves in danger. Nobility did not look favourably on peasants who lied to them, and there could be consequences.

"I promise ye, Piers, the moment I can walk, I will leave and be out of yer lives."

Piers laughed. "Ye saved Ollie's life. If ye hadn't come along that day, she'd be dead. Ye stay here as long as ye need. We'll manage."

Cathal silently vowed that he would do the right thing for these people as soon as he had recovered. Their unselfish kindness shouldn't be forgotten, and he had a glimmer of an idea.

Each day saw an improvement, and Cathal felt assured his wounds wouldn't fester. The healing process had begun, and with it, his confidence returned.

After another week had passed, Cathal was anxious to try and stand. He requested the Isolde wrap the dressing tighter and fetch him some rope. With care, he wound the rope firmly around his chest and abdomen so that when he stood, his stomach wouldn't distend and rupture the wound. It offered him support, and with help, he finally managed to stand on wobbly legs. It had been sixteen days since the fight, and Cathal was anxious to be on his way.

"Why the hurry?" Piers asked as he and Isolde gingerly lifted him to his feet.

"I fear the knights, and I believe they will return and seek me."

"Ye won't be walkin' fer 'nother few days yet," observed Piers with a laugh as Cathal struggled to take a single step.

Some days later, a lone knight was seen in the area asking questions, and Isolde dashed into the byre to inform Cathal.

"We must do what we can to hide ye, Cathal," she stated as she scooped up Cathal's bag and staff.

Cathal knew he couldn't defend himself; his walking had extended to only a dozen pain-filled paces, and then, only with the aid of his staff. He had no choice but to hide.

Like any peasant byre attached to a cruck, the animals were sheltered inside at night and during bad weather. They were valuable, and if left unattended, they could be stolen. After a week or two, dirty straw in the byre was tossed out and replaced with fresh straw.

"I will hide under the straw." Cathal pointed to the pile of soiled straw near the gate outside.

Isolde helped Cathal to the heap and, with a pitchfork, began to pile excrement-covered straw over him until he was completely hidden. Only moments later, a solitary knight rode up to the cruck.

The knight saw a tired-looking woman cleaning soiled straw from the byre with a pitchfork. When she saw him, she touched her hand to her forehead in respect to the nobleman and lowered her gaze.

The knight remained mounted and looked around. Not seeing anything of interest, he turned his attention back to her. "Woman, I seek word on a man fatally injured a short distance from here, on the road to Dearthington. I believe over two weeks past, what became of him?"

Isolde tucked away a strand of hair that became dislodged from beneath her head covering. "I saw some goin ons," and pointed towards the road. "T'was there, an I remember well, Milord, but what happened is of no business to me or my man. We likes to keep outa trouble, Milord."

The knight adjusted his seating position. "And what did ye see?"

"Oh, Milord, there was an injured man, and we took a gander, but then some other men came, land like yer good self, they had swords and chased us away. We don't want trouble here, Milord and we obeyed our betters as we should."

"Tell me woman, who saw what happened to this man?"

Isolde shook her head. "No one, Milord."

The knight looked at her with suspicion. "These men, did they have horses? Were they knights?"

"Oh, Milord, I can't recall, only that they had swords and told us to bugger off, s'cuse the language, Milord, but it was what they said."

"Interesting. Did they take the body, and which direction did they go?"

Isolde scratched her head. "I expect they took the body, don't know fer sure. But we was pleased when they left. I thinks they went that way, Milord," Isolde replied and pointed towards Dearthington.

Cathal could overhear the conversation, and Isolde was playing her part perfectly. She even changed the way she spoke.

"And they rode horses?" asked the knight, seeking confirmation.

"They might have done, Milord." Isolde looked intently at the knight. "If I remembers, I can tell ye, but don't know where to find ye."

Cathal held his breath – this was crucial. Would the knight divulge his name?

"Of course, I am Sir Guy of Lancaster. But that is too far away for ye. If ye wish to pass on a message, any knight in Dearthington knows of me."

Beneath the filthy straw, Cathal grinned.

Isolde brushed away the filthy straw that covered him. "Ye spoke well, Isolde and said what we planned, but I have worry," Cathal stated.

Isolde paused from her task.

"Why leave me to die and then return and ask what happened? It makes no sense."

"Could he just be curious?" she asked.

"I believe they will return, and I must take my leave. If more knights come, they will do a thorough search, and they will find me, and then Piers and ye will be at risk."

"Why are we at risk? We have done no wrong."

"Because ye saw what happened."

Isolde started into Cathal's face. "And ye will leave?"

"Aye, I must. Even though I am not fully recovered, I must leave and put distance between us."

Isolde felt disappointed; she would miss her enigmatic patient. She felt her face begin to flush and turned away.

"I think it best I leave during the night, and I will seek refuge during the day."

Cathal wound cloth tightly around his abdomen and chest to reduce the discomfort and prevent his chest and stomach from expanding and causing more pain. Although there was no longer a risk of corruption from the wound, the knight who had cut him had severed his stomach and chest muscles, and they needed ample time to heal.

To disguise his appearance, Isolde had made him a loose-fitting robe that masked the bulkiness of the cloth wrapped around him. She'd put a lot of care into sewing the garment and was proud of her effort. He found the robe comfortable and pleasing to wear as it didn't restrict his movements.

The evening was still when Cathal exited the byre. He had his bag and, with the aid of his staff, gingerly walked away. Isolde and Piers had been unselfishly kind, and he enjoyed their company and would miss them. He'd said his goodbyes earlier and promised to return when fully recovered. Little Olive, the dear girl, had wept when he said farewell to her.

With the aid of the moon, he walked down the short path to the road. Left would take him to the uplands, and right, back to Dearthington. He turned left and then stopped. He felt the presence of another.

He turned and squinted into the darkness and saw her. Isolde, her outline highlighted by the moon, stood a short distance away. *Why was she outside*? He exhaled slowly and raised his hand in farewell. He doubted she saw, but then he saw her arm wave in response. He couldn't linger and needed to create distance between himself and here. With measured, slow steps, he walked away.

CHAPTER FIFTEEN

Mormaer, Harald Maddadsson, the Viking ruler of Orkneyjar, preferred to sit in his great hall rather than venture out. Old battle wounds and age had taken their toll on his toil-worn body, and most afternoons, he would lay down and rest for a while. A simple pleasure and an indulgence he looked forward to. He wearily rose from his seat as it was time to sleep when Nels One-Ear entered the hall with unusual urgency.

From his mannerisms, Harald feared the worst and fully expected news of an invasion or that the volatile Scots had united and raised arms in preparation to attack.

"I have news, Harald," began Nels One-Ear.

Harald could see Nels was clearly agitated and steeled himself for what was to come.

"Do ye recall the woman and the boy ye sought years ago?"

Harald felt relief the cursed Scots weren't attacking and shook his head.

"The Irish woman–"

"Of course, what of it, hurry fer, I have important matters to attend to that require my attention," Harald harshly responded.

"The priests have had visions. They see him…"

"Who?" Harald queried.

"The boy, or rather he is no longer a boy, the son of the Irish woman we seek, but now he is a man. I am told he isn't too far from here in Jórvík[28]."

It dawned on Harald, whom Nels spoke of. He'd forgotten.

28 Jórvík – What Vikings called modern day Yorkshire.

"Are ye sure, and this isn't foolery? The priests are too fond of their wine and blather on about nought just to please us."

"Nay, Harald, fer I questioned them endlessly."

"Why now? After all these years nothing, and then now ye tell me…"

"Aye, I asked this question too. The priests tell me this man has powerful energy, and it prevents them from seeing him," Nels explained. "They liken it to a fog that surrounds him. But that fog has mysteriously lifted, and now he is revealed." He began fidgeting while waiting for a decision.

Harald stroked his full beard and considered the importance of what had just been disclosed. "Aye, take one other with ye, a priest with proven vision who can see this young man. Find him and take his life without delay."

Nels looked shocked. "Only one other and a priest? I was going to suggest a score of men."

Harald smiled. "Ye are so young and impetuous. Two Norsemen travelling in England will not attract attention. A score of Norsemen will create questions, fer people will worry about their safety. Ye will be observed and may not be able to move freely. I am right, Nels, have faith in me. Take one other, a priest, because he will guide ye so ye can kill this man quickly, fer I feel time is running out.

This wasn't what Nels expected. *A priest*? But then again, what Harald suggested wasn't reckless. One man or even two could more easily remain hidden.

He selected a youngish priest, who, he believed, would not have difficulty sleeping outdoors or travelling on foot. A man who could even fight if needed. Two days later, when Nels went to depart and arrived at the temple to collect the priest, he found him sitting atop a hefty chest.

The priest explained the chest contained an assortment

of small statues and figurines of Gods. He added how he'd thoughtfully packed other various implements and devices to perform sacrifices and other necessary rituals during their journey.

Nels shook his head and looked down at the priest from the back of his horse. "How do ye expect we can transport this?" he asked, pointing to the chest.

The priest looked incredulous. "A cart, of course. How else? I don't expect fer ye to carry this on yer back." He looked skywards, rolled his eyes, grasped the Thor's hammer pendant that hung around his neck and wondered how the gods had allowed him to travel with such a fool.

"Take only what ye can carry on horseback. If ye can't carry it, then it remains here," Nels instructed with finality.

The young priest who'd insisted on being called Raven briefly considered disobeying the order to journey with Nels One-Ear. The hardships he would endure were not something he welcomed, and then to trust his safety to a *dunga*[29]. But the consequences of refusing Harald's order shouldn't be dismissed either. He sighed loudly and stood with a scowl.

As planned, Cathal hid during the day and walked only when it was dark. His body was weak, and he was disappointed at his progress and doubted that he'd travelled more than five miles in two days. Yet each night, when the greyness of dawn seeped across the eastern sky, he was relieved and eagerly sought shelter to rest his aching body.

He had food, slept fitfully throughout the day, and hadn't encountered a soul. On the evening of the third night, as he set out along the main road that would take him to the Uplands, he heard the sound of someone steadily approaching from behind, and he tensed. He'd not been vigilant, and now it was too

29 *Dunga – Viking word for a useless person.*

late to hide. He stepped to the side of the track to give room and allow the person to pass and he kept his head bent low so he couldn't be recognised and later identified.

The sound of footsteps grew louder, but another sound mingled with the steps caused him to look up in alarm. It was the muted sound of sobbing. The figure materialised from the early evening gloom.

"Isolde?" he questioned.

She walked towards him and stopped close. He could feel her breath on his face and see glistening wetness from tears. "Isolde." He spoke her name not to question her but as an exclamation of pity. He knew there could only be one reason for her to be here and then fought to control his emotions as he reassuringly reached out to gently clasp her shoulder.

Isolde pushed away his hand and embraced him. Her painful wails cut through the early evening stillness, the despair of a grieving mother so chilling and stark. Despite his discomfort, he held her close; his physical hurt melded with her emotional pain, and together they stayed that way. He knew what had happened.

Comfort and time helped; the spasms that wracked through her body eased. Her breathing began to settle, and he could feel her return to lucidity. She hadn't spoken a word, while the only word he'd said to her was when he called her name. He felt the suffering of her pain and loss, and like the spreading corruptness of a festering wound, he wanted nothing more than for her to be rid of it.

They stood together for an age, both in understanding that their unspoken words heralded tragedy and stained memories of sorrow that could never be forgotten. She eventually released him and looked up at his face for answers and relief. A responsibility he was unprepared for.

"Why?" she asked, her voice cracking.

"I am not wise to the world, Isolde, but I know there are men who seek power. Power feeds on fear, which is built on the foundation of desperation." Cathal knew his words couldn't offer her the comfort she needed.

"Why desperation?"

"Because someone must have spoken about what they did to me. The Church doesn't look kindly on acts of brutality, and its opinions and judgements can tarnish the glow of a respected family or knight. They wanted to silence me and anyone else who witnessed what they did. These men have become desperate and dangerous."

Isolde seemed to accept Cathal's answer. She reached out for his hand and led him to a bank where they could sit. After a moment or two of silence, she spoke. "I never heard them come and seen them only when they were leaving. There was four o' them on horses, and I recognised them; they'd been 'ere a'fore." Isolde paused to collect herself and continued. "I couldn't warn them, Cathal." She wiped her eyes. "And they rode through the field to where..."

Cathal remained silent and allowed her all the time she needed.

She sniffed once and continued after wiping away tears. "To where Piers and lil' Ollie were harvesting carrots. I wasn't there, and sweet Ollie was helpin' Piers. I'd taken carrots to trade fer some onions. When I came back, I saw them knights set the cruck ablaze before riding off. Piers had been struck by a sword, and–"

Cathal patiently waited until she had the strength to continue.

"And Olive ... dear lil' Ollie, she'd been trampled or kicked by one of them horses."

Cathal felt her back begin to heave. "When did they come?"

"After ye left, mid-mornin', I reckon," she sobbed.

"Did they talk?" he asked.

Isolde shook her head, "I don't know. I hid, and those bastards never saw me. But I should have taken her with me, but she loved to help Piers harvest, and I should never of left her. Now, everything – my Olive – everything has gone."

The moon had risen, and they were bathed in its soft, reflective light. Somewhere in the distance, a dog barked. Otherwise, it was still.

"What do ye wish to do, Isolde?"

"I want to be with ye, Cathal, where I feel safe."

"And yer family?"

"Nay, fer they have no room and fear the knights will return."

"And his?"

She shook her head. "They think I'm responsible, that I am the cause."

He thought carefully and couldn't think of why she shouldn't come with him, after all, he couldn't leave her alone. He nodded. "Aye, be best fer now."

They sat silently, both lost to their thoughts and despair before Isolde rose, tugging on his arm and sniffling, "We shouldn't tarry, eh."

Together, they walked into the night towards the Yorkshire Uplands, where Cathal wanted to return to the only place he'd ever called home. He thought of his mother, Lohier, Gryffen, and others who'd come into his life and died.

He felt warmed by having Isolde at his side, patiently helping him. She must have been exhausted, but she never complained. She didn't speak much, but he knew she grieved, and he allowed her that luxury because, more often than not, other things took precedence.

Would the knights who slaughtered Isolde's family and torched her home continue their search for him, or would they just give up? He walked on, each step a cruel reminder of the horrendous injuries he'd received at the hands of those evil men. He tried to put aside his emotions and think logically, concluding that the knights believed he posed no physical risk to them. Did they fear that he would report their unchristian-like behaviour? It was possible, but then he didn't know who they were or what influence they wielded. Were their respective families important nobles? The more they had to lose, then the higher the risk. If they were willing to kill innocent peasants and children … he firmly believed they would continue looking for him and seek his death.

He couldn't falter; he needed to be vigilant, not take foolish risks, and, more importantly, he felt a duty to keep Isolde safe. That was a new and unfamiliar responsibility, but one he was ready to embrace. It gave him purpose, and it felt good.

They pressed on, mostly in silence but not in moody sullenness. Isolde had to come to terms with her loss, and Cathal knew that deliberation provided acceptance. He could attest that the feeling of grief or loss never went away; it was something you became used to and learned to accept.

She had found a way to link her arm through his, and it gave him added support, easing his pain. They shuffled onwards into the night with Isolde lost to her grief, their wounds raw and inflamed but not festering. Cathal's senses were finely honed, and he listened for anything untoward. He heard and saw nothing.

Albert Pickens did. Although at his age, his hearing was not as it should be, and so it was understandable that he failed to hear two people walking along the road not far from his cruck home and the small plot of land he cultivated. It was his cow who alerted him. His dear, old cow. She was too weak to walk into the byre and lay down on the grass not far from his cruck. Cows were an asset; they were valuable beasts, and he could ill afford to lose her. Every couple of hours, he ventured outside, hand-fed her and gave her water in the hope it would give her some strength.

The moon was high in the evening sky, and this was the third time tonight he'd gone outside to check on his beloved cow. He was still optimistic she could regain her health. On this occasion, he noticed she was a little more alert and readily ate the hay he gave her and even drank water from a bucket; there was some hope. But as he was about to return inside, his cow's ears flicked, and she turned her head towards the road. Ever cautious about brigands who roamed the forests and roads, Albert crawled on hands and knees to a nearby tree, carefully stood and strained to listen as he peered into the darkness. He was about to give up when he saw movement, then, a moment later, he heard footfall and saw the dark outline of two people walking. From their height, he could see one was a man, and from how he walked and his awkward shuffle, he assumed he might be elderly. The other person walking close to his side, almost blending together, was a smaller figure he determined was a woman. He didn't hear the metallic clink that suggested they carried weapons or wore armour, so he relaxed and waited for them to pass. Albert found it strange that they'd be walking in the dead of night, shrugged, returned to his stricken cow and thought nothing more about it.

CHAPTER SIXTEEN

Lord Oliver Hansard had returned to Dearthington and his home, Walworth Castle, and along with his wife, were enjoying their evening meal with their esteemed guest, Bishop Chlodomer Dunhelm. They sat in a smallish room heated by a roaring fire that was more intimate and comfortable than the great hall.

The bishop tossed the last remaining delicate rabbit bones onto the table and belched loudly. "Nothing like a good rabbit, eh?"

The lord looked up and grinned as he devoured the remaining morsels he held. His wife, Lady Brenna, had finished some time ago and quietly sipped wine from a goblet.

"I have heard a few disturbing rumours," began Bishop Dunhelm during a pause in their conversation.

With their curiosity piqued, Lord Oliver and Lady Brenna turned their attention towards the bishop.

"There have been a few reports. Unsubstantiated, of course," continued the bishop with a smile, "concerning some rather brutish behaviour from some young knights."

Lady Brenna's face clouded over, and she leaned slightly forward in her chair. Lord Oliver wiped his mouth with a sleeve. "Continue."

"Ye know how spirited young men can be, and far be it fer me to judge. However, some priests have come to me with, uh, a concern or two."

"Does this involve Lambert?" asked the lord.

Bishop Dunhelm raised a hand dismissively. "I know not. However, if the archbishop hears of these … er, whimsical tales, then I am bound to investigate and take action. It isn't acceptable fer nobility to mistreat peasants without cause, and as ye are aware, King Henry has implemented reforms…"

"What have ye heard, Bishop Dunhelm?" interrupted Lady Brenna. "Mistreating peasants? What is this ye speak of?"

The bishop looked a little uncomfortable, the recent pleasures of his rabbit quickly forgotten. "Some, er, peasants have disappeared, gone missing fer no reason. Others claim they have been unfairly treated fer sport. Perhaps some have been cruelly tortured and even slain."

"This behaviour must stop," replied Lord Oliver. "Ye are correct to bring these abhorrent crimes to me."

The bishop nodded. "This is where it becomes murky, Milord, as yer fine son … Sir Lambert may be implicated. He and others–"

"Nonsense, he wouldn't act in such a, an, unchristian like way." Lord Oliver turned to his wife for support. "Who makes these accusations, yer Grace?"

Bishop Dunhelm knew he needed to de-escalate the situation, or it would quickly become out of hand. "Nay, nay, milord, please understand, er, as such, no formal accusations have been made. These things are nothing but hearsay and gossipmongering. But the prattle can't continue." He shook his head to reinforce his point and focused on Lord Hansard. "It may be best that ye speak to yer son, ask him to subdue his, er… temper his enthusiasm until things have calmed down. We can't have the archbishop asking questions that neither serves your or my interests well, Milord. Er, I'm sure you understand the gravity of my predicament."

Lord Oliver sat back in his chair and considered the bishop's advice. He knew the bishop spoke wisely, and if the archbishop were displeased, it would certainly reach the ears of King Henry. He turned to his wife. "Where is Lambert, fer I have not seen him?"

"I believe he is with his friends. They spoke of a hunt," she shrugged, "Boar, I believe."

"Upon his return, have him come to me. I will speak with him and curtail his, er, enthusiasm as ye suggest," scowled Lord Oliver."

Bishop Dunhelm was eminently satisfied.

Sir Lambert had been spoken to by his father, and of course, he vehemently denied any wrongdoing or that he'd even been involved in any altercations or grievances with peasants. Once dismissed, he'd immediately rendezvoused with his friends, three other knights of similar age who'd grown up and trained together. They'd sworn oaths to their lords and to uphold the time-honoured traditions of chivalry, but as yet, they'd not faced an enemy. With time on their hands and ample resources from their wealthy families, these virile young men exuded arrogance and haughtiness that frequently brought trouble upon themselves.

Sir Lambert disliked Bishop Dunhelm and privately considered him a meddlesome old fool. However, fool or not, he was still an influential bishop and wielded power with the same might as he carried a sword.

While Sir Lambert may be young, inexperienced, and reckless, he wasn't without nous and fully understood the significance of his father's stern warning, which echoed the bishop's voiced concern. Unfortunately, he found it challenging to temper his blood lust, and his solution to the problem, as explained to him by his father, was to be more circumspect and restrained.

What alarmed Sir Lambert was that people had begun to talk about his recent activities, and mere whispers could turn into an uncontrollable gale of accusations and finger-pointing. Aided by tankards of mead at a local Inn, Sir Lambert and his friends vowed to destroy anyone or anything that linked them to far-fetched tales of intimidation, torture and death. They reasoned that if peasants were haughty beyond their social station, openly defiant, and disrespectful, then exercising discipline was justified. Defiance had consequences, and if handled appropriately, as he and his friends had done, there couldn't be repercussions. But someone had talked, and one loose end remained vexing. Whatever happened to the body that had been almost eviscerated outside of Dearthington? There had been no sign or word of what had happened to it.

"Who buried the corpse?" Sir Lambert questioned.

Sir Guy shrugged.

"We silenced the farmer, and one of the horses kicked the runt of a girl," added Sir Robert coldly. "But the farmer's woman has also vanished."

"Aye, so now we must find her and that corpse. If the bishop hears of this, we will be shamed and face a reckoning before the Church and our lords. That corpse must not turn up, and we must find and silence that peasant woman. If she speaks of us or complains to someone..." Sir Lambert drained his tankard. "She was probably hiding and saw what happened to her man and runt of a daughter," he added, turning to each of his friends. "She poses a risk to us."

"And more'n likely, the corpse ain't a corpse and survived," laughed Sir Robert.

"Aye, so pack yer things; we will travel on the morrow at dawn," instructed Sir Lambert. "We will find out what happened, even if it takes a day or two."

"Yer never knows, we might even make sport," laughed Sir Crispin.

Sir Lambert grinned. "Aye, we are going on a hunt."

Sir Guy looked away; he wasn't as enthusiastic.

Four knights and two pack horses departed Dearthington as the first rays of sunshine speared above distant hills. The knights were jolly and in high spirits as they charged away from Dearthington, scattering peasants too slow to make way for horses. The knights retraced their route from days earlier and questioned everyone they encountered. When they came to the holding where the farmer had been slain and the little girl struck by a hoof. They saw the farm was deserted. Neighbours were unhelpful, and intimidation and threats did little to pry open the mouths of stoic, hardworking men. Women were worse, their baleful expressions and brazen insolence tested the patience of the young knights while filthy children stared at them in open hostility. Learning nothing, Sir Lambert and friends continued onwards in a north-westerly direction towards the uplands. In their wake lay injured men, some with broken bones, others with painful wounds. The disrespect shown to them by peasants they encountered justified their actions and were explainable - they felt no guilt. It would take time for the affected families to recover, and the reason behind the wanton violence would never be answered. Fear would fester and grow, and hatred and mistrust would pass from father to son.

The young knights believed it was their God-given right to discipline unruly peasants who were no better than animals. Peasants had no real value; they were poor because they were lazy and contributed only to crime and pestilence. They needed to learn to respect their betters and offer unquestioning loyalty and servitude without griping or sullenness. Devotion and hard work were expected, and through fear, harsh control, and punishment, lords could ensure unquestioned compliance and servitude. A practice Sir Lambert passionately believed and enjoyed.

The knights approached yet another unremarkable hamlet, similar to the last one, and the one before that, and saw a lone figure toiling in the sun digging a hole. As they approached, the knights saw the remnants of a cow carcass. Everything of value had been stripped or cut from the beast, and all that remained was for the waste to be buried. They watched the farmer from horseback in malevolent silence.

Albert Pickens paused from his digging and looked up at the four knights. He wiped his sweaty brow with an arm before leaning on his spade. "Morn'n Milords," he offered in polite greeting. The courtesy of a response wasn't returned, so he shrugged and prepared to continue his arduous task when one of the knights spoke.

"It is most impolite to turn yer back on yer betters, Churl," spoke Sir Lambert.

Albert ignored the slur, sighed, and turned to face the four men. "How can I be of help to ye?" he asked.

"We seek a woman, a peasant woman. She may have passed by here in the last week or so. Have ye seen her?" asked Sir Robert.

"Nay, Milords, only women I've seen pass by live 'ere. Do ye have a name?" Albert asked.

"She would be a stranger to ye as she lives many miles back, closer to Dearthington," informed Sir Lambert.

Albert nodded and scratched behind his ear. There was something… if he could only recall.

"Then you've seen her?" Sir Robert asked.

"I might have, am trying to think, Milords."

"Perhaps a foot up yer arse will help ye to remember,"

prompted Sir Robert, which caused his three friends to laugh.

"Out with it!" instructed Sir Lambert. "What have ye seen?"

"I don't knows what I seen. It was a week, some nights ago now… Aye, might have been longer, maybe nine or ten nights ago. T'was late, moon was high, and I was tendin' to her when she was poorly." Albert pointed to the fly-covered carcass. "It was her. She heard a noise first, and then I did too, and I seen two people walkin' real slow like, up the road, that away," Albert swung his arm around and pointed in the direction of the road."

Sir Lambert urged his horse to step closer to the old man. "Then ye saw a woman? Was she young, old, tall or short? Out with it, or are ye a fool?"

"I figure the man was old as he walked slow like 'e was labourin' and at 'is elbow was a woman. She can't have been tall cause she came up to his chin. That's all I saw. T'was dark, and she wore a hooded cape, Milords."

"The man, was he old, or could he have been injured?" Sir Crispin asked. Sir Lambert shot him a surprised look.

Albert again scratched behind his ear. "Oh, I wouldn't know and hadn't gave it any thought. I s'pose he could'a been hurt. He walked like he was old, but then, he could'a been injured as ye say."

"Ye aren't very helpful," Sir Lambert snapped.

Albert inclined his head.

Sir Lambert pointed up the road. "And they went in that direction?"

"Aye, ten or so nights ago, Milord."

"Then I suggest we hasten, if we hurry, we may yet find them," Sir Robert advised as he swung his horse around.

The entire time Albert had been speaking, he'd slowly inched his way closer to the tree and retained his spade. He didn't trust these knights; if the need arose, he would defend himself to the best of his limited ability. He saw the closest knight, still astride his horse, observing him carefully.

"Ye'd be wise to offer respect and avert yer eyes, Churl!" shouted Sir Lambert.

Albert wisely lowered his head and hoped these men would soon leave. If the knight charged, the tree would offer some protection and likely only delay the inevitable. He couldn't hope to fight four armed knights with a spade. But hoped he could leave a mark or two. He stared at the ground at his feet and smiled.

"Come, we must hasten!" Sir Robert urged.

Sir Lambert looked a moment longer at the insolent peasant, then suddenly wheeled his horse around and trotted to the road.

Albert breathed a sigh of relief and spat at the departing knights.

CHAPTER SEVENTEEN

They rested in a forest glade surrounded by towering trees and soft, dappled light. Colourful butterflies flittered here and there, which created a facade of peace and tranquillity that they both knew was temporary at best. Cathal lay propped against a tree trunk, and Isolde sat close beside him with his hand held in hers as they talked. The contact provided comfort as the weeks since the death of her daughter, Olive and her husband, Piers, had been difficult. It wasn't her first child who'd died; she'd lost a daughter shortly after birth and another during pregnancy. Losing a child was never easy to reconcile and was a tragic, common occurrence most women faced in their lives. Notwithstanding his horrific injury, Cathal had provided support, and they'd spoken about life, death and what it meant to them both. Talking helped, and with Cathal's encouragement and patience, she hesitantly began to express herself in an outpouring of pent-up emotions, which ultimately turned into a torrent of tears and more stark revelations.

She hadn't loved Piers; marriage hadn't been about love, that was a costly luxury afforded to nobles, but he had been a good provider, and that's what mattered. For the most part, he'd kept her and Olive warm, safe and fed, and in turn, she'd worked hard and been an obedient wife. "What more could a woman want from a man and a man from a woman?" she'd asked Cathal.

He had no satisfactory answer for her and continued to listen as she recounted her life and the hardships she endured. He enjoyed the sound of her voice; it was smooth, and she had a way of phrasing words that made her impassioned monologue sound almost melodic. Like a discordant note, the pain of her experiences harshly cut through the sweetness of birdsong, emphasising her lifelong struggles.

When emotionally spent, she pushed him to talk and express his thoughts. He was self-conscious at first and unused to speaking, let alone sharing his deepest feelings, but loosened up when he learned she didn't judge or force her opinion. These purging sessions often occurred during the day when they rested after a tiring night of walking.

Lately, he'd woken and was surprised to find her wrapped in his arms with her head nestled on his chest. It wasn't awkward or disturbing; he believed it had to do with their developing bond and trust. He didn't object, and like everything else about his life, Cathal pondered the complexities of their relationship and tried to make sense of his changing sensitivities.

These were new thoughts, new feelings, and new experiences to reflect on, and they candidly discussed them. She had a way about her that made him feel comfortable talking about himself, and when they journeyed on the road, he found himself walking as close to her as possible. Frequently their shoulders touched, and it was charged, like lightning.

There was a naïve honesty to Isolde, and she had a way about her; her mannerisms, how and what she said that challenged his previous and limited understanding of women. For the first time, he saw her beauty, and it wasn't just physical. It was an incomprehensible blend of her personality, her voice, appearance, and attributes. This was different; it was new and endearing, and he warmed to the pleasure even if it was confounding. It would take many months for him to comprehend it was her sensuality, and for the first time in his life, he considered what the feeling of love meant.

As the days passed, Cathal's strength continued to improve. He couldn't have survived without Isolde, who was dedicated to her unselfish care of him. The savage wound that slashed down the centre of his chest and abdomen remained free of corruption but not physical pain. Muscles had been severed and took time to heal and recover.

Their progress was slowed by his injuries and stamina, and when he told her it was time to rest, she never complained or challenged him. She foraged for food, kept him clean and cared for him. Not from a sense of duty or debt, it was an acknowledgement of newly admitted, previously unexperienced feelings, as unfamiliar to him as they were for her.

He now saw her differently, the way the early morning light of a new dawn reflected from her dark hair—the blush of her skin – her face when she looked at him. The blueish-green hues of her eyes mirrored intimacy and untold passion, which were new, untested aspirations. When she walked, he saw her form hiding from beneath her shapeless dress. She wasn't heavyset like other women with broad child-bearing hips, Isolde was slender and lithe and moved fluidly in rhythm to an unheard melody. The first time he found himself staring at her, he felt his heart race and thought he'd been stricken by a malady of sorts. She had a profound effect on him, and as he discovered, to his surprise, she was fully aware of it and didn't admonish or chastise him as expected when he told her of his affections. Instead, she held his hand tightly to her chest and whispered that the feeling was mutual. He closed his eyes and basked in the unexplored joyful wave of emotion that washed over him.

They'd recently entered the forest fringes of the Uplands and rested. The uphill trek would test Cathal's stamina, and they decided to remain for another day and give his body a chance to recover from the arduous journey they'd been on.

While Isolde checked on traps she'd set, Cathal tipped out the bones from his bag and studied them carefully. What he saw didn't portend well, and when Isolde returned, she immediately noticed something amiss.

"What ails, ye, Cathal?" She dropped the rabbit she'd snared, crouched down and looked at him in question.

"Men come, and they will arrive from the north and south," he pointed with a hand and then lowered it to rest on hers.

Isolde was perplexed, "North and south? Ye mean from Dearthington and…?"

"Aye, the knights who seek us will ride this way." He sighed loudly, "And from the north, the Vikings come."

With both hands, she firmly grasped his. "Then we will do everything we can to make sure they fail in their quest, eh?"

Cathal held her gaze. "I am still weak. Every passing day sees an improvement, but I cannot defend myself against one man… more than one man is impossible."

"Then what do we do?" she asked.

Cathal smiled, "We will continue up into the hills to the house where I lived with Gryffen. There are weapons and other things there we can use to defend ourselves. This area is familiar to me, while they have no knowledge of the terrain or forests. It gives us a small advantage."

"Ye said the house was destroyed, burned…"

"Aye, but there will be enough there to serve our needs. I only hope they don't come at the same time. Each day gives me more time to regain my strength to prepare for them, and the longer it takes fer them to arrive, the better fer us." He smiled at her, hoping it would offer her some assurance.

She looked determined. "Then we should leave as soon as it is dark."

"Nay, rest fer me is more important. He cupped her face in his hand and gently stroked her cheek. "We will journey during the day instead of night, fer travelling through the forest when it is dark is dangerous." He removed his hand, and his face hardened as he thought about what he'd just said. It gave him an idea.

Isolde stared into Cathal's eyes. When he turned his head to look away, she gently raised a hand to his cheek and turned his head back to face her. "Do not be frightened of me looking at ye, Cathal," she whispered.

"I am not frightened of ye, Isolde. I fear what ye will see in my face … the horrors yet to come," he replied softly. "Ye may not like what ye see."

Later, under the stars, Cathal thought back to Gryffin and all the martial lessons he'd been taught and hoped he could suitably account for himself to keep Isolde safe. There was an ache in his heart for the man who had been like a father and for others whom he'd loved and tragically died.

Lord Oliver Hansard proudly watched his son, Lambert, as he practised tirelessly with a wooden sword against a post in the courtyard of his castle in Dearthington. Lambert had been at it for some time; his body was sweaty, and his breathing laboured from the effort. The lord straightened from the wall he leaned against and ambled towards his son, who paused from his training to wipe his brow with a cloth.

"Ye need to move your off-arm back out of the way. A clever opponent will see that and strike at the arm, it becomes an easy target."

Lambert threw the cloth aside and loudly exhaled. "Aye, so I have been told," he said breathlessly.

"When a warrior is fatigued, then his weaknesses are highlighted and more easily an advantage gained by an opponent," wisely counselled his father.

Lambert grinned and bent over, resting hands on his thighs.

Lord Hansard took a step closer to his son and lowered his voice. "Have ye taken care of the problem that the bishop is so concerned about?"

Lambert shook his head. "Nay, Milord, fer I know the source of my problem has now moved into the Uplands. It will take more time to hunt her down." He looked up at his father, his expression grim. "We were only a few days away from finding her and had to turn back. So we plan on departing at the week's end fer an extended time, and we will be better prepared."

The lord's eyes narrowed. "Ye must end this, Lambert. This violent behaviour must stop." He thrust a finger at his son's chest. "Ye put my honour at risk. Do not allow this person or persons to have a voice, fer the Church and the king have ears, and believe me, they are listening. Whomever ye seek - silence them and see to it with urgency and haste. End it quickly and ferever."

"That is my intention, Milord," Lambert replied, standing straighter and glaring at his father. It was a less-than-subtle challenge intended to remind him that he was taller and that his physical build was more imposing than few in Dearthington could equal.

The lord bit his tongue and silently acknowledged his son's defiant assertion. He believed Lambert would one day challenge and fight him for his claim to title and lands, however, for the present, his son might be stronger, was an excellent swordsman, but he lacked diplomacy, wisdom and the required martial expertise to be completely effective against someone with experience. He let the flash of annoyance pass. "Do ye need anything before ye leave?"

Lambert relaxed and shook his head, "Nay, Milord."

"Godspeed." Lord Oliver Hansard spun and strode away.

Lambert watched his father walk away with indifference. He had no real affection for the man, and there was no paternal bond between them. He was a stranger at best, a man whose modest influence and power had seen him journey to far-off places and battle other men, also with power and influence. *To what end*? Wondered Lambert with a slight shake of his head. He was away more often than not, and his absence from Walworth Castle was expected. His mother tolerated the absences, but he believed she couldn't care less about his father. She enjoyed the prestige, the comfort and privilege but nothing else.

Lately, his father had insisted that he accompany him on some of his journeys, but these were diplomatic visits to strengthen alliances or petition for favours. In those situations, he saw the mighty Lord of Dearthington, Oliver Hansard, bow subserviently to greater lords as he postulated about territories, boundaries, and treaties, arguing the letter of the law. He saw his father humiliated before a royal court, scolded by Earls and laughed at by battle-hardened knights. Sir Lambert was embarrassed by his father, who ruled inconsequentially over a small region of Yorkshire and only at King Henry's whimsical pleasure.

Lambert was repulsed by his father, Oliver Hansard, and he'd vowed, some years ago, that he would never, ever, be laughed at or humiliated by either serf or royalty. And when the day came that he finally inherited lands and titles from his father, he would show the king and others and demonstrate what it was like to be respected and feared. He would govern over his lands, exude power and restore dignity to the family name Hansard, and God help anyone who stood in his way.

He picked up his wooden practice sword and began striking the wooden post in a series of powerful strokes, slashes, and thrusts. The wooden sword was deliberately heavier than his steel sword, and his arms ached as he repeated the intricate moves over and over again. He wasn't motivated by the desire for self-improvement; he was driven by the fear of humiliation and anger. It was pure rage that distorted his outlook on life, and he imagined destroying anyone or anything that cast doubt on his name or status, and he wouldn't be looked down upon like his weak-kneed servile father.

From high above, partially obscured by a rampart, Lord Oliver Hansard observed his son and felt shamed. He knew of Lambert's violent passions. Spies kept him informed of his son's thirst for brutality and his unchecked ardour for bloodshed and violence. It wasn't a new development; as a boy, he'd been unnecessarily cruel to animals, his friends and even towards serfs who worked in the castle and the villeins who toiled in the fields. The only partial consolation was that Lambert had learned to moderately disguise his sadism. Age had tempered his overt needs, and he'd been more circumspect but no less violent when an opportunity presented itself. His peculiar behaviour had drawn attention to the family, and he, as lord, had to smooth things over and keep the peace countless times, often at great expense.

People, mostly peasants, had gone missing and were later discovered, disembowelled, mutilated, and some almost unrecognisable. In nearly all instances, they were left alive to suffer a slow and painful death. As Lord Oliver learned some years ago, it wasn't actually killing someone that excited Lambert, it was seeing people suffer through extreme and inhumane mutilations.

Priests had attempted to curtail Lambert's enthusiasm and

spoke to him about his unchristian-like behaviour, but it had little effect. As a father, and on the counsel of priests, he'd taken the boy aside and punished him, given him a few beatings, but that, too, made little difference.

Of considerable concern, Lord Oliver prayed that word of Lambert's behaviour wouldn't spread outside the boundaries of Dearthington. With the news that he intended to travel into the Uplands, rumours would soon surface of atrocities, and as always, Lord Oliver hoped they wouldn't be linked to Lambert.

He watched a moment longer as Lambert continued to train, then walked back into the castle shaking his head. He had little hope for his son.

CHAPTER EIGHTEEN

Nels One-Ear wasn't a happy man. The priest, who he'd been forced to take with him on his search for the Irishman, the son of the woman they'd sought for years, was as useless as a teat on a bull. Not only was he bone lazy, but he'd also avoided doing any form of work whatsoever. After their first day of travelling south, when Nels called it a day and made camp, Raven, the priest, refused to rub down his horse and insisted Nels do the required task. When asked to gather firewood, the priest adamantly refused, saying that gathering wood was women's work and beneath him to perform such menial and demeaning chores. A well-placed foot up his arse saw the priest adopt a rapid change in attitude but not in griping.

Progress was painfully slow as the priest claimed his bottom was chaffed raw from riding all day in the saddle and demanded frequent rests. Unused to the rigours of manual labour, Raven had a woman's soft, small hands and, Nels determined, the attitude to match. When Nels questioned him about his fighting skills, Raven felt no compunction about boasting of his abilities, so when Nels suggested a challenge and demanded they practice together with swords, Raven had no option but to accept.

Nels acceded Raven was reasonably adept and showed technique but lacked the strength and stamina that would put an end to a lengthy fight. The man was simply unused to any form of physical activity and had no hardiness. Had he a choice, Nels would have sent Raven back to Orkneyjar after the first day, but he didn't want to earn the displeasure of Harald Maddadsson.

However, Nels wasn't without some deviousness, and while Harald Maddadsson insisted two Norsemen wouldn't attract undue attention on their journey, he never said others couldn't follow or ride in advance. That simple omission was as good as an approval, and prior to their departure from Orkneyjar, and without informing the priest, Nels picked two trustworthy men who would ride ahead, reconnoitre and act as scouts. During the evenings, Nels departed camp, explaining to Raven that he wanted to walk and stretch his legs. He would casually stroll from the camp and meet his men to discuss the route and any obstacles they would encounter the next day.

Much to Nels' surprise, Raven had delivered on his ability to offer guidance on which direction to take, and in agonising slowness, they eventually arrived at a village that sat at the foothills of the Uplands. Nels arranged to meet his scouts at the inn later in the evening, and after three torturous weeks of travelling, he looked forward to an uninterrupted and peaceful sleep indoors.

They followed a solitary knight and his squire shepherding a wagon and three men who looked to be miners from the tools they transported, into the village. The inn was easy to find; a large sign above the door advertised 'The Wanderer'. Beneath the sign, a small leafy tree branch was suspended, indicating wine was also available. The interior was large, and The Wanderer offered an assortment of food and, if needed, chambers to sleep. The knight and his squire found a table in a corner, and the miners sat at a neighbouring table. To the delight of several rowdy patrons, a troubadour sang bawdy ballads while the far side of the inn was mostly empty and quieter and more suited to having a natter without being disturbed. Against one wall, a fire spluttered, but it was more for cooking than to heat the interior, as the evenings were still warm and pleasant.

Sir Robert nudged Sir Lambert, "There, that Dane..."

With casual interest, Sir Lambert nonchalantly turned to look at the Dane at the adjacent table. He could see the Norseman made no secret of his interest in the patrons who were in the inn and scrutinised everyone. "He's looking fer someone," Sir Lambert replied.

"Aye, as are we," Sir Crispen said, then downed the last of the ale from his tankard.

"Methinks we should return to Dearthington, we'll never catch sight of the woman, it's been weeks, and she could be anywhere."

Sir Robert leaned over towards his friend, "Ye are welcome to return home anytime ye wish. But fer now, it's yer turn to get the ale." He slammed his tankard on the table as Sir Lambert and Sir Guy emptied theirs.

Nels One-Ear turned his attention from the miners and the knight he'd been scrutinising towards the four young men who sat near him. They were knights, he was sure of it. But they weren't dressed as knights. He'd watched them carefully since arriving, and one knight in particular, a large young man with hooded eyes, caused him some concern. He'd seen people like that before. Men who hated everyone but themselves. From their cocky, aggressive demeanour, he determined they thought of violence as entertainment, as pure pleasure. It was the subtle things that gave him away. Facial expressions, the way he compulsively touched the hilt of his sword, and anytime someone in the inn raised a voice in disagreement, the young knight would sit up and smile like he took pleasure in another's discomfort or hoped for conflict.

Although Nels felt some apprehension, he wasn't frightened of the young knight and thought nothing more about him as his two scouts entered the inn.

"Two more," Sir Robert stated.

"Aye, any more and I'd say we being invaded," replied Sir Lambert with a grin. He watched as the newcomers sat down with the Dane, who had a missing ear.

Sir Lambert knew they needed to mingle, talk to locals, and find out if anyone had seen the young woman. A coin or two would loosen tongues. "We need to split up, ask around. Someone will have seen her."

Sir Crispin finished what ale remained in his tankard as Sir Lambert and Sir Robert stood to question the locals. Sir Guy took a hefty swallow and followed his friends.

Sir Lambert sauntered towards the miners, and as he approached, he saw their guardian assessing him carefully. "Fare thee well?" Sir Lambert greeted the knight, then looked towards the squire, who was also observing him. The miners paid him no interest.

"Aye," simply grunted the knight in response. He kept his head lowered.

"I seek a woman, a comely thing. A farmer's wife," Sir Lambert asked. "Would have passed through here some weeks ago."

The knight shook his head.

"Perhaps yer squire…?"

The knight inclined his head. "Petrus?"

"I have seen many a woman," the squire grinned, "But ye will need to tell me more."

Sir Lambert felt uncomfortable; his cockiness had suddenly deserted him in the presence of the knight and his squire, and he felt very self-conscious. "She may have a companion, a man, and they travel slowly, fer this man may be injured."

"Injured, ye say." The squire shook his head. "Then, to be sure, I have not seen who ye seek.

The knight remained silent and drank wine from a mug.

"Perhaps, ye could..."

The knight twisted on the seat and raised his head for the first time. "We can offer ye no more help."

Sir Lambert was struck by the intensity of the knight's steel grey eyes.

"Er, aye, very well. With thanks to ye both," Sir Lambert dipped his head and retreated. The knight had not been hostile, but he was formidable, and he instinctively knew the man and his squire were not someone to trifle with. Even the squire, a man similar in age to himself, had a presence.

Nels observed the four knights as they split up and wandered around the room, speaking to clientele. He observed that some were willing to talk and others not. He turned to the scouts. "Have ye seen these men a'fore?"

Both shook their heads. "Nay," said one of them. "They did not come from the north."

They watched as the brash young knights intimidated a couple of patrons.

"They'll come here to us, so perhaps we can find out, eh?" stated Nels as he saw Raven enter, glance around the room, and then walk towards them. "Here comes trouble," Nels said, "Let me do the talking as he'll wonder who ye are and what ye are doing here."

As predicted, Raven paused when he saw the two strangers sitting with Nels.

"I thought yer arse was sore, and ye wanted to rest," Nels said with a laugh.

Raven wasn't amused and stared at the two men.

"Ah, these fine fellows are my scouts."

Raven turned and glared at Nels. "Harald said there would be only two of us."

"Aye, and there are only two. Leif and Bragi have been riding ahead of us and ensuring we avoid trouble."

The priest turned back to the scouts and scowled before sitting on the bench beside Nels

"And now it is our turn," Nels whispered as he saw one of the young knights approaching.

"We seek a young woman, a farmer's woman travelling alone," Sir Crispin asked. It was uncommon fer a young woman, even a peasant, to travel without a male escort, and Sir Crispin believed his basic description would be enough.

"From which direction did she come? Is she on foot?" Nels asked. "Is she comely, fer such a fine young woman would easily be remembered?" The two scouts laughed. In contrast, Raven directed his ever-present scowl at the knight and remained silent.

Sir Crispin folded his arms. "She's been travelling northward, and aye, she is comely fer a peasant."

"Then I would recall such a vision, but I have not seen this woman ye speak of." Nels turned away to continue his discussion with Leif.

"Begone, leave us in peace," snarled Raven.

Nels silently cursed at the priest's uncalled hostility.

Sir Crispin looked over his shoulder towards his friends, who were all talking to patrons. He turned to face Leif and Bragi. "Have ye seen her?"

"Are ye deaf?" Raven spat. "Begone."

Nels placed a hand on Raven's shoulder, a subtle hint to keep quiet. "Best be on yer way," he advised the young knight. He then focused his attention on Raven and lowered his voice. "Unless ye want trouble, say nothing more. We are not to draw attention to ourselves," he warned.

Leif and Bragi felt uncomfortable and readied themselves to leap to their feet if needed.

Less than thrilled at the rudeness directed at him, Sir Crispin unfolded his arms and lowered them to rest a hand on the hilt of his sword.

Nels One-Ear reacted quickly. "Fergive my friend, he is foolish. His tongue is quick, and his mind slow. He speaks without thinking, we mean ye no offence."

"Ergi[30]!" Raven yelled and rose from his seat. The guttural pronunciation left no doubt to Leif and Bragi that the slur was intended to insult the knight and fully expected him to retaliate. They leapt to their feet and stood with hands on sheathed swords. Nels knew enough about the priest and understood the affront was directed at himself and not the young knight, but the others were not aware of the priest's surly disposition and animosity towards him.

From across the room, heads turned at Raven's loud exclamation, and Sir Crispin's friends hurried over.

'Sit," Nels ordered the scouts to return to the bench and then struck the priest across the side of his head with the back of his hand. "Yer mouth may cost ye yer life," he hissed.

Led by Sir Lambert, the knights hurried over and positioned themselves in a semi-circle around the table and glared at the four Norsemen. He noticed one of them rubbing the side of his face as he stared hatefully at another.

"What goes on here?" questioned Sir Lambert, turning to his friend for answers.

Sir Crispin was confused and shook his head.

Nels determined that the largest of the four knights represented the obvious and most dangerous threat. Slowly, he rose from his seat and stood to his full six feet two-inch height. He kept his hands away from his sword and assessed the four young knights as he spoke. "My friend offered insult to me,

30 Ergi – Old Scandinavian word for coward.

and to me alone." He shook his head. "We have not seen the woman ye seek, as we came from the north. We come in peace and do not want trouble."

"The Norsemen are brusque, offensive and offer no respect," Sir Crispen suggested, feeling more emboldened now that his friends arrived.

The knights arrogantly faced them, and Nels believed they sought pleasure from conflict. He made eye contact with Leif and then Bragi and saw them tense while Raven glared at him in loathing. Casually, he moved his hand out of sight behind his back.

It was a standoff, and any experienced warrior would know that in the blink of an eye, the situation could alter drastically and quickly turn into a bloody brawl – or worse. Already, the innkeeper and some curious locals were rushing over to de-escalate the matter. The knights and Danes knew fighting with swords inside a building limited their ability; swords were best used outside in open spaces. Nels hoped the knights decided to walk away and avoid any conflict.

As the group leader, Sir Lambert's friends turned to him for a decision. That was until Raven hawked onto the floor near the feet of Sir Crispin.

Sir Lambert was the first to unsheathe his sword, his intentions plain and obvious. Nels One-Ear's hand reappeared from behind his back, clutching a savage-looking knife. With an underhand flick, the blade flew across the short distance and struck Sir Crispin, who was still fumbling with his sword, piercing the thick leather vest he wore, embedding in his right shoulder. Nels didn't intend to kill the knight; just wound him. He took a quick step back to avoid the slashing blade of a knight as Sir Crispin shrieked in pain.

"Enough!" shouted the Innkeeper, and bravely pushed his way through the knights to stand between them and the Danes.

"Ye'll take this outside. There won't be any fight'n here."

"I'm wounded," Sir Crispin wailed.

The Innkeeper turned to look at Sir Crispin. He could see his leather vest had protected the young man and prevented any serious damage. "Is a small wound, ye'll recover."

Sir Robert stepped over and pulled the knife from Sir Crispin's shoulder.

Leif and Bragi grinned. The knight was nothing more than a boy.

Sir Lambert was deciding what to do. He'd never previously fought anyone in anger who was capable, with actual fighting experience. The Dane standing before him was a large, battle-hardened, and tough-looking warrior who appeared quite fearsome. For the second time that night, he doubted his ability.

"Out o' here! Out, the lot of ye!" shouted the Innkeeper. He wasn't allowing anyone to shed blood in his establishment. Behind him, local patrons murmured in agreement. The miners, knight and squire silently watched.

Sir Lambert knew his familiar and proven intimidation tactic wouldn't be effective inside the inn. He had no choice but to leave. "We need to tend to the wound." He gave the large Dane a long, hard look and raised his sword to point it at him. "And I'll see ye again."

Once the Innkeeper had shepherded them safely outside, he turned to Sir Lambert, "O'er there, near th' hearth, the man there will tend to his wound. Don't come back."

Sir Crispin complained bitterly about his injury while the man the innkeeper recommended tended to the wound. He cleaned the small gash and poured vinegar over it before suturing and binding the shoulder.

"Ain't bad," said the man. "Ye won't be able to wield yer

sword fer a week or two without it hurt'n," he laughed, which ended in a fit of wet hacking.

Sir Lambert leaned against a table inside the filthy home. He couldn't wait to leave.

It was a single-roomed dwelling, a fire burned in the hearth and a large tallow candle sputtered on the table, sending clouds of soot upwards into the foul-smelling air. Sir Guy and Sir Robert waited outside and kept watch as Sir Lambert expected the Danes would come for them. Fortunately, and so far, they hadn't seen them.

Once the man's coughing fit had subsided, he continued. "What brings ye this way, then?"

"We are looking fer a woman, a farmers woman," eagerly replied Sir Crispen, repeating the lines he'd already asked countless times at the inn earlier in the evening. "She is likely travelling alone."

"Oh, and when would she 'ave been 'ere?" asked the man.

To Sir Lambert, the man was far too cheerful and had no reason to be. Seeing the job was done, he dropped a penny on the table as payment so they could leave and walked to the door.

"Oh, then I can't helps ye," the man replied. "Only woman I saw was, er..." He lifted his cap and scratched his head. "Be 'bout a month ago now, but she was with a man who looked poorly. I remembers cause I thought I could help him, but the stranger said he didn't need help."

Sir Lambert paused and turned around. "What did this stranger look like, his appearance?"

The man shrugged, "He was tall and thin-like. Didn't say much, but I sees he ain't well, either sick or wounded, I'd day. I, uh, have a good eye and know these things–"

"Did ye happen to see which direction they were headed?" interrupted Sir Lambert and smiled at Sir Crispen. He broke eye contact and stomped to the man as Sir Crispen rose from his seat.

The man nodded, raised an arm and pointed. “Of course, that away, they were headed into the hills, the Uplands.”

CHAPTER NINETEEN

When Cathal and Isolde finally arrived at what remained of Gryffen's house, he was thoroughly heartbroken. Not only had he physically suffered due to the gruelling climb into the hills, but the memories of the man who'd essentially raised him, the good times they'd shared, all resurfaced when he saw the charred embers of the house he'd called home for so many years.

Isolde instinctively knew Cathal's injuries were more than physical; his mind had also been damaged, and she felt ill-equipped to help. Common sense suggested that if Cathal spoke openly of his emotional pain, it could help him adjust to the loss. All she could do was encourage him to talk.

For the first two days after they arrived, Cathal could do little but rest and recover his strength. While he slept, she set traps, searched through charred debris to salvage what she could to help them be more comfortable, and when possible, she gently urged him to speak of his pain.

In the many weeks since they had been together, their bond strengthened. She'd better understood the esoteric young man, and that realisation had grown into what she believed was called love. As she discovered, love was powerful and, at the same time, frightening as it exposed her own frailties and needs. She lived for Cathal and believed he was innocent and, at times, almost childlike – naïve, and she wanted nothing more than to nurture and protect him, not as a mother for a child, but as a woman for her man.

She knew Cathal had been fiercely protected by his mother,

and like her, he had a desire to help people, and he simplistically believed people wanted his assistance. But not everyone wanted his help, and he suffered those disappointments easily. He was remarkable because he knew more about the human body, healing and remedies than anyone she'd ever met. If you didn't know Cathal, people falsely believed he cast spells or had magic potions and concoctions because it is easier to believe in magic than a logical explanation for a wonder experienced. Isolde thought Cathal secretly liked being mistaken for a druid or a mythical wizard because they would take him seriously and listen, notwithstanding the fear of being turned into a frog.

When she asked about his abilities and vast array of skills, he cryptically told her that his fate was assured, that his existence was to serve a higher purpose. When questioned about whom he served, he couldn't or wouldn't elaborate. When she probed further, he explained that he didn't fully understand it either – but he just knew.

In the last week or so, Cathal's strength had begun to return; his ghastly wound, now a savage red scar that ran down the length of his torso, was an unpleasant reminder of the evil of man, but he felt close to being healthy. He'd been able to focus more on their safety and how they could overcome the challenges they had yet to face with the impending arrival of the Norsemen and knights.

Earlier, they'd cleaned themselves in the nearby brook that ran close to Gryffen's home, washed soiled clothing, and, as shadows lengthened, feasted well on wild pork expertly caught in a snare. Darkness descended over the uplands, and the mysterious and indistinct sounds of a night-time forest drifted to where they lay beside an unburned wall of Gryffen's house. Occasionally, as wood settled in their fire, a shower of sparks drifted upwards, flames danced, and its orange glow cast eerie moving shadows over the standing wall while the sound of crackling, burning wood dissolved into the evening forest ambience. They hadn't spoken in a while and lay together on their backs with shoulders touching, staring up and into the heavens through large gaps in the forest canopy.

"I have seen them, the men from the north, and the knights–"

Isolde rolled over and placed a finger over his lips. "Now is not the time, Cathal," she said. Her voice, a mere whisper.

He felt the heat of her breath on his cheek, her lips almost touching his. Her hand moved to cup his face, and she caressed his cheek with her thumb as her unbound hair tumbled down. Cast in shadow, he could see the outline of her head highlighted by the twinkle of orange flames reflecting from moist eyes.

He could feel her heartbeat, its rhythmic cadence perfectly synchronised with his own. He didn't question the peculiarity of his observance, instead, and ignoring protesting stomach muscles, he slightly raised his head. Their lips met in an explosion of unfamiliar sensations. Any pain or discomfort he felt was lost in the wilderness of rapture and his uncharacteristic abandonment of self-awareness and constraint.

He gently rolled her over and now looked down at her face, his breath heated as his eyes feasted on her. In the flickering light, he saw her as if, for the first time, the flawlessness of her lips, nose, eyes, and blemishes. The imperfections made her perfect, highlighting beauty as he'd never seen before. His eyes welled in overwhelming joy as he accepted Isolde was no longer just a pleasant travelling companion and a confidante. Like a veil lifted, he looked at her with the euphoria of discovery, she was perfection. He lowered his head and kissed her again, surrendering his heart and soul to her.

Together, their bodies connected, and they learned from each other, communicating without speaking, as words weren't needed. They felt each other and responded eagerly. Their actions were potent yet gentle and accompanied by an understanding as fulfilment created an awareness of each other's needs. Time, discomfort, and the forest around them meant nothing, they were lost and oblivious to everything except each other. While the future heralded uncertainty, they were entwined in the present that dominated a cruel and merciless past.

The forest and its inhabitant creatures gave them space and undisturbed privacy. It was universal, Cathal thought. The absoluteness of intimacy and the beauty of love were accepted and respected by all.

When the morning song of birds heralded a new dawn, Cathal opened his eyes, absorbed his surroundings and marvelled at the perplexities of life. Beside him, Isolde still slept. A leg and arm were draped protectively over him, and he smiled at last evening's memory and the expectation of pleasures to come. He felt different – for the first time in his life, he was complete and content, and even the lingering irritations of his injuries had lessened. Isolde stirred and attempted to edge even closer to him, but it wasn't possible; they couldn't get any closer, and he carefully turned his head and kissed her. With a smile, he turned back to face the greyness of dawn; *this past night was the best of my life*, he thought.

More so than at any previous time, he knew he must protect Isolde, even if it cost him his life. He thought back to the painful lessons Gryffen taught him about swordsmanship, archery and mastering the trusty quarterstaff, how Gryffen had explained the confusing logic behind martial tactics and how to exploit weaknesses, especially when faced with overwhelming numbers. He reaffirmed why he'd brought Isolde to this place and how he could use his knowledge of the uplands to his advantage.

"Loss is experienced only by the living," he said aloud.

Isolde moved in response. "Cathal?" she asked.

He turned his head to marvel at her, and like a war drum, he could feel his heart pounding furiously. Her eyes searched his face, questioning.

He felt her fear and sighed. "We must prepare."

Raven demanded frequent stops for rest and to consult his religious relics, and often, they'd have to backtrack as he insisted they were headed in the wrong direction. Much to his frustration, the new path was even more complex and physically challenging than the other. However, Nels One-Ear took no satisfaction in seeing the priest struggle; he was becoming more anxious about what he would find when they arrived at their destination, wherever that was. His two scouts now travelled with them, which made Nels feel a little safer, but progress was painfully slow, and the priest complained and constantly whined.

They'd abandoned their horses two days ago and left them for safekeeping at a small hamlet, where they would retrieve them on their return. Nels preferred to be on foot; a warrior could fight best on his feet, be agile, run down his enemy, stand shoulder to shoulder with his brothers and celebrate victory as one.

Yet, as much as Raven complained, he was dedicated to the mission, and even when resting, he consulted the few religious relics and trinkets he was permitted to bring and provided continual guidance. Nels also began to see a picture form.

If a man wished to hide, then this high country was where he could do it. If the Irishwoman's whelp son wanted to evade them, this part of Yorkshire was most suitable, and, reasoned Nels, if he hid in these hills, then he was frightened.

Nels sat on a large rock and waited for Raven. The priest had refused to travel further unless they could catch a live animal, the bigger, the better, he'd said. He'd insisted on making a sacrifice to the Gods and offering a small creature like a hare or a dead animal was an insult that would displease them. The delay had cost them three entire days, but eventually, they'd caught a good-sized sow, kept her alive until Raven was ready and then sacrificed the beast in a bloody ritual. The only consolation was that everyone ate meat that night.

Feeling empowered, with a blood-marked face, Raven gathered his tools so they could set out and venture further and up into the forested hills. Nels had sent his two scouts ahead a little way with instructions to report back to him about the terrain and obstacles. He'd also had them look for signs of men.

Finally, Raven stood beside him and pointed the way with a stick, "There we will find the one ye seek."

Nels inhaled deeply and looked up into the hills before setting off. Something wasn't right.

Sir Lambert was fed up. Climbing the remote Yorkshire uplands was not what he expected to be doing. He preferred to feel his courser between his thighs where he could control the beast and look down on his adversary. Walking was for soldiers and peasants, and it was when a man was most vulnerable. He could exude power from atop a mighty destrier, control the weak and vanquished, and force his will – or so his fertile mind imagined. The only will he'd ever asserted was on lowly peasants and women. Still, the feeling of power was extraordinary and intoxicating, and he imagined the ecstasy would only magnify when doing battle.

There were few people in the hills, and certainly, if he encountered anyone, they'd not be of a mind to challenge him. The miners and knight had departed the inn early and, thankfully, headed in a different direction. However, after the minor altercation at the inn, he'd not seen where the Norsemen had gone, but after a day, he'd encountered their tracks and, within a short time, caught up to them.

A willing peasant had been tempted with a shiny coin and confirmed a man and a woman had passed through here some weeks ago. The man explained that he remembered that the traveller appeared injured and had walked in pain with the aid of a woman.

Sir Lambert and his friends were thrilled. They'd found the woman and the man they'd previously thought dead after being gutted and left to perish alongside the road. If the man and woman were dead, then word of his deeds would never reach the ears of the bishop.

They'd kept their distance and ensured they didn't get too close to the Norsemen. It was easy to keep track of them because they travelled so slowly. Of interest to Sir Lambert was that one of the Norsemen was a priest of sorts, and during one entertaining evening, he and his friends watched the priest perform a gruesome and bloody ceremony. The performance was exhilarating, and Lambert was thoroughly aroused by the carnal spectacle and decided he would enjoy the opportunity to create his own version of a sacrifice with the Norsemen. He still had a personal unsettled score with the large man with one ear, and he intended to seek retribution and perhaps enjoy some sport at his expense. There was little chance of discovery in the uplands, and despite the warnings from his father, he believed it was unlikely that word of his spirited activity would ever reach the bishop.

Lambert didn't know why the Norsemen ventured into the hills, but they were headed in a similar direction, and Lambert believed the Norsemen were up to no good. Sir Guy suggested they were looking for someone, but the route the Norsemen took was away from regular hunting trails and where people were likely to be. *Was it a coincidence they travelled in the same direction,* Lambert wondered? When he finally had the large Norsemen begging for his life, he would take pleasure in asking them why.

Feeling more energised, Sir Lambert decided that they should pass the Norsemen, overtake them, and look for a suitable place to set an ambuscade. The slight injury Sir Crispin suffered at the inn was minor, nothing more than a nuisance, and he was fortunate that it wasn't worse and could even have been killed. But now, Sir Crispen was quite willing to exact revenge and, along with the others, fully supported Sir Lambert's plan.

Passing the Norsemen was not difficult as they took frequent rests. The four knights headed away from the Norsemen, then fought through thick forest, circumvented a treeless rocky hill and reappeared at the top of a steep rock-walled ravine. There was no sign of the Norsemen, and Sir Crispin suggested they may have taken another route. It wasn't until a short time later they heard shouting and cursing; the harsh guttural sounds of the Norse language drifting up to them confirmed the Norsemen were coming.

But not this day. Unpredictably, the Norse stopped early in the afternoon and made camp.

Seeing what the Norse were doing, the knights also decided to make camp, and they split up to set snares and find a suitable place to build a fire where smoke wouldn't drift down, alerting the Norsemen of their presence. They didn't know that Nels had dispatched his two scouts to look ahead.

Leif and Bragi were chosen by Nels One-Ear because they were experienced and good at their work. When they left camp, they did so quietly. Rags were tied around anything metal they wore to avoid any clinking sounds that could be identified as man-made, and they silently communicated with hand signals. They were stealthy, observant, and excellent swordsmen, and Sir Guy was utterly unaware of them until he felt a sword pressing into his back.

CHAPTER TWENTY

Sir Guy dropped the twine he used to build a snare and slowly stood, raising his hands to shoulder level. The Norsemen had caught him by surprise, although it shouldn't have been unexpected, Sir Guy and his friends were not expert trackers or woodsmen, they were gallant knights, taught in the art of battlefield warfare, on or off horseback, and not on the finer skills of bushcraft.

"Why do ye follow us?" Bragi asked, with an economy of words.

Sir Guy quickly gauged the two men. Neither looked formidable, and while large, they didn't appear to carry much weight or have the physique of swordsmen. He carefully weighed up his options. Without any warning, he suddenly leapt back while unsheathing his sword. He'd been preparing a snare between two smallish trees. The gap between them was wide enough to spring through, and at the same time, the tree trunks would protect him from being struck by a sword as he made his desperate move.

The Norsemen were also quick, and rather than follow the knight, they ran around the trees. Bragi faced the knight, who was wildly swinging his sword, while Leif tried to circle and position himself behind the Englishman.

Fully aware of what the Norsemen were trying to do, Sir Guy quickly took a few more steps away and spun back to face them with his sword still extended.

The Norsemen slowly advanced on the knight, separating to create some distance from each other. Their sword tips moved in lazy circles, forcing the knight to split his focus as he knew they could lunge at any time. The sword blades probed, looking for weakness.

Sir Guy continued to retreat, step by step. Then yelled, “Norsemen! Help!” He hoped it was enough to scare the two men away and warn his friends, but they didn’t run.

When the knight yelled, Bragi saw the briefest lapse in concentration, and for the agile Norseman, it was enough, so he sprung forward, thrusting outward with his sword. He was too quick for the knight, who was caught completely off guard. He cried out as the razor-sharp blade penetrated through his clothing, slicing easily between ribs to fatally pierce his heart.

Before the body stopped moving, Leif and Bragi crouched down and listened. They knew the three other knights were probably already rushing towards them, and they needed to make their escape, but they weren’t sure from which direction they would come.

Bragi made a circle with a finger and pointed. Leif nodded, and both men stealthily crept away as they heard the first sounds of the three remaining knights coming to support their friend.

Nels One-Ear was livid and paced backwards and forwards at their camp. “Why, why did ye kill him?” he shouted at Bragi. “Now we have to fend off three angry young knights who will seek to avenge the death of their friend.”

“I ain’t afraid of them, we can take ‘em easily,” Bragi confidently stated and stood straighter, thrusting out his chest.

It took considerable effort to control himself and not run Bragi through with his sword, but he needed the man. “And now they will come fer us,” He sighed in frustration and turned to Raven, who was seated on a log caressing a figurine of a God-like child playing with a toy. “Gather yer things, we leave.”

Raven was about to protest but wisely decided against it. He would complain about the lack of respect shown by Nels towards his beloved Gods when he returned. The thought of sacrificing Nels One-Ear on an altar held considerable appeal.

Nels put aside his anger, unsheathed his sword and thrust it at Bragi. "Keep ahead of us and keep watch, that way," he swung the blade away from the path they'd been on and pointed it towards a narrow ravine. He looked at Leif. "You watch our rear. Both of ye, stay close, within reach of us."

Nels was still seething as they veered from the main path and onto a seldom-used track that led them deeper into the forested hills. He looked over his shoulder at the priest, who struggled to keep pace. "We no longer search for the Irishwoman's whelp; we climb into the hills to avoid being killed by those brash young knights. It would behove ye to move quicker if ye don't want to lag and be slaughtered."

Sir Lambert crouched down and stared at the lifeless body of his boyhood friend. He covered his face with his hands and wondered how to explain Guy's death to his family. He had a duty, an obligation to seek vengeance against the Norsemen, and no one would care how many he killed in the name of retribution. Crispin, Robert and he had to preserve Sir Guy's honour and to accomplish that duty, they needed to find the cowardly men who'd skulked off into the forest and serve justice.

"What do we do?" asked Sir Crispin when he returned from searching for a sign of the Norsemen.

"We cannot take Sir Guy home; we must bury him here and offer prayer. Then, we will find those cowardly Norsemen and take their heads to Guy's father. We are honour-bound and have no choice." Privately, Sir Lambert was pleased. He now had a mandate to wage war on three Danes, and no clergyman in the land would challenge his actions. For the first time in his life as a knight, he had a purpose. "Find Sir Robert, we must bury our friend."

Not that far away as the crow flies, but at least a day's hard travel on foot and high above on a rocky outcrop, Cathal watched four men slowly make their way up the ravine. Every morning, as soon as it was light enough and the sun shone down into narrow crevasses, Cathal would spend time at the outcrop looking for the men who came for them. This morning, he wasn't disappointed and saw their ponderous, slow climb. He could see that one of the men had no stamina and was holding them back. At their rate of progress, it would be a day and a half before they approached the site of Gryffen's home. It made no difference to Cathal, he was as ready as he could be, although no amount of consoling appeased Isolde, she was terrified.

His dull clothes blended into the greyness of rock, and even if the Norsemen looked upwards, they'd never see him watching. Cathal stayed motionless for some time watching before losing interest, eased back from the precipice, and crept away. He jogged along a ridgeline, down the other side, through a stand of trees, and up again to stand on another outcrop where he had an uninterrupted view, this time towards the south. What he saw gave him pause.

Five men in total, two on horseback, one driving a wagon, and two more walking, were making their way upwards towards a narrow pass at the summit. Once they crested the summit and began to make their way down, they would discover that the trail was impassable for horses, let alone a wagon, and they'd have to turn back. These five men had taken an extraordinarily long and impractical route to reach this point, which meant they had a purpose and that worried him.

He continued to observe their movements and, from some distance, saw that two men were knights, the others were labourers, yet they searched for something. Periodically, a man would dig at the ground, and then everyone would come to inspect whatever he found. Then, he would move on again and repeat the process all over at another location. Cathal was perplexed, perhaps they were miners, he thought.

He risked moving closer to them and crept over rocks to better see. Like the Norsemen, the men didn't look up and were too engrossed with what was on the ground to have interest in what was above them.

One man was a knight, and he carried the mantle of authority that became evident. The other armed man wasn't a knight as he first thought, but perhaps a squire or a sergeant. It all made sense now. The three labourers were miners and were exploring for minerals or ore and they posed no immediate danger to himself or Isolde. However, would they involve themselves in any altercation with the Norsemen or the young knights who came for them?

It was time to return to Isolde; he'd been away longer than expected, and she'd be concerned. As he jogged back, he thought about the young knights whom he'd not yet seen but knew they couldn't be far behind the Norse. The appearance of the miners changed everything. Would they become involved, and who would they assist, or would they not involve themselves in another man's affairs? More importantly, would they crest the summit and venture down this side before the Norse came?

The following morning, armed with a bow and quiver, Cathal returned to his vantage point to look for the Norse and see their progress. As he anticipated, they travelled slowly, too slowly and he could now see the culprit was, as expected, a Norse priest. He'd come across them before and found them to be arrogant and entirely self-serving, and through his observations, determined this priest was no different than others he'd encountered. While they had knowledge, that learning was never shared with their people to help, it was deliberately withheld, which gave them power and control. The reason for the priest being with the Norse warriors was clear. The priest provided vision; he had sight, which was why the Norse had found him. The priest was the most dangerous.

Without making any sudden moves to attract unwanted attention, Cathal reached for the bow, slid it across, and then extracted an arrow from the quiver, inspecting the fragile shaft and fletching with care. Satisfied, he notched the arrow and looked outwards at the treetops gauging the wind. Today was mild, yet the breeze predominantly blew from the south, over the summit and down into the ravine. His arrow would have the wind behind it, and shooting downwards always required an extra level of skill.

He eased himself upright and pulled the big Welsh longbow close to his side as he watched and waited. Cathal was vehemently opposed to killing either man or beast unless its death filled an empty belly or saved a life. As he surveyed the men slowly climbing the ravine, his thoughts were for Isolde, she was in danger, and he couldn't protect her if the Norse killed him.

As expected, the weary priest began to lag again, and Cathal knew the man would find a suitable rock and sit while rebuked by his fellow countrymen. It mattered not, he knew from his observations that the priest would only continue when he was ready and able, not because he was being yelled at.

The priest paused, bent over with both hands resting on his

thighs, gasping for air. Only steps away was a suitable rock to sit and rest. Cathal extended his arm and with protesting muscles, began to draw the bowstring back. He still didn't have the strength to shoot an arrow over a great distance, but his target was well within his range and ability.

Unbidden, Gryffen's voice filled his head... *feet, Cathal, place yer feet... good lad... now breath easily... that's it.... and relax.*

The priest took a couple of steps to the rock, eased himself down and raised his head to inhale much-needed air. He easily saw the figure standing high above him holding the bow, however, he failed to register that the arrow was aimed at him. For the briefest of moments, he stared in curiosity.

Cathal let the drawstring slip from his fingertips, and the arrow accelerated from the bow at unbelievable speed. Around the time the priest realised he was in imminent danger, the arrow struck him hard, piercing through the animal hide cape draped over his shoulders and then skewered him diagonally down through his sternum before the impact flung him backwards over the rock he sat upon. On its brief journey through the priest's body, the arrowhead eviscerated vital arteries and organs before appearing through his lower back.

Nels, already hurling abuse at the lazy priest, stopped midword as Raven was flung from his seat. By the time he looked up, there was nothing to see and, in pure reflex, screamed, "Archer!" as he ran for shelter.

Cathal didn't loiter and, once out of sight, ran along the ridgeline to his next location behind a large boulder perched on the edge of another outcrop high above the ravine.

The boulder had been sitting here for years, and Gryffen and Cathal had painstakingly moved it using wedges they hammered beneath it. Eventually, they rolled the boulder until it sat balanced at the edge. The only thing preventing it from toppling onto the ravine were two larger rocks jammed against its base. Cathal had already battered away one of the rocks, and now he gripped a wooden club and belted the remaining rock. Nothing happened. He struck again, and still nothing; the weight of the big boulder prevented the smaller one from moving. He scrambled furiously for a suitable sharp-edged rock, placed it beside the small boulder, and struck the sharp rock with all his might, hoping to crack and weaken it. With relief, the impact shattered the smaller rock, and with a grinding sound, the large boulder slowly tipped forward. With his back against the boulder and using his legs, Cathal shoved with all his might, and the large boulder toppled from its perch high above the ravine.

CHAPTER TWENTY-ONE

The boulder was as tall as a man, then half as much again, and its weight incalculable. On the side that faced away from the sun, it was covered in a variety of lichens and moss, which clung desperately to the base where it once sat partially embedded into the earth. The boulder silently descended, rotating in colourful splendour as it plummeted, end over end, from the cliff top. It wasn't a solitary descent, other smaller rocks of varying sizes dislodged from the boulder's base accompanied it, some trailing, others leading. The immense boulder landed with an explosive crack as it impacted obliquely onto an unforgiving granite slab at the base of the ravine. It splintered into two large pieces with dozens of lethal rock shards spraying outwards.

Bragi stood momentarily frozen in disbelief in front of the group as he watched the boulder hurtle down to impact onto the granite seven yards away. Realising the danger, he scrambled away, but not quick enough as sharp fragments pelted his body. A large shard struck the back of his head, causing him to stumble before one-half of the boulder ricocheted towards him. He was prone and struggling to regain his footing when it collided onto him, crushing his head and body before bouncing haphazardly down the ravine.

Nels One-Ear and Leif watched in horror as the boulders cannoned from the ravine's granite sides in an erratic, unpredictable course. In a panic, and like Bragi, Leif slipped on lichen-covered rocks and fell. He wasn't quick enough to avoid the tumbling boulder, which struck his lower legs, crushing them both. Nels One ear, further back, had time to scamper away but, in his haste, slipped, twisting an ankle. Once the boulders passed, he saw the carnage and, unable to walk, painfully crawled across rocks to help Leif, who was shrieking in agony.

Sir Robert looked up when he heard the crash, followed moments later by the pitiful sound of a man screaming. Masked by the forest, the sound of the cascading boulders that carried down to them was indistinct and unidentifiable, and he turned to his two friends in fear. They heard the explosive crack, and the aftermath of a man's painful cries gave them chills. They'd already lost one friend on this journey, and their bravery was tenuous at best and supported only by youthful naivety and the fact they outnumbered their adversary.

Their terror was absolute; what lay ahead was unknown, and their haughty quest suddenly seemed less important. Sir Robert turned to Sir Crispin in silent appeal for support, then resolutely faced Sir Lambert. "I do not relish this," he looked up towards the ravine when the tortured cries suddenly stopped. "I'd see us return safely to our families, what say ye?"

Sir Crispin rubbed the wound he'd received at the inn. "My injury causes me some discomfort; I cannot wield a sword..."

Both knights faced Sir Lambert, who pretended to consider what they had suggested. Privately, he didn't want to continue either, but admitting that to his friends was inconceivable. "The peasant..." He shook his head in forced solemnity and looked at his friends earnestly. "Aye, if we must, we can return home and live to fight another day, and when we have our strength, we can return for the scoundrel."

Thus motivated, the three young knights quickly turned and began their laborious descent. They couldn't leave quick enough.

The miners had stopped prospecting and were staring upwards towards the summit after hearing the indiscernible noises. The sole knight supervising their exploration had also heard the muted sounds, and his eyebrows furrowed in puzzlement. “Petrus!” he yelled to his sergeant, who was farther down the hill.

“Sir?” questioned the young sergeant when he arrived.

“Did ye hear that?” asked Sir Hyde.

His sergeant shook his head.

“Crest the summit, find out what is happening. I heard noises.” He pointed up the slope. “Take care, and best ye walk and remain unseen.”

Petrus nodded and turned away.

“No risks, Petrus,” warned Sir Hyde with a chuckle. His impetuous sergeant had no fear and was known to frequently push the limits of even his considerable expertise.

No trees were near the wind-swept summit, only large clusters of boulders scattered amongst wild grasses and a few low-growing, hardy bushes. With caution, Petrus crept to a large outcrop of rocks that offered concealment and looked down and waited. There was nothing to see or hear. After a while, he angled down towards the nearest stand of trees.

Again, he saw and heard nothing. Ahead, he saw a break in the trees, which he hoped would provide an unobstructed view of the valley below. He silently crept down and was about to venture towards another cluster of boulders when he smelled smoke.

He knew the source of the smoke couldn’t be far away because of the direction of the breeze. Tracing the source of the smoke, he turned left and entered the forest fringe when he saw what remained of a burned house once constructed of logs in a clearing. The house had originally been crudely built, and much of it had burned, although temporary repairs had been made to offer some basic shelter. With Sir Hyde's warning still fresh in his ears, he didn't venture closer and crouched by a tree, waiting to see if he could see anyone.

He heard her first, the sobbing breaking the peacefulness of the forest, and moments later, a couple walked into the clearing. He easily identified a young man about his age and a young woman who was distressed. The young man offered comfort to the woman and had an arm over her shoulders, leading her back towards the fire and charred remnants of the log house.

A sword swung from the young man's belt, a large bow was looped over his shoulder, and a quiver was tied to his back. Petrus scratched his chin. The man wore a robe but was not like a priest, nor did he appear to be a knight. Peasants weren't typically armed in such a manner, *who was he*? The man was tall and lean, and moved fluidly, like a hunter. Food in this area was scarce, and growing crops this high in the uplands was impossible. Hunting game was the only real option to fill empty bellies, which explained the bow the young man carried. *Why would anyone live this far up here*, he wondered.

Suddenly, the young man stopped and turned in his direction to where he hid. Petrus knew he was well hidden and couldn't be seen, but the way the man looked... it was like he sensed him here. Uncomfortable, Petrus carefully backed away and, once out of sight, jogged back to the opening in the trees where he could look down into the valley. He gasped when he looked. It wasn't a valley as he expected, but a narrow ravine gouged from the hill and curved downwards in a series of bends. Because of the unscalable granite rock faces, Petrus calculated the only way to exit this part of the uplands was to descend through the ravine.

Amongst the boulders littered on the ravine floor, he saw three bodies, or what remained of them. One was more of a red smudge where he had been mutilated by something. A few yards away, two other bodies lay side by side. One man's lower extremities were covered in blood, and his lower torso and legs were disfigured and a shredded bloody mess. From his high vantage point, Petrus couldn't see any physical damage to the other man, who appeared to be dead. But then he moved. The man slowly sat up and began massaging his lower leg. From his clothing, Petrus could see he was a Norseman, as were the others. They looked familiar and remembered them from the tavern.

He heard a noise and turned to look up the ravine. He saw the young man who had previously been with the woman slowly descending alone into the ravine, climbing from boulder to boulder towards the bodies. He saw no sign of the woman and determined she must still be at the log house.

Petrus's master would have preferred his sergeant to return to him at this time and report his discoveries, but the impetuous young sergeant wanted to know what tragedy had befallen the Norsemen and why were the young man and his woman living in isolation this high in the uplands. Petrus shook his head. *It made no sense.* With his mind made up, he retraced his route towards the log cabin and knew there must be a path nearby that led down into the ravine.

The path was well-used, and it was easy to navigate his way into the rocky gorge. He did not attempt to hide his approach and nimbly hopped from rock to rock as he saw the man in robes bending over, tending to the only Norseman who remained alive.

"Hail friend!" he yelled. He kept his sword sheathed. "What happened?"

Cathal straightened and stepped back. He'd already consulted his bones and knew the man posed no threat, but he couldn't be sure. His hand went to the hilt of his sword, but like the stranger, he did not unsheathe it. He'd seen the man earlier and, for the present, felt the man posed no immediate threat.

Nels One-Ear grunted, the pain from his ankle excruciating.

"Ye are in danger," Cathal responded to the stranger as he returned to the side of the ailing Norseman."

Petrus looked around and saw that the man with the crushed legs had a chest wound, and he presumed he'd been killed by his friend, a mercy killing. Then he saw another body behind a rock he'd previously missed. He stepped closer and saw an arrow protruding from the Norseman's chest. "Do tell, what tragedy befell these men?" He repeated his earlier question and watched Cathal as he inspected the Norseman's ankle.

"Not far from here, three knights seek my death, and these men from the north also prefer to take my life."

Again, Petrus looked down the ravine and saw nothing. "Then ye must be disagreeable to have six men climb into these hills just to kill ye. What foul deeds have ye done to deserve such attention?"

Cathal ignored the question and turned back to the Norseman. "Who are ye?" he asked. "Why have ye come all this way fer me? Who sent ye?"

Petrus searched for a clue as to what misfortune struck the two men and saw nothing as he curiously waited for the injured Norseman to reply.

Nels-One turned his head and grimaced before looking at Cathal then at Petrus, and then hawked weakly at Cathal.

"I think it only fair that ye answer the question," insisted Petrus.

Nels One-Ear clasped the pendant that hung from his neck

and stared at Cathal with pure loathing.

Cathal slowly eased himself upright.

"Are ye known to this man?" Petrus asked.

Cathal shook his head. "Nay, fer we have never met."

"Was it ye who killed them?" Petrus waved his arm in the direction of the mutilated corpse and then at the man with the arrow in his chest.

"He killed his friend, but the other," Cathal shrugged. "I pushed a boulder from atop." He pointed to the top of the cliff. "A boulder fell."

"And he? Ye killed him?" Petrus pointed to the man struck by the arrow.

Cathal nodded.

It made sense to Petrus. One man had been completely crushed and the other partially.

Petrus didn't trust the Norseman. "Why do you hunt this man?"

Nels snarled and hawked at Cathal again.

"I can help him, for the bone has not broken, his foot twisted," responded Cathal as he again bent down to tend to the Norseman's ankle.

Petrus looked down the ravine, wondering where the knights the young man spoke of were. A movement caught his eye, and he turned to see a knife appear in the hand of the Norseman.

Cathal was engrossed in tearing strips of cloth from the Norseman's breeches to bind the ankle and wasn't aware of the threat.

"Nay!" Petrus yelled.

It happened within a heartbeat. Petrus roughly pushed Cathal aside with his thigh, simultaneously drawing his sword. The knife slashed across Cathal's shoulder at the same time Petrus swung at the exposed neck of the Norseman. It was a fatal strike, and a geyser of blood spurted outwards. For Nels One-Ear, his mission was over. After a loud gurgle, he lay still.

"I made an error," said Cathal, slowly rising to his feet. "Placing trust in a man directed by priests." He shook his head as blood began seeping from the gash in his shoulder. He undid the top part of his robe to inspect the wound and exposed his chest from the waist up.

Petrus gasped. He'd never seen such a savage and jagged scar that ran the length of the young man's chest to disappear below his waist. It wasn't an old scar, this was new, raw and red. "Who did this to ye, for such a wound is surely fatal, yet ye live."

Cathal raised his head. "The knights who hunt me, they did this and seek to complete their task, fer I am witness to their horror. This new wound is not serious."

Petrus and Cathal both heard the yell simultaneously and looked up at the cliff top, seeing the outline of a man.

"Yer master hails," said Cathal.

"Aye, he will want to know of this," replied Petrus, wiping his sword on Nels One-Ear's breeches before sheathing it. "Do ye need help with these men?"

"Nay."

"Petrus!" shouted Sir Hyde.

"I must leave, er, do ye need my help, yer wound?"

Cathal shook his head. "It is nothing."

Petrus turned and began clambering over rocks towards the path where Sir Hyde impatiently waited.

"Look after yer knee," Cathal stated.

Petrus paused and looked back. "My knee?"

Cathal had already turned back to the dead Norseman and didn't respond.

"Who is the liege of these knights? These knights are the same young men we encountered when we were in the tavern," stated Sir Hyde when Petrus breathlessly arrived and explained what he had discovered.

Petrus shrugged, "He didn't say. And aye, the Norsemen were also at the tavern."

"What perturbs me is the Norsemen; why are they here in the Uplands?"

"The peasant suggested they were looking fer him."

Sir Hyde's steel blue eyes scanned the ravine, looking for signs of life and saw no movement. "The peasant, he's gone."

"He was there moments ago," added Petrus.

"I'd like to look closer at those bodies. Show me the way down. Petrus."

Sir Hyde bent down and inspected the Norseman killed by the arrow. "This man is a high priest, I have seen them before. Look, see what he carries. Idols, the Gods the Northmen worship." He straightened and then looked up towards the cliff tops where Petrus pointed to where the peasant had pushed the boulder from. "Do ye think the peasant was lucky with his shot, or is he skilled?" Before Petrus could reply, Sir Hyde continued. "Methinks our mysterious woodsman is much more than a simple peasant."

"There's nothing on these bodies to offer us any clue why they seek the peasant," Petrus responded after going through the few possessions the Norsemen carried.

"Aye, and I'd like to meet this peasant. How could he have disappeared so quickly?"

"A most peculiar fellow."

"Come, Petrus, let us return, we have work to do," Sir Hyde said, casting one final look around.

Cathal knew the knight would want to see the bodies of the Norsemen when the sergeant explained what he'd learned and didn't want to be anywhere near them when they ventured down. Quickly, he searched the dead men and found their purses. The man with one ear that the Sergeant killed had two bulging purses; it was substantial, and after pocketing them, he scampered back up the ravine to Isolde. It was time to leave.

Isolde didn't protest, she knew they could no longer live here, they weren't safe, and she fully expected the knight and his sergeant to come for them at any moment. As she waited for Cathal to return, she packed what few possessions they owned in a large leather satchel and waited.

There was another way down into the ravine that Cathal knew of. It required climbing down through a narrow fissure in the cliff some distance from the burned house. It was partially hidden by the branches of a fallen tree and difficult to see from above and below. In the event of an emergency, he and Isolde had practised descending the fissure until she was comfortable and knew exactly where to place her feet and hands. The rocks at the base of the fissure were sharp, and a fall would prove fatal.

As rehearsed, Cathal descended first and cautiously guided Isolde down. She was tough and resilient and gave no outward sign that she was frightened, but he knew she was terrified. With patience, she managed to step safely onto the ravine floor around the bend and out of sight of anyone near the bodies of the Norsemen.

They clambered over boulders to descend from the hills and then veered towards the protective safety of thick forested hills where they would camp for a few nights.

Sir Hyde had looked closely at the bodies and now stood

with hands on hips, gazing around the ravine. Petrus was dragging the body of the Norseman who'd been shot with an arrow towards the others.

"Leave them, Petrus, can't bury them here," shouted Sir Hyde to his sergeant.

Petrus grunted in acknowledgement, then lay the body down beside the others.

"Why would these men travel with a priest?" Sir Hyde asked.

Petrus sat on a boulder to rest. "From what I saw, these men had no love for the peasant, milord. I believe the peasant was who they were after."

'I suppose we will never know the reason, eh, Petrus. Come, we must return to the miners; we have been gone too long, and the peasant and his woman have long taken their leave." Sir Hyde turned and began walking towards the path that wound out of the treacherous ravine.

Petrus Bodkin watched his master for a few heartbeats, shook his head, then hoisted himself up and followed.

CHAPTER TWENTY-TWO

Isolde had never been aboard a boat before, and she found the journey to Frankia frightening. Under an onslaught of gales and high seas, large green waves cascaded over the ship's bow and pushed the vessel to the limits of seaworthiness. While Cathal did his best to appease her fears, the crossing was appalling, wet, and she was violently sick. The events over the last few weeks had been testing for them both, and Cathal wanted to depart England as quickly as possible and leave their past behind. Privately, he believed the young knights would continue to hunt for them to unleash the terror they took such perverted pleasure in.

Dry, firm land was welcome, and the Norseman's bulging purses Cathal had taken contained a fortune in gold coins, so they had no need to worry and could purchase anything they needed. After landfall in the ancient Frankian seaport town of Bononia[31], Cathal immediately bought two hackney horses and paid an exorbitant price for a mule to carry newly purchased provisions.

"Where are we going, Cathal? This country, this land is foreign to me, the language, the people…" she said as they lay down to sleep after safely departing Bononia and its confusion of people and crime.

The fire crackled and spat, and a few glowing flecks drifted up to be carried away by the gentle breeze. The horses and mule were hobbled and stood quietly together behind them.

31 *Bononia – Modern day Boulogne-sur-Mer, northern Frankia.*

Cathal rolled onto his side to face her. His eyes sparkled in the firelight, "I have heard of an immense forest, the black forest of the Swabi. There, we can live amongst them in peace."

"Swabi? Are these people savage? Will we be safe?"

"Some call them Alemanni, but they are no different than the people of home. There will be good and bad amongst them."

Isolde gave Cathal's words some thought before she spoke. "Is it far?"

"Everything is far."

She remained quiet, and Cathal raised his head to see her better. Her arms were wrapped around her stomach, and she looked uncomfortable. "Does the sea voyage still trouble you?"

"A little. But I will fare better on the morrow," she forced a smile and Cathal scooted closer.

The days were long, and Cathal determined they travelled an average of twenty miles daily, always heading south-easterly. However, over the last few days, Isolde began complaining of tiredness, and Cathal made camp early as she rested. He became increasingly concerned as he believed her humors were out of balance. She denied being sick when he asked, but he wasn't sure. Without making it obvious, he inspected her stool for clues, and one day, she unexpectedly vomited, and he looked closely at her stomach's contents.

He was frustrated and couldn't determine the reason for her lethargy and mysterious symptoms she adamantly refused to acknowledge. Cathal believed that the balance of the body's humors, blood, phlegm, yellow bile, and black bile must be proportionately balanced. From what he witnessed, they weren't, and he found that troubling.

As they sat beside the fire that night, he raised the issue

again. “What ails ye, Isolde, fer I have seen all is not hale, and ye bravely suffer. Speak to me fer then I can help,” he appealed.

A blanket was draped over her shoulders, and she looked small and frail. She hadn’t been eating as much recently, and she seemed pale.

She sighed and turned to him, and slowly shook her head. “I know not. Fer, I know my body well, and I am unsure.”

“Do you suffer from pain?” he asked, relieved she spoke up.

This time, she nodded. “Some days I do, other days I feel no pain but am overcome with tiredness.”

“Where is this pain? Tell me Isolde, fer then I can treat it.”

She removed the blanket and gently rubbed a hand around her stomach. “Not from one place, but from all over.”

Cathal instructed her to lay on her back, and with care, he probed and gently pressed on various parts of her abdomen. She winced. He pressed an ear to her stomach and listened for gurgles and other sounds indicating she’d eaten something tainted or foul. But what he heard sounded normal. The tenderness came from all over, and he suspected her organs had swelled. But the cause of her discomfort eluded him.

In the morning, he had her eat some ginger root, which changed nothing and only confirmed that it wasn’t anything she’d eaten. Today, she seemed more energetic and told him she was without pain. While she felt good, they cleared their camp, mounted their horses, and continued.

The Black Forest was close, and Cathal was eager to arrive so he could focus on Isolde and find the cause of her ailment.

Throughout their three-week journey, they encountered many peasants who were polite but cautiously kept their distance. Many groups of heavily armed warriors often gave them a long hard look because Cathal and Isolde looked like peasants, yet he was armed, riding a horse, as was his woman, and they led a heavily laden mule. The mule was a prize possession and a luxury most peasants could ill afford. But they weren't accosted, nor did they have to account for themselves; the warriors always let them continue. When they finally arrived at the forest's edge, Isolde was exhausted.

In contrast to the flat lands of Frankia, they were finally surrounded by thickly forested steep hills. A flat valley lay ahead, and Cathal made camp in a sheltered area away from well-travelled paths. He scouted for locations offering isolation, security, sun for growing food, and a nearby water supply where he could build a home.

The next day, they rode into the hills until they could ride no more, then they dismounted and led the horses and mule higher. Isolde struggled, but with determination, she valiantly forged on without complaint until Cathal saw the perfect place to build their home. They'd arrived in the Duchy of Swabia[32], and unknown to Cathal, this land had been contested for centuries, and many lives were lost through historical conflict between Frankia and Swabia.

Since they no longer journeyed on horseback, Isolde seemed to fare better and regained some of her strength. Cathal felled trees and, with Isolde's contribution, planned their home. They were happy, content and consumed by each other. Using the horses, Cathal cleared flat ground by removing tree stumps, where he could construct a home and grow food. As the weeks passed, a house began to slowly take shape that was loosely based on Gryffen's log home. It was crude, and simple, but it would be dry and warm and protect them from the cold and wet when the seasons changed. They came into contact

32 Swabia or Suebia – South-western region of modern-day Germany near the Swiss and Frankian borders.

with no one, and as far as they were both concerned, they were the only people in the entire world. Sadly, her health continued to deteriorate.

Cathal continued to administer potions and remedies he hoped would improve Isolde's worsening condition. It may have helped a little, as her physical deterioration slowed, and for a few weeks, she even appeared healthy and hale. As the season began to turn and their home was finally completed, they could both relax a little more.

Nervous of aggressive knights or bands of outlaws stumbling across them, Cathal focused on defensive measures. He couldn't do much, but through his experience with Gryffen in the Uplands, he knew the benefits of taking precautions and did everything he could to keep them safe.

Besides Isolde's mysterious condition, Cathal was the happiest he could ever remember being. He was no longer running and hiding; he felt the unconditional love from Isolde and returned it in equal measure. There was abundant game, and their planted winter crops had already germinated and sprouted. They had want for nothing but each other, and most of all, they felt safe.

Cathal had slain a large boar and used one of his horses to drag the carcass back to their home. On returning, Isolde did not rush out to greet him as she usually did, and with a sinking feeling, he entered their crude cabin to find her lying on their bed. The expression on her face was enough. "Your stomach?"

She nodded. "It hurts Cathal," she told him between clenched teeth. It was the first time she'd ever admitted to the pain. "It's worsened and there is blood."

He lay beside her and comforted her as he considered what to do. He had used all his knowledge and experience to help

Isolde, but none of his treatments or remedies achieved any noticeable improvements to her worsening condition - he was out of ideas. "In the morn, I will ride out, and perhaps I can find someone who can help ye, Isolde. Fer, I have no notion of what to do."

She forced a smile. "The light of a new day will see me improve, and I need ye here, with me." She rolled over, and they embraced.

"If ye continue to worsen, as I fear, then I cannot leave ye. What am I to do? Now, at least I can find a village or someone who can help and return quickly." Cathal hated the thought of leaving her alone, but he had no choice.

She knew arguing with him wouldn't work. When he had his mind set on something, nothing or no one could change it. "Then depart in the morn and return before sunset, promise me this, Cathal," she pleaded.

He nodded. "I will return before sunset.

Not far from Cathal and Isolde's home was a large rock spur that jutted out from the hill and offered an unobstructed view of the valley and behind them back towards Frankia. He and Isolde had spent much time standing on the rocky outcrop, guessing where the nearest village or neighbours were. He had an idea, and before the sun had fully risen, he saddled a horse and departed, heading in a northerly direction.

The village was closer than he expected and hidden from his view by a range of heavily forested hills. He cautiously entered the village, dismounted near a goatherd, and offered a greeting.

"Hale, friend."

The goatherd assessed the tall stranger with piercing eyes, his leathery skin a witness to a life outside tending to goats. He nodded, then hawked, preferring to remain silent.

"I seek a *laech*[33]. Is there one nearby?"

The goatherd seemed to relax, then coughed, a wet, sickly hack and pointed to a cluster of cruck houses. "Second one," he hacked again.

Cathal nodded and led his horse towards the crude homes, tethering his horse to a rail outside. "Greetings!"

Moments later, a filthy curtain was thrust aside, and an elderly woman appeared and gave Cathal a once-over look. Like the goatherd, she said nothing.

"I am in need of a *laech*, can ye help me?" he asked.

"Not fer ye, for ye are hale," she responded like it was an accusation.

"My woman is unwell, and I am not without some knowledge, but nothing I do helps," he appealed.

The elderly woman sat on a bench with a loud sigh. Her thick eyebrows furrowed. "What ails her?"

Cathal explained all he knew about Isolde's condition, and the old woman listened with growing interest.

"Ye have done more than I could have; yer knowledge is great, but I cannot do more than ye," she said.

Cathal was heartbroken.

"Two days ride north, in the Palatinate forest, there is a monastery at Disibodenber, close by, there is a *Frauenklause,* a female hermitage which is part of the monastery. The women there have great knowledge. They should be able to help."

"A convent?" Cathal asked.

"Call it what ye like, but the women have learnings," she volunteered.

"Is there no one closer, someone here who can help me?"

She shook her head. "Your woman, she has *oncos*. No one can help her, perhaps only a miracle from God."

33 *Laech or leech. In medieval times, a practitioner of Roman medicine*

Cathal lowered his head into his hands. She confirmed what he refused to accept. He knew *Oncos* was Greek for swelling and was part of a more serious untreatable condition. A miracle was what Isolde needed. Perhaps the women at *Frauenklause* had access to miracles.

She read his mind. "Be wary, for *Raubritter*[34] will roam the paths between here and Disibodenberg and take yer coin fer taxes.

He raised his head. "Thank ye, fer I will take my Isolde to this *Frauenklause."* He stood and dipped his head in respect.

"I wish ye well," she croaked.

Cathal mounted his horse and turned back to her. "What are ye called?"

"Cäsarea."

He nodded and departed the village as quickly towards home and Isolde.

34 Raubritter – German for robber baron or robber knight.

CHAPTER TWENTY-THREE

"Am I going to die, Cathal?" Isolde asked when he explained what he wanted to do.

It was difficult for him; he didn't want to be untruthful and offer hope when there was none. He wouldn't lie – he just couldn't lie to her.

She saw his expression and teary eyes and didn't need an answer. "I have faith, Cathal. I know ye will do yer best, but hope is all we have. I can't make ye promise to heal me, fer that is unfair." She wiped her eyes as Cathal stood beside her. "We will leave in the morn for this *Frauenklause* place. Perhaps these women have a spare miracle fer us."

He lowered himself to lay alongside, gently pulled her close, and remained silent. She knew what was in his heart, and words weren't needed. His love was healing, giving her the strength to fight what ailed her, but it wasn't enough.

"When is it enough?" she asked, her voice a mere whisper.

He struggled to find an answer. "When all else fails," he breathed, as his eyes filled with tears.

Isolde couldn't travel that morning as she had taken an unfortunate turn for the worse. The pain in her abdomen kept her bedridden and immobile, and she couldn't eat. With Cathal's insistence, she finally drank water, but that was all. There was more blood in her stool and he inherently knew her organs were damaged and failing, and her body was beginning to shut down, and if he couldn't find someone to treat her soon, she would die.

The golden hues of a sunlit dawn revealed a glorious day,

and Isolde felt better, and with some gentle urging, she ate a little. It was fully light when they departed, leading the horses down the narrow path until the spaces between trees widened, and with some difficulty, Cathal assisted her onto her horse. She was weak, and while she appeared in good spirits, he knew she struggled. However, once mounted, she showed her resolve and determination.

Once clear of the valley, they turned and headed north, where the elderly woman had indicated they would find the monastery at Disibodenber.

With the old woman's warning of *Raubritter* preying on unwary travellers still fresh in his mind, Cathal brought only enough coin he anticipated needing, nothing more. He was attentive to their surroundings and, when possible, took secondary paths to avoid more frequented main routes where he thought bandits could be found.

As expected, they encountered peasants and some merchants, and he inquired if it was safe ahead. They greeted him suspiciously and informed him there were no bandits in the area before hurrying off.

The trails were well-used and easily ridden, and Cathal believed they had ridden more than twenty miles on the first day. Camp was made beneath the base of a cliff behind some fallen trees, and they ate and rested without a fire. Isolde was exhausted but still claimed she felt well, and the next morning, they headed off just as the first rays of sun lit distant hilltops.

Again, there were no signs of bandits, and without a fire, they ate and rested. Isolde woke during the night in distress and vomited. He inspected her stomach's contents and saw the blood. She couldn't sleep, and in the morning she struggled to stay upright on her horse. It was obvious she couldn't travel, and Cathal hobbled the horses and lay at her side, providing comfort and support while Isolde dozed with the occasional groan slipping from dried lips.

That night, she managed to sleep, and in the morning, she told him she was strong enough to remain seated without sliding off her horse. Progress was slow, but they were encouraged by a jolly merchant they encountered who told them Disibodenber was only a mile away. After saying farewell, they pressed on, desperate to arrive and seek help.

Cathal had dismounted and was leading his horse as he walked beside Isolde to ensure she didn't slide off her horse when a guttural command brought him to a sudden stop. Ahead, four armed horsemen blocked the path.

"What have we here?" questioned the group leader, then urged his horse to walk closer.

Cathal fought the impulse to panic and tried to appear unconcerned at their sudden appearance. He was willing to do anything to protect Isolde, but he hoped the horsemen could see their sorrowful plight and avoid any violence. His staff was tied to the horse, and his sword was belted to his waist. If the need arose, he was fully prepared to use them. He took a deep breath and resisted the temptation to lower his hand to its hilt, hoping diplomacy would see them unmolested.

"Hail, traveller, where are ye headed?" asked the leader as he stopped directly before them. "Looks like the lady is stricken," he said, smiling for no apparent reason.

Cathal met the gaze of the horseman, then looked at the hostile faces of the other three before speaking. "We seek care from convent *Frauenklause.* Ye can see my woman ails."

"The *Frauenklause!"* exclaimed the horseman, who turned to look behind towards his friends, "They are going to the *Frauenklause!"* He turned back to face Cathal. "Methinks the good *frau* there *will* be able to help ye." He smiled again.

"Then we will be on our way, fer we are weary and travel

with urgent haste."

"Of course, fer we have been most impolite and blocked yer way."

Cathal felt the relief and nodded in thanks.

"But, er, first ye must pay the tax."

The relief was short-lived, and Cathal tensed. "How much is your tax?"

The three horsemen walked their horses closer to surround Cathal and Isolde.

"Oh, that depends on how much coin ye travel with. You see good sir, the more coin ye have, the less the tax you pay because the more ye will spend in my liege lord's lands. And he welcomes travellers to stay for a few days and spend coin." His friends all laughed.

Cathal knew this was a game, these bandits would rob him of every coin he had. Coin he needed to pay for Isolde's treatment if the women at the convent charged a tariff. Thankfully, he had brought only a little coin and had hidden his coin reserves back at their house. Isolde coughed and almost slipped from the horse. When she was again steady, he reached into the folds of his robe and pulled out a small purse. "I am happy to pay the tax, but we must leave urgently. Ye can see my woman needs care."

One of the horsemen dismounted and stepped up to Cathal to take the offered purse. He then undid the string and emptied its contents. "This will do fer ye, but we need more coin to pay fer her. Ye are free to continue, but she must remain."

"I have no more, I cannot pay," Cathal appealed.

The leader shook his head in mock pity. "Ah, then that does present a dilemma." The other three bandits nodded in agreement. "We are reasonable men and will take yer horse as part payment."

Cathal thought furiously. He couldn't leave Isolde. The moment he walked away, they would use and then kill her.

"Is there a problem? Do ye find our terms unreasonable?" queried the group leader. He no longer smiled, and his hand now rested on the hilt of his sword.

The bandit holding Cathal's purse took a step closer.

"Wait, I have more coin," Cathal stated. "It is hidden, let me…"

Cathal twisted his body as if to reach into his robe and quickly sprung sideways, unsheathing his sword. It slashed cruelly across the nearest bandit's stomach. Blood and entrails spilt out as the man collapsed. He was now within striking distance of the group leader, who had yet to unsheathe his sword. Cathal screamed a shrill, piercing cry, and the horses shied in fear, causing the leader to use both hands to control the frightened animal. Cathal's sword speared over the neck of the agitated horse and deep into the chest of the leader. Without pause, he leapt towards the third bandit, still fighting to control his horse.

Isolde's horse had recoiled like the others, and without strength, the sudden, unexpected movement caused her to fall. From his peripheral vision, Cathal saw her sit up. Thankfully, she appeared unhurt.

He heard the unexpected whoosh sound that came from behind and saw a bright flash and simultaneous explosion of pain before succumbing to the darkness.

Two men and an unknown woman were buried in accordance with Christian practices, and the service was presided over by Father Gotfrid and attended by a score of devoted nuns. At the conclusion of the brief homily, the nuns returned to the convent and the *Domus Dei*[35] , where a new patient desperately needed their skills. The young man had been severely wounded and abandoned by local bandits known to loiter around the outskirts of Disibodenber. Usually, the *Raubritter* only robbed and extort-

35 Domus Dei – The house of God. The hospital was a house because it was always part of a religious community, a household with God at the head

ed travellers to pay unreasonable levies imposed by local lords, however in this case, as a witness had come forward and told Father Gotfrid, the robbery had taken a violent turn when the victim surprisingly challenged the *Raubritter* and managed to kill two of them.

In retaliation, they had brutally slain the young woman and left the victim for dead after stabbing him repeatedly. Father Gotfrid believed the victim was deliberately left alive, so he would endlessly grieve, knowing his woman had suffered cruelly by their hand in revenge for the deaths of two of their own. Meanwhile, the young man hovered somewhere between limbo and purgatory, neither alive nor dead, and his fate rested at the hands of Almighty God and the handful of nuns who dedicated themselves to the Church and took pity on the wretched and poor.

Father Gotfrid and Abbess Mathilt stood at the stranger's bedside and silently observed him.

"He is not long for this world, Father," finally stated Abbess Mathilt.

Father Gotfrid's lips were pursed as he considered the patient. He waited a moment longer, grunted in response, turned and departed without saying a word.

A nun entered the room, respectfully acknowledged the Abbess and, with a wet cloth, dabbed the dry lips of the young man who remained unresponsive. With a rustle of skirts, the Abbess spun and left the room. Now alone with the patient, the nun began to quietly sing *Magnum salutis Gaudium, Great joy of salvation*, a hymn commonly sung to the ailing to bring salvation to their pitying condition.

The words were soft and soothing and sung in an unfamiliar language. The cadence and delivery were peculiar. The lyrics came and went in the chaos of awakening senses… pain, despair, but no light. He involuntarily kept his eyes firmly shut. It was confusing, tormenting … he wanted to resist but couldn't … he needed to help and protect. "ISOLDE!" he shouted, and again, he succumbed to the welcoming and numbing darkness where he could hide.

The nun recoiled at the unexpected outburst and, in fear, immediately sought the guidance of a more experienced colleague.

Cathal was trying to make sense of what happened, but his thoughts were addled and consumed by the events of the robbery and Isolde falling from her horse. "Isolde?" he croaked.

He felt someone gently touch his shoulder and opened his eyes, hoping to see her. Instead, he saw a youngish woman about his age seated beside him and an older woman hovering close by, frowning.

"Isolde? … My woman," he asked and tried to sit up, but the pain from his head and neck quickly changed his mind. He sunk back into the bed and felt more pain from his back. "Where is she?"

"Drink this," offered the younger woman, holding a mug to his lips.

The older woman bent down and whispered into the younger's ear and left the room only to return a few moments later with another. The younger stood and moved from her chair, allowing the newcomer space to approach the bed.

"I am Abbess Mathilt of *Frauenklause,* and ye have been wounded and are under our care," she stated solemnly. "What are ye called?"

Cathal looked at the faces of the three women standing in the room. *Frauenklause*? he thought. "My woman, where is she? Isoslde?" he queried, hoping they would know. His voice sounded stronger, and he waited for a response.

"Please, sir, may we have your name?"

He closed his eyes tightly to gather strength, then opened them to focus. "I am Cathal, and I seek the whereabouts of Isolde. We travelled together; she was unwell. I hoped you could attend to her fer healing as her cure is beyond my knowledge."

The abbess took a step closer and lowered herself to the chair recently vacated by the younger nun. "Ye have been injured and suffer deep wounds to your back and have been struck hard on the head. Ye need rest, Cathal," firmly stated the abbess.

The pain and discomfort he felt made sense. Now that she told him, he understood why he hurt. "I travelled with a woman, her name is Isolde. Is she also under yer care?"

The abbess toyed with the rosary beads she held and moved them one by one through her fingers with practised ease. She looked down at the beads as if to inspect them for flaws and remained silent a moment before looking up at the expectant face of the young man. "Isolde did not survive the attack. I am sorry, she passed before ye were found."

His expression was of disbelief. "I saw her before... before I was attacked. I saw her – she fell from the horse, and she sat up. Isolde was alive... could ye be mistaken?"

She shook her head. "We buried her two days past. She suffered a severe wound to her abdomen, probably from a sword. A stronger woman may have survived, fer the woman we buried was in failing health. She appeared to have been suffering from *carcinos*[36] and would likely have passed in a day or two."

Cathal looked away from the abbess, his face devoid of expression. He felt guilty and believed he could have done more to help Isolde. If he was to believe what the abbess said and Isolde was dead, then the blame was solely his to bear.

"God has taken pity upon ye, Cathal, and ye survived," smiled Abbess Mathilt.

Her words offered no consolation, and he tried to sit up but couldn't; he was weak, and his entire body ached. The exertion

36 Carcinos – Greek for carcinoma or crab and crayfish.

was too much, and he succumbed to exhaustion and despair that overcame him.

CHAPTER TWENTY-FOUR

Nuns took turns sitting with him as his body healed. It wasn't a quick recovery, wounds on his back became corrupted and wept foulness. He suffered from mindlessness, and the attending nuns genuinely believed he wouldn't survive. During brief moments of lucidity, he convinced a young nun named Sister Hildegard to venture outside and gather various flora needed to treat his festering wounds. Initially reluctant, and after seeking approval from her superiors, she followed his precise instructions, blending them with mortar and pestle to create a paste that she applied to his wounds. Within days, and believing it was a miracle from God his condition miraculously turned.

This morning, it was again Sister Hildegard's turn to sit with her patient, and Cathal enjoyed her company. He found the young nun to be extremely quick of mind, and she had a beautiful voice. To bring joy and lift him from the despair that consumed him, she would sing and teach him chants and songs she'd composed. Sister Hildegard encouraged him to sing and told him his voice was beautiful and his natural tone was rich, melodic, and expressive. It was the first time anyone had ever complimented him on his singing. He sang to honour Isolde; his passion and expression surfaced from a broken heart.

Most unusually and pleasing to him, she expressed curiosity in nature, healing, and they would discuss remedies that progressed into philosophy that broached a subject she called mysticism. A theme close to his heart and familiar with, but he never knew its name. This was the first time he had ever had an opportunity to expound on his founded convictions on this new word, mysticism, to anyone, and this vibrant and open-minded nun that sat with him listened and then shared with him her learnings. Frequently, she tested her radical ideas on him before espousing them on the more discerning wider abbey audience.

While she was enlightening and stimulating company, his heart was consumed by sorrow, and he saw Sister Hildegard only as a preceptor. Her informal lessons and their unmoderated conversations were a distraction which temporarily shelved his undiminished grief and heartache. He missed Isolde so much; her passing was like a wound that wouldn't heal - and almost too much to bear.

Abbess Mathilt, fully aware of the open discussions between the convalescing patient and Sister Hildegard, encouraged the free-thinking young nun to challenge the heretical hypothesis espoused by her patient. Privately, she believed the arrival of Cathal wasn't the result of a simple accident – a robbery gone awry. Instead, it was a covert evaluation designed by God to test the devoutness and teachings of her abbey and determine if young and pliable minds like Sister Hildegard and others like her could be easily swayed by the perverted ramblings of a demented and Godless soul.

Within the sanctity of the abbey, many lively exchanges of views took place, and Sister Hildegard was permitted to speak and expound on the developing, fanciful and unsupported ideas she adapted from Cathal. While in response and through robust debate, older, more mature and learned nuns sought to temper her theories and wild speculations, yet the young nun had a talent for convincing others to accept her suppositions and postulations, and the subsequent discussions became increasingly worrisome for Abbess Mathilt. The abbess prided herself on allowing novices and nuns to question accepted norms, she permitted frank and open conversations because it gave her the opportunity to educate and instruct and put right when the young strayed from righteousness and God. However, and most unfortunately, this wasn't presently happening.

Sister Hildegard sat on a crude chair beside Cathal's bed and looked at him closely before continuing their latest open exchange. "Some years past I set my hand to writing. While documenting my thoughts, I sensed, as I mentioned to ye before, Cathal, about the deep profundity of scriptural exposition. Raising myself from illness by the strength I received from God, I finally brought this work to a close – though just barely – and it took over ten years. And I spoke and wrote these things not by the invention of my heart or that of any other person, but as by the secret mysteries of God I heard and received in the heavenly places. And again, I heard a voice from Heaven saying to me, 'Cry out, therefore, and write thus!"

"And did ye write these words?" he asked.

She nodded and smiled at the recollection. "Aye, and I call my first written work *Scivias,* and I will write more." She raised her head to face him. "Can ye write, do ye know words?"

He shook his head. "Nay, fer I have never learned."

"Then so be it, I shall teach ye how, fer I believe ye have much to write, Cathal. Yer mind is curious, similar to mine, and we think the same. Yer thoughts should be lasting and be a divine account that others can learn from."

"Who will know what I have written? What does it matter?"

She laughed, the sound of her voice delicate and a painful reminder of Isolde.

"Ye will know what words to choose; that is the beauty of being a creator." She leaned forward in her chair. "Cathal, ye have spoken of healing in ways I know nothing about. Others can learn from ye. Your words can be a gift to all of humanity."

"I could not heal Isolde," he said, feeling shame and looking away.

"Nay, ye could not, and neither could anyone else here, not the nuns or monks. *Carcinosis* is a mystery to us all, we have no remedy, Cathal."

"Perhaps not yet, but I will try to find a cure. I am debited to Isolde and everyone else who suffers from it."

"Then, I will teach ye to write so ye may document what ye learn. How ye will do this? What say ye?"

"Ye speak of a divine account, but I do not love the God you pray to. My words, if I could write with the beauty you describe, will not support your holy teachings."

Sister Hildegard was not shocked by Cathal's frank admission and laughed. The stark warnings of the abbess were foremost on her mind. She bravely pressed on regardless. "Cathal, then who is this God you love? For ye have spoken many times of God."

Cathal tried to sit up a little straighter as he thought of a suitable response to satisfy an inquisitive and educated mind. "I have not the learning to speak convincingly to you about my beliefs."

"You worry I will mock you?" she asked.

Cathal shook his head. "Nay, fer ye are not that way."

"Then tell me, fer I must know."

"And risk the wrath of the abbess or the Church?"

Again, Sister Hildegard thought of the abbess, who believed if Cathal spoke to her truthfully, she was honour bound to convince him that he was wrong. "I want to learn from ye, Cathal. I have discovered ye are most unconventional and have so much to give. I want to hear your words so I can ponder and reflect on yer wisdom. Ye are young, but yer mind is not. Here ye are safe; this is a place of learning. No one will make jest of yer beliefs, but they might challenge ye in debate. Is that what ye fear?"

This time, Cathal offered a rare smile. Sister Hildegard saw his expression soften; the façade disappeared, and she saw him, vulnerable, tormented, and lonely. Not because he lost his dear Isolde but she felt his suffering and pain extended over a lifetime of grief. She fought to hold back her tears as he began to speak.

"God is everywhere," he began, his voice soft and rich. "God is the energy around us. Energy we can feel and see. God isn't a man, woman, cow, or bird and doesn't rule on a throne like a king over his dominion, nor does he sit on a cloud above us to watch and guide us. God *is* the cloud; God is the essence of who we are and what ye are. God is Mother Earth that nurtures us - the plants and trees, fish and animals and even insects, all God's creations. God provided us with all these plants and animals to give us food and nourishment; they keep us alive and can also heal. God isn't a single divine entity as ye see him. Do ye understand?"

Sister Hildegard's eyebrows furrowed, "Please continue."

"My relationship to God is individual and peculiar only to me, just as my relationship is to my mother, to Isolde or even ye, Sister Hildegard." He took a deep breath and continued when he saw the young nun listening attentively. "A stranger or a priest cannot speak to me of God as he believes, nor can he know what is in my heart or know the intent of God. He cannot stand before me and interpret what God bids or wants me to do."

Sister Hildegard listened with focus; his delivery was mesmerizing, and the rhythm of his words was melodic and expressive. However, the words he spoke were contrary to her beliefs and the holy life she'd dedicated herself to. But his passion was real … It was captivating like he was singing the praises of God – a supreme being he obviously loved – the feeling so close to her own heart, yet miles away through interpretation.

"The presence of God leaves us clues to its existence, the proof so many people want to see. It's here; it's everywhere and all around us."

"What proof, Cathal?" she whispered.

"Love, joy, happiness, even sadness. What we see, taste, hear and feel allows us to love. Can a rock feel love? Does a dog feel love when it mates? People have been given the gift of love by God, fer without God there can be no love and without love there can be no God." Cathal met the nun's quizzical expression. "You doubt me?"

"Nay, nay, for ye have me thinking."

"About what?"

"You say God is everywhere, in everything?"

"Aye, God is life, all life, in everything that lives."

She looked down at her hands in her lap and then back up at him. "What is the Church's role with God?" she whispered. Then quickly glanced back over her shoulder at the door.

Cathal exhaled slowly. "I shall speak openly to ye, Sister Hildegard, fer I have no motive to be untruthful. The Church, a creation constructed by men, uses God to further its own needs. The Church uses good people like yerself to serve its purpose."

The nun raised a hand to her mouth in surprise at Cathal's statement. 'You say I deceive people?"

Cathal reached across and placed a hand reassuringly on her shoulder. "Nay, fer ye are not a bad person, and ye and other good people like ye support the belief that the Church's role is to spread the word of Christ."

Sister Hildegard sat back in her chair. "Then you do not believe in Christ?"

"I have no reason to doubt he lived and was a good man. The Church gave him divinity, not God."

"He is the son of God. How can ye doubt that?"

Cathal lowered his voice. "Who was it that said he is the son of God?"

Her mouth opened, but she remained silent as she thought of a response. "He did, and he performed miracles. There were witnesses, the bible."

"That proclamation did not come from God, did it?"

Her eyes were wide open, and he could see her fighting to control her emotions. "I am not trying to upset ye, Sister Hildegard, but offer ye a logical perspective."

After a moment, she relaxed and smiled. "I still have much to learn about debate, fergive me."

"I apologize if I spoke out of turn."

"Ye are a truly special man, Cathal, thank ye. If I may, I will dwell on this and return with questions." She rose to leave.

"Wait, please. Do not share what I have spoken about; it will anger many, and the Church will not approve."

She smiled nervously, thinking of the abbess, and quietly departed.

Convalescing at the convent *Frauenklause* wasn't a complete gift to those in need and didn't come without a cost. When a patient was able to walk, they were given light duties, and as their condition improved, they undertook more responsibilities to tend to a variety of tasks that included building repairs, livestock, gardens and household duties. It was a form of repayment. When fully recovered and the patient had sufficiently contributed to the convent's wellbeing, they could leave, and Cathal was no exception.

Because of his horticultural knowledge, he was tasked with developing a new garden containing medicinal plants and herbs. The fertile land around Disibodenber was ideal for propagating plants, and Cathal, initially with limited physical ability and with help, fully immersed himself in work. Sadly, Sister Hildegard wasn't permitted to help him as she had other responsibilities, and he quietly believed it was deliberate.

He saw Abbess Mathilt infrequently. As a layperson, he dined and slept separately to the consecrated nuns, a couple of monks and a priest. The few times he did see the abbess, when she wandered around the expansive abbey grounds inspecting work, she was polite asked pertinent questions, but he felt she was distant and aloof.

Tending to his new garden gave him time to dwell on the matter, and he came to believe the abbess was keen to see his departure. He hadn't seen Sister Hildegard in days and hadn't talked to her in a couple of weeks, and then only briefly. The intimacy of their previous chats was like an embarrassment, and when he saw her, she looked away after a polite nod in greeting. He came to learn that the young nun was highly regarded and thought of as special. The laypeople he talked to spoke of her as uniquely gifted and, with no exceptions, revered her. He understood why and hoped he could one day talk candidly with her again.

His injuries had mostly healed, but his strength had not fully returned. He still felt weak but knew within another two or three weeks, he'd be close to his usual self again. The shade beneath the large expansive tree was welcome, and he quietly pondered his future as the late afternoon sun would soon descend behind wooded hills.

CHAPTER TWENTY-FIVE

The birds provided a warning someone approached, and shortly after, he sensed her presence; he didn't turn around.

"I often come here to reflect," she said as she walked around the tree to stand before him.

Seeing her face as she stood with the sun at her back was difficult. She was cast in shadow – dark.

"The solitude and peacefulness..." she sighed loudly. "So beautiful."

He felt the intensity of her gaze upon him, which confirmed his suspicions. He silently acknowledged the purpose of her visit and reached for his staff to aid him in standing.

"Wait, let me speak," the abbess commanded.

He brought his knees up, close to his chin, and waited, his staff lying at his side.

"*Frauenklause* is more than a convent or a female hermitage, as some call it. It's a place of worship and learning where we can exercise our belief in Christ, our saviour. Before we came here, a Celtic temple existed, and rightly so, fell to ruin. Against adversity, we built something special here, and it's founded on our unwavering belief in God Almighty. While I believe ye are a good man, Cathal, you threaten our existence. Your vaporous conjectures have poisoned the innocent minds of our sisters and even lay people." She shook her head to emphasise her point. "Your words slash at the life-giving blood of our ideology and the tenant of holiness that proudly courses through us."

She lowered her head slightly, and Cathal saw her ardent scrutiny.

"Ye look at me now and doubt the soundness of my mind, fer I can see it." She separated her clasped hands and pointed a finger accusingly. "It cannot continue, it won't continue, and I will see the heresy end."

She turned her head and looked briefly over her shoulder at the setting sun, and he saw the shine of glistening tears marking her cheeks. They could have been rivulets of blood from wounds he'd created, and he knew he'd overstepped. He'd come into the domain of these devout Christian followers and, through his arrogance and self-assuredness, tried to impart his convictions on this holy community when they had done nothing untoward and only helped him when he was in dire need. These women of *Frauenklause* hadn't deserved the pain he'd brought them. He'd wrongly challenged their faith, and they merited far more. For the first time in his life, he felt shame. *What have I done*? He wondered. He looked away from her and down at the leaves that carpeted the ground

Abbess Mathilt looked down at the young man and felt pity. From his reaction, she sensed genuine remorse. "I know ye meant no harm," she said. Her voice conciliatory and sincere. "The brashness of the young such a potent aseptic against wisdom and learning."

Cathal raised his head and met her gaze.

She bent down close to him. "We fergive ye, Cathal, and we offer ye the sacrament of baptism. Allow Father Gotfrid to baptise ye and accept Jesus Christ into yer heart and life, what say ye, Cathal? Dost, thou renounce Satan, all his works and all his pomps?"

He had yet to speak, his mind a whirling maelstrom of conflicting emotions and guilt. He took a deep breath and slowly exhaled as he sought the right words. "I offer ye my sincerest apologies, Abbess Mathilt. My arrogance blinded me to common respect and courtesy. I was wrong to speak openly about my views, and I hope I have not upset the balance of life at *Frauenklause*. What

I spoke was not intended to create disharmony or challenge yer belief in the Christian faith. I spoke sincerely from my heart and was allured by the opportunity to speak frankly, and I unwisely took advantage of that. Sister Hildegard has a gift, an innocence, but also an inquisitive mind. I was seduced into speaking my sentiments when I had no cause or right."

Abbess Mathilt straightened and stood assessing him with hands again clasped. She believed him. For all his faults, the young man before her is a good man. Confused, stricken by grief, and Godless. Yet, motivated to help people. He would make a fine priest.

With some discomfort, Cathal reached for his staff and rose to his feet. "While I spoke out of turn, my beliefs are my own. What I have learned as I have travelled across lands, what has been taught to me, and what I have come to accept as *my* truth is what I hold most dear to me, fer it is all I have. To my mind, I spoke no mistruths, uttered no lies, and deceived no one. I spoke from my heart as ye have done to me." Cathal dipped his head in respect to the Abbess. "Yer offer of baptism is generous, but I cannot accept. I will take my leave on the morrow as the sun rises. Please pass on my apologies to all the sisters, the lay and Sister Hildegard, whom I will never forget. She is a most remarkable person, and I have learned much from her."

Abbess Mathilt's expression momentarily hardened, then softened. "I wish ye safe travels, Cathal." She walked away, leaving him alone.

His few salvaged possessions were handed to him. They weren't much: his sword, a blanket, a leather bag that contained a mortar and pestle and an assortment of clay jars containing dried herbs that he was using to treat Isolde and his small pouch of bones. Remarkably, his horse had been found and been cared for by the convent. But nothing else; none of Isolde's clothes had been spared and were either burned or buried with her. With a heavy heart, he departed *Frauenklause* and resisted the temptation to look back. He felt the uncensored gaze of Sister Hildegard staring at his back.

His wounds, still not fully healed, caused him pain when he sat astride his horse. He decided to walk and lead the animal as he slowly ventured from *Frauenklause.* The thought of returning to his home nestled deep in the Black Forest offered little consolation. There was nothing there except memories, and it heightened his frustration that he'd not been able to cure Isolde of her malady. The despair added to the accumulated grief of those he cared for who had passed - people he'd loved: death - such a cruel and faithful companion.

His recovery at *Frauenklause* had not been unpleasant; the nuns had been friendly, and he'd learned much about philosophy, mysticism, the Christian faith, and even about himself. The biggest disappointment had been his lack of self-discipline. He'd spoken brashly with unfettered arrogance about his views on the Church and offended those who'd committed with vows to their staunch beliefs. He'd challenged their faith, and he shouldn't have. He'd been wrong and chastised himself again for his lack of consideration.

As he plodded along well-worn paths, he solemnly vowed never to speak of his philosophical or mystical beliefs to anyone again. Such was his simmering anger, his focus targeted solely on a self-deprecating cauldron of loathing that he never heard the horseman approach from behind. He didn't pause, didn't turn, and slowly continued on his laboured journey.

It didn't take long, and the rider overtook him and reined in, blocking his way.

Cathal surveyed the rider. He was well armed; a sword hung from a belt at his waist, and an unstrung recurve bow was affixed to the saddle. At least two lethal knives of varying lengths were tucked into his belt, and although he didn't wear chain mail, Cathal believed the man was a knight. The stranger pulled at his full beard and remained silent.

Cathal tugged on the reins of his horse to lead him around the knight, but the man gave an unseen command to his horse, and the animal obediently stepped backwards.

"Aye, it is ye," he finally spoke. "Ye were the one who slew my brother."

Cathal had nothing to offer in response and remained silent, although he remembered the face from when he and Isolde were attacked by the *Raubritter* three months ago. This man was a bandit acting for the local lord.

"Have ye nothing to say?"

Cathal shrugged - he didn't care.

The knight continued toying with his beard. Coming to a decision, he pointed to Cathal's sword.

Cathal unfastened his belt with a sigh as the knight reached down to take it from him. He could easily have struck the man with his staff and knocked him from his horse, but he didn't. He waited for the next instruction, and when it came, it wasn't a surprise.

"Mount up," he pointed down the path in the same direction Cathal had been travelling. "That way."

It was difficult to climb into the saddle, and with the aid of his staff and an involuntary grunt of pain, he managed to slide onto the back of his horse.

The brief ride was made in relative silence. The only words from the knight were in which direction to ride. It wasn't long before they approached a hamlet dominated by an extravagant large stone lodge, too small to be a castle but too big to be a manor house. People stared as the two riders entered the main thoroughfare, then quickly hurried away, not willing to become involved in anything that drew attention to themselves.

They pulled up outside the lodge when the knight instructed him to stop. Cathal looked around the hamlet and noticed a couple of inns, a baker and a few other merchants selling wares from crude buildings. From a safe distance, a small crowd began to gather. They watched with cautious interest.

Large, heavy wooden doors swung open, and half a dozen armed men poured out and stopped to stare. Another man appeared, older and much larger than the others and through his deportment and fine clothes he wore, Cathal guessed he was the lord.

"What have ye here, Bartke!" yelled the *Gutsherr*[37] in a booming voice.

Cathal took an immediate dislike to the loud man who seemed full of self-importance.

"He was heading south, and I found him near the convent, *Gutsherr*. This is the man who killed Heinke and Dirske."

The lord placed his hands on his hips and glared hatefully at Cathal for a dozen heartbeats before nodding towards one of the knights who stood nearby. "Is that so."

In response, the knight rushed over and, without a word, grabbed Cathal's robe and roughly jerked him from his horse. With a cry, Cathal landed heavily on the hard-packed ground with a howl of pain.

He was dragged to a barn and tossed into a stall. The familiar and comforting smell of horses was the only thing he welcomed. A door slammed shut, and he was alone in the darkness. Since encountering the bandit, no one had questioned him, and he hadn't spoken a word - he had nothing to say. With his hands, he felt around the stall and found a bucket that contained water,

37 Gutsherr – Lord of the Manor

and from the odour, it was fetid and had been in there a while. His throat was parched and unperturbed, and he drank greedily. He was tired, his wounds hurt, and he lowered himself onto the filthy straw, hoping they wouldn't delay killing him.

Gutsherr Gotfridus Brisigavi gnawed on what remained of a leg-bone bone from a wild boar hunted and slain four days earlier. With him at his table sat his trusted advisors, mostly senior knights, who had finished eating some time ago. However, Gotfridus was well known for his voracious appetite and continued feasting long after everyone else's bellies were full.

"What will ye do with him, *Gutsherr*?" asked Bartke, who'd captured the peculiar man and brought him to the village.

Gutsherr Gotfridus Brisigavi threw the bone to a hound at his feet, wiping his greasy hands on his tunic before looking towards one of his best and most accomplished knights. "We will kill him, Bartke, what else?" replied the lord.

"Fergive me, *Gutsherr*, but how?"

Gotfridus's small black eyes narrowed. "*Gehängt, gestreckt und gevierteilt*[38]"

In reaction, all heads turned to their lord in surprise. There hadn't been a dramatic execution of this magnitude in many years.

"And ye, Bartke, will have the pleasure of overseeing the spectacle. The people need entertainment, a healthy distraction from hard times, eh?" replied Gotfridus, smiling before picking away debris from his meal lodged between his teeth.

Bartke dipped his head in acknowledgement of the honour. "*Gutsherr*, when would ye like to have this done?"

The lord leaned back in his chair and belched. "We will need to hunt fer a boar or four, prepare a feast and ready the village–" He inspected the morsel he'd discovered between his teeth, then flicked it away. "Anticipation, Bartke, that is the solution to a suc-

38 *Gehängt, gestreckt und gevierteilt – Hung, drawn and quartered.*

cessful execution – fourteen days."

Bartke again dipped his head. "As ye command, *Gutsherr*."

Gotfridus sat forward and rummaged through the scraps of their meal, hoping to find another tasty treat to chew on. His advisors began peppering Bartke with questions about what he knew of his prisoner or where he came from. While Gotfridus appeared to be unconcerned, his advisors were far from comfortable. They knew nothing about their condemned captive or where he came from. He might belong to a powerful tribe, and executing him in a spectacle as their lord demanded could have unpleasant consequences. The last thing any of these knights wanted was to be attacked in retribution by a powerful force.

He'd been in the stable for two days, and no one had come. They didn't bring food or clean water, they didn't clean the stall when he had to defecate in the corner, and Cathal considered ways to end his life quickly. He didn't have much, perhaps his only option was to use his robe and hang himself from a rafter.

Without warning, the stable door was flung open and Cathal covered his eyes, blinking in the harsh light as three armed knights entered. They reacted to the stench by covering their noses.

"Take him outside, eh," suggested one knight as he stepped back towards the door for fresh air.

Cathal recognised the knight who'd captured him. "Get up," instructed Bartke and pointed to the door.

Weak from lack of food, Cathal stood with difficulty and stumbled towards daylight.

CHAPTER TWENTY-SIX

The German village nestled in the hills of the Black Forest was poor, life was hard, and their *Gutsherr* was a cruel and unforgiving man. To feed money into his coffers to pay for his excessive and underserved lifestyle, Gotfridus Brisigavi frequently sent his knights onto the trails and paths to waylay travellers, imposing unreasonable levies on and earning the dubious distinction of being called *Raubritter,* which somewhat irked the self-important lord. It was how Cathal and Isolde came to meet these unkind men and where she suffered a cruel and incongruous fate. Death for a traveller wasn't desirable for Gotfridus as he preferred to impose outrageous taxes rather than explain an unwanted slaying to a neighbouring lord. In the brief and violent exchange between his men and the stranger he now held captive, two of his valuable knights had died, and as he didn't have many knights to speak of, the attempted extortion had been costly.

Providing food and drink to celebrate an execution was another unwelcome expense that Gotfridus wasn't thrilled about and, as he usually did, sent his men out onto the trails and paths, hoping to encounter some wealthy travellers and continue to impose his unjustifiable taxes upon them. The village needed the distraction of a spectacle; morale was low, and his spies had delicately enlightened him that the people had lost confidence in his ability to lead and keep them safe. A vain main seldom sees the flaws in his own character and freely directs blame at others or circumstances, and with that mindset, Gotfridus admonished neighbouring lords, the weather, and even Christians for their current misfortune. To anyone who would listen, he extolled his virtues and preached of his righteousness and probity, believing he could bring about loyalty and obedience by announcing a feast and an execution. Or better yet, multiple executions. Few were impressed with his oratory discharge, but most agreed that a feast would be welcome, even if it came at the expense of another's life.

Gutsherr Gotfridus Brisigavi's knights returned to the village at the end of the day with two prisoners - brothers who had openly defied the knights, refusing to pay the levies. While the brothers were large and healthy men, they were not skilled warriors and fought with emotion rather than skill. They were easily overcome, and to the *Gutsherr*'s relief, without loss of life. Although one brother was wounded, but that was of little concern. The brothers carried a substantial amount of coin and could pay the tax, but they chose not to. Gotfridus never questioned why the brothers had so much coin, and he simply decided they would be executed along with the stranger he already held captive, bringing the total to three. They were tossed into the stable along with the stranger. Gotfridus was happy, the day's earnings were substantial.

Cathal observed the two new prisoners with feigned disinterest. The brothers were suspicious of him, and they spoke together in hushed whispers and ignored him. While it was dark in the stable, filtered late afternoon sunlight seeped through small gaps in the walls and roof to provide just enough illumination to make out most details. Cathal fervently hoped the two men could put an end to his consuming misery and end his life before the brutality of the execution.

During the next day and night, the brothers did not speak to him and kept their distance. However, during the night, one brother became delirious, and Cathal realised that he was wounded and the injury, as usual, was corrupt.

It was automatic, and without consciously thinking about it, Cathal wanted to heal the man. Because the day of the execution was still eleven days away, the water in the stable was replenished, and recently, basic food was provided. Fortunately, Cathal's condition didn't deteriorate, and through rest, he'd regained some strength, but he was treated worse than a village dog. The boy who came with water daily was the only person who showed him kindness. It was the same boy, Hans, who began bringing food, and Cathal suspected no one knew or even cared what the boy was doing.

In anticipation of Hans's daily visit, Cathal positioned himself as close to the water bucket as possible. A guard always stood at the door and prevented them from talking.

Not long after daybreak, the stable door was thrust open, and as he always did, Hans appeared carrying a bucket of water. Nervously, he entered the stall, avoiding coming into close contact with the prisoners.

"Hans?" whispered Cathal.

The boy turned his head in curiosity to look at the dishevelled man.

Cathal flicked his eyes towards the guard who stood watching.

"Bring me Marjoram. Please, bring Marjoram," he softly repeated.

The boy looked puzzled.

"Marjoram," he implored.

Hans finished emptying his bucket and turned to leave.

"Ask your mother, is for his wound," Cathal indicated with his head to one of the brothers who lay in a troubled sleep.

Hans dropped the bucket outside the stable and returned to the corner where another bucket sat filled with human waste. Too heavy to carry, he dragged it from the room, emptied it and brought it back. As Hans turned to leave, he made brief eye contact with him before the guard slammed the door shut. Cathal took a mouthful of water; he could do nothing more.

Sometime later, Cathal wasn't sure how long it had been when he heard a scratching noise behind him. He moved out of the way and peered down. Someone was on the other side of the wall. Through a gap, small leaves were being passed through. From the distinctive smell, Cathal knew the boy had done as asked. When he thought the last leaf had been pushed through, there were more. Tightly wrapped small bundles of sage were being pushed through. For the first time in weeks, he smiled. He knew the boy's mother understood the reason for his request. "Thank ye," he said softly, but he doubted the boy could hear. But one of the brothers did, and he looked up in puzzlement.

Cathal scooted closer towards him. "This is for his wound. He will die if we don't do something."

The wounded brother woke. With his back to the door, Cathal swept away the filthy straw from the floor to clear a small space, then, with water from the bucket, cleaned the area of the wood floor as best he could. With all the marjoram leaves held in both hands, he crushed them together until they became a small, mushy ball of leaves. Both brothers watched him closely but remained silent. He then placed the leaves on the cleaned floor and mashed them with his thumbs and body weight into a pulp. The sage was more difficult, but he broke the small leaves into smaller pieces, crushing them and combining them into the marjoram paste, continually kneading the mixture and infusing them together. A mortar and pestle would have been helpful, he thought. The smell was potent, and if anyone came into the stable now, there would be no disguising what he was doing.

"Remove yer tunic," Cathal instructed.

The man didn't respond.

"Yer wound - is corrupted, this will heal it," he explained.

The man turned to his brother who nodded.

With the shoulder wound revealed Cathal could see the corruption. It didn't look good and had been left unattended for too long. Using water and his fingers, he patiently cleaned the inflamed area as best he could to wash away the seeping foulness. He didn't hurry and took his time, knowing he had nowhere to be. Time meant nothing.

Satisfied the wound was free from unwanted filth, keeping a wound clean was something his mother had repeatedly stressed to him, and with a gasp of pain, he pried open the wound and applied the pulpy concoction. With the wound bound by a torn strip of fabric, Cathal sat back against the wall.

"Why do ye help us?" asked the uninjured brother.

Cathal didn't know; he had no answer, so he shook his head and silently considered the question. "Because I can," he finally answered.

Both brothers looked at him like he was a simpleton. His answer was concise and honest; to Cathal's mind, it didn't need explaining.

"What are ye called?" asked a brother.

"Cathal."

The brother nodded. "I am Engel, and this is Urs," said Engel, pointing to his injured brother.

Cathal nodded.

"Thank ye fer what ye have done," offered Engel.

Cathal shook his head. "I have done nothing yet. Time will tell if his life will be spared from this injury, but if Urs recovers, then at least he will be healthy when we are executed."

The unkind reminder prompted no further discussion, and Cathal rolled over to sleep.

The next day was a repeat of the last. Hans came with water, took out the waste and left some food, not much, but it was something. He said nothing, but a short time later, he passed Marjoram and Sage through the small gap in the wall just as he'd done the previous day. There was no change in the brother's condition, but Cathal attended to the injury as best he could. This went on for two more days until Cathal noted a remarkable improvement. Urs was recovering. Engel thought it a miracle. Cathal told him it was no such thing and purely a result of creating ideal conditions for nature to heal.

They didn't talk much; the impending date of execution was fast approaching and weighed heavily on all three men. Cathal was trying to decide how he could convince Engels and Urs to kill him. The thought of being hung, drawn, and quartered was disturbing, as was the fact that the lord of the manor had shown no interest in questioning him or the brothers. He had not shown any curiosity, which was equally perplexing. other than they would be providing entertainment for the day. It was a foreboding sign: if the lord had no interest in them, then they were of no value.

"Does anyone know ye are here?" asked Urs.

"Nay, not a soul," Cathal replied.

The afternoon passed in typical silence. Each lost in the darkness of their thoughts.

Bartke and his men were again patrolling the main roads and tracks that headed towards Disibodenberg. Three other knights with him obeyed Gutsherr Gotfridus Brisigavi's instructions to continue their practice of charging unfair levies. They had not had a productive day, and while they had encountered a few travellers, they'd taken very little coin. The *Gutsherr* wouldn't be happy, and the four knights chatted amongst themselves as they waited for their next victim. If no one came soon, they would return to the village as it was late in the afternoon.

The rumbling of an approaching cart drew their interest. Wealthy merchants frequently used carts; the distinctive sound was a good omen. As expected, a cart pulled by an old horse appeared carrying a single person, and Bartke broke from cover and approached the nervous merchant.

"Hail friend," Bartke cordially greeted.

The merchant appeared frightened, which was another good sign, thought Bartke. The more scared they were, the easier they'd hand over their purse.

The cart ground to a halt.

"Where do you go?" the knight asked.

"To, er, *Frau, Frauenklause,* the c, co, convent," stammered the man.

The man did not have the appearance of a typical merchant. Merchants treated everyone like a customer, hoping to make a sale. They were zealous in the protectiveness of their wares, and their eyes spoke of cunning and deceit. This man was different.

"I'm sure ye shall fare well, the convent is kind to merchants," began Bartke. He urged his horse to take a step closer to the cart so he could better see his wares. "You may continue on yer way, good sir, but first, there is the simple matter of a traveller's tax."

As rehearsed, the three companion knights rode from concealment and blocked the cart's path as Bartke reined in his horse near the merchant. The threat was clear.

Without question or protest, the merchant reached into the folds of his clothing and produced a purse, he extended a hand, offering it to the *Raubritter.* "This is all I have, take it. I want no trouble."

Bartke took the purse and looked inside. It wasn't much coin at all. He secured the purse and studied the man.

"Ye can search me. As God is my witness, I have nothing more to give."

Bartke motioned to one of the knights, who dismounted and searched the merchant's possessions and wares. He found nothing.

"It is as I said, ye have all my coin. May I be on my way fer the sun is going down, and I would prefer not to be here?"

Bartke made eye contact with his friends. It was late, and he wanted to return home. "Aye, be on yer way fer these roads are not safe at night," Bartke ironically suggested.

When the wagon was out of sight, Bartke wheeled his horse around, and the four *Raubritter* were only too happy to return to their village."

Not far behind them, a single man on horseback, a scout, covertly followed the four knights, and behind him, nearly a full score of heavily armed men trailed.

CHAPTER TWENTY-SEVEN

Bartke and his three companions unknowingly led the trailing men directly to the hamlet. With care, the twenty-armed hid in the forest near the village and planned their attack. No one, least of *Gutsherr* Gotfridus Brisigavi, was aware of the carnage to follow.

Cathal's eyes opened, and he lay still, trying to determine what had woken him. Engels or Urs snored, but it wasn't them. He sat upright and scooted back into a corner to listen. There were no clues or tell-tale signs anything was amiss, but Cathal trusted his senses; something was wrong.

A dog barked, then another. Someone yelled an obscenity at them, which did little and another, further away, began baying. Cathal cocked his head and focused.

A woman's scream pierced the night and, for a brief moment, silenced the dogs, then another scream, a man. Then pandemonium. He closed his eyes.

The violence was vivid. The baleful bawls of armed men and pitiful answering pleas went unheeded and were abruptly silenced without compassion. Cathal imagined mothers with babies held tightly to their chests and clasping children's hands, running in fear for their lives. He heard them - he lowered his head and felt their fear. The sickening sound of steel against flesh, blade against blade, pealed like an ominous bell that heralded death. He felt ashamed; nothing justified such wanton bloodshed, most of all to this extreme; there was no logical rationalisation for men to dispense such uncaring cruelty on others. The horrisonous symphony intensified then climaxed with a single wailing appeal for mercy only to be silenced with a hateful curse. Even the dogs' previous vocal warnings now obvious by their absence, added to the stillness but not peacefulness.

He couldn't see them, but the brothers, their fear palpable, stood with backs to the wall waiting. For what? Cathal didn't know, and he couldn't care less.

New sounds emerged: the crash of doors being kicked, cries of discovery, and a lone brave dog now barked in earnest protest. Beyond the confines of the stable, the sound of footsteps approached, and they were no longer light and hurried; the footfall were heavier, measured, and deliberate. He brought his knees to his chin and waited. It wasn't a long wait, perhaps a dozen valuable heartbeats, before the stable door crashed open, accompanied by bright light and two wild-eyed men carrying raised swords.

Their eyes, wide open and alert, passed over him without pause and stopped at the brothers. Engels and Urs stared with open-mouthed terror at the two warriors. Nothing was said, not a word spoken. Cathal saw the guilt; their expressions were as clear as words on parchment. Contrition was a language that needed no translation.

Two more men entered the stall and paused. Like the first two, they spared not a moment for him, their morbid attention focused on the brothers. The larger of the warriors turned over his shoulder to another. "Did yer find it?"

"Aye, and plenty more," the warrior confirmed.

Without pause, the larger man nodded, leaned forward and ran his sword through Engels. Before Urs could react, he felt the coldness of a blade through his chest. The brothers were dead. All four warriors finally focused their attention on the man seated on the floor and looked down as if seeing him for the first time.

Cathal didn't turn away and remained silent. Anything he had to say to these men would offend them.

The largest of the warriors took a step closer, and Cathal saw blood dripping from the tip of the dangling sword.

"Why are ye here locked up with them?" he asked. His voice gravelly and harsh, and his eyes blazed.

"Does it matter to ye?" Cathal asked.

"Nay, perhaps not," he replied. His three associates wandered outside the stall. They'd already lost interest.

Cathal heard the unmistakable sounds of looting. Whoever these men were, they were systematically going through the decimated village, taking anything of value. He doubted anyone remained alive. He had no desire to live and hoped the warrior would quickly end his misery. He smelled smoke; they were burning buildings. "Ye are free to take my life."

The sword arced down and stabbed into the wood floor. Cathal tensed. With a creaking of leather, the warrior crouched and looked intently into his eyes.

He wasn't a young man as he first appeared, and Cathal surmised he was the group leader.

"Ye don't fear death?" the warrior asked.

Cathal shook his head. "I welcome death, fer there is nothing to live fer."

One hand firmly gripped the sword still impaled into the floor, and with his free hand, he rubbed his thick, full beard.

"Anno!" someone yelled.

The warrior turned his head and looked out the door before refocusing on Cathal. "The brothers were bad men." He looked over his shoulder at the two lifeless bodies on the floor. "They stole coin from us." He waited a couple of heartbeats and, with a grunt, slowly stood, towering over Cathal, pulled his sword free, turned, and walked from the stable.

Cathal remained unmoving as the village was systematically destroyed. Eventually, a warrior entered the stall and instructed him to leave. The stable wasn't spared and set alight. Outside, what he saw was no different from what he had imagined. The entire village had been looted, and all buildings had been torched. Bodies, men, women and children lay where they'd been slaughtered. It was sickening. Nothing and no one, except himself, had been spared. In a daze, he wandered away from the carnage and headed into the forest to seclusion and safety, where nature had order, purpose, and design.

It took some time, but he eventually found his way to the cabin he'd built for Isolde and himself. Since their departure weeks or months ago, he wasn't sure, nothing had been disturbed; it was how they'd left it. Isolde's presence was strong. Her possessions, smell, and her clothes… the ache in his heart and the emptiness as confronting as the horror he'd witnessed in the village a week ago. He lay upon the bed he'd built for them and again considered ending his life.

Without Isolde, his existence had no meaning. He'd been unable to help and come to her aid when she needed him. Without complaint, she'd suffered and endured the relentless consuming pain as her organs, one by one, ceased to function. His helplessness and inability to heal and cure never more apparent. He knew his fragile and tenuous life was gratuitous and now understood that he no longer served a purpose. Consumed by despair and exhaustion, his eyelids grew heavy, and he succumbed to the inevitability of despair, exhaustion, and sleep.

In abject sadness, he woke, touching his face as if feeling the sharp sting of a slap in the dawning familiarity of his surroundings. Unsettling dreams and visions of his mother, Macha, scolding him for his folly and self-pity haunted him. He couldn't shake free from her impassioned voice rebuking him for his weakness when faced with adversity and challenge—the fierceness of her argument as real as if she'd slapped him. He couldn't ignore.

He ventured outside and set traps for game. While overgrown, his garden contained plenty of food, and a day turned into two. A week into four, and sun and warmth into cold and snow. His body, not long ago, injured and frail, healed and recovered, and his mind, uncertain and erratic, became resolute and determined. He turned his frustrations at not being able to cure Isolde into a desire to learn more about the body and nature so he could help people heal and recover. His night of terror in the village reinforced his newfound belief everyone had a right to live, himself included. From their frequent discussions, Sister Hildegard had planted the notion that if you took a step back from a problem and became objective, a different perspective and solution would present itself. He used that concept to analyse his treatment of Isolde. He still missed her and always would, but he adjusted to her absence and accepted her death. His foolish words to the warrior that night in the village were ill-considered, and he was grateful to Anno, the warrior, that he refused his request. One thing was certain, and his resolve was firm: he couldn't continue to hide from people.

Fully recovered from past injuries, he began to hone his defensive skills and practised endlessly with sword, bow and staff. Gryffen had been incredibly skilled, had mastered many weapons, and patiently taught Cathal everything he knew. He'd often comment that Cathal had unusually swift reflexes and exceptional coordination, making him not just good at weaponry but superior. Any lord would welcome a warrior with these skills, he told him. While vehemently against needless killing, Cathal knew self-preservation was crucial to survival, and he would ensure he would not succumb to the brutality of those who sought to take advantage. With that mindset, Cathal practised tirelessly and didn't just hone his skills, he improved them.

Of growing interest, he heard more people passing through the forest. They weren't merchants or peasants, and on closer inspection observed, they were fully armed knights. Some came in large groups accompanied by squires, attendants, and servants. Others travelled alone yet their demeanour was festive and didn't portray the sombreness or false bravado of men preparing to do battle. Curiosity had the better of him, and he made his way down to the trail to inquire as a lone knight drew near.

Cathal stepped out from behind a tree some distance from the approaching knight.

Instantly on guard, the knight's hand went to the hilt of his sword, and his head rotated, anxiously looking for signs of an ambush.

"Hail, good, Sir!" Cathal greeted. He carried no weapons besides his staff and waited for the knight to approach."

The knight reigned in about twenty paces and kept his hand on his sword. Wary, his eyes flicked from tree to tree, looking for danger. "Greetings," he responded with suspicion.

"In recent days, many knights have travelled along this path. Should I fear a battle?"

The knight laughed. Cathal noticed he had removed his hand from his sword.

"Nay, fer we travel to a tourney in Dijon. The Duke of Burgundy is hosting a tournament with great prizes. I seek to make a name fer myself," smiled the knight.

Cathal scratched at his face. "Dijon is some distance; it must be a big purse."

"Aye, for winners, the prize is substantial, but I seek victory in contests of skill to make myself known fer I am a valiant swordsman and a most competent adversary for the unwary."

Cathal nodded. He knew knights were vain and wanted nothing more than to be acknowledged as superior and skilled in combat. "When does this tourney begin?"

"At the next moon," replied the knight.

"Then perhaps I will see ye there and wish you well, good Sir."

The knight laughed again. "Why do you intend to go? Will ye enter into contest?"

Cathal's expression didn't change. "Nay, fer I will come to the aid of those who need care from injury."

"Are ye a Barber?"

Cathal shook his head. "Nay, I am a healer," he proudly stated. "I wish ye well."

The knight squeezed his legs, and his destrier responded and began to walk closer. "I hope I shall not be in need. What are ye called?"

"Cathal."

"It would heed ye well to remember me, fer I am Sir Gerhart from Frankenfort[39]."

Cathal was impressed. The knight was journeying some distance to attend this tourney, so it must be important. "If it pleases ye, I will call on ye in Dijon, Sir Gerhart."

The knight responded quickly, and his laugh thundered through the forest. "Not to administer to my care, eh, Cathal."

Cathal didn't understand the humour. "Good day, Sir." And he trudged back into the forest towards home as the knight continued on his way.

The bones told a story. Just as his tutor Lohier had taught him all those years ago, Cathal tipped the old bones from a small cloth bag. The scattered fragments fell haphazardly to the ground, and he squatted beside them to study and interpret their random alignment. It had become second nature to read the bones, and from what they told him, it was an easy decision. If he dedicated his life to healing, then a tourney would be the perfect place to

39 Frankenfort – Modern day Frankfurt.

begin. With his mind made up, he prepared.

The pride and ego of men saw them enter contests, testing each other in various martial contests. The intent wasn't to kill but to best an opponent, claim victory, be rewarded with a healthy prize and hopefully enhance your reputation. Unfortunately, every competition saw a loser, and often the defeated were injured. Sometimes mildly, other times severely, which generally required the attention of a barber. Cathal disliked barbers; in his opinion, they were brutal, unskilled men with little to no knowledge of the human body and, with enthusiasm, went about removing limbs and body parts without consideration or care. He'd seen the results of their handiwork before and was disgusted at the results. More often than not, needless amputations killed many undeserving men. In memory and in honour of Isolde and his mother, he would journey to Dijon and save lives.

However, one thing was perplexing: the bones reminded him about his past and an injured Templar knight. As far as he could recall, there was only one such instance when he and his mother twice encountered a Templar knight and saved his life on both occasions. Cathal had no understanding of the significance of this knight, and if he still lived, he would be quite old.

With no intention of returning to his forest home, he sorted through his meagre possessions and took only what he could carry; everything else was left to whoever discovered his modest dwelling. As the sun rose, he left his forest sanctuary, the place of such happiness and grief, and headed south towards the Frankian town of Dijon some distance away.

CHAPTER TWENTY-EIGHT

Cathal determined it would be a lengthy thirty-day journey before he arrived in Dijon, quicker if he could purchase a horse along the way as his horse had been taken from the village. He still had the coin he took from the Northmen and would rather buy a horse than carry the coin's weight when travelling by foot.

Along the journey, he had time to think and contemplate his tumultuous past, a confused present and a tenuous future. Reading the bones guided him but never painted a complete picture and, as always, left him questioning his fleeting relationship with the Templar Knight all those years ago.

It was on his fifth night, after having eaten his evening meal and he was laying beneath the expansive branches of a large tree when it dawned on him. Something he'd missed earlier, and it centred around the Norsemen. He'd never really learned the whole reason why they had come for him, and when he thought back, he understood, at least in part, their motivation. They'd come to kill him, and they'd brought with them a high priest, someone trained in similar skills that he had for observing and interpreting the signs of nature.

They had no personal motive to see his death; it was more than that, and the Norse priest had been influenced by what he'd seen. He recalled his mother telling him that his fate was assured. *What fate*? He wondered. Reading the bones only reinforced what she'd repeatedly told him, that he was destined to help and save someone's life. Someone who the Norsemen didn't want to survive? *Who*? he questioned, whose life would he save? Undoubtedly, the person was linked to the Templar knight, but it wasn't the Templar. Answers didn't come, and Cathal didn't push it, he knew at the right time, he would understand.

After the second week of his journey the bones provided a clue. A baby! He understood now that it was the son of the Templar knight; he was the key to this mystery and perhaps a link to his fate. The bones shed no further light on the subject, but that was enough for now. He made a mental note to be on the lookout for Norsemen, as they might try again. This time, and if they came, he'd be ready for them.

He'd made exceptionally good progress. As his second week of travelling drew to a close, he saw more and more people. He'd avoided contact with communities for most of his life, choosing to remain safely in the protective leafy shadows and be unseen rather than be vulnerable out in the open. Macha, his mother, had been cautious, and after she died, he continued the practice, especially after the incident with the young knights who enjoyed torture and savagery. But now, he remained in the open. It was uncomfortable at first, but then he realised that you could be in full view of everyone, and people wouldn't see you, they looked right past. You could hide in plain sight unless you acted in a way that drew attention to yourself.

That night, a young man entered his campsite and asked if his master could join him. The young man, a squire, informed that his master, a knight, had developed an illness, was too weak to ride a horse, and was now being transported in their wagon. One night was all he asked, and they would be on their way in the morn.

Cathal's interest was piqued, and he readily agreed. A short time later, a wagon rumbled into his camp along with the squire, another youngish lad, and an attendant wagoneer, a surly, uncommunicative man. Too weak to sit, the knight was laying in the back of the wagon and groaning in distress.

With help, Cathal moved the knight close to his fire and made him comfortable before closely studying him.

"What can ye tell me about his illness," Cathal asked the squire.

"Six days ago, he complained of a gut pain. The next day, it worsened, and he couldn't eat or drink. I tried to gives 'im water, but he would take only a mouthful, nothing more."

"What was the last thing he ate before becoming sick, and did ye eat what he ate?" Cathal asked, suspecting tainted food was the simple cause of the knight's misery."

"Nay fer Sir Joss, ate in a tavern, we ate elsewhere," said the squire, looking at his young associate for affirmation. "We didn't know what to do."

Both youths looked concerned, and rightly so, Cathal thought. If something happened to their master, the boys would have nothing and must fend for themselves.

Gut problems were commonplace, and Cathal had ample leaves and berries to treat the routine malady. He put water to boil and prepared to make a potent medicinal tea. While waiting, he cut a small piece of ginger root and gave it to Sir Joss to chew on. The ginger would settle his stomach and allow the knight to drink the tea made from pulped leaves and berries to combat the canker in his abdomen.

By sunrise, Sir Joss was feeling better, and Cathal instructed him to drink as much water as possible, by midday, the knight was assisted back into the wagon, and they all set off together for Dijon.

Sir Joss regained his strength, and by the next day he was again riding his horse. Cathal learned that Sir Joss was the second oldest son of Rudolf of Rheinfelden, the Duke of Swabia. As

Sir Joss explained, his father, Rudolph, was an unforgiving, cold man with no time for his children, except the oldest son and heir to whom he was devoted.

To Cathal, that explained the wagon with all the supplies, equipment, the spare horses and the two young squires. Sir Joss had no shortage of coin, and as he explained, he wanted to prove himself in Dijon and, in acclaimed victory, sought the love and attention from his father.

They'd travelled some distance and were only a day's ride from Dijon when Sir Joss reigned in beside the wagon where Cathal sat. After a short time, he edged his horse closer. "Why is it ye travel to the tourney in Dijon?"

"I must be somewhere, and people will need my help," he shrugged. "Dijon is as good as any place."

"That is the only reason?" asked the knight.

Cathal remained silent.

"Ye carry a sword, a bow and a staff, yet no armour, and do not present yerself as a warrior, it begs the question, that is why I ask."

"I carry weapons only to protect myself, not to fight or kill for a liege lord or coin," Cathal offered.

It was Sir Joss who remained silent and studied the enigmatic man in the wagon. What Cathal said made sense, however, and by all appearances, Cathal appeared as a peasant, but he was educated, he just didn't know what he was educated in. His first thought was the Church, but there was nothing about the man that suggested he had links to them, and so far, he'd not spoken of God or any religious matters. At first, he thought he may have been a mercenary who sold his fighting skills for a purse. But again, Cathal had been clear that he had no liege and had a disdain for fighting and killing other than in defence.

Sir Joss was perplexed, in his world, you were either a warrior, peasant, merchant, or with the Church. Cathal was neither. He showed no subservient characteristics of a peasant, had not the silky patter of a merchant… but to pry wasn't considered polite, and Cathal had been adept and ridding him of his gut ailment and proven he was a healer. *Perhaps that's all he is*, thought the knight - a healer. Sir Joss turned away from Cathal and spurred his horse to canter to a rise just ahead to see what lay beyond.

They arrived in Dijon two days before the first contests were scheduled to begin. Huge tents were erected where colourful battle flags proudly flew. Knights and their entourages were camped everywhere, and there were hundreds of them, too many to count. Typical of such a spectacle, merchants came peddling wares, peasants sought work, blacksmiths set up shop to repair broken equipment, and whores and troubadours vied for attention and coin. Bards, artists and poets congregated and, with typical aloofness, judged people with whispered convictions of their liberal beliefs.

As Cathal anticipated, it truly was a wonder, and he stared in undisguised wide-eyed disbelief. He had never seen so many people gathered in one enormous group outside of any town he'd visited. The confusion was astonishing. There were brown-skinned people, black, yellow and every colour in between. Some were short, others tall, and many were enormous in overdeveloped muscular bodies. He saw shifty-eyed men, women and children casually loitering in shadows, looking for opportunity and advantage, and he frowned disapprovingly at hawkers peddling magical remedies and potions.

Sir Joss invited Cathal to camp with him and believed they would be safer from thieves if they remained together. While Sir Joss rode away to reacquaint with friends, Cathal set up his meagre possessions as the squires and Wagoneer erected Sir Joss's modest tent on open ground.

There were disagreements aplenty, arrogant knights with their perceived honour easily offended sought justice, and a simple dispute escalated into an unsanctioned contest which attracted curious onlookers. Already, injured men were carried away to be treated by barbers, and the tournament had yet to begin.

Cathal mingled and took in the sights. He saw Norsemen; their skin markings and garish adornments affixed to beards stood out in contrast to others. They were part of larger Norman groups, and he instinctively knew they weren't a threat to him. He ignored them and continued past and observed a barber beneath an open-sided tent about to remove an arm from an injured knight. The barber, a large muscular man, wielded a saw and waved it around, laughing with an associate as the knight screamed and pleaded to spare his blood-soaked arm. Friends held him down as he writhed in sheer terror. Oblivious to the emotions of the fearful knight, the barber continued with his light-hearted jest.

Cathal couldn't help himself and stepped closer to inspect the injury. It was an ugly wound, and as best as he could tell, a sword had sliced down the lower forearm, cutting through flesh, sinew and muscle, scraping alongside bone. A flap of skin hung from the exposed wound as blood streamed onto the ground.

"He will die unless ye stop the blood," he said to the barber, who only just saw the stranger bent over inspecting the injury.

Perhaps it was the authoritative tone of his voice or his confidence that caused everyone to stop what they were doing and stare at him. "Bind his arm," Cathal added. The timbre of his voice rich and smooth.

A man, possibly a squire, found a strap and immediately wrapped it around the knight's upper arm following Cathal's instruction.

"Be gone, away with ye!" shouted the indignant barber and

stomped towards Cathal, waving the saw like an axe.

Two other knights, friends of the stricken knight lying on the table, weren't sure what to do and gazed uncertainly at the stranger and the impending clash with the much larger barber, who was less than thrilled with the interfering interloper.

It appeared to everyone watching that the stranger would lose his head as the barber attacked. Cathal straightened. In a blur, his staff rotated, stopped horizontally to the ground, and then firmly struck the barber in the middle of his upper chest. The barber dropped like a felled tree, gasping for air. Cathal didn't spare him another thought. The knights looked at each other in total surprise.

He saw a pile of cloth torn into strips on a nearby table, and he placed the flap back over the exposed wound and bound it to the consternation of the injured knight.

"What are ye doing?" asked the confused knight between uncontrolled gasps of pain.

Cathal quickly looked at the barber, who still lay full length on the ground, trying to recover his breath. "Do ye want me to save yer arm?"

"Can ye?" asked another knight. "Have ye the knowledge?"

"Aye, but if ye want me to help, then bring him to my camp," Cathal instructed.

"Save my arm!" appealed the knight.

Feeling better, the barber cursed loudly as he rose unsteadily to his feet. One of the knights stepped closer to the red-faced barber and slowly extracted his sword. "Ye will leave well enough alone," he instructed.

The knight was placed on a litter, and Cathal led the small procession back to his camp where he immediately began making a poultice to prevent the savage wound from corruption. He sat on a blanket beside the knight and ground various herbs and roots into a pulp with his mortar and pestle.

One of the knights stepped up and crouched down beside him. "What are ye called?"

"Cathal."

"Irish?" asked the knight.

"Does it matter?"

The knight shrugged and pointed to his friend, who lay in agony and bathed in sweat. "Sir Virgil is a powerful lord and will reward ye well if ye can spare his arm."

Cathal paused a moment to look up at the knight.

"If he dies, his family will not look kindly upon ye," continued the knight.

"If he dies, it is because the wound became corrupt and sepsis prevailed, not because I killed him," Cathal added and then resumed the grinding. His concoction had turned yellow.

"What is it ye are making," asked the knight.

Cathal sighed. "A paste to prevent the wound from becoming foul."

"It appears to me that it might kill."

"Frankincense and Tumeric will ease his pain, and the Yarrow will help stop the bleeding. Witch Hazel and lavender will prevent corruption - do ye want to know more?" Before the knight could answer, Cathal continued. "Ye might be best to leave me to attend to yer friend fer then if he dies, I will tell his family ye are to blame."

The knight smiled. "Thank ye fer what ye are doing. I will leave ye to yer magic." He eased himself upright and stood back to give Cathal space.

A small crowd followed the procession to Sir Joss's camp and now gawked to see what was happening. They watched intently as Cathal removed the temporary bandage and cleaned the wound as best he could with water infused with lavender. Satisfied, and with the help of Sir Virgil's friends who held him down, Cathal applied a thin layer of paste to the open wound as Sir Virgil screamed in agony. With a sharp piece of bone and thread, he began to suture the loose flap back to his arm. The unconscious knight had stopped writhing as he applied more paste on top of the wound before wrapping his arm in a clean cloth.

Sir Joss and his squires arrived just as Cathal finished and were surprised at the group of people assembled at his camp. "What have ye done, Cathal? Have ye been in contest already and maimed a knight?" he teased.

"Ye know this man?" questioned Sir Virgil's friend.

"Aye, he spared me from a wicked gut ailment and travelled with us. This is my camp," answered Sir Joss. "Who might ye be?"

Fergive me, I am Sir Michael, and here lies my liege, Sir Virgil Paganel, lord of Birmingham Manor, in England. Sir Virgil was wounded in a fight with a German ruffian, and a barber was about to remove his arm. Cathal appeared, and, er, here we are."

Sir Joss looked thoughtful. "But his arm remains?"

Sir Michael smiled. "Cathal took exception to the barber's methods and insisted the arm could be saved."

"Doesn't surprise me. I am Sir Joss, son of Rudolf of Rheinfelden, the Duke of Swabia."

"Ah, then I am familiar with yer brother, Rudolf. It is an honour to make yer acquaintance, Sir Joss."

At the end of the second day, another unlucky victim of an unfortunate incident with a sword sought Cathal's help. As far as Cathal was concerned, the injuries were minor, but if not treated with care, the price of such a misfortune could cost a limb or, even worse, a life.

While Cathal was loath to admit it, he was in his element. A few people came to him seeking advice, not just because of his expertise but because he was sober and his answers succinct.

Seeking coin for his services wasn't his objective, as he wasn't motivated by greed or ambition. Cathal's sincerity and dedication to helping those in need became evident, and word began to spread.

CHAPTER TWENTY-NINE

Sir Joss stood near his large tent with hands on hips and looked around at the four injured men receiving treatment from Cathal. "These men are fortunate, Cathal. Not only have ye saved their lives, but also their dignity."

Cathal didn't reply. He had nothing to add to the statement. As he understood it, it was a fact and, therefore, accurate.

"I hope I do not return here this afternoon upon a litter but firmly on my two feet, fer if you tend to me, then surely I would have been defeated in my first contest and likely injured."

Cathal tore his protective gaze away from the men under his care and faced his new friend. "If ye keep dropping yer right elbow, I'll have a place ready fer ye."

Sir Joss's eyes widened. "What say ye?"

"I saw ye practice. Yer right elbow. When ye defend, ye lower it, preventing yerself from counterattacking with strength. For yer opponent, he sees it as a weakness and yer right side becomes his target." Cathal walked away to attend to a knight in distress and left Sir Joss somewhat perplexed.

Sir Joss followed two steps behind. "What do ye know of swords and contests of skill? By yer own words, ye are a healer, not a warrior or a knight. What does a healer know of technique, strategy, combat and honour?"

Cathal remembered being held captive in the hamlet not that long ago and how the knights came and slew everyone without mercy. *Where was their honour?* he questioned to himself. He chose not to answer Sir Joss's question and helped a knight to drink water, then looked up at Sir Joss. "Think upon my words as healing. If ye don't drop yer elbow and win, then I have healed ye." He offered a rare smile.

Not every knight who lost a contest was injured. There were established rules, and a knight could yield to his opponent if he felt he couldn't win. Yielding wasn't a preferred option, but it spared lives and injury, and yet it took a knight's dignity, which, for many, was a cost too high to pay. Knights contested each other in various disciplines, and some events were completed on horses, others with feet firmly on the ground with an assortment of lethal weapons. As the first few days passed and preliminary bouts began, reputations were already enhanced, and crowd size increased as competitors arrived from everywhere, including England.

Lord Oliver Hansard of Dearthington had seen fit to ensure his son, Sir Lambert, and his two closest friends, Sir Robert and Sir Crispin, were well-funded and equipped for their journey to Dijon. The Duke of Burgundy was an acquaintance of Lord Hansard, although not close, but it was important for Lord Oliver Hansard to have his son represent him at the tournament. Success would reflect well upon his standing with the duke, and Sir Lambert did not need to be persuaded to attend and compete. As many in Dearthington could attest, Sir Lambert's level of confidence was well-known and often stated. The lord had ensured his son had suitable staff, servants, and equipment so Lambert would be comfortable and represent him to the best of his ability. As the lord confided in his wife, Lady Brenna, "Lambert has remarkable skill with a sword, and unfortunately, fer him, he knows it. This tourney could offer him a valuable lesson and perhaps, when he competes with others, teach him about humility in victory."

While Lord Oliver Hansard was not an influential English lord with wealthy, productive manors, he did outlay considerable coin for this venture to Dijon, which was more than was deemed wise and certainly more than he could afford.

Sir Lambert had spare horses, a cluster of tents for dining, sleeping, and ample equipment for training and competitions. Attentive servants saw to his care and well-being and he even had the added luxury of a blacksmith. Anyone unfamiliar with Sir Lambert incorrectly assumed his liege and sponsor was powerful and wealthy.

After spending the morning training with his friends, Sir Lambert, Sir Robert and Sir Crispin went on a walk to explore the temporary town the Duke of Burgundy created. There was much to see, most of all, Sir Lambert was interested in the quality of the opposition he would face, and together the three knights wandered through the encampment, stopping to chat with other knights.

There was a haughtiness and arrogance to Sir Lambert that did not warm him to others. If Lord Oliver Hansard expected his son to forge new alliances and strengthen existing bonds, he would have been bitterly disappointed.

By mid-afternoon, the sun was hot, and Sir Lambert suggested they return to their camp and enjoy some wine in the shade when Sir Crispin stopped to stare at something in the distance.

"Come, Crispin, my throat is parched," grizzled Sir Lambert.

"It is he. Do ye see that peasant," he raised an arm and pointed toward a small campsite where several men stood while others lay on cots or on the ground. "I believe he is familiar to us. Is this not so?"

Sir Lambert and Sir Robert looked in the direction their friend indicated.

"I wouldn't believe it had I not witnessed it. It's that peasant we had sport with," exclaimed Sir Lambert.

"What business could he have here?" asked Sir Robert.

Sir Lambert continued to watch the man. "I do believe we have some unfinished matters to settle with him."

"He should have died," added Sir Crispin.

"If I judge him by what I witness, then he is a barber. That explains why he survived," stated Sir Lambert.

"Is it wise to pursue a vendetta against him?" Sir Robert continued, "He obviously has friends, and this could prove awkward fer us."

"Only if he were to die in an underhanded way, but if it was a fair contest fer all to see, then that would be different." Sir Lambert turned to face his lifelong friend. "Have ye not the stomach, Robert?"

Sir Robert didn't have the appetite for the savage games Sir Lambert called sport, but he didn't want him to know it. "It matters not to me; I care not if a peasant lives or dies."

Sir Lambert turned to Sir Crispin and waited for his response.

Sir Crispin shrugged. "What do ye have in mind?"

"Come, let us honour our dear friend Sir Guy with wine and recall how he died while I ponder how to solve our problem with this heathen," he clapped Sir Robert on the back, and the three knights headed towards their camp some distance away.

Cathal felt the hair on his neck prickle and, without making it conspicuous, sought the cause of his discomfort. It didn't take long before he saw the three knights, and it sent a shiver down his spine. He recalled their cold and sadistic penchant for brutality and knew there would be a reckoning. He believed the three knights would come fer him and finish what they had begun.

Three days passed, and he never felt their presence again, yet he knew they were nearby and would come for him when he least expected it. Unfortunately, he didn't have time to dwell on the appearance of the three sadistic knights. More injured men came to him for care as his reputation as a healer grew just as much as the knights who claimed victory in contest.

He didn't ask for coin from those who sought his expertise, yet it became a point of honour for knights to insist on payment. The higher the gratuity, the more respect a knight received from his peers. As such, Cathal could afford to hire help. There was no shortage of people looking to earn a little extra or to fill empty purses, and he cautiously selected the most suitable.

Dafydd was a jovial, calm and understated Welshman with a ready smile and quick to offer a kind word. He'd once been a priest, had learning, and an insatiable curious mind. Unfortunately for some, Dafydd was also rather amorous, and he'd upset local villagers in Abertawe[40], where he'd been involved and caught in numerous passionate trysts with local married women. In fear for his life, he'd wisely fled and travelled extensively through England and Frankia until he wore out his welcome through his habitual and untethered cravings.

When Cathal spoke to Dafydd, he was taken by the Welshman's honesty. He freely admitted his shortcomings, spoke about his interest in healing and expressed a genuine need to learn more to help the unfortunate. Cathal believed him and, with some certainty, was sure women wouldn't be coming to him for care at the tournament, so he employed the Welshman as a *Medicus*, a job description Dafydd suggested. Cathal didn't care what Dafydd called himself as long as he followed instructions and did exactly as he was told. As it turned out, Dafydd was liked by all and genuinely cared for the men who needed help.

In contrast to Cathal's personality, who was reticent yet unrestrained and, at times, brutally honest in expressing himself, Dafydd was the opposite. He had an outgoing, gregarious personality, was quick to laugh and possessed a wry sense of humour that the knights under his care warmed to. However, what wasn't

40 *Abertawe - Swansea, Wales*

contested was Cathal's knowledge and absolute ability to heal.

On the first evening, after eating their evening meal, Dafydd sang—his powerful voice melodic, and expressive. A small crowd gathered, and Dafydd engaged everyone and welcomed them all, including Cathal, to join in chorus. Unused to such forms of social entertainment, Cathal was initially reluctant, but memories of his mother's talent and voice returned, and he soon joined in. It was afterwards, when the crowd dispersed that Dafydd remarked on Cathal's silky intonations.

"Ye have a glorious voice, Cathal. The natural timbre is unlike anything I have heard. Yer voice is healing fer the spirit, and yer gift is truly a blessing from God."

Cathal shrugged. "I have no time fer wistful ballads of fair maidens or the dank green valleys of Wales."

"Aye, and yer skill at healing injuries is seen as a miracle by many. But we both know that skill is from learning, but yer voice can bring joy and heal the mind, fer ye have no potions or poultices for treating the melancholy. Yer voice is like a tonic for those afflicted and brings joy to those in need."

"And sadness." Cathal rose to check on a knight. He turned back over his shoulder. "Singing is for the idle."

Dafydd followed a step behind. "When ye see the faces of men listening, it isn't sadness, Cathal, they are memories. Memories of a time past, of loved ones and experiences. Those memories are what keeps us in touch with who we are. That is what I see in the faces of the men who listen."

"I see injured men who need care, Dafydd. See they all have water."

Whenever Cathal left their camp, he wore a sword and always carried his staff. He had no illusions that the three knights would leave him alone and fully expected they would do something; he just didn't know how or what. He couldn't stay confined to his campsite, he had to venture out to visit merchants and purchase food for the ailing. He had to replenish his supply of herbs, plants and other essential things to aid in the quick recovery of wounded men. He even had to pay merchants to deliver water. The coin he received as a gratuity was being rapidly spent.

Sir Lambert became obsessed with Cathal. He felt an inherent jealousy that he couldn't explain or rationalise. He observed how all knights courteously respected the peasant, irrespective of their status. No one said an unkind word to or about him, which irked the young knight to no end because the peasant was receiving more attention than himself. Yet he had already proven himself victorious in contests and easily won four competitions with sword on foot, and while some had acknowledged his skills, he felt the praise was polite and insincere.

He wanted to impress and excite powerful lords and knights with his abilities, but he couldn't explain to himself why others didn't warm to his charms and evident superior martial skills. He'd made a few new friends, but they were shallow and largely inconsequential in a place where power and influence were status.

He knew his name; everyone did; he was simply known as Cathal. Where he came from, no one knew, and it didn't matter to others, but it did to him. *What of the peasant woman who helped him? What became of her*? he wondered.

Of interest to Sir Lambert was the sword Cathal now wore when he left camp. Being armed changed the rules considerably and allowed for opportunities where none previously existed. He discussed it with Sir Robert and Sir Crispin, but even they seem to have lost interest in exacting punishment on a most deserving man.

Every day, Sir Lambert passed by his campsite. He didn't care if the heathen peasant saw him, but there was no indication if he had seen him walk by. This only caused frustration because he wanted to experience and know Cathal was frightened and afraid of him. The thought of the peasant cowering and shaking in abject fear as a sword tip pressed into his flesh, that feeling of power and control, was intoxicating and erotic. He wanted to hear him plead and beg for mercy. At night, back at his camp, he would lay on his cot and imagine the carnal thrill of repeatedly slicing through Cathal's flesh and watching his organs spill out and life-giving blood slowly drain from his body - it gave him a shiver of pleasure. He licked his lips as he could almost taste it.

CHAPTER THIRTY

Sir Joss was scheduled to fight at first light, and he invited Cathal to observe. He wouldn't be the only one contesting, and sixteen knights would face one another in eight contests of skill.

Even Dafydd encouraged Cathal to go. "I have matters well in hand here, Cathal. Your friend invites ye to attend to him. Respect the friendship and go."

Dafydd has such a pleasing disposition. It's no wonder women have a weakness for him, Cathal mused. The Welshman's presence in Dijon had been enlightening; after all, Cathal acknowledged, he'd spent much of his own life secluded from communities and hiding, and he'd begun to learn more from Dafydd about interacting with others and how not to offend. "Very well, but if something happens, if a knight's condition worsens, send word."

Dafydd smiled. "As ye command, Cathal."

An entourage of Sir Joss's friends and supporters walked through the encampment with Cathal following. As always, he had his sword on his hip and his staff firmly in his grip. They arrived at the field where the contests were to be held, and other groups of knights and supporters were already there preparing.

Cathal saw the three young knights immediately, and unconsciously his hand went to his chest, where one of those knights had slit him open from breastbone to groin and had smiled in perverted pleasure whilst doing it. He still recalled the horror of seeing the gratification on the knight's face as he was slit open. He knew the perversion wasn't normal, that to experience joy while committing such a brutal act was the behaviour of a tormented soul. Cathal didn't seek revenge, he didn't want retribution, he just felt pity for the young knight, and as the sun rose, that knight now stood twenty paces away, already drinking mead, brazenly watching him with undisguised loathing.

After the formality of agreeing to the rules, all contestants stood anxiously facing each other in designated areas marked by flags. Sir Joss was paired with an English knight, Sir Crispin, who was largely unknown to most but had acquitted himself quite well in previous preliminary bouts. Cathal noticed Sir Crispin's two friends were not competing in this round. He stepped up to one of Sir Joss's friends.

"That knight, yonder, standing with one other, do ye know his name?" Cathal didn't point but inclined his head.

"Aye, Sir Lambert is English. His liege and father is Lord Oliver Hansard of Dearthington, and he is making a name for himself here as a swordsman, but alas, he is rather arrogant and fond of himself and his abilities. The other, on the right, is Sir Robert; his liege is also Lord Hansard. Both fought previously and won and will contest today's victors in two days."

Cathal didn't ask any more questions; he'd heard enough.

The contest began, and sixteen knights cautiously evaluated their opponents with tentative strokes and parries. Sir Joss looked to have an advantage over the younger and quicker Sir Crispin because of technique and experience. As Cathal had previously warned Sir Joss, his right arm was held too low, and Sir Crispin had already seen the weakness and sought to capitalise. A quick slash and Sir Joss was struck on his hip. Not serious, but enough to cause some concern.

All contestants were skilled, but fatigue soon took its toll. Rather than risk an injury in defeat, many took a knee to yield. Sir Joss fought well and, having learned an early and painful lesson, adjusted his right arm position as Cathal had previously advised;

no one could tell if the slight injury on his hip caused him difficulty as he began to slowly dominate his rival. Sir Crispin showed signs of fatigue, having spent his energy early and was starting to struggle under the relentless onslaught of Sir Joss's methodical attack, but he stubbornly refused to yield.

Spectators yelled encouragement and applauded the victors, while at the last remaining contest, Sir Joss pressed his growing advantage. Cathal watched Sir Lambert yelling frantic instructions to his beleaguered friend while others tut-tutted, knowing that failing to yield at this point could result in a serious injury. Yet Sir Crispin adamantly refused to concede. Cathal wondered if pride or the need to impress his arrogant friend prevented him from acknowledging defeat. Sir Lambert continued to yell advice, but it was pointless; Sir Crispin was spent.

While exhausted, Sir Joss had held himself to good account, and Sir Crispin could do nothing more than weakly defend. The battle was lost, and everyone watching could see the frustration on Sir Joss's face as his opponent stubbornly refused to surrender. After evading another wild, uncoordinated swing by Sir Crispin, Sir Joss charged in, placed a foot behind Sir Crispin and shoved. The young knight fell back onto the ground, and Sir Joss stood over him with sword raised. "Do – ye - yield, - Sir?" he yelled between tortured breaths.

Sir Joss's friends were closest to the two duelling knights, and Cathal clearly heard Sir Crispin, even though he spoke softly. "Aye, I yield."

"Nay, ye fool," cried Sir Lambert angrily. "ye could have had him!" He threw a mug of ale onto the ground and stamped his foot in fury.

The contest was over. Sir Joss drove his sword downwards into the earth and placed both hands on his thighs as he sucked in lungsful of needed air.

Sir Crispin was still seated on the ground and as Sir Joss bent over, Sir Crispin flicked up the tip of his sword and attempted to drive it into the side of the victorious knight. Sir Joss saw the unexpected move and grabbed his sword as he lunged sideways to avoid the thrusting sword tip. In a single powerful response, slashed at Sir Crispin's exposed neck. Everyone witnessed the move, and all spectators fell silent in horror as blood erupted from a severed artery. Sir Crispin collapsed, falling backwards as his hands tried to stem the blood flow.

Cathal ran over to help the stricken young knight, but it was too late; there was little he could do. The blow was fatal, and Sir Crispin died within moments.

"Ye killed him!" cried Sir Lambert as he ran over. "Ye killed him! The contest wasn't over! Ye murdered him!" he screamed in rage.

Sir Joss's expression said it all; he was horrified. He'd just defended himself against a competitor who'd cheated. He'd heard him yield, just as many had, and then the young knight had attempted to stab him when the contest had ended. As any competing knight would have done in a similar situation, and as the rules allowed, Sir Joss acted purely in self-defence.

Sir Lambert rushed towards Sir Joss, roughly pushing aside onlookers and stopped, their bodies almost touching. "By all that is holy and by Saint Michael the Archangel, I will have ye, and ye will suffer by my hand."

Sir Joss wasn't having any of it. "Yer man surrendered, and I accepted his plea to yield, and then he tried to stab me. Yer man cheated and I committed no foul, and it is within the rules. I have a right to defend myself."

A chorus of support swelled, and Sir Lambert suddenly realised he was surrounded by Sir Joss's sympathetic supporters. There was nothing he could do.

"I will protest," Sir Lambert stated. He turned to walk away, saw Cathal, stopped, raised an arm, and pointed to him. "And ye, yer thief, I will take yer life too."

Sir Joss was lying on his side, and Cathal was treating his numerous minor injuries, "Ye know this knight? Ye have history with him?"

Cathal wasn't sure how much to divulge. He was happy and willing to help these men and treat their injuries, but sharing details of his life with them was another matter.

"He called ye a thief, Cathal."

"I am no thief," he responded but added nothing more.

As Sir Lambert promised, he protested the contest and the adjudicator subsequently decreed that Sir Crispin had distinctly yielded. Sir Joss had acted within the rules and had the undisputed right to defend himself. Many knights had come forward and affirmed they had heard Sir Crispin concede. As the adjudicator affirmed, the victor was the only person who needed to hear his opponent yield. When Sir Joss drove his sword into the ground, that proved enough that Sir Crispin had conceded victory to his opponent. As far as the tournament adjudicator was concerned, the matter was over.

Back at his campsite, Sir Lambert seethed and, fuelled by mead and unwavering loyalty from Sir Robert, swore he would exact revenge on the cowardly knight who took the life of Sir Crispin. He'd lost two of his closest friends, Sir Guy and now Sir Crispin, and that filthy heathen barber had been involved in both their deaths. He vowed to Sir Robert that he would enjoy seeing the knight and the peasant suffer cruelly by his hand.

Cathal was attending to other patients, men who'd suffered wounds from other contests and his supply of herbs and plants was almost exhausted. Dafydd volunteered to collect more and, with detailed instructions, departed with a sack. Nearby, Sir Joss was closely inspecting his newly sharpened sword and saw Cathal taking a break and stretching his back. He walked over.

"Ye have yet to tell me why that knight accused ye of being a thief?"

"I am no thief," Cathal curtly replied.

"Aye, as ye said. I do not believe ye are, but that knight does. Ye are known to him, so why is it he has no love for ye?"

Cathal watched as Sir Joss took some practice swings with his sword. "Yer hip, does it bother ye?"

Sir Joss twisted his torso a couple of times. "Nay, it is nothing. Cathal, that knight, Sir Lambert, causes me more concern and I feel he will seek to hurt ye. I do not want to see you injured or killed. I worry fer ye."

"Ye need to worry fer yerself. I have no fear of that man."

Sir Joss sheathed his sword, "Then tell me why. What happened?"

Cathal turned to walk back to a patient.

"Nay, Cathal. Answer me, fer your past involvement with him affects me too. What do ye know of this man?"

Slowly, Cathal turned back to face his friend and breathed deeply. "In England, he tried to kill me fer nothing more than sport. I was unknown to him and had done nothing to offend him."

"Fer sport?" clarified Sir Joss.

Cathal held his gaze and pulled his robe apart.

Sir Joss gasped. The horrific red, jagged line descended from his upper chest and continued down to disappear below his waist. A smaller horizontal scar marked his chest.

"He did this for pleasure, to satisfy a need… then he left me to perish beside a road."

"And ye survived this?" Sir Joss shook his head in astonishment. "Do ye think he will come fer me or you, or is he talk and bluster?"

Cathal rearranged his robe and looked at his friend. "When a man is driven by the heat of his emotions, he is unpredictable, which makes him dangerous."

"He and I may contest each other in the next bout…"

Cathal shrugged. "I have never seen him fight with sword. If he has already won contests here in Dijon, then I fear he has skill, and ye need be wary."

"Aye, is what I feel too. I will speak to others who have seen him fight and learn what I can."

"And look over your shoulder, fer Sir Lambert has a troubled mind, and he will take unfair advantage when he can," Cathal warned.

Sir Joss waved and wandered off.

Dafydd had not yet returned, and Cathal was becoming increasingly anxious. He needed those herbs, and any delay would increase the likelihood of corruption manifesting in the wounds of his patients.

One of the young water boys Cathal hired, Aloïs, whose job was ensuring water was always available, returned carrying another bucket. "Find Dafydd, tell him to hurry, fer he will likely have found a woman and forgotten my need. Quickly now." Cathal told him precisely where to look.

Only too pleased to do the bidding of his generous employer, Aloïs ran off, and Cathal returned to his endless task of caring for the injured. Of some consolation, many of the least skilled contestants were no longer competing, and the number of wounded knights seeking help diminished noticeably; however, those that did come to him had more serious injuries that required careful treatment. Already, that afternoon, he had to remove the arms of two knights who'd suffered serious wounds. He hated performing amputations, but at times, they were necessary, but without his medicinal concoctions, lives could be lost.

By late afternoon, Aloïs had not returned, and Cathal believed something dreadful had befallen Dafydd and the boy. Sir Joss graciously offered to send his squire and wagon master out to search for them. As instructions were given, the frantic cries of someone yelling could be heard, and Aloïs appeared. He could hardly speak and was distraught. With Sir Joss watching, Cathal gave him water, sat him down and questioned the young lad.

CHAPTER THIRTY-ONE

By following Aloïs's directions, it didn't take long to find Dafydd. As Aloïs finally explained, he'd had no luck locating the Welshman and had been searching farther into the forest where he presumed Dafydd had ventured. Upon hearing the sound of riders, he'd hidden and allowed the horsemen to pass. That was when he saw Dafydd. His hands were securely tied, and he was on foot, led by two mounted knights. Eventually, he tripped and, unable to regain his feet, he was dragged to a secure place and stripped naked and hoisted by rope over a sturdy tree branch where he hung by his arms. That was how Cathal and Sir Joss found him.

The amicable and jolly Welshman was dead. No one could have survived the atrocity and savagery inflicted on him. When Cathal and Sir Joss first saw the hanging corpse, Sir Joss retched and was violently sick. Cathal stood unmoving, in silent anger. He knew what Dafydd experienced; he'd suffered the same, but it had been much worse for the poor and likeable Welshman.

Dafydd had been sliced open from his breastbone down to his groin, and the depth of the cut had been precise, where internal organs had not been damaged. Then, his entrails had been scooped out and hung obscenely from the eviscerated carcass of what had once been a living, breathing man. Beneath his swinging feet, blood dripped, and lying on a bed of leaves lay his heart.

"I have never seen such horror. Who would do such a thing?" said Sir Joss as he wiped his mouth. He couldn't look at the body and turned away to face Cathal. "It, it, is the same… the same wound ye showed me. This is what they did to ye?"

Cathal saw how pale the knight appeared, and he retched again. "Aye, the evil of man shows no boundaries or limits," his voice a mere whisper. "They would have done this to me, except they had no tree to hang me from."

"Sir Lambert," simply stated the knight.

Cathal didn't reply as he cut the rope.

Without tools to bury Dafydd and from the light of a fire they built, they covered the body with heavy rocks so animals couldn't interfere, and when completed, Sir Joss felt compelled to offer a brief and moving prayer. Cathal remained silent and brooding and didn't utter another word on their return to camp. The shock of what they had witnessed was unsettling and disturbing, and Sir Joss wondered at the mind of a man who could do such a thing.

Cathal had devoted his life to healing and felt restoring an injured or unwell body to full health was a privilege he enjoyed. He believed everyone deserved to live. His difficulty was comprehending the unseen illness that influenced a person's behaviour. He wished someone could advise him on the health of the mind, for he had little to no experience in such matters. Sir Lambert was unwell, of that fact Cathal was certain. He believed the knight's penchant for atrocity was borne from past experiences, much like bruising a shin against a rock. For days after, the pain of the injury could be felt, and he believed the mind of man was no different. However, where a contusion could be treated, it was generally accepted that the mind couldn't be cured. In contradiction, Cathal didn't believe that notion and felt the mind and the way man thought could be altered. The propensity for Sir Lambert to commit brutality and revel in the pleasure was obscene, and something needed to be done - he just didn't know how. Left to his own devices and unchecked, Cathal also believed the level and frequency of violence would increase. How many innocent people would fall victim to Sir Lambert's unrestrained savagery?

Sir Joss and Cathal never spoke together about what they witnessed ever again, yet it dominated Cathal's thoughts. Perhaps because he'd been a victim and seen the expression on the knight's face as he cruelly sliced into his body gave him a different perspective… One thing was sure, the sickening behaviour had to end, or more people would cruelly suffer.

Sir Joss was equally disgusted by what he had witnessed. While knights are no strangers to the savageries of battle, and he'd witnessed first-hand the variety of grotesque ways men could die, but what he saw hanging from the tree branch was more than troubling. Knowing that he could face the knight who'd committed the heinous butchery in a contest was unsettling. *Would Sir Lambert try to mutilate him if they fought*?

Sir Joss knew he was a better-than-average swordsman and stood a good chance at finishing high in the competition and perhaps even winning outright. However, the contest wasn't about killing your opponent; it was about using skill to defeat them, so the death of Sir Crispin had been avoidable and unfortunate. He sought advantage by cheating and lost his life as a result. Sir Lambert saw it differently, and Sir Joss firmly believed Sir Lambert sought retribution and would do so cruelly and savagely. Sir Joss didn't want to die in that way. The death of Cathal's *Medicus*, Dafydd, affected him profoundly, and he and Cathal had no evidence to link Sir Lambert to the horrific murder. Reporting Dafydd's death wouldn't change anything. That night, Sir Joss considered withdrawing from the contest.

The next day, Sir Joss stood on the field of contest and felt relief that he did not have to face Sir Lambert. Instead, he was scheduled to fight Sir Lambert's compatriot and friend, Sir Robert. There were only eight contestants and four bouts planned, and each swordsman nervously awaited the sound of the horn, which would announce the start of the latest contest.

Cathal stood behind a flag marking the boundary and closely watched the competitors. While he believed and hoped Sir Joss would prevail, he focused on Sir Lambert in the other contest and carefully observed. He watched his style, the moves, feints and thrusts. His stance, foot position and defensive technique. The knight had talent, strength and skill, yet he was also confident and assured, which made him highly competent, but he also saw his weakness.

Switching back to Sir Joss's contest, he predicted Sir Robert would be victorious. However, Sir Joss did not fight with conviction as he'd done previously. His fighting style was not smooth and deliberate as he demonstrated in earlier contests. Today, he defended with only enough skill to remain unharmed - his heart wasn't in the contest. Cathal was disappointed. He believed Sir Joss was the better swordsman and deserved victory.

It was apparent that Sir Robert was an accomplished swordsman and fought well, and sadly, he anticipated that Sir Joss would soon yield. Looking back towards Sir Lambert, he could see the contest had swung in Sir Lambert's favour. The competing knight, a local Frank, had suffered a wound to his leg and lost mobility, and Sir Lambert took advantage. With a groan of disappointment from the onlookers, the Frank took a knee and yielded to Sir Lambert. Spectators collectively held their breath when it appeared Sir Lambert would run the Frankian through. To everyone's relief, at the last moment, he stopped himself.

Friends of Sir Joss were yelling encouragement, urging him to fight with more vigour, but the support did little to motivate the German knight. It was no surprise when Sir Joss lowered himself and crouched with a knee touching the ground. It was an honoured acknowledgement of defeat. Sir Robert recognised the gesture and, in victory, suddenly spun and walked away to join his friend. Victors often said a conciliatory word as a sign of respect to their defeated opponent and frequently offered a hand to help them to their feet, but not this day. Sir Robert's actions went against established protocols of chivalry, and by not speaking, Sir Robert did not endear himself to those who watched. A few unsavoury comments and insults were hurled at the departing knight in response to his unsportsmanlike behaviour.

Sir Joss wasn't hurt and refused to discuss the contest with Cathal. He went to his tent, and even his two squires and wagon master were instructed to leave him in peace.

With no patients requiring his urgent care, Cathal ventured into the forest, where solitude and nature provided comfort and assurance. He sat beside a brook and absorbed his surroundings - the birds that flittered by, even small animals, the flora and fauna and the splendour of nature's design. Trees with immense leafy branches that towered high above, the colours and shapes of small plants and even the earthy smell. He breathed it in while the nearby stream babbled incoherently, its language yet to be learned. He could name the largest trees and even the smallest, seemingly inconsequential plants. The familiarity of nature and the environment gave him clarity of thought and helped his mind to place order in the jumble of unanswered questions and incomplete thoughts that littered his thinking; for Cathal, it was like returning home.

After a while, he stood, removed his robe, stretched and began loosening his body in a series of slow practised movements. His body responded well, and the exercises became fluid, coordinated and deliberate as he focused on different parts of his body, just as Gryffen had instructed him when he was a boy. His breathing was deep and measured as the tempo increased. He sweated profusely and pushed his body, finding the limits of endurance, strength and willpower. When finished, his body glistened with sweat, and he went to the stream to drink and wash.

When he returned to camp, his eyes sparkled with vitality, and the spring in his step could have heralded an ominous warning. Sir Joss was still lost in self-pity and despair and had not resurfaced from the protective cocoon of his tent. Cathal ignored him; it was safer for him to remain cloistered and inebriated.

Most competitions had concluded. Victors were paraded around like conquering heroes, and reputations had been enhanced or created. Friendships forged through the commonality of martial skills were genuine, heartfelt and frequently lasting. The defeated fought honourably and were often seen in the company of the victorious as the bonds of battle held firm. Honour and respect were held in high regard, while grudges and ill feelings were harboured by the few unworthy and hopeless. The tournament had been a success, and the Duke of Burgundy was imminently pleased. A couple of contests were still to be decided, and the conclusion would highlight a profitable and worthy event.

All other preliminary contests had concluded, however, one particular and popular contest was still to be decided, and Sir Lambert would challenge the Duke of Burgundy's champion, Sir Alexandre. He was a man of no great stature. Still, he possessed remarkable speed and agility that saw him easily defeat all opponents in the preliminary bouts and was heavily favoured to win.

Sir Joss had eventually resurfaced and was friendly and cordial, although Cathal noticed a subtle change. He lacked confidence and was quieter, preferring to remain in his own company rather than socialise with his numerous friends.

With all his patients under the care of their squires and servants, Cathal had time to wander through the makeshift township and take in the sights, looking at merchandise hawked by overbearing, overdressed men with silken tongues and slick patter. Lords he didn't know, with an extravagant entourage of servants and vassals in tow, nodded to him as they strutted by. Knights, barons and officials greeted him with a smile and a kind word. Not only had knights made lasting reputations for themselves in Dijon, but Cathal, through his dedication and ability to heal, had also become known, for those warriors never knew when they would need the services of a most capable and trusted healer.

The attention didn't affect him; Cathal remained an enigma. While his standing within the temporary community was high, he remained aloof, guarded and careful. People who tried to initiate a conversation with Cathal found him unresponsive. Yet a genuine interaction about a malady or injury was productive and fruitful and only enhanced his reputation. There was a way about him that was different and unusual, and when he walked through a crowd, a space opened, and people made way for him. As one overheard conversation stated, Cathal wasn't liked, he was respected.

Cathal had a plan, and his wanderings around the temporary community weren't aimless; he wanted to be seen; he knew Sir Lambert and Sir Robert weren't finished with him, and Cathal wanted to learn more about the two knights who sought his death. Of equal concern was Sir Joss, who'd lost confidence in himself and his abilities.

On return to his campsite, Sir Joss was having a loud disagreement with one of his friends. Cathal didn't interfere, it wasn't his business, and he allowed them to yell at each other, and he hoped some good would come from it as Sir Joss had become surly and, fuelled by mead, belligerent.

The yelling escalated, and within moments, both men were on the ground grappling with each other. Cathal rushed over and, with the help of others, separated the two men.

"Leave me, Cathal, this isn't yer concern!" Sir Joss pushed Cathal away and stomped into his tent.

"Yer well-being is my concern, fer I am a friend, and I seek yer best interests," Cathal replied without raising his voice.

Sir Joss didn't respond, and Cathal allowed him to soak in his misery.

Sometime later, Sir Joss ventured from his tent. "Er, fergive me, Cathal, it was wrong of me to speak to ye in such a way."

Cathal raised an eyebrow. "Ye spoke how ye felt, it did not offend me. But methinks we have a need to talk. What is ailing ye?"

Sir Joss looked around, and Cathal could sense that he wanted to talk but as Cathal expected, he preferred somewhere private. He turned his head as if looking for secluded space and saw something disturbing. He didn't react. "I must collect some herbs in the forest, come with me."

He was reluctant at first but agreed. Cathal gathered his things and was about to walk from their camp and noticed the knight wasn't armed. "Bring yer sword, fer I feel it is better to have protection…"

Sir Joss gave him a long, hard look; their last venture into the forest ended badly. He returned to his tent and came back, strapping a sword to his waist. After informing his two squires and Wagon master where he was going, he and Cathal strolled from the camp towards the forest.

Cathal remained silent and gave his friend the time and space to speak when he was ready. It didn't take long, and within moments, Sir Joss was gushing.

Watching them walking from the camp towards the forest, a young girl turned and ran through the temporary township towards the far side of the encampment. She arrived breathlessly at Sir Lambert's tent.

"I done as ye asked, Milord," she began after recovering her breath. "The healer, Cathal and a knight, they'd be goin into the forest."

Sir Lambert took a deep breath and slowly exhaled. "Where?"

The girl raised a filthy arm and pointed. "That way, Milord."

Sir Lambert turned to his friend. "Are ye ready fer this?"

"Aye, now is as good a time as ever," replied Sir Robert as he reached for his sword.

Sir Lambert handed her a coin. "Be off with yer and say nothing."

CHAPTER THIRTY-TWO

For Cathal, the familiarity of the forest was comforting, while for Sir Joss, the forest provided places of concealment where an enemy could remain hidden and launch an unexpected attack. The gloominess was ominous, and being on foot made him feel vulnerable. He could see how effortlessly Cathal adapted to the forest environment and quickly led him to a bank beside a stream where the warmth of sunshine removed the chill and darkness. Cathal stretched out, lay on the bank with hands behind his head, and invited his friend to sit and relax.

"No one is near, and ye are free to speak," he suggested, and under his breath muttered, "at least for a while."

Sir Joss stepped to a nearby tree, plucked a leaf from a branch and leaned against the trunk, toying with the leaf.

"Why did ye choose to fight that knight when ye know ye shouldn't have?" Cathal asked.

Sir Joss pulled his gaze from the leaf to make eye contact with Cathal. "How did ye know? Was it that obvious?"

Cathal raised an eyebrow and said nothing.

Sir Joss began to talk and disclosed his thoughts and fears, and Cathal quietly listened. He offered no opinion, made no judgment, nor provided advice.

Sir Lambert and Sir Robert didn't want anyone to see their destination and took a non-direct route to the forest, choosing to ride horses instead of walking. They dismounted at the forest edge, where he believed the healer had likely entered, hobbled their horses and began looking for signs.

Cathal's eyes were closed as he listened to Sir Joss. He wasn't asleep; his mind was focused and sharp. When his friend took a long pause, Cathal sat up. "I believe that Sir Lambert and Sir Robert may have followed us here."

Sir Joss dropped the mangled leaf he'd been fidgeting with and stepped away from the tree as his hand dropped to his sword. "What? Ye know of this and said nothing."

"I know nothing, except Sir Lambert has had people watching us. When we departed camp, a young girl ran off. Methinks to inform Sir Lambert. What would ye do if ye were he?"

Sir Joss's head swivelled from side to side as he nervously peered into the forest. "I would follow."

Cathal eased himself to his feet, retrieved his staff and adjusted his sword. "Aye, that is what I would do."

"Ye do not seem worried. If Sir Lambert had followed us, he wouldn't have come alone. Sir Robert will be with him. Two highly skilled swordsmen and only the two of us. I cannot protect ye, Cathal; remember, Sir Robert defeated me."

"Ye allowed Sir Robert to win, and ye are the better swordsman, but did not fight with yer mind, fer it was elsewhere. Ye fought with despair and fear. Ye said so only moments ago," Cathal reminded him.

Sir Joss laughed, but not from mirth. "Aye, but Sir Lambert faces the duke's champion in the final contest. If he wins or loses, he is, at worst, the second-best swordsman here. I cannot save ye, Cathal - I am not that good."

Cathal stepped up to the knight. "Ye take care of Sir Robert and leave Sir Lambert to me." He pat Sir Joss on the shoulder and retraced their steps from the forest. "Come, let us see if they followed us." He pulled the hood of his robe over his head.

Sir Joss shook his head in anguish and reluctantly followed a step behind, believing Cathal led him to a cruel and violent death.

Cathal walked silently. The earthy hues of his robe blended into the shadows, rendering him almost invisible. Sir Joss struggled to keep up and remain stealthy. Never had he seen a man move through the forest with such fluidity. Cathal appeared to float from shadowed tree to tree without pausing or making a sound. Yet he did it with speed, and Sir Joss found himself running to keep up. Only when they approached the forest edge did Cathal slow and then stop to listen.

"No one is here," Sir Joss confidently whispered in Cathal's ear.

Cathal slowly raised a hand, indicating he wanted silence, then cocked his head, listening. After a few moments, he crouched behind a large tree trunk and turned to the knight. "Someone is yonder beyond the small bushes, and they are hiding."

Sir Joss looked at his friend in surprise. "And what now?"

"Ye wait here, and when ye hear that I have been discovered, come quickly from that direction," Cathal pointed. "If it is Sir Lambert and Sir Joss, then Sir Robert will come when he sees ye, creating separation which suits us. We must not allow them to stand back-to-back."

"And what do we do, defend and cry fer help?" Sir Joss asked.

Cathal's expression hardened. "Nay, we kill them, fer those two knights are diseased, just as we cull sick animals from a herd." Sir Joss looked uncertain. Only days ago, he'd lost to Sir Robert in fair contest, and now, Cathal expected him to fight the man again and, this time, kill him. He swallowed away the fear.

"Ye are the better swordsman; yer experience will see ye well. Remember, Sir Robert habitually attacks for the midriff and feints with a strike to the shoulder beforehand. Do not drop yer elbow, or he will see the weakness and attack as he did last time."

Sir Joss still felt the effects of the slight injury to his hip. It was a good reminder. "But Sir Lambert is the better swordsman. Ye can't fight him and expect to win."

"Why not?" Cathal replied and then turned and ran towards their unseen enemy.

He saw Sir Lambert hiding behind a low bush. His attempt at concealment was laughable, and Cathal approached him from behind. Sir Lambert was unaware that danger lurked so near, but a sixth sense alerted him, and he turned.

In horror, Sir Lambert saw the healer quickly approaching, and he leapt away, at the same time yelling a warning to his friend as he unsheathed his sword.

Sir Robert rose from behind a leafy bush with his mouth open in surprise, but he was ten paces away and posed no immediate threat to Cathal. As planned, Sir Joss appeared behind Sir Robert, who turned to face his assailant with his sword drawn. As much as Cathal wanted to watch, he needed to contend with Sir Lambert, who had assumed a fighting stance and was preparing to launch an attack on him.

Cathal stood facing Sir Lambert and was relaxed and calm. He had watched the knight fight with a sword to know his technique and how he would attack. He was predictable, and Cathal was ready. However, he wouldn't fight Sir Lambert on his terms; he would engage the knight on his own.

As Sir Lambert leapt forward, Cathal spun his staff horizontally, trapped one end under his arm, gripped the staff firmly and quickly stepped forward just as he'd done countless times in the past with proven success. The end of the staff connected with the upper chest of the attacking knight and stopped him dead in his tracks. Sir Lambert yelped and looked winded and, to his credit, didn't fall. He stumbled backwards to create some distance between them to regain his breath rather than remain stationary and be attacked.

Cathal didn't wait and stepped forward again, pressing his

temporary advantage. This time, the staff swung from right to left, connecting with Sir Lambert's sword-wielding arm at the elbow. Cathal knew the blow hurt.

"Ye heathen cur!" spat Sir Lambert, shaking his arm to ease the pain.

Cathal didn't relent and leapt from his feet at Sir Lambert to deliberately slide along the ground with his feet extended. The staff was a blur as it struck the knight on the back of his legs, and Sir Lambert howled in agony as his legs buckled and he crumpled to the ground. Cathal regained his footing and swung at the knight again, hoping to strike him on his head. In reflex, the knight raised his sword to fend off the blow and struck the staff firmly. With a crack, the staff snapped.

Dropping the staff, Cathal shot to his feet. Without pause, he unsheathed his sword and stepped forward, fending off a few quick strikes from Sir Lambert, who was still struggling to rise. Behind him, Cathal could hear Sir Joss and Sir Richard; their clashing swords offered some satisfaction that Sir Joss was alive and fighting well.

Cathal knew he'd hurt the knight with hard, fierce blows and needed to finish him off quickly before he recovered and began to counterattack. He changed his grip on the sword, now clasping it with both hands and swung with all his strength. Typically, such a move was not considered wise because he was fully committed and his body would be fully exposed, but because Sir Lambert was already suffering from the effects of repeated blows from the staff and was caught off balance, Cathal believed the powerful strike would work. Both swords clashed together, but the power of Cathal's swing forced Sir Lambert's sword arm backwards, exposing the entire mid-section and left part of his body. With momentum and continuing his motion, he pirouetted, spinning quickly as his sword arced through the air and sliced deep into the exposed abdomen of Sir Lambert. The cut was deep and extended horizontally across the knight's entire stomach.

Cathal knew the wound was serious but not fatal. However, Sir Lambert's bravado and confidence deserted him.

Sir Lambert looked down at the reddening gash with his mouth open in disbelief. "Ye cut me, yer whoreson!"

Cathal chose the point of impact carefully and drove his sword into the heart of the injured knight. He felt no satisfaction or emotion; it was a necessary task, just like any unpleasant job that required doing. He extracted his sword and quickly walked towards Sir Joss, who was fighting for his life.

This was no contest with rules and structure. Sir Joss and Sir Robert fought, each to stay alive, and Cathal had no qualms about ending it. Sir Robert was just as guilty as Sir Lambert of committing atrocities on people for no reason other than to satisfy a carnal lust. It wasn't an unsupported opinion; Cathal had experienced his savagery and survived while many others hadn't. He stepped behind Sir Robert and swung his sword as hard as he could at the neck of the unsuspecting knight, almost severing his head.

Sir Joss dropped to a knee to regain his breath and looked incredulously at Cathal. "How, how-" he panted, "did ye defeat him?"

Cathal's expression was grim. He took no pleasure in killing and had done so with the same mindset as culling a diseased pig or chicken. Those two dead knights were no different. "I believed I could," he simply stated.

Sir Joss rose to his feet. "These knights will be missed, questions will be asked, what do we do?"

Cathal had thought it through carefully. Sir Lambert had cleverly ensured no one knew where he was going or for what purpose. He didn't want anyone to know that the reason he departed the encampment was to torture and kill two men. "Nothing. We will walk through the forest and appear back at camp from a different direction."

"Sir Lambert was to fight the Duke's champion on the morrow..."

Cathal shrugged, "Then the Duke's man can claim a victory." Cathal bent down and wiped the blood from his sword on Sir Robert's clothes. Then, he fumbled for the knight's purse, which he found and took. He saw the expression on Sir Joss's face. "When they find the bodies and no purses, they will claim it's a robbery. That thieves in great numbers lay in wait and robbed two skilled knights who fought valiantly and died."

Cathal walked back to Sir Lambert's unmoving body, took his purse, retrieved both pieces of his staff, and began to walk back into the forest. Sir Joss followed.

"Will we be suspected?" Sir Joss asked.

"That ye, who lost to Sir Robert in a contest and I, a healer, defeated two knights? Nay, methinks not."

Sir Joss shook his head. This man, this healer, was a riddle. Sir Lambert was recognised as a highly competent swordsman, and Cathal faced him one-on-one and defeated him in mere moments. *How could it be*, he thought? He stared at Cathal's back and hoped he'd never have to face him in battle.

As Cathal and Sir Joss returned to camp, no one spared them a second glance. They wandered between rows of tents adorned with colourful pendants and flags that proudly flapped in the afternoon breeze as they headed towards their camp. A troupe of minstrels were performing, and both men stopped to listen, and Cathal was reminded of Isolde. He felt the emptiness of her passing as the poignant lyrics spoke of lost love and heartache. He wasn't the only one affected. The passion of the balladeer moved others who'd also stopped, and he could see some hardened knights wiping moist eyes. Poor Isolde, he missed her so, and she had painfully suffered so much. It seemed unfair, unjust and undeserved; if only he could have helped her. After returning to camp, he spent the rest of the day thinking about his future.

The bones provided clues but no answers. Again, the interpretation of how the bones lay spoke of his past and future. Past events were linked to future events and people. His mother had spoken of it countless times and stressed that his future was destined – *But how*?

Helping the wounded and sick had filled a void, and attending the tournament here in Dijon had been worthwhile. The bones pointed northwards to a castle or large structure. But what was north? And castles were plentiful.

He raised the question with Sir Joss. "What is north of here?"

Sir Joss stroked his beard as he thought of a suitable answer. "North is home, fer me and in a couple of months or so, I will return unharmed and not victorious," he laughed. "Beyond that is the land of the Rus. A cold and forbidding place. Do ye wish to go there?"

Cathal shook his head.

"If ye wish to journey northward, it isn't quite so simple, fer ye will need to avoid Chaumont-sur-Epte," warned Sir Joss.

"Chaumont-sur-Epte, what is this place?"

"The English, King Henry, lays siege to Chaumont-sur-Epte, a castle owned by Louis of Frankia. It is a formidable castle, and it will take some time for the king to take possession of it. There is much fighting, and I am told Louis is defending it quite well."

A castle! Cathal's interest was piqued. "How far is Chaumont-sur-Epte from here?"

"Ah, it is a three or four-day ride. I will avoid the place as I return home, fer I have no desire to involve myself in such political matters."

Cathal had no interest in politics, but if men fought, they

would also require healing. "Then I shall go to this castle."

"Ye do not wish to ride with me back to Rheinfelden in Swabia? The women are the most beautiful in all the lands. Big strong women who will work hard and give ye lots of children."

Cathal had seen the women of Swabia, and they were not beautiful, but they were indeed large. He shook his head "Nay, fer my future lays at this castle."

Sir Joss seemed genuinely disappointed. "When will ye leave here?"

It all made sense to Cathal now. The bones had been precise; Chaumont-sur-Epte was where he was meant to go. "I will depart on the morrow."

CHAPTER THIRTY-THREE

Cathal arrived alone at Chaumont-sur-Epte without incident after a leisurely four-day ride from Dijon. He wasn't the only person travelling to the castle. Many others ventured northwards, intrigued at the opportunity to seek work as mercenaries or in other non-fighting support roles. As he quickly learned from people he spoke to, Chaumont-sur-Epte was described as a sprawling castle draped over a low hill where Louis of Frankia stored weapons. Eminently displeased, King Henry II attacked the castle in retaliation for Louis's continued encroachments and attacks on his land.

Men of all descriptions wandered everywhere. Knights, men-at-arms, sappers, engineers, archers, smithies and clerics. Each man had something to do and somewhere to be. If the tournament in Dijon was structured and organised, King Henry's siege at Chaumont-sur-Epte was chaotic disorder and it showed.

Row upon row of tents sprouted from grassy fields like mushrooms, and roped pastures kept horses secured. There were stables and sweaty blacksmiths who hammered away, their tireless clanging dissolving into the background clamour of merchants, hawkers, and bards. As in Dijon, coarse women plied their trade, and the atmosphere was almost jovial. Yet here, men were wounded and died violently because they followed orders by well-meaning lords and a dominant king.

It took Cathal a week or two to make sense of the confusion; unlike Dijon, where his campsite was his base, and people came to him for help, here, he went where he was needed - to the stricken. There were large areas where he was forbidden to go, and zealous guards ensured no one broke the rules.

Word of his skills spread, and people greeted him by name, nodding as they walked past, raising a hand and waving with a smile. For some, Cathal was a living talisman who brought luck to the unfortunate through healing.

Not every person Cathal attended to was wounded from fighting; some were injured at work or in accidents. Any time people gathered in significant numbers, outbreaks of disease and pestilence would claim many, and death was an unpleasant and undignified outcome.

Cathal wandered around Chaumont-sur-Epte, administering care and remedies to those in need and the days blended into weeks. There was plenty to do and no shortage of people who needed care. He saw two Norsemen who looked out of place, which caused him some concern, but they had no interest in him, which was a relief. He didn't suffer fools and was often abrupt and dismissive to those who sought advantage, and he had to defend himself from frequent attacks by thieves. Even the criminals learned, and eventually, they left him alone, for they, too, had need from time to time.

However, the reason for being here in this place of violence was still unclear; the bones provided no clues, and Cathal surmised that patience would be rewarded. He had coin; in fact, he had plenty but never charged a tariff for his services and occasionally accepted a donation to pay for consumables he used in his treatments.

He was administering to a young boy with a corrupted lesion on his leg when he felt the presence of someone observing him. With the boy's leg now wrapped in a bandage, Cathal's work was done, and he packed things into his large bag so that he could attend to the next, wherever they were.

"Be on yer way, lad. Find me in two days, and I will replace the herbs and bandage. Do ye understand?"

The boy nodded.

"Keep it clean," he warned and helped the lad to his feet.

"Thank ye, Master," the boy said before limping away.

"I'm not yer master." Cathal grumpily yelled after him, then turned to the priest in question.

"You do a good service to these people," the priest stated.

Cathal scrutinised the young priest. He did not wear the robes of a parish priest and appeared out of place. He didn't reply to the comment and, with the bag packed, grabbed his new staff and stood.

"Please, Cathal, fer that is how ye are called, is this so?"

Cathal's eyes narrowed. He had no fondness for self-serving priests and their predisposition to talk endlessly about something without a measure of truthfulness. *What did this priest want?* "I am he."

"Ah, then I am pleased fer I have found who I seek."

Again, the vagueness. Cathal sighed.

"Aye, er, can ye accompany me? Someone wants to speak with ye."

Cathal was instantly suspicious. "Who?"

"Er, he prefers to remain unknown," replied the priest with practised gravity.

Cathal looked around to see if the priest had brought anyone with him. Seeing no one, he faced the young man. "If ye require healing, tell me what ails ye, but I have no interest in ye or the Church." He turned and wandered away, leaving the priest standing.

"I must insist!" yelled the priest.

Cathal continued on ignoring the pleas.

An engineer had suffered an unfortunate accident when constructing a *trebuchet* for King Henry's forces and lost an arm when a heavy wooden brace fell onto it. The arm had to be amputated, and the engineer, a young man with a family, continued work the following day. Needing income, he believed he could still work and be productive. However, Cathal was concerned the stump was becoming corrupt and needed to apply a poultice to the raw wound and replace soiled bandages. In Cathal's opinion, this task was far more important than the needs of the priest.

The young engineer was in much pain and was struggling to work with only one arm, and Cathal performed his duties by cleansing the wound, packing a poultice onto the stump and rewrapping the bandages. Before leaving the engineer, Cathal gave him two gold coins, some of which he had taken from Sir Lambert and Sir Robert. In disbelief at the gratuity, the engineer refused the gift, thinking unreasonable conditions were attached.

"Nay, Luke," Cathal explained, "I have no need of yer woman or daughters. Take the coins, fer they will see yer family provided fer until yer arm heals and ye can learn to work again."

"I, I can't repay ye," stated the engineer.

"Cathal shook his head. "It isn't a debt, the coins are a gift." He placed them on the table beside the engineer, packed his jars into his bag and turned to leave.

"God bless ye, Cathal. Ye are a good man."

"I'd rather God blessed ye, fer ye need it more than me," he added before leaving.

Each day, Cathal encountered more people who needed help with various medical issues, and his knowledge and expertise increased. He experimented when he could, trying different combinations of healing with potent herbs, sometimes with success and other times not. He became efficient at ministering to those who suffered and, when he felt it appropriate, gave coin to the wretched and took the recompense offered by those who could afford to pay for his services.

It was becoming late, and Cathal decided to return to his campsite, some distance from the village on the outskirts and well away from the rows of tents occupied by King Henry's forces. While still in the village, he rounded a corner and found his path blocked by sword-wielding knights. The young priest who'd approached him a week earlier was issuing instructions. "Take him!"

Cathal was stunned and could do nothing. Against his will, his sword, staff and bag were taken, and his hands were tied securely behind his back, and he was led through the village to a small parish church. On arrival, the guards pushed him inside, and the priest followed.

Cathal was furious and let the priest know how he felt. It made no difference, and he was taken to a chair and seated. A guard remained behind him with a sword pressed into the side of his neck. Any wrong or sudden moves and Cathal knew his life would end immediately. Without providing answers, the priest wandered away.

The church was old, dimly lit, and smelled of soot and unwashed bodies. It was no wonder people became ill, he thought as he waited. He had no idea of the reason for his abduction, and when the opportunity presented itself, he would ensure his captors knew of his displeasure.

He didn't have to wait long. The priest and another returned, and an extra chair was placed in front of him so the stranger, also a priest, could sit.

"I apologise for taking ye away from yer work, Cathal. However, God's work is also important."

God's work? Cathal wanted to leave. He remained silent.

"I am Monsignor Stratton, an emissary for Bishop Dunhelm of Dearthington. I understand you may recall your, er, rather unpleasant visit whilst there."

Cathal certainly did remember what happened in Dearthington. The bishop had killed Gryffen, and Sir Lambert had gutted him like an animal. He felt a chill and knew this Monsignor was dangerous. *What was this all about?*

The Monsignor adjusted his robes, and the younger priest stood subserviently at his side. The sword at this neck was a cold reminder he was entirely at their mercy. The poor light made it difficult to see faces clearly, but Cathal had seen enough to remember the man if he had the good fortune to live through this encounter.

"His Eminence, Bishop Dunhelm, has asked if I would come to Frankia to find ye. He is poorly and finds travel rather taxing," began the monsignor. "Ye may not be aware, but recently, employees of Lord Hansard returned home to Dearthington. A blacksmith and a handful of servants, I believe. They were attending to Lord Hansard's son, Sir Lambert, who ye are acquainted with, at a tournament in Dijon."

Cathal stared at the monsignor, but his expression gave nothing away.

"Are ye willing to listen to what I have to say, or will ye resist?"

Cathal thought quickly. If he were being accused of murdering Sir Lambert and Sir Robert, then he would either be dead or sitting in a gaol. He nodded. "I will listen."

Monsignor Stratton waved the guard away, and Cathal felt relief as the sword was removed from his neck. No one else appeared to be in the church besides himself and the two priests. The three of them were alone.

"The servants all reported that Sir Lambert and Sir Robert were found dead near the forest where the tournament was held. Reports state they died defending themselves. Some people claimed they were killed by thieves. Or rather, that is the account given to Lord Hansard. No foul play."

This was becoming more perplexing by the moment. *What is this all about*? Cathal wondered.

Monsignor Stratton leaned forward in his chair. "Of concern to Lord Hansard is that your name and another, a knight called Sir Joss, were repeatedly mentioned. Sir Lambert feared ye, Cathal. Would ye like to tell us why?"

Cathal quickly considered various options. Anything he said could be used to charge him with a crime. "Untie my hands, and I will show ye."

The monsignor looked up at the priest, who nodded in affirmation, then stepped away to untie Cathal's hands.

"If ye harm us, ye will not leave this church alive," warned the Monsignor as Cathal's hands were freed. He rubbed his wrists. The priest returned to his place, standing beside the monsignor.

Cathal's heart was racing, and he thought of how to escape from the church. Even if he succeeded, he knew they would come looking for him. He would never be at peace. He slowly stood, untied his belt and pulled his robe apart, revealing the savage scar.

The young priest gasped, and his hand flew to his mouth. Monsignor Stratton didn't flinch and remained impassive.

Cathal retied his robe and sat.

"It is as I thought," finally responded Monsignor Stratton.

Cathal was furious. "Ye knew! Ye knew he was committing such brutality on others, yet did nothing to stop it? This is why I do not respect the men who govern the Church. Ye have a care of duty to protect yer people, not to ignore their plight."

The monsignor leaned back in his chair. "Sir Lambert's father knew. It first came to the attention of the Church, and Bishop Dunhelm discussed it with Lord Hansard, believing he could end the mutilations and not soil the lord's reputation and implicate his family."

"It didn't work," Cathal snapped.

"Nay, it didn't," replied the monsignor. This is why I am here. Was Sir Lambert and Sir Robert's death a direct result of his, er…"

"Sickness?" Cathal interjected

"Aye, sickness," continued Monsignor Stratton.

Cathal took a deep breath. The way he answered could have massive consequences if the monsignor had lied to him. Both priests waited for his response. "My *Medicus*, Dafydd, was gutted in Dijon just like I had been, except worse. His heart had been removed and placed beneath his feet as he swung by his arms from a tree. Dafydd had not known Sir Lambert or committed any deed to offend him. They were strangers. The mutilation was revenge because I survived the torture and knew that Sir Lambert was a tormented man. He wanted to end my life to keep his secret safe. He and Sir Robert came to kill me."

Cathal could see Monsignor Stratton was distressed as he rubbed his face with his hands.

"Bishop Dunhelm seeks confirmation of why Sir Lambert was killed. I think you have provided the answer. When I report back to the bishop, he will talk to Lord Hansard and inform him." The monsignor paused, considering his words. "You may well ask, why did he send us here?"

Cathal inclined his head.

"Because the bishop has received complaints by parishioners who seek answers. Those complaints can no longer be ignored. What you told us verifies what the accusers said and what Sir Lambert did. We, or rather Bishop Dunhelm, recognise that Lord Hansard knew of the mutilations and murders and was unable or unwilling to prevent them. This matter can no longer be ignored."

"How many died?" Cathal asked.

Monsignor Stratton appeared troubled. "Over the years, there were dozens that we know of."

"And now will I be accused of murder and face judgment by the Church?" Cathal asked.

Nothing moved, and the room was silent except for the chair's creak as Monsignor Stratton slowly leaned forward. "I have not asked ye if ye killed Sir Lambert and Sir Robert, and ye have not admitted to killing them. I won't ask, and fer yer sake, do not confess." Monsignor Stratton rose from his chair. "Ye are free to go, Cathal, and we will return to England."

CHAPTER THIRTY-FOUR

The two priests departed, and Cathal remained seated in the church as he contemplated what he'd just learned and experienced. Unconsciously, his hand went to his neck, where only a short time ago, a sword pressed against it. He felt some relief, believing that if the Church wanted to see him punished for the death of Sir Lambert and Sir Robert, then accusations would have been forthcoming. As much as he mistrusted priests, he believed the monsignor's explanation for coming to Frankia. If they held Lord Hansard accountable, there would be serious repercussions, so the two priests were sent to find him to confirm the allegations. Before any action was taken, they needed to corroborate the accusations against Sir Lambert. The monsignor was correct; he hadn't asked if Cathal had killed the two knights, and in turn, he had not confessed to them. The Church did not seek to find and punish the man who'd killed them, the questions they asked were only to verify. He rose from the hard wooden chair, rubbed his bottom and walked to the door where he found his possessions. Exiting the church, notwithstanding the fresh and clean air, he felt better, lighter, and freer. The two Norsemen he'd seen some time ago walked past, and again, they paid him no mind.

It was just another day, like the countless days that had already passed, but when Cathal awoke, he knew it would be different. The bones that fell from the small cloth bag seemed to land haphazardly, but he knew better—the soothsayer Lohier had taught him how to interpret the position of how they landed. Lohier had patiently instructed Cathal on the nuances and minor details of how the bones rested after being upended from the bag. Today was marked as special, again, the bones told of the past and merged with current events that linked the future. Cathal didn't know in what form this would become apparent to him. As he placed the bones back into his bag, he muttered under his breath about life's uncertainties and his inability to understand details. *Why was everything so vague*? he questioned in frustration.

Someone informed him that a knight sought him. He was seeking help for an injured friend, travellers who had encountered problems whilst journeying here. Cathal told the man that he could be found near the village centre if anyone was looking for him.

He introduced himself as Sir Renier after finding him near the fountain, and the knight explained how his fellow traveller had been struck by a sword near his armpit, and the wound had festered. Cathal silently acknowledged this was a serious life-threatening injury and followed the knight to his campsite.

It was a small camp, and the travellers did not come to Chaumont-sur-Epte to fight for King Henry or Louis of Frankia but for other matters that were unclear to Cathal. It mattered not their reason, of concern was the injury.

When he saw the man, bathed in sweat and suffering, Cathal paused momentarily – his face. It was familiar to him, but he didn't know from where. He thought back to this morning and the reading of the bones…

The extent of how the body was being poisoned by corruption needed to be determined, and he checked the patient's urine, studying it carefully. Someone had crudely attempted to sew the gash together, but through swelling, it only made the injury worse and more painful. The wound was a ghastly mess and had been left untreated for too long. As usual, Cathal did the best he could.

Not long after tending to the injury, another member of the group returned to the camp. He was a young man, and Cathal paused briefly from his work and looked up at him. By the flickering flames of the campfire, he saw his face. Inquisitive eyes stared back, and they spoke of wit and intelligence, although he returned his look with sadness and despair. He wasn't a knight or squire but wore the clothes of a peasant farmer. Most peculiarly, everyone treated him as an equal, and he did not behave subserviently as expected.

Cathal's heart raced, and he turned back to his patient in growing confusion. It came to him, the wounded man - his face. It was a long time ago, but it was the squire who came to help him when the Northmen came to the uplands. His own appearance had changed considerably since then. His hair was long, he caried more weight and a full beard now hid his features; it was unlikely the patient would remember him. He turned back to the young man who still stood watching.

"I will fetch more wood fer the fire," the young man said and turned away.

"Odo, take care do not wander far," replied Sir Renier.

Odo? Odo? Odo? Cathal questioned. *Could it be?*

"I'll go with him," volunteered Squire Thomas and ran off.

Cathal turned back to his patient and continued cleaning the wound, but his mind was elsewhere. It was back to a time when he was just a young boy with his mother. The knight Templar with the injured leg, then years later, the injured priest near the stream with a knife wound. He thought hard from memory and tried to piece together the puzzle.

He returned to his campsite more confused than ever. Sleep eluded him as his mind tried to recall everything his mother and what the bones told him. By morning, he was no closer to understanding and returned to Sir Renier's camp, hoping to learn more.

As he suspected, the young man called Odo wasn't just a freeman herdsman but also a landowner whose land ownership was disputed and claimed by the Church. He'd come to Frankia to seek an audience with King Henry and obtain a judgment on his dispute. He consulted the bones again, and after, he felt supportive of the young man. The bones spoke of honesty, integrity and dogged determination—qualities he'd seen in his brief interaction. But the bones also suggested there was more, that Odo would positively impact England – his lineage was crucial to the outcome. His future was integral; if he lived, his life would change much for the people in the north. Cathal recounted what his mother told him, and slowly, he began to understand, the picture was clearer. Odo needed a guiding hand, a mentor to help overcome obstacles and his obstinate self. The ailing priest with the knife wound could only have been Odo's father.

Cathal was taught not to believe in destiny. Instead, he thought that events and people were linked for the greater good and that fate predetermined lives. He questioned if it was his fate to meet the Templar knight and again later when he was a priest. Was fate that brought him here to Chaumont-sur-Epte? All those countless events, some small and insignificant and others monumental, they all brought him here, and even Isolde's death may have played a role. Had she not perished from illness, he would never have come to Chaumont-sur-Epte. He felt closure and now understood. He cherished their time together, and now he knew it had only been temporary. If he tried to piece the puzzle together, then indirectly, she led him to this young man called Odo; could that have been her fate? He wasn't sure. There were too many missing pieces and merely a series of coincidences.

The bones gave him insights but not answers. The answers Cathal knew had to come from within.

The mood at Sir Renier's camp was dour. Odo had not found support from King Henry, and while the monarch hadn't ignored him, the King wisely informed Odo that he could not come between him and the Church. The outcome of his meeting with the King had seen Odo become a messenger, a task Odo took seriously and wouldn't divulge the context of his meeting even when pressed by the patient, Reeve Petrus. Petrus Bodkin, reeve to Mellester Manor, was a likeable fellow with a dry wit, little patience and a strong sense of values and he was recovering nicely, just as he knew he would. There was never any doubt.

Sir Renier had come to Frankia to swear fealty to King Henry, and having completed that duty, the group were preparing to depart Chaumont-sur-Epte and return to the small village called Mellester Manor that Cathal had never heard of.

He returned to his camp exhausted and slept little. Something wasn't right. It was still dark when he arose and felt troubled.

Shortly after dawn, Sir Renier, Reeve Petrus, the squires, and Odo would return to England. Should he go with them, he questioned? Was his fate tied to Odo Read? While the story behind Odo was rather unusual. The young man was only a herdsman, and the bones had told him about a powerful man who would positively affect the people of the north for the greater good. Cathal felt that Odo couldn't possibly be that person. That person was still to enter his life. He packed up his small camp and readied himself to leave. He wouldn't accompany them to England, instead, he would return to the Black Forest. That was his fate.

It was still dark when he wandered to the roped pasture where horses were kept and looked for his horse. He wasn't the only one awake at this early hour, and he saw two men saddling horses. They were talking and didn't see him standing nearby.

Cathal identified them as the Norsemen he'd seen a couple of times earlier. They never seemed to be far away… had they been watching him? If they had, then they would have seen him at Sir Renier's camp treating Reeve Petrus, and they would also have seen him talking to Odo. If the young Englishman were indeed the person they sought, then they would kill him at the first opportunity. Or was it just another coincidence? Yet on the same morn that Sir Renier and Odo were leaving Chaumont-sur-Epte, these two Norsemen were also saddling their horses and preparing to depart. For the present, there was only one thing he could do, watch them carefully.

As Chaumont-sur-Epte woke to a new dawn, the two Norsemen rode quickly out of town and headed onto a nearby wooded area on a low hill that gave them a good view of the road. Some distance behind, Cathal followed, circled back behind them, hobbled his horse and, crept close to their position and waited.

Cathal was in his element, in a forest, in his home, and they had no notion of his presence.

The sun had fully risen when the Norsemen stirred. From his hidden vantage point, Cathal looked down at the road and saw the five riders, Sir Renier, Reeve Petrus, Odo, and the two squires riding single file from the town. He had to look again. Odo was riding a pure black stallion, a beautiful, impressive beast that many would covet. How does a herdsman own such a fine horse? He had no time to ponder what many other men had previously asked when the Norsemen reacted. They spoke in their mother tongue, a language Cathal couldn't understand and made for their horses a little distance back.

To Cathal, the Norsemen's intent was obvious, they intended to attack the unsuspecting riders. Two Norsemen against five? The knight Sir Renier was the only capable fighter, the reeve wasn't capable of fighting and the two squires were no match… He made his move and leapt from cover, blocking the path to their horses.

"Why do ye intend to attack those men?" he asked, speaking Frankish. His sword hung loosely from his hand.

Ignoring his question, the Norsemen, angry at the intrusion, unsheathed their swords and separated, creating enough distance to have the freedom to fight within the confines of the forest. They began to aggressively circle him. To Cathal, they looked fearful and hesitant.

Cathal asked again. "What business do ye have with those riders?" this time, he spoke German, and they turned to exchange a quick glance, and he knew they fully understood. Cathal had already assessed which of the two warriors posed the biggest threat and leapt forward at him, his sword a flashing blur as it swept upwards, diagonally across the Norseman's body. Unable to defend against the unexpected move and with no option, the Norsemen leapt backwards, and Cathal pressed his attack, spinning quickly and swinging his sword downwards. The large and muscular Norseman wasn't lithe and quick enough to avoid the razor sharp blade as it sliced through leather, clothes and into his chest. With another quick strike, Cathal struck his sword, and it fell from the Norseman's grasp. Cathal kicked it away as the warrior, in total surprise, slumped against a tree.

The other warrior was slow to react and stood frozen as he watched his friend so easily overcome. Enraged, he now charged Cathal, who stood ready and waiting.

Cathal leaned away from the whooshing blade as it swung by missing him by a whisker. The warrior intended to collide and overpower Cathal, and would have if he'd still been standing there. Instead, Cathal stepped aside and kicked out with his foot, tripping the warrior, who fell heavily. Before he could rise or reposition his sword, Cathal stood over him with his sword tip pressed onto his neck.

"Why do ye seek those men? Cathal asked again. He pressed

the sword harder, and the warrior grunted in pain. "Why?" he repeated.

"Is Harald Maddadsson," finally answered the Norseman.

Cathal was puzzled, "Who is Harald Maddadsson?" Cathal pressed harder, piercing the skin and a warm trickle of blood ran from warrior's neck.

"He, he, is the *Mormaer* and rules *Orkneyjar* in the north of Scotland."

"Why is it so important? What do you seek by attacking those riders?" Cathal spared a quick glance towards the road and saw Sir Renier and the group had already ridden past.

"Is the boy."

"There is no boy in that group," Cathal responded.

"No, no, he is a young man. Priests foretold it, and Harald has had men searching fer, fer…"

"Fer who?"

"Fer ye," gasped the Norseman. "It has been many years, and we remembered what Harald told us. It was luck we found ye, and it was ye - ye led us to him. Ye would lead us to the boy, er, the young man, and with yer death, ye couldn't protect him. We should have killed ye when we had the chance."

Harald Maddadsson of *Orkneyjar*, Cathal thought. It all made sense to him now. This is why the Norsemen had sought the death of his mother and then himself. He drove the sword into the neck of the Warrior, severing his spine. He turned back to the warrior against the tree, who was still alive. Cathal ended his life, cleaned his sword, and untied their hoses, leaving them free to roam.

Astride his horse, he rode from the hill and chased after Sir Renier. He understood it all; his fate *was* linked to young Odo. Norse priests had foretold it. Where Odo's fate would lead him, he didn't know, but he would be at his side the entire time to nurture and protect.

As usual, Sergeant Thomas spotted the rider approaching from the rear. “Someone approaches, Milord.”

All heads craned to look, and it soon became evident the rider was known to them all.

“It’s Cathal,” stated Sir Renier. “Did he not check yer wound last night and kiss yer goodnight?” he teased.

“Perhaps ye forgot to pay him,” replied the reeve with equal wit.

The small group pulled to a stop and waited for Cathal to ride up.

He rode past everyone and pulled alongside the knight where they talked. Finally, Sir Renier spoke. “Cathal will join us to England. He wishes to accompany us to Ridgley Manor and then to Mellester, where he intends to make his home.”

Strangely, Odo found the healer’s presence reassuring and was secretly pleased. The reeve had no issue whatsoever with him. Now numbering six, the group rode for Wellebou, and Cathal drifted back and rode in solitude a few horse lengths behind the squires

And so began their journey back to England.

...to be continued

AUTHORS NOTES

As a writer of historical fiction, I attempt to weave historical facts into my stories as much as conveniently possible. Sometimes, it may only be a small detail; in other instances, it could be significant and dramatically advance the plot. The Templars are a prime example and have become integral to the Falls Ende story. They are also known as the Poor Fellow-Soldiers of Christ and of the Temple of Solomon, or if you are familiar with Latin, *Pauperes commilitones Christi Templique Salomonici*, or in French, *Pauvres Chevaliers du Christ et du Temple de Salomon.* For the sake of simplicity, I refer to them within this book as Templar Knights. Whatever name you prefer to call them, they were a French military monastic religious order approved by the Pope to initially protect travelling Christian pilgrims from bandits and marauding highwaymen. They preyed upon the Christians as they journeyed from the coastline at Jaffa, near the modern-day city of Tel Aviv, to the Holy Lands, a distance of 85 miles or 135 km's, as the crow flies. The medieval Holy Lands is roughly located between the Mediterranean Sea *and the eastern bank of the* Jordan River, within the biblical Land of Israel and the region of Palestine.

Like most devout religious orders, the Templars swore an oath of poverty, chastity, and obedience and renounced the world, just as other religious orders of that time did. They were frequently found in prayer and expressed particular devotion to the Virgin Mary. They were not allowed to gamble, swear, or become drunk and were required to sleep in a shared dormitory and eat basic meals together. They adopted a traditional monastic attitude towards women, being strongly anti-feminine and believing women contaminated them. The Templar's 'Rule of Order', laid down by Saint Bernard of Clairvaux, expressly forbade women from joining the Order and went so far as to set rules that kept the members of the Order as far from the temptation of women as possible. There could be no female Templars.

Joining the Templars was not a commitment to be taken lightly; the knights could hold no property and receive no private letters. They could not be married or betrothed and could not accept any vows from any other Order.

Historians claim that 'The Templar Rule of Order' no longer exists, and I believe the 'rules' have most likely been modified and translated with many inaccuracies over the years.

For poor Odo, life with the Templars' was challenging when he had to consider the following –

> *We believe it to be a dangerous thing for any religious to look too much upon the face of woman. For this reason none of you may presume to kiss a woman, be it widow, young girl, mother, sister, aunt or any other; and henceforth the Knighthood of Jesus Christ should avoid at all costs the embraces of women, by which men have perished many times, so that they may remain eternally before the face of God with a pure conscience and sure life.*

> *If a brother is found guilty of lying with a woman, and we hold guilty the brother who is found in a wicked place or in a wicked house with a wicked woman, he may not keep the habit and so he should be put in irons, nor shall he ever carry the piebald banner or take part in the election of a Master.*

> *We prohibit and firmly forbid any brother to recount to another brother nor to anyone else....the pleasures of the*

flesh that he has had with immoral women; and if it happens that he hears them told by another brother, he should immediately silence him; and if he cannot do this, he should straightaway leave that place and not give his heart's ear to the pedlar of filth.

In contrast, cleromancy, augury, or divination practiced by Cathal was not as heathen as most would think. Divination is defined as the prophetic divining of the future by observing natural phenomena—particularly the behaviour of birds and animals and examining their entrails and other parts - but also by scrutinising man-made objects and situations. Cleromancy *is a form of sortition (casting of lots) in* which an outcome is determined by means that usually would be considered random. In Cathal's case, he used the random casting of *lots* (bones) to determine an outcome.

In the New Testament of the Bible, in The Acts Of The Apostles 1:23–26, the eleven remaining apostles cast *lots* to determine whether to select Matthias or Barsabbas to replace Judas. The Eastern Orthodox Church still occasionally uses this method of selection.

Some would argue that the practice is nothing more than witchcraft practised only by shaman and street pedlars. In 44 BC, Cicero wrote *De divinatione (*Concerning Divination), which is known as a respected source on ancient divinatory practices. In China, for millennia, many have sought guidance from the *I Ching (*"Book of Changes") before making important decisions. *I Ching is an ancient Chinese* divination *text that is among the oldest* Chinese classics and is believed to have been written around 220 BC. *I Ching was the basis for divination practice for centuries across the Far East and was the subject of scholarly commentary. Between the 18th and 20th centuries,* this text was influential in Western understanding of East Asian philosophical thought.

If the Catholic Church believed Cathal's practice of cleromancy warranted punishment, he could very well have been excommunicated, as was Gryffen. The Catholic Encyclopaedia defines Excommunication (Latin *ex*, out of, and *communio or communicatio*, communion — exclusion from the communion) as the principal and severest censure by the Church. It is a medicinal and spiritual penalty that deprives the guilty Christian of all participation in the common blessings of ecclesiastical society. By the 12th century, excommunication was the most commonly used and harshest form of censure. Within the context of Falls Ende–Sextus, Gryffin had the severest version of excommunication, *vitandus,* imposed on him by Bishop Dunhelm.

I have been harsh on the Catholic Church in the Falls Ende series of novels. History has judged the actions of the clergy during that time, and I feel my interpretations of the clergy have not been balanced without including some notable historic people devoted to their faith who acted for the common good of the Church and humanity. One such person is the most remarkable Sister Hildegard.

Hildegard of Bingen, *c. 1098 – 17 September 1179,* became Mother Superior at the convent at Disibodenberg, the same convent where Cathal recovered from his injuries. She was also known as the Sibyl of the Rhine and was an active writer, composer, philosopher, mystic, visionary, medical practitioner and medical writer during the High Middle Ages. She is one of the best-known composers of sacred monophony (A tune sung without accompaniment or a melody played by a single instrument). Many scholars have considered Sister Hildegard, the founder of scientific natural history *in Germany.* How wonderful that Cathal had such an influence on this incredible woman.

For Cathal's character to develop, I believe he needed more than his mother, Macha, could teach him. He needed a structured environment to expound on his beliefs, debate them, and learn from those he respected. In Falls Ende–Sextus, Sister Hildegard offered him that opportunity. I honour Sister Hildegard by using a paragraph of her own writing in Chapter 24; I changed a few words to adapt her actual translated text into context.

> *"Some years past I set my hand to writing. While documenting my thoughts, I sensed, as I mentioned to ye before, Cathal, about the deep profundity of scriptural exposition. Raising myself from illness by the strength I received from God, I finally brought this work to a close – though just barely – and it took over ten years. And I spoke and wrote these things not by the invention of my heart or that of any other person, but as by the secret mysteries of God I heard and received in the heavenly."*

Despite the grief of losing Isolde, I wanted Cathal to leave Disibodenberg, a much different person than when he first arrived. His views on the world were expanded, he was taught to read and write, and he came to respect the devotion of others committed to their faith. More importantly, Cathal learned of his own shortcomings, and this moulded and shaped him into one of the most enigmatic and complex characters in the Falls Ende novels.

If we, as Falls Ende fans, had been transported back to that era and met Cathal, we probably wouldn't have liked him. To us, he would appear uncommunicative, perhaps almost rude and arrogant, but when he spoke, everyone would stop and listen because his words were uncensored, and he told the absolute truth. We may not like Cathal, but for everyone who meets him, his presence is lasting, his integrity is unquestioned, and his knowledge is superior.

Thank you for reading Falls Ende – Sextus.
Paul W. Feenstra

Other books by

Paul W. Feenstra

Published by Mellester Press

Boundary

The Breath of God (Book 1 in Moana Rangitira series)

For Want of a Shilling (Book 2 in Moana Rangitira series)

Gunpowder Green

Into the Shade

Falls Ende short story eBooks

1. The Oath
2. Courser
3. The King

Falls Ende full-length novels.

1. Falls Ende – Primus (eBooks 1,2 & 3)
2. Falls Ende – Secundus
3. Falls Ende – Tertium
4. Falls Ende – Quartus
5. Falls Ende – Quintus
6. Falls Ende – Sextus

Leonard Hardy Series

A Sinister Consequence

A Questionable Virtue

A Gentleman at Heart

www.ingramcontent.com/pod-product-compliance
Lightning Source LLC
Chambersburg PA
CBHW020256030826
48979CB00026B/1285/J

* 9 7 8 1 0 6 7 0 1 0 1 5 7 *